LIKE THE MOON

A PORTAL WORDS NOVEL

DAWN J BRAITHWAITE

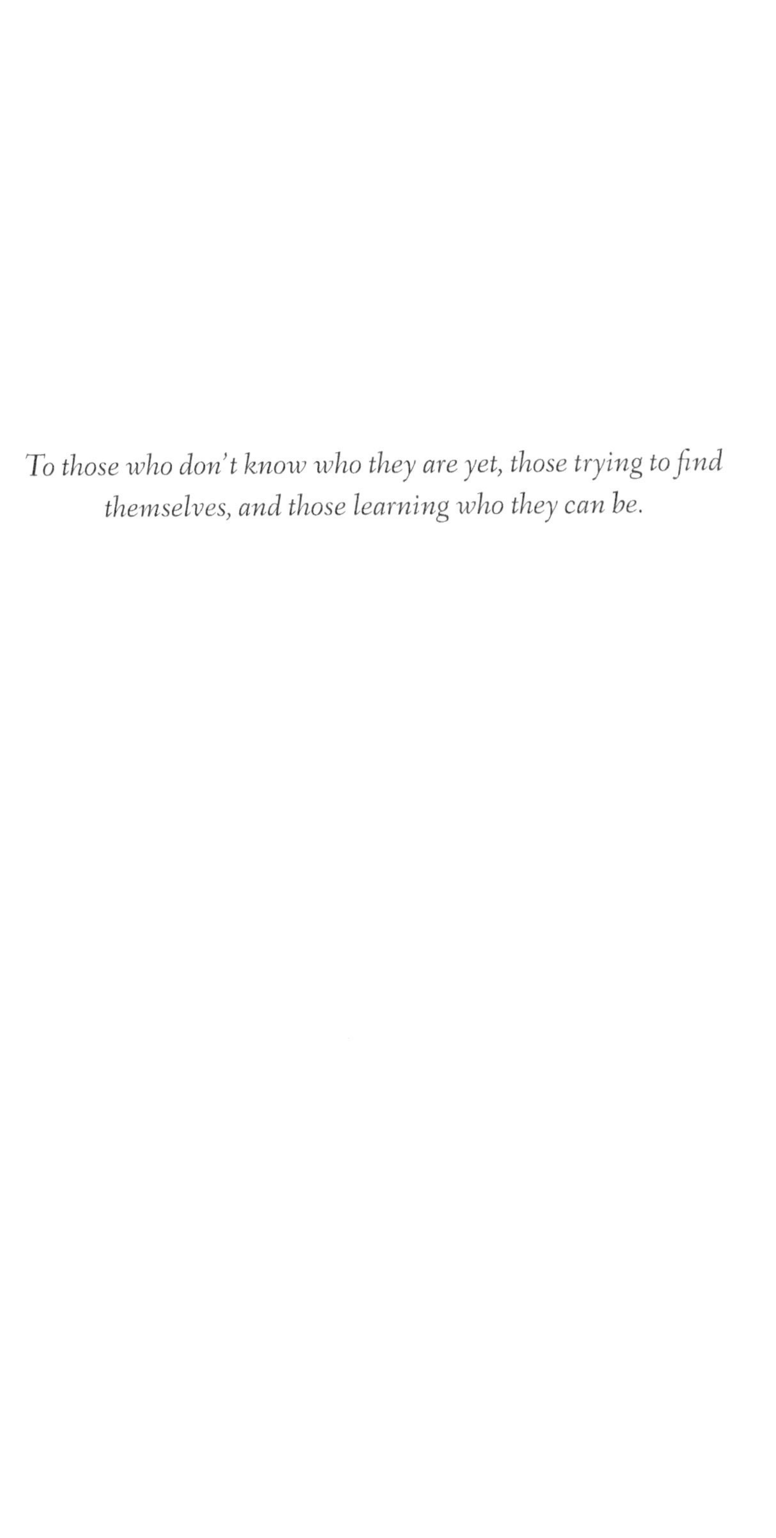

To those who don't know who they are yet, those trying to find themselves, and those learning who they can be.

PART 1
MOONSTRUCK

ONE

ALLOW ME TO INTRODUCE MYSELF

"ELLE! Hurry up or you'll miss the bus!"

"Coming Nikki," I shrugged on my thick, black pea-coat as I flew down the stairs, skipping several in the process. Nikki watched me from the bottom of the banister, her deep auburn hair pulled back into a messy bun. Loose hairs lit by the pale autumn morning light streaming into they foyer took on a halo effect, making her look like the angel she was. With one hand on her hip, she held out the other. In it, one of her specialty breakfast sandwiches. My stomach twisted in anticipation and the corners of my mouth lift as the smell of it hit my nose. My favorite, a spicy sausage and egg with roasted peppers and spinach. So freaking good. With my food addiction, I kind of lucked out with this family having a chef for a mom.

Nikki ran a quaint cafe called Main Street. One of those hole-in-the-wall places, impossible to find unless you were in the know. Which was pretty much everyone that lived in a five mile radius. An off day for Main Street meant the line stretched a few feet out the door, rather than down the block. The sign of awesome food anywhere; a line long enough to rival the lines at the best amusement park rides.

Nikki's famous soups and sandwiches, made on buttery herb bread, had made her cafe a hot spot for all ages. Her nominal prices, pulled in patrons from all walks of life while still making more than you'd expect a hole-in-the-wall to make. She could have easily afforded to expand her cafe into a fancier restaurant, or open another location. Nikki refused to do that. She loved the Mom and Pop charm of her cafe, and wouldn't change it for anything. Her small town upbringing had to play a big part in that, as well as her strong Christian beliefs. Which also was a small part of her only flaws.

Nothing against Christianity, but sometimes some of their rules can be, well, less-than Christian.

"How many times do I have to tell you that you can call me Mom?" She offered me the sandwich as I landed next to her. My stomach growled the moment my feet hit the oriental rug at the bottom of the stairs, greedy for the spicy, warm goodness to come. There was no hesitation on my part in snatching up the greasy parcel. The oozing warmth greeted my hand with the promise of sating the rumbling in my belly. At least for a few hours.

"I know, I know. I try. I really do, I'm just not used to being in one place so long." A pang of guilt stabbed at me. I wished I could allow myself to bond with her, but my strange past, and my strange condition, kept me from doing a lot of things most people did as easily as breathing.

Nikki McIntyre was one of many foster moms that I've had in the past nine years. I liked her well enough. She really cared for me, no question about it. The rest of the family though; let's just say the jury was out on them from the get go. Mr. McIntyre, Greg, was nice enough. Kind and hardworking were the words best used to describe him. His flaw? His obvious favoritism. His daughter got the best of the best from him. Not to mention her innate ability to manipulate him. Somehow every time he got mad at her, ended up with me getting into trouble. If this family were a business, I'd definitely have suffered from the effects of nepotism.

Amanda, Greg's pride and joy, had some bug up her ass about my presence. I'm pretty sure it had to do with, well, everything about me. Having a freak in the house ruined her perfect, cliche, cheerleader reputation. She, and her pep squad cronies, never let me forget it either. Almost every sentence she deigned to utter to me began with, "Before you came around".

I'd been with them for almost seven months, a lot longer than any other family for sure. Other than Amanda's blatant disdain, they had been the kindest and most understanding of my problems out of any of the families I've been placed with. Well, Nikki had been. I'd been places in a lot of homes. Each one gave me up almost as soon as they got me. My special needs proved too much for all of them.

Even though Nikki had been the closest thing to a mother I would probably ever have, I never allowed myself to let my shield down and let her in completely. Calling her "Mom" would've only broken my heart in the end. That's why I never let myself get too comfortable. I knew better. Any day they could've decided that dealing with my issues wasn't worth the trouble and sent me packing. It was only a matter of time, in my experienced opinion. My place-ment history was proof of that.

"Well, I have absolutely no intention of giving up on you," she pulled me into a light hug, which to me felt like an ill fitting coat. After nine years of rejection and little affection from people that were supposed to care about you, hugs really weren't my norm. "Now, hurry up. And tell Amanda I need her to come home right after school, please."

"I will," I winced inwardly knowing how well that would go over. Amanda wouldn't listen to me, I knew that. She wouldn't listen to me if I had an endorsement from Harry Styles. She called it selective hearing. I called it bitchy. Like I said, she really didn't like me. She let me know as often as possible, out of Nikki's hearing range, of course.

I skipped out before Nikki could rope me into something else that would be pointless. The cool air nipped at my face the moment I stepped out the door. Not even mid-October, and the temperatures were already frigid. It wouldn't be long before a frosty layer of white blanketed the town. I hoped I was wrong, even though I knew I wasn't.

Snow had never been my favorite. Snow and winter were at the top of my "if I could wish it away, I would" list. As far back as I remembered, which wasn't more than about ten years, the winter always brought me a string of troubles and heartache. Firstly, that's when kids really upped their game in calling me names. I'd heard it all in the past: Snowflake, Frosty, Snow Queen, Ice Princess. Not to mention kids telling me not to go out in snowstorms because I'd get lost. Those weren't much more creative than being called Moony, Granny, Spook, or Ghost the rest of the year, but somehow hurt worst of all.

To put that in perspective, I'd always been pale. Well, maybe pale didn't quite cut it in my case. Pale would've been tan for me, being practically translucent from head to toe. White hair and pale gray eyes on top of my light, pretty much glow-in-the-dark, skin. Even in the warm summer months my skin stayed the same, no matter how much time I spent in the sun. Tanning beds? They were no help there either. I didn't tan, I burned. From cherry red to pink to white again, all in a week. I accepted that I was meant to be pale, no matter what, almost instantly. Whenever anyone commented on my monochromatic look, all I wanted to do is thank them for the reminder of my weirdness.

Memories of being picked on weren't the only things that make me dislike winter so much. I always felt so alone and afraid during the long cold season. The time of year where family and warmth took precedence over everything, heightened my isolation. While families gathered to celebrate, I was only reminded that I didn't belong.

On top of it all, my condition always seems to get worse with the first snow of the year. I didn't know why, but that's how it was. It was definitely not fun, or cool, to have some strange, undiagnosable mental condition with traumatic memory loss. That's the long and short of my unseen oddities, or at least that's what I'd been told.

From what every doctor and psychologist has said to me, something bad had happened to me when I was a kid. I had no idea what, not even after all their prodding and hypnotic attempts, but it had to have been bad. I was found wandering the streets late one night in a tattered nightgown. My arms legs and face were marred with scratches, bruises, dirt, and tears. My hiccuping sobs broke the still night air. I had obviously been through something atrocious. Whatever it was, made me forget everything about my life before, even my name.

I was found by a kind woman, Reubenesque and middle aged. She stooped onto the cold wet pavement and wrapped her heavy blue tweed coat around my tiny shoulders. I remembered snuggling into her warm chest and breathing in the floral perfume that surrounded her. She fretted over me, soothing my fears. She was the one that named me. Elle, the name she found embroidered on the tattered hem of my gown. El, to be more precise. The rest had been ripped away in whatever ordeal I went through to end up there. For all I knew, my real name could've been Ellen, Elenore, Eloise, or some other name that began the same. Heck, it could even have been just Elle.

She almost took me in as her own. But, when the hallucinations started she had been quick to hand me off. The fear of dealing with my different-ness rearing it's head for the first time had me at the step of social services faster than lighting. Families had been handing me off ever since. No one seemed able to handle a girl that saw and heard things that weren't there, almost all the time. They didn't want to, more like it. Once they realized my meds weren't working, they gave up on me and handed me off to Mrs. Wembley, my social worker, who eventually handed me off to a new family that would just do exactly the same thing a short time later. I'd been in dozens of foster homes in nine years. That much rejection and bullying became pejorative, case in point; I had trust issues.

A gust of wind whipped through the autumn speckled trees. The added chill settled deep in my bones and I clutched my heavy coat a little tighter. As I walked down the leaf scattered sidewalk, I chomped heartily into the breakfast sandwich Nikki prepared. The spicy, peppery flavor warmed over my tongue in a moment of sheer delight. Words couldn't describe how happy it made me. Serious thoughts of marrying it crossed my mind. My relationship with food was always better than with people. Food never judged.

I savored the sandwich until I got to the bus stop, at which point I scarfed the remaining bites down in a hurry. The last time I ate on the bus, the driver tried to make me throw my food away in the tiny garbage behind his seat. I refused, defiantly shoving the final chunk in my mouth all at once. That was a big mistake. The bite was too big, and I ended up choking and subsequently losing all of my breakfast all over the driver. I got in major trouble. After that day, I made sure my breakfast was gone before I got to the stop. I didn't need the extra trouble. Trouble meant more attention I didn't want.

The handful of overly bundled teens at the bus stop ignored my arrival, as per usual. Not that expected anything else. I probably would've died of shock if they did anything else. In turn, I took my usual isolated stance away from the rest of the small group that happily gossiped with each other. My mind kept occupied examining the cracks in the cement and eavesdropping on the mindless conversation happening five feet from me. Suddenly, I knew the innocuous scene at the street corner was about to get uncomfortable, for me anyway. It began as it usually did, with a heavy feeling forming in my head, fuzzy and swirling as though I'd just spun in circles in an attempt to make the world spin. Pro-actively, I sat on the dirty, half-frozen ground. I'd learned long ago when that feeling crept into my head, I'd better sit my ass down if I didn't want to crash to the ground. My breath slowed, as I prayed this episode would be a short case of vertigo, rather than a full blown trip inside my head. Soon, though, that hope proved fruitless.

The chatter in the air quieted, taken over by the unmistakable sound of crying. A woman crying. My insides froze at her wailing and my muscles tensed in preparation for what I knew was coming, a full on vision. A hallucination. The bane of my unique existence. The reason I'd been shoved out of so many homes.

The wailing woman, one of the voices I heard more often than I'd like. The voices that came that came before so many of the visions. My heart clenched every time I heard the wailing woman, and I heard her more than any of the others. She sounded completely broken every time. Lost even. Whatever she was going through seemed awful. Every time I heard her, my instincts told me to comfort her. Of course, I never could. She wasn't real. Her sadness, more than likely, was a bi-product of my trauma. One psychologist even suggested she was me, an embodiment of whatever had caused me to be the way I was.

Her sobs faded, making way for the vision. My visions never revealed anything huge or meaningful. Despite being out of focus, I could always tell what things were supposed to be. It was like looking through a sheet of privacy glass. Blurry gardens and structures. Sometimes I saw figures too. Unfocused bodies going about their business completely unaware my brain had dreamed them up.

This hallucination was no different. The world frosted over. A bright light filtered through the frost, bringing to mind a sunny day ahead instead of the clouded sky on the brink of the winter that reality held. A figure sat near a large monolithic structure of some sort. A decidedly feminine figure.

The glittery light flared, blinding me. When the light dissipated the vision is disappeared. Reality set back in and my heart sank at what it revealed to me. Before me, the black exhaust of the bus swirled in the air. The bus was pulling away down the street without me, the faces of my peers jeered out of the dirt crusted windows.

Shit.

I knew it'd be useless to walk back to the McIntyre's to hitch a ride to school. Nikki had already left for Main Street. Greg worked an hour away. Amanda was already at school, and wouldn't give me a ride if her life depended on it.

Standing, I hitched my bag up and started to walk.

TWO

SCHOOL OR TORTURE

THERE WAS no rush to get to school, so I took the slow route. My bus always arrived just before the morning bell, barely giving me time to get to my locker. There's no way I would've made it on time on foot. I decided to make the most of it and miss my first class, History. Mr. Granger, the history teacher, was so over zealous about his small goat farm, that he prattled on about it for half the class. Anyone that complained about it caught the ire of the kids that wanted an easy ride. Since they were the popular kids, no one dared risk the social suicide by doing so.

I even had time to stop into Cuppa for a nice cup of hot tea to keep me warm on the way. Cuppa, almost as popular as Main Street, made the best drinks in the county. Not to mention their fast and reliable service was always done with a smile. The baristas working there knew every one of their customers by order. A nod of the head was all the confirmation they needed to start an order of that customer's usual. By the time the customer got to the counter, their order was ready. All they had to do was pay. My order was almost always a hot ginger and turmeric tea with honey and lemon. That day, it didn't change.

I was so tempted to hang out in the coffee shop all day, drinking tea and eating delectable pastries. I couldn't though. I needed good grades in order to get a much needed scholarship to be able to afford college. No foster family would put me through college, and a part time job would nowhere cover tuition. Even with money for school that the state promised, I needed scholarships. Missing too many classes was something I couldn't afford, not with attendance and participation being a small percent of the grade in over half my classes.

Trust me, I'd much rather not go. If college wasn't so important to survive in this world, I wouldn't. School never had been high on my list of things I liked to do. Aside from it being a cesspool of bullying and over-rampant hormones, I found it boring. Not stimulating, at least not outside of the classic novels assigned by ELA teachers. I loved recreational learning. Other than that, school was only a mildly tolerated obligation. That was the only reason I left the little shop and continued on my way.

I made it to school with fifteen minutes until first period let out. I wasn't surprised to find my best, and only friend, Q, hanging around the commons sipping on his own caffeine-infused drink. His addiction to the stuff ran far deeper than mine. He slurped down the last drops as I plopped next to him. It was all but guaranteed he'd skip off later in the day for another.

"E tu, Q?" I joked about his being late with me. Q got his name from his double Q moniker, Quentin Queen. I had no idea what his parents were thinking saddling him with a name like that. I just knew I felt eternally grateful to them for his constant presence in my life, and their complete and total acceptance of, well, everyone that deserved it. He'd been raised the kindest person I'd ever met. We were pretty much inseparable from the moment we met when we were ten. We kept in touch whenever my foster situation took me away to different schools or towns. His existence made me unbelievably happy.

"Actually, I was here on time today but figured there's no use to sitting through Mr. Granger's boring lecture about either the great American experience or his amazing goats without my BFF to suffer with me. So I left, got my mocha and came back to wait on your beautiful, late butt." He brushed his bright pink hair out of his eyes and finished with a wink.

"I like the pink, by the way."

"Thanks, I did it last night. You know, you should let me do your hair. You know I'm dying to make it look like your silvery mane has been dipped in unicorn farts."

I laughed at his comment and snorted tea into my nose; not a pleasant feeling. "Yeah, that's not happening and you know it," I said when I finally recovered from the citrus attack on my sinuses. It's not that his desire to make my hair look like gasses from a mythical creature's ass wasn't amusing to me, I just couldn't. I wished I could change my hair, but, as with my un-tannable skin, it proved impossible. I tried to dye my hair a few times. Nothing crazy or fun, just brown. It was a low point, the bullying was getting to me and I thought that giving my hair some color would help. The dye washed out before the weekend was over. I thought it was a fluke and tried again with a different, stronger, brand. Two days of brunette bliss followed by crushing defeat. I felt certain not even the most permanent of the most chemical filled dyes would save me.

"You are no fun, girl."

"Shut up. You know how much I would love to have colorful hair, it just never takes. Lord knows I could use something to make me look normal-ish."

"Normal is overrated." He leaned over and planted a friendly kiss on my cheek. "Now, let's do our nails before the zombie masses are released from their cages and swarm our sanctuary. Do you want purple glitter or holographic?" He dug about in his messenger bag for a minute before coming up with said prizes.

"Holo, for sure. Then my nails will match my vision this morning, super shiny."

"You are twisted, my friend. That is why I love ya."

"I love you too, Q." I did. I loved that he stood by my side, and that he never pried for details when I had episodes. He merely accepted me, no matter what.

The next few minutes were pure therapy. Q painted a shiny layer of polish on my nails with the same level of expertise and flair as a professional, the whole time gossiping about cute boys and mean girls. If I could've, I'd have frozen time, just to spend the whole day like that.

My heart sank at the shrill bell that called for the end of class. It didn't take long for the commons to explode with hustling students traversing the school in herds that rivaled scenes from a zombie movie. We looked at each other and knew we thought the same thing. Q rolled his eyes and imitated the undead. School.

"Shall we join the herd?" Q laughed while giving one last admiring glance at his now shiny nails.

"Do we have a choice?"

"No, sadly. Come on, darlin'," he offered me a hand up, "arm yourself, and don't get bit."

"All right," I stood, laughed, and slung my bag over my shoulder. "If we survive, meet me here for lunch?"

"You know it."

THE SECOND HAND on the classroom clock threatened to travel backwards. Every class had felt that way, making lunch an eternity away. When the bell ending fourth period finally rang, I couldn't leave my seat fast enough.

Despite my best efforts, the commons was crowded by the time I made it to lunch. Scanning the area for Q, disappointment settled in me. Q's bright hair was nowhere in sight. I assumed he got held up, as usual. Unmoved by the promise of what either line offered, I picked the closest one and joined in.

It took a minute, but soon after getting in line I realized it was a bad choice. Amanda's sleek, signature high-ponytail, a copycat style of her favorite pop-star's, gleamed before me. Nikki's request to speak to her rang in my head. I debated doing it. Talking to her at school was a kiss of death. She'd either ignore me, or find some way to humiliate me in front of half the student body. On the other hand, if I didn't tell her, I risked getting in trouble with Nikki. The one person in the McIntyre household I felt certain actually liked me. I didn't want to do anything to hurt that relationship in any way. Even though I hesitated in opening up in return. Part of me hoped there would come a day, far in the future, that I would; if not with Nikki, then at least with somebody.

Humiliation was the only option. I tapped Amanda on the shoulder. Her golden hair swished as she turned. Her vain smile disintegrated into a sneer when she realized I stood behind her. The eye-roll she gave me, before whipping back around, could've won awards, if there were awards for eye-rolling.

"Amanda," I tapped her shoulder again, and braced myself for the tiger to pounce.

"What makes you think I want to talk to you at school, loser?" Her voice carried over her shoulder without her having to turn. Her lemming friends cackled at her remark. They were witches with a capital B. Amanda, being their leader, was the funniest girl in the world; to them at least.

"I don't," I came back at her. "I'd rather have a hallucination than have a conversation with you. I'd lose less brain cells."

Amanda turned with fire in her eyes. "Then what is your problem?"

"Nikki says to come home right after school, Your Vainness." The words tumbled from me almost too fast to comprehend.

She glared back, mouth hanging wide. No one else in her life had the audacity to call her anything but perfect. Sure, to the pedestrian and sheep eyed population of teenagers at school, she was. Perfect hair, perfect teeth, flawless skin, and a perfect body. She was popular and pretty. All that was superficial. Those few of us that saw the inside, knew better. Her perfect hair came from a bottle. The perfect teeth were bought and paid for. Anyone could have perfect skin if they spent most of their time preening themselves. As for her body, well that was purely based on opinion.

After a beat she forced her friends to leave the line for another. I saw their protest in their eyes, but they didn't dare defy their queen.

As if the encounter with Amanda wasn't bad enough, I soon got a glimpse of the gourmet muck waiting at the end of the line. Chipped beef and fries. Yuck. My stomach churned like a raging sea in a storm as I wondered what horror lay at the end of the other line that made Amanda's cronies think this was preferable. I watched, half mourning for my stomach, as the lunch lady slopped the white, meaty gravy over the golden fries on my tray.

There was no worse death than that by creamed meat. Poor fries.

I sat in mine and Q's favorite spot and pushed the mess around on my tray with absolutely no intention of eating it. I was ready to abandon ship when my lunch was saved.

"Never fear, I am here." Q announced, plopping next me. He set a brown paper bag on the table in front of me and another before his self. The smell of the delicious contents seeped through the bag and I knew what hid inside without opening it. "I saw the horror show that is school lunch and decided to save us."

"Carlitos! You are my hero right now." I tore into the bag to find just what I expected; a veggie and chicken burrito with a side of spicy pickled avocados. The first time Q took me to his favorite food truck during lunch I was adamant that I would not like the healthy fare. Riced broccoli and cauliflower instead of real rice just didn't sound appealing at all. Tacos and burritos were supposed to be greasy and full of all the things bad for you, but one bite was all it took to hook me. Carlito was a magic man. "This is just what I need to get through the rest of this day."

"Wanna tell me about it?"

"Nothing, really. I had to talk to Amanda."

"Gasp!" Q exaggerated his sarcasm with a hand to his chest. "Did she explode?"

"No," I replied between bites of my upgraded lunch. "That would have been a real tragedy, I would have gotten her ick all over me. I might have been infected."

Q mock-shuddered as he stole one of my avocado slices from the red checkered paper tray.

"Hey, get your own!" I swatted his hand away.

"Never. Stolen avocados taste better," he popped another in his mouth and grinned maniacally. "You need to stop worrying about Amanda so much, not worth your time."

"I only do it for Nikki. She's the best foster mom I've had so far. Greg's tolerable. Amanda fell far from those trees for sure."

"Or she was dropped on her head."

I giggle-snorted with the grace of a cave troll, "That would explain it."

"Coming over after school?" Q changed the subject.

"Of course. Where else would I go?"

Lunch seemed to be over all too soon. Isn't that how time always worked? The fun things passed by so quickly while the work took an eternity and then some to be done. All I could do was plan to count the tedious minutes until the end of the day came.

THREE

THE WORST THING I COULD DO

My eyes struggled to stay open, lulled by the low hum of the projector and the dim glow of the black and white film it displayed. The exceedingly outdated and boring health video Mrs. Carvey picked for our viewing pleasure, didn't help. For some reason, the school figured these outdated films didn't need replacing, despite the fact much of them had been distorted by time. Cheap bastards.

I wasn't the only one not watching. No one paid attention to the plight of Billy playing out on the white screen pulled down in front of the white board. Half the class chatted amongst themselves. Others busied themselves by drawing, reading, or some other activity by the low light. Not even Mrs. Carvey paid attention to the video, or the class for that matter. She busied herself with some project on her laptop, likely grading or some other boring task. Part of me suspected she moonlit as an erotic romance author, writing spicy love scenes that would make the most experienced lovers blush. She was so buttoned up and pristine in her appearance all the time, like she'd just stepped out of one of the heath videos she tortured us with weekly. Yet, there was something in her eye that hinted at a secret wild side.

After only ten minutes of fighting it, sleep claimed me. It didn't take me long to find myself in an old familiar dream.

LOW LYING branches scratched like clawed hands desperately grasping at my ankles. My steps echoed the pounding panic in my heart. I had to get away, the man in the black robes was closing in. I could almost feel his fingers at my back. I knew deep down that he would catch me again, he always did. He had the advantage of being grown over me, the advantage of having full use of magic.

A wall of trees sprouted up out of nowhere, blocking my escape. The dark figure closed in, but not all the way. The space left between us terrified me. It could close at any moment. The figure's hands became engulfed in flames, just before he flung those flames at me with a growl. My arms rose in a feeble attempt to guard myself. I didn't know how, but the fireball veered off into the thick woods. There was no relief though, the figure remained and advanced, stretching his claw-like hands out to grab me. Before it could, I pushed at them and they tumbled away.

A high-pitched screaming crept into my mind, growing louder and louder. The trees and bushes protecting me began to fade away. In moments the world around me changed from dark woods into the top of the stairs of the commons in my school. I should have been hunched over my desk in health class. What the heck?

As the dream continued to fade from my mind, I was met with erratic, hushed commotion. It's only when I became fully aware of reality that I saw the crowd of students standing frozen, feet away from me. Their faces full of judgment and horror. The silence broke into cries and yells.

"Oh my God! Elle, you are such a freak!" a girl shouted over the din.

"What did you do?" a passing voice accused, laced with panic.

My eyes followed the frantic form of a teacher I recognized, but didn't know her name, down the stairs. I couldn't see what she rushed too. There were too many people gathered around the bottom of the stairs. I didn't have to see to know my freak sleepwalking episode made me do something awful. Something I feared more than anything. I'd hurt someone.

Part of me wanted to run. Run and never look back. What would that make me though? A monster? A monster that had no control of what had happened. Morbid curiosity compelled me. I had to know who bore the brunt of my damaged brain. Even though I didn't want to know.

The jeering cries of the surrounding student body muffled with my invisible cotton in my ears as I got closer to the crowd. The seconds ticked by like molasses, slow and steady. I pushed my way into the crowd, shoving my way through in desperation. Many of them shouted accusations at me with angry eyes as I passed them, but I couldn't hear them. All I could hear was the pounding of my heart.

I shouldered my way through remaining cluster of people. Each person I passed turned to me with horrified and hateful glares. My stomach sank deeper with each step, until finally I reached the center and saw exactly what I had done. Who I had hurt. Amanda. My foster sister was the first victim of my sickness. I knew instantly how it looked from the outside. Everyone knew we didn't get along, everyone heard the rumors she spread about me. This was bad. Very bad.

My eyes clamped shut against the ugly scene and I shook my head, hoping I had seen wrong. Desperately, I opened my eyes and rubbed them, hoping the scene would fade away. I wanted it to be nothing more than another hallucination. The scene remained, as I knew it would. My foster sister lay unconscious on the cold linoleum floor of the commons. Her arms splayed out awkwardly and one of her legs was obviously broken; a bone protruded grotesquely from the middle of her shin.

No. Oh no.

I froze there, unable to move, speak, or hear clearly. My whole body trembled. I was in so much trouble. When the EMT crew rushed past me, I stumbled to the side. Yet, I was still in a daze. It was only when someone physically pulled me away that I began to come out of it.

Panic filled me as my senses came to. I looked over my shoulder, expecting to see an officer or a teacher ready to take me away for my crime. Instead I saw Q. Unlike the rest of the room, he wasn't mad. His fists didn't shake at me in accusation. All he did was sit me against a wall and try to calm me.

The gravity of the chaotic ordeal finally fully processed. The dam broke and all my consequential emotions came pouring out. My sobs came out thick and heavy, barely giving me air to breathe. The crowd growing behind Q only made things worse. I looked in to each face, desperately looking for some sympathy. Only Q had any for me.

Two uniformed men joined the faces peering down at me. Their grave expressions set my panic into overdrive. I struggled past the rising panic, finally managing to say, "I didn't mean to. I'm sorry. I didn't mean to."

FOUR

FROM GHOST TO PARIAH

"Amanda's going to be just fine. It will be a long recovery, but she will be fine," Q kept reassuring me. "It was an accident. Everyone knows that."

I scoffed, "Tell that to all the kids at school. They don't care that I'd never sleepwalked before, or that I had no control over it. Most of them are on Team Amanda, and drink that kool-aid wholesale." After the incident, my classmates avoided looking me in the eye. Walking through the halls, they treated me like a predator. A shark alone in water, left wanting from the hasty parting of the minnows when I approached. Whispers drifted back to me. Gossip about why I really pushed Amanda. Some said I was jealous of her so pushed her on purpose. Some went as far as saying I faked my illness to get away with doing whatever I wanted to.

I became more of an outcast. That was painful. At least before, people were willing to be nice to me if they had to be. Even teachers eyed me warily after what happened. Nobody trusted me.

"Everyone that matters." He pulled me into his side and hugged me. "The McIntyre's are great people. I'm sure this isn't going to affect how they see you, or your place with them."

"Greg barely looks at me. I'm out. I know it." Being bumped from my foster home wouldn't be ideal. Being transitional would keep me out of school for a while. My school work would suffer and I'd miss out on much needed scholarships.

"Give him some time. Just remember it's not your fault."

I wasn't convinced. I still had a terrible feeling that severe consequences hung over my head. I pulled my knees to my chest and hugged them. A few fresh tears welled in my eyes. I wished I were normal. Things like that didn't happen to normal people.

Q noticed my worry and began to rub my back, "You still have me. Always. Weirdos for life, right?" Q was undoubtedly too good for this world. I didn't know what I did to deserve his loyalty.

I chuckled halfheartedly, "Yeah."

Q's mom, Janice, called from downstairs, letting us know that dinner was ready. My cue that it was time to go. I knew the Queen family were more than happy to let me stay and join them. They were amazing, and totally understanding about my situation. I often wished they had been able to foster me, then I'd have been Q's sister for real and I wouldn't have had to worry about my illness getting me kicked out of my home. There were a few reasons they couldn't foster, Janice's arrest for public indecency for one. She'd been arrested in her young adulthood for protesting in the nude. Her flippant attitude towards the judge, and probably stripping down in court, earned her some time to serve. Not a lot, but enough for her to have a record.

"I better get back to the McIntyre's."

"You sure?"

"Yeah, with all that is going on I shouldn't be breaking their rules. You know, home by dinnertime and all that jazz on school nights." The McIntyre's were pretty strict about their rules.

We descended the stairs slowly. The incredible smell of Mrs. Queen's Tuscan inspired chicken pot pie made me regret Nikki's rule about having to eat as a family. I'm not even sure why she still enforced the rule. No one was there anymore. Amanda was still in the hospital and Greg and Nikki were always there with her. Nikki had been making me simple meals to heat up at dinnertime, or making sandwiches for me and leaving them in the fridge. I ate alone and went to bed before anyone was home.

Q walked me to the door, "Hey, find out if you can have a sleep-over this weekend. We'll gorge ourselves on Tom Hiddleston movies and chocolate while doing makeovers."

"You know they don't let me do sleep-overs here. You're a boy, blah blah blah."

"Please. They know I play for the same team as you."

"But we have raging hormones that we're dying to experiment with," I said with sarcasm, imitating the answer Nikki gave me every time I asked to sleep at Q's.

"You know it, baby. I'm just dying to get in your pants," he waggled his eyebrows in jest. "Who knows, maybe they'll say yes this time, with everything going on and all."

"Maybe."

"Need me to walk you home? Ma won't care if I don't eat right now."

"Nah, I'm good."

"Sure?" concern shone from his eyes.

"Yeah."

Q wrapped me in one of his famous bear hugs and left a kiss on my cheek. "Love ya, sweetie."

"Love ya too, Q."

Walking down the street, I couldn't shake the feeling that something bad was heading my way. I had to keep telling myself that those were the words of my guilty conscious eating away at me. To stop being paranoid, but, I couldn't help it. I always expected the worst, that way it never hurt so much when it happened.

❄

BOTH OF THE McIntyre vehicles were in the driveway when I got home. The unexpected sight left a lump in my throat, and turned my insides to stone. There was no way that this was a good thing.

"Shut up," I scolded myself. "This could be a good thing." Maybe they had good news about Amanda. Maybe Amanda was home. I played out eating dinner as a family and apologizing for the millionth time in my head. Even Amanda forgave me and became the sister I always wanted. A dream that never would come true.

I knew I'd never be forgiven.

The nagging at the back of my mind that something bad lay behind the front door wouldn't leave me. I had to calm myself before going in, or I'd have been a blubbering mess before I could say a word. I stopped and started a five things countdown to cool my racing mind. Five rocks, tiny stalagmites decorating the neighbor's yard. I heard birds in the trees, a car horn honking, a dog barking, and kids playing down the street. Four. I felt the cold wind bite my ears, the ground under my feet, and the lining of my coat pockets. Three. I smelled the crisp autumn leaves gathering on the ground and Mrs. Baral's exotic cooking wafting from across the street. Two. One, I tasted the bitter bile that threatened to rise in me, smear across my tongue.

My nerves mostly calmed, I took a refreshing breath and made my way into my foster home.

"Sorry, I'm a little late," I called as I hung my jacket and backpack on the coat rack by the door. I wasn't late by much, only a minute or two. I even called ahead while I walked home when I realized I was going to be late, leaving a message on the machine when no one answered, but I didn't want to upset them anymore than I already had. I was covering my ass.

I rounded the entryway corner and go into the dining room. The lump I'd banished moments before, returned to nest in my throat.

Greg and Nikki sat at the dining table with Mrs. Wembley, my social worker. We'd already had out monthly visit a week before the incident. She sat there for another reason, and not a good one. Her presence definitely meant something bad. I should've known better and trusted my gut.

"We need to speak with you, Elle." Greg took on a serious and somber tone. He wouldn't look at me, flitting his eyes everywhere else in the room. I knew he had grown to hate me. I'd hurt his precious baby girl.

Dread knotted in my stomach again, and tears jumped into my eyes. I wiped them away furiously. "Oh," was the only thing I managed to say. Even though I expected that particular shoe to drop sooner or later, it still stung like a bitch.

"Do you want to sit down?" Nikki asked.

I shook my head, wrapping my arms around me. There was no point in it.

"We think," Nikki started but choked on her words. I could tell she was broken hearted. It didn't matter though. After a moment of composure collecting she managed to finish, "We think it is time that you move on to another home."

I knew it. I buried my face in my hands to fight the oncoming tears. I didn't want them to see me cry. My feelings obviously didn't matter, wouldn't change anything. Despite how good I'd been, and all of the apologizing I'd done since that day, I got tossed away.

"It's not that we don't love you. We do, a lot," her voice cracked.

Nikki's words stung. No, they didn't love me. They wouldn't get rid of me if they did. People didn't throw people they loved in the trash when the chips were down. "No, I get it. I'm too dangerous now," my voice quiet, muffled by my hands.

"No, Elle..."

"You don't have to say anything else, Nikki. We all knew this was coming," I uncovered my face to glare at her and Greg. My hurt became greater than sadness. It became anger. "I'll go pack and leave with Mrs. Wembley. You don't need to worry about me anymore. It'll be easier."

I turned on my heel and stormed off to my room. No, it was not my room anymore. The room that I had been using.

"Greg, can't we reconsider. She's so fragile." I heard Nikki plead tearfully as I headed up the stairs.

"Nikki, no. Amanda needs to feel safe. She won't come home with Elle here. My daughter comes first," Greg replied, anger peppered in his voice. Yeah, he hated me. His angry words motivated me to pick up my pace. I ran the rest of the way to the room where my stuff sat.

Instead of beginning to pack, I threw myself on the bed and pulled my cell out of my pants. My fingers flew through my contacts. I had to text Q.

ELLE: *I knew it!*

Q: *What happened?*

Elle: *Greg and Nikki were home when I got here. Mrs. Wembley too.*

Q: *What?!?!*

Elle: *Yeah. Her car must've been around the corner. Complete surprise.*

Q: *Does that mean you're out?*

Elle: *:(Yup*

Q: *:(Need me to come help you pack up?*

Elle: *No. I have to be fast. Apparently Amanda is ready to come home, but won't with me here.*

Q: *I'm sorry. Call me when you get settled in your new place, k?*

Elle: *K. Later Q. Thanks for having my back.*

Q: *NP. <3*

Elle: *<3 U 2*

I SHOVED my phone in my pocket only to take it right back out. I remembered it belonged to the McIntyre's, not me. My fingers deftly pressed icons, deleting everything of mine from the device. As an afterthought, I started a factory reset on it. All traces of me were off of it once it finished. Goodbye phone. I didn't need it anyway. I knew

Q's number by heart and I didn't have pictures on it. I put the now empty phone in my pocket and got busy packing. Everything I owned fit in the giant gym-bag I kept under the bed, ready to be filled at a moment's notice. Even with the few items of clothes Nikki bought me, plenty of room remained in the bag. It took me a mere ten minutes to finish.

My feet spun me around to take in the room one last time. There were no long off memories fogging my eyes, or visions of good times playing back at me. I had to make sure nothing of mine got left behind. I had to make sure I wasn't forgetting anything that was actually mine. Nope, nothing.

I turned my back on the room I called mine and marched away. Yes, I'd hoped that bed would have been the last I'd lie my head in before entering the adult world. Even the most messed up kids in the system dreamed of permanent homes. We just knew not to get our hopes up too much. In the end it was always, *"Thanks for the bed and food, even though you couldn't love me."*

Back downstairs, I handed Nikki the cell phone. "I'll be outside when you're ready to go, Mrs. Wembley," my eyes didn't dare look in hers. I could barely interact with her. Interaction with Greg fell off the table the moment I learned this was Amanda's stipulation. With him wrapped around her perfectly manicured little finger, she held all the power in the house. Nikki did what Greg wanted. Greg did what made Amanda happy.

"Elle," Nikki started after me as I headed to the door, but I didn't stick around to hear what she had to say. Of all the rejections, this one hurt the most. Anything she said would only make it hurt worse. I didn't want any more pain. Despite not getting close to the McIntyre's, this place had been the best home of them all, if only for Nikki's sake.

I hoped the next one didn't suck.

For the time being, I'd be staying in the group home yet again.

FIVE

HOME SWEET PSYCH WARD

"Where are we going, Mrs. Wembley?" I didn't like how long we'd been in the car. Every minute fortified the lead sitting in my gut. We'd been driving for quite some time, a lot longer than it should have taken to get to the group home. The route had no familiarity other than the towering pines lining the road, it looked like any other. Pines were all the same here, you couldn't throw a rock without hitting one. "Am I being put with another foster family already?"

"No, Elle. No foster family," pity laced her voice, which wavered with emotion. I liked Mrs. Wembley, she was kind to me. Even though it was her job to be, I liked to think she was one of the few adults who actually cared what happened to me.

"Then, where are we going? A placeholder?" my response clung to my lips, afraid of the answer. Her tone made me wary, that something worse waited around the next bend. When she didn't respond, I grasped at answers to where she could be taking me. "A hotel? A different group home? Where?" My heart began to pound harder with each passing moment of silence.

Mrs. Wembley looked at me in the rear-view mirror, her eyes brimmed with concern and hesitation. After a long minute she sighed, "Elle, listen, honey. I didn't want to spring this on you before, at the McIntyre's, because I know how much you liked them. Leaving them the way you did had have been really hard on you."

I already didn't like where this conversation led, something felt really off. "Yeah, and?"

"Well, with what happened with Amanda McIntyre, the state doesn't feel that it would be appropriate for you to go into another home. You need to go somewhere where you can have your condition supervised properly; treated and monitored."

"What are you saying, exactly?" my eyes narrowed. I knew what she meant. I just wanted to hear her say it.

"You are going to a place called The Kendrick Institute." Mrs. Wembley paused and sighed again, "It's a private hospital."

There it was.

A hollow and heavy feeling took up residence in my body. A hospital. They were admitting me to a psychiatric facility. A loony bin. Every ounce of my being crumbled. I didn't want this. This wasn't right. It was an accident, I hadn't meant to hurt anyone. I never had before. I wasn't dangerous. They condemned me to the worst possible place for me, for one mistake.

I would've jumped out of the car if I didn't think it would kill me. Instead, I stared, dejected, out the window as a new batch of fat tears began to stream down my face. The towering pines lining the road blurred with the evening clouds rolling in. We were in for some harsh weather.

THE RECEPTION AREA of The Kendrick Institute felt cold and unwelcoming. Everything from the walls to the chairs were shades of icy white or stormy gray. The only color came from the super pink receptionist and the decorative plants, but even the flowers seemed muted. Perhaps my perspective made it seem so. Perhaps everyone else saw it as clean, quiet, and calm. Healing.

"Welcome to the Kendrick Institute." The receptionist greeted us cheerfully the moment we walked through the door. Everything about her was pink. From her baby pink clothes, to the shiny lip gloss on her lips. She even had strawberry blonde hair styled into a high ponytail. I guessed that the bubble gum she chomped away on was pink too. Her name tag read Kimmie. Even her name was too perky for the sterile lobby surrounding her.

"We're checking in, Elle Smith." Mrs. Wembley responded. "She's been referred by the state."

Kimmie's long pink fingernails clicked on the keyboard as she searched up my name. A shadow of worry crossed her face as she read what pulled up. Violent patient, I presumed. "Oh, yes. I see here," she said off-handed, trying to cover her concern. "Give me one minute to call a nurse up for you."

Moments later a small group of medical personnel were buzzed into the front lobby; a woman and three men. One of them was obviously a doctor, the long white coat and snazzy tie gave that away. He was short with a silver crew cut and dull brown eyes that sparkled with false interest. The woman was slender with olive skin and dark brown hair hanging down her shoulder in a thick braid. She wore light green scrubs and a great big smile, although it was fake because it didn't reach her eyes. She seemed as cold as the lobby felt. The other two were large men in the same light green scrubs. They were carbon copies of each other; short hair and dead eyes. They made me nervous.

"Hello, Elle," the doctor greeted me by name. I knew he didn't really care, he only cared about the money he'd be getting from the state for treating me. His false warm greeting meant to give me comfort, didn't. I could smell sleaze-ball all over him. "I'm Dr. Preble. We are happy to have you here at Kendrick Institute."

I scoffed inwardly. Yeah, happy to have the state's money.

"This is Carina," he motioned to the woman with him, "and these are Geoff and Henry." He didn't indicate which of the men belonged to which name. Maybe he couldn't tell them apart either. "If you'll come with us we will show you around." Dr. Preble extended a handed out, not really offering it to me. It was an invitation to join them. He would've been a good politician.

I looked to Mrs. Wembley for any form of reassurance. Any sign that being there would be good for me.

"It will be all right, Elle. I'm right here with you."

"Actually, Mrs... What's your name?" Dr. Preble asked with indifference.

"Fiona Wembley."

"Mrs. Wembley, I'm afraid we can't allow you past the security doors to the patient area. Only patients and personnel are allowed past those doors. A safety issue you see, many of our residents are agitated by too many strangers."

A hurricane churned my insides, sweeping away the butterflies in my stomach with its destructions. The safety net of Mrs. Wembley being pulled away from me, terrified me. I didn't want to be alone, surrounded by strangers in that sterile place.

Mrs. Wembley handed me my bag and offered a wavering smile. I knew she meant to reassure me, but I saw right through it. She'd been in my life longer than anyone else, including Q. I knew her too well. Her smile couldn't cover the sadness in her eyes or the worry in her voice when she said, "Go on, Elle."

My legs rooted themselves in a sea of molasses, each step dragging as if in protest. It didn't help that the faces of these people I was meant to trust now all stared at me with varying degrees of annoyance, like I wasted their time. The moment I stood within a foot of Dr. Preble, Carina flanked me. Geoff and Henry took up position behind us. Tension built in the air around me from the toxic waves they emanated. I felt they were just waiting for me to lash out and try to fight them off. They craved the violence advertised to them that was not there. That's why the state sent me there, after all. I'd become a violent mental health patient to the rest of the world.

Even though I saw it coming, I jumped at Dr. Preble's hand dropping onto my shoulder as he began guiding me toward the security doors. His touch felt wrong and alarming. "I know this is scary, but I promise The Kendrick Institute is a good place. I know you are going to be happy here." His words held no comfort. They were a judge's gavel ushering in a verdict, sending the cold chill of injustice down my spine.

My last ditch effort to see something comforting failed miserably. Peering over my shoulder only solidified the dread spreading through me. Instead of seeing a sure and confident Mrs. Wembley, sending me courage through her own, I caught glimpses of her sniffling into a handkerchief. "Mrs. Wembley!" I called out in desperation. The plea in my voice broke the poor woman. She turned on her heel, likely to keep me from seeing her tears, and shuffled towards the doors.

The doors opened with a shrill, teeth jarring buzz, pulling my eyes forward again. The sound resonated deep inside of me, and reaffirmed the prison feeling I'd picked up on. As the security doors closed behind us, I heard Kimmie in the lobby, "Have a good day. Bye now."

The facility beyond the doors showed nothing of the sterility of the lobby. There was no question of it being clean. The harsh cleaner smell made that blatantly obvious. But the patient area wasn't as well cared for as the lobby. The floors were nicked, torn, and stained. The walls had mismatched patches of paint where they'd been repaired. Nothing adorned them except a few small holes, scratches, and scribbles. Nothing homey or comforting could be seen anywhere. The true interior of The Kendrick Institute was a blank canvas that would never be painted. The powers that be obviously placed all their effort and money in what the general public was allowed to see.

They led through the bland halls. Marching along, walled in by the nurse and orderlies, drew the attention of the patients we passed. Their curious faces turned to see me, the new patient, in wonder. I knew they were curious about me, what disease of the mind brought me into their ranks. Some seemed afraid. Perhaps they saw my pale appearance and thought me to be a ghost. Others appeared to be sizing me up, determining my threat level. Would I upturn their status in this place?

It felt like being the new kid at school all over again. How long before they began taunting me too? For once, it didn't bother me much. How could it? My situation trumped any name calling and strange looks. All the same, I battled tears the whole time. I didn't want to be seen crying. Sympathy was the last thing I wanted. Nor did I want to be seen as weak.

Carina kept talking and pointing to areas of the institute as we passed them, oblivious to the fact I barely paid any attention. All my effort was focused on keeping it together until I was alone. Fortifying myself. Her words garbled together into nonsense, like the adults in a kids cartoon. A broken trumpet repeating itself.

I snapped to when we stopped at a simple wood door with a small window in it. The number on the wall next to it read 89S. Carina huffed as she opened the door, revealing a very thin young woman with red hair and freckles sitting on a simply made bed, humming to herself, playing cards.

"You aren't supposed to have the door closed right now, Elise," Carina chided, her voice stern and cold. Elise said nothing. She stared at Carina, in innocent defiance and kept humming. "Do you want to lose your door?"

"No, ma'am," Elise responded to the threat, her eyes shifting nervously between the nurse and the hulking orderlies. "It's just a kid down the hall was screaming and my head hurt." Her voice pitched up, trying to garner sympathy.

"No exceptions, Elise. You know the rules."

"But,"

"Keep your door open unless it is bed time," Carina enunciated each word slowly.

Elise crossed her arms, pouting and defeated. The few loose strands of her hair fell over her face.

One of the orderlies shoved past Carina, engulfing most of the free space in the middle of the small room. He hovered over Elise, watching her carefully like he expected her to do something. The gesture read as ridiculous, she was so small compared to the lumbering man. One look at her and it was easy to see he terrified her.

Carina turned to me, I made sure to pay attention. Her ire was quick and dangerous."This is your room, your roommate. Don't follow her example and break rules." She pushed past me to march back down the hallway, off to some unknown task. The nurse's brusque manner left me stunned.

When I didn't move immediately into the room after Carina's departure, the orderly in the hall shoved me in. My feet stumbled, but I managed not to fall on the short walk to the bed. I lowered myself onto the bed, hugging my bag on my lap, the old springs inside groaned in protest from the added weight. After a moment I noticed the sterile scent of the institute faded away, replaced with a funky smell. Something rotten. My insides churned over the odor while I prayed it would disappear. With nothing to take in, I kept my eyes on my new roommate. Her eyes met mine briefly before falling back to her lap.

Before he left, the orderly in the room faked a lunge at Elise. She cringed and squeaked, a mouse in the presence of a monster. The man laughed at her fearful hiding behind her skeletal fingers. His enjoyment of the situation switched something in me. I couldn't sit idly by and play nice with these people. As I stood to confront the bastard, I dropped the bag from my lap to the floor. Elise must've known I was about to butt in. She shook her head at me with wide bambi eyes. The orderly didn't miss the gesture and turned on me.

"What?" he sneered. The crazed power in his bloodshot eyes wilted the courage blooming in my chest. Derangement lived there, unsteady and volatile. He wouldn't be above hurting me, and lying about it. I backed down, sitting back on the squeaky bed. "I thought so." He left snickering, and gave his buddy at the door a high five. Their laughs could be heard far down the hall.

It was clear to me those two belonged in a place like this, but not as orderlies.

The silence left behind by Carina and her goons was heavy with awkward feelings. Elise continued to stare at her lap, occasionally flipping one of her playing cards with her spider-like fingers. I watched her, trying to get a feel for her before introducing myself. Trying to figure if she'd reject me for the same reasons everyone else had. Once in a while she looked up at me, her face full of uncertainty and anger. I wondered if she blamed me for something?

Long, awkward minutes passed. I realized watching her was useless, I wasn't learning anything. But, I wasn't ready to take the first step in introductions. The toll of the emotional day blanketed my desire for anything. I was in no mood to talk, and I could tell she wasn't either.

I turned my attention to studying the room, not that there was much to it to look at; misty gray walls with patches of white where the paint had peeled away, cold tile floors, and absolutely no personal touches. They probably weren't allowed. The only furniture in the room were the two beds, made with plain white sheets and a thin gray blanket, and a single wardrobe with four drawers placed directly between the two beds. Obviously, we were expected to share.

Standing, I plopped my bag onto the bed and glared at it with hesitation. The last thing I wanted now was to unpack it, like unpacking made it really real. I knew it was silly, that no matter if the bag was empty or full this was my reality. But, that was how I felt. Defeated, I pulled the zipper back and reached inside.

"Don't bother. They're gonna go through your stuff, probably tomorrow during your first appointment. They decide what you keep."

"Oh. I guess I'll wait." I turned to look at my roommate. "I'm Elle."

"Yeah, you don't get any of the drawers anyway. The dresser is mine. I need all of the drawers," Elise's face remained directed at the cards on her bed, uninterested in anything else.

She shocked me. I didn't expect her to switch from scared little girl to bitch in three seconds flat. Her warning me not to confront the orderly must have been more or her sake than mine."Excuse me?"

"The dresser's mine, and don't bother filing a complaint either. They don't care enough to do anything about it." She flipped a few more cards before looking up at me, "If you challenge me about it, you'll regret it."

I checked off the box in my mind saying Elise and I wouldn't be BFFs. "Whatever," I mumbled, shoving the shirt in my hand back into the bag. I zipped it and kicked it under the bed. It was that moment it was clear to me that I was on my own at The Kendrick Institute.

With nothing to do, I flopped onto the bed still refusing to give in to the tears wanting to break free. I stared at the water-stained ceiling and let my mind wander. Life had dealt me a shit hand and kept on piling it on. My sadness evolved into something akin to grief. Angry grief that finally broke the dam holding back my tears.

Elise made a gagging sound, mumbling about being roomed with a cry baby. Her bed squeaked right before I caught a glimpse of her lanky form leaving the room.

Good riddance.

SIX

ALWAYS A PATIENT

THEY LIKED to get things done bright and early at The Kendrick Institute, starting with a nice loud rap on the doors to wake up the patients. Too early for my weary mind.

I woke up feeling dried out. I ached all over. My eyes burned from all the tears I shed; keeping them open was difficult, to say the least. I didn't want to either. What I wanted was to stay in bed, no matter how creaky and uncomfortable the springs made it, and pretend that yesterday didn't happen. Heck, I would've taken being permanently stuck in a hallucination over being stuck there.

A loud buzz filled the room, forcing me to cover my ears. "What is that?" I asked Elise when she sat up lazily. Whatever the noise was, she had grown immune to in her time here.

"Wake up call, duh. You have five minutes to get dressed in privacy before the door rules take effect."

"Door rules?"

"Doors have to stay open unless it's bedtime, remember?" her eyes rolled as she talked down to me.

Her rude warning was enough to get me moving. I had no desire to get dressed with the door open for everyone to see. I was a freak enough already, I didn't need to add exhibitionist to that too.

The door rule had to be the most ridiculous thing ever. At least in my opinion, I knew the reasons behind it were probably good, and for safety, but it was still inconvenient for those that liked their privacy. I definitely liked my privacy almost as much as I liked my food.

I dressed faster than ever before in my life, slinging on my faded *"nerd"* t-shirt and a pair of stonewashed jeans. I finished pulling on my boots seconds before a nurse I didn't know opened the door and called, "Breakfast in ten girls. Hurry, hurry," as she disappeared.

Elise wasted no time shrugging into her blue, over-sized, institute issued sweater, and followed the nurse's disappearing act. I however, needed motivating.

Breakfast wasn't what I wanted. Even though I was starving. I hadn't eaten since the afternoon before at Q's. I wanted a time machine. There wasn't anything I wouldn't give to go back to that day in health class and not fall asleep. Hell, I'd take it back further than that, to before whatever made me this way happened. Maybe I'd have a home and family that were actually mine. Perhaps I'd be considered normal.

A girl could only dream.

With reluctant steps, I followed Elise, staying several feet behind the whole way to the dining room. The moment I laid eye on the glorified cafeteria, bustling with patients being watched over like children by orderlies and nurses, I couldn't will my feet to go any further.

The squeak of rubber abruptly stopping on tile floor seemed to echo over the utter chaos taking place in the room. Confirming my suspicion, every head snapped towards the sound, every eye fell on me. Leave it to the mad masses to have supersonic hearing.

I froze, with an all too familiar small feeling roping me into submission. Somehow, their attention felt more intimidating, more penetrating, than those of the herd of hormone filled teenagers that I encountered at school. Like they could see into me and knew everything about me instantly.

Like their instability recognized the instability in me. A neurodivergent namaste. I hated it.

"Screw breakfast," I muttered to myself, even shocking myself those words came out of my mouth. Without a second thought about it, I turned to march myself back towards room 89S, only to find myself face to face with Dr. Preble.

"You know, breakfast is very important, Elle. Sets the tone for the day, if you will. Beginning our day with a 'screw this' attitude sets you up for a bad one." His smile was saccharine, in-genuine.

My teeth pressed into my lip, "It's not that I don't want to eat breakfast. I love breakfast. Food, really. I'm just not that hungry," I lied, eyeballing the crumble-topped blueberry muffin in his hand. Just as I said it, my stomach exposed me, rumbling audibly.

"Not hungry?" he chuckled, taking a huge bite out of it. Rude.

"I don't feel ready to mingle. People aren't my strong suit. Especially new people," I fessed up.

"That's understandable, Elle. With your history, that is." He bit into the muffin again, letting crumbs fall on his white coat. He guided me back around, placing his free hand on my shoulder. "How about I walk you through the line, and you can bring your breakfast with us to my office. You can eat while we get started on your assessments. And," he added after a pause, "you can take your meals in your room for a week or so, until you feel ready to join the population."

"Yeah, thanks," I swallowed hard as he ushered me towards the meal line, feeling myself shrink more and more with each second. I drew so deep within myself, guarding myself from the stares I felt boring into me, I barely noticed the crying before the world started spinning. I stumbled right into Dr. Preble just as the everything frosted over.

Two figures sat in the garden my visions so often showed me. Their presence felt somber, would have felt that way even without the sad woman's crying. Soon, they were joined by a third figure that appeared more shadow than not. Dark and flowing. Its presence changed the air. Cooled it with something I couldn't put my finger on before the vision faded back to reality.

Dr. Preble's face came into focus next to my own. His muddy eyes held a look more of fascination than concern. I fascinated him. "There she is."

"I'm so sorry," I stammered, righting myself. Even though Dr. Preble was a doctor, I felt embarrassed by my episode.

"No need to apologize, Elle. Let's get you that breakfast and to my office. We can talk about it there."

I stayed silent the rest of the time in line, embarrassment suppressing my voice. Nothing else needed to be said anyway. I wasn't there to make friends with my doctor.

SEVEN

NEVER A FRIEND

I CAME BACK from my day of testing wiped out and feeling a little like a lab rat. A lot like a lab rat. Dr. Preble had me poked and examined, running about every test in the book. The worst of it had been the brain mapping. It took hours for them to induce a hallucination, and hours longer to do it again in order to double check their findings.

At least Elise was nowhere in sight when I got back to the room. I barely knew her, but I knew that she wasn't going to be pleasant to live with after the minimal amount of time spent with her.

Waiting to greet me, though, were my exciting new clothes. A small pile of institute issued pants, short sleeve shirts that matched the pants, long sleeve undershirts, a big drab gray sweater with pockets, a few slipper socks, and regular socks, and a pair of white sneakers without laces sat on my bed. Best of all, a neat little pile of underwear that were little more than glorified paper. I wasn't looking forward to those. A quick inspection of the main clothes was all I needed to see the same number stamped onto each piece, my patient number. My file of grievances grew by the length of that number, because that was who I became once I put them on. No name, just a number.

The pile of clothes reminded me what Elise had said the night before about my things. I wondered what else they decided I got to keep. I pulled my bag out from under my bed and searched it. They took everything, Most notable, they took my stone necklace away. I hadn't had time to put it on this morning. A decision I regretted every minute I didn't have it to soothe me. Finding it gone completely, devastated me.

I paced, fuming over the loss and the very limited wardrobe they provided. It got me to wondering why Elise said she needed the whole dresser. There was no way she had enough clothes to fill the drawers with what little the institute allowed us to have.

Storming over to the dresser, I threw open the top drawer. It was filled with socks and paper undergarments. Okay. I moved to the second drawer, it held the issued shirts and pants. I counted them, same as what I'd been given. So what was the deal?

I opened the third drawer and nearly got floored by stench. What appeared to be a bunch of small packages filled the drawer. I mean filled. Every last inch of it. Against my better judgment, I poked at one. It squished and oozed, releasing more stench. I immediately shielded my mouth and nose with my elbow, to keep from throwing up. There was no force on Earth that could've closed that drawer quick enough. Mustering my strength I took a quick peek of the last drawer to find more of the same.

Everything added up to one thing about her. Elise hid food, but not for consumption. No, she'd been hiding at least some of her meals, pretending she'd eaten her food. She'd been doing it for a long time too from the look of it. From the smell of it. Elise had an eating disorder, in a major way. She obviously lied to the staff about what she ate and didn't eat. I had to pay the price two-fold. My things "had" to be stored in my bag, not that I wanted a drawer anymore. Those were pretty contaminated. Plus the smell, I knew had to have permeated the room. Nothing would ever make it go away.

Nasty.

Despite everything going on, the dresser became the most important. I stood there for a long time staring at it, debating if I should tell someone or not. Did I really want to give Elise a reason to hate me? A real one? I didn't really care, but sharing a room with her just might be worse than Hell if I did.

I peeked in one of the offending drawers again, and instantly regretted it. The answer became clear. I could handle living out of a bag, I'd done it before. But, I couldn't handle the smell. Especially now that I knew where the smell came from. Rotting food. It just wasn't sanitary, not to mention, those little packets would haunt me constantly. My stomach churned at the notion.

My mind made up, I started out of the room to find a nurse. I got a few feet down the hall before seeing one of the orderlies from the day before. They looked so much alike, I had no idea if it was Geoff or Henry. One look at him and I remembered the fear etched on Elise's face when the orderly taunted her. It was enough to make me second think telling on her.

She may have been a bitch, but no one deserved to quake with fear the way she had. It would've been better to give her a choice in the matter, be more open to communicating with her. I hoped that it would help us forge some sort of bond, enough of one that we'd trust one another.

I turned back to wait for her to return to our room. I didn't have to wait long.

Elise sauntered into our room giddy, something had put her in a good mood. She wore her sweater, even though the heating system kept the institute toasty; the pockets bulged with what I assumed were more packets of uneaten food. Her face faltered the minute she saw me. Since I knew her secret, part of me thought it wasn't me that she didn't like. The real problem was having a roommate.

Elise groaned and flopped on her bed. Her plan to empty her pockets foiled. Her food packets were a secret and she couldn't empty her pockets with me there.

"Hey, can I talk to you?" I asked with hesitation. I prepared for her to reject me, which she did by carefully rolling onto her side to face the wall with another groan.

Of course she had to make this harder than necessary.

A nurse I didn't know yet appeared at the door, announcing she had my dinner. The idea of eating it turned my stomach. Knowing there were dozens of packets of rotting food sitting nearby, made food the most unappealing thing ever. I regretted asking to have my meals away from the cafeteria for a few days until I adjusted to being here. As adjusted as I could get that is. She brought the steaming tray to me, instructing me to leave it outside the door when I finished. Part of me wanted to tell her just to take it away, but the chance of consequences prevented me from doing it.

Out of curiosity I opened the lid on the tray; although, I didn't have high hopes after the bland breakfast this morning. That muffin was nothing but a lie. Dr. Preble had likely brought it from home.

The food on the plate could barely be considered food. Some gooey block of something brownish with green flecks sat in the middle of the plate. Meat, possibly? A pool of watery sauce covered a pile of limp potato slices and a pool of almost yellow creamed corn flanked the meat thing. I slammed the lid back over the plate, my appetite completely gone.

I was going to starve to death.

"You're not eating in here." Elise's voice pulled my attention from the tray of maybe food.

"I might, I have permission to."

"Wasn't a question, Whitey. It's a statement. You. Are. Not. Eating. In. My. Room. It's disgusting, and it smells." The slur stung, as they always had. But, she had no idea what I knew. That took some sting out, enough for me to stand up for myself. Words couldn't shut me down. Not this time.

"That's rich. I can barely smell it over the rotting food in the dresser."

Elise's eyes flared. In moments her face hovered right in front of mine. "You looked in my dresser? You have no right to go through my things!"

"Your things? Rotting food is sitting in the two drawers that are supposed to be mine! I have no idea how no one has figured it out that you're hiding food instead of eating it. It smells like death in here. The only explanation is that everyone here is dumber than you."

"You told on me!" the anger in her eyes edged with fear.

"No, I didn't."

"Elise stepped back, "What?" A look of genuine shock came over her. She couldn't believe I didn't rat her out.

"But I will, if you don't get rid of every packet in those drawers, or if you continue to hide food in here. This place is hellish enough without having to deal with the stink of rotting food day in and day out." I narrowed my eyes at Elise, hoping it drove home my serious stance.

Her eyes narrowed right back, "Are you threatening me?"

"No, I'm giving you an option. You can get rid of your gross hoard and find some other way to trick Dr. Preble, or you don't and I'll be more than happy to complain about the smell coming from the dresser. You'll be forced to eat and actually get better. I'll even consider starting to eat in the cafeteria now, instead of when I'm ready to."

After a minute of considering my proposition, Elise smiled, not warm or friendly, more snide. "Fine. But, I can't do it all at once. It'll look suspicious." She stepped to the door, "I'll start with what's in my pockets now. Tomorrow I'll do some more, until it's all gone. I promise."

My body slumped onto the bed, exhausted after she left to throw away the food in her pockets. I couldn't believe I'd just done that. Confrontation had never been my strong suit. The fact I'd just stood my ground and won bewildered me. Made me proud. But I still had no appetite.

I smiled to myself as I placed the tray of maybe food on the floor just outside the door to be picked up. The high of actually speaking up when I needed to finally feeling real enough to celebrate. Did it mean that Elise and I were friends? No, not by a long shot. But at least we stood on even ground. She knew walking all over me wouldn't happen, and I knew I could keep it that way. It felt good to stand up for myself.

There was nothing else to do, and I didn't really care about changing into pajamas. Part of me wanted to hang on to what I had left of my own belongings as long as possible. Enjoy wearing real underwear for a little longer and force the institute to wait. Plus, my body wanted rest. Lots of rest. I curled up onto the bed and fell into a deep sleep.

I'd only been asleep for a few minutes it seemed when my bed began to violently shake, startling me awake. Instead of an earthquake, like my brain imagined, the source was much more human. Carina's face blurred into focus, along with her goons towering behind her.

"Get up. Dr. Preble wants to see you. Bring your things."

"My things?" my voice graveled with sleep. "Why?"

"Dr. Preble will explain further."

I looked over at Elise, who stood quietly near the foot of her bed hugging her elbows. She looked small and nervous, perhaps a little scared even. But it wasn't the same real fear she wore when the orderlies were after her. Suspicion niggled at the back of my mind. After all, there were two of her. Scared little girl Elise, and bitch Elise.

There was no real need for me to pack. Everything I owned not on my body was already tucked into my bag, thanks to not having any drawers. Carina eyed me curiously as I lugged it out from under the bed. No doubt she wondered at what I was up to, what motive I had to be packed and ready.

As I left, I gave a last look at Elise. I didn't know what I was looking for really, perhaps a nod of solidarity with our truce in place. I thought I saw a smirk hiding behind the shower of hair over her face. A second glance showed her as wary as before. My anxiety must've made me see wrong. At least that's what I told myself.

The feeling that something was up wouldn't leave me alone though.

"Ah, Elle. Here you are." Dr. Preble met us by the doors of the long term wing instead of his office, and dismissed the nurse and orderlies. "Walk with me," he placed a hand on my shoulder, guiding me along with him as I fell in step. "I must say, I'm disappointed, Elle. Less than 24 hours in treatment and I've received a complaint about you already."

"A complaint?" I asked, confused. I hadn't interacted with anyone today, aside from the doctor, nurses, orderlies, and Elise. Then it dawned on me. Elise. That smirk I wrote off. She turned the tables on me, instead of keeping her end of the deal. My insides simmered. I should have known better than to trust her.

"Now, don't play dumb. It's beneath you. Elise came to me after dinner with the dismaying news that you harassed her about her condition; made fun of her even."

"But,"

"It's not productive to her treatment if her roommate is going to bully her," he interrupted. "So, we are moving you to a new room. But we only have an available bed in our short term patient wing, so you'll have rotating roommates. I hope you treat them better than you did Elise."

"I didn't,"

He interrupted, "Why would Elise lie? She has nothing to gain from it, and we've never had a problem with her. You, on the other hand, do have a history of unsatisfactory behavior prior to coming here." He referred to the one incident that landed me here as if it were multiple incidents. It sucked.

"I won't," I promised, knowing it's what he wanted to hear. Beneath the surface I boiled. Falsely accused of harassment and not allowed to defend myself messed with me even more than what I'd done to get here. It told me all I needed to know. At the Kendrick Institute, my word was valued less than anyone else's. I didn't see me making any progress at the institute if that kind of treatment was what I could expect. I saw no reason to be super cooperative being offered.

I kept my head down the rest of the way to my new room, not saying anything. Not even responding to questions from Dr. Preble. My mind was raging with my new, new reality.

"Here we go, your new room," I looked up from my internal ranting to see we'd arrived at room 22N and Dr. Preble presenting it to me like I'd won a new car on a game show, big fake smile and all. Whoever I was sharing with wasn't there, all for the better. I'd already decided not to bother trying to know my roommates. There'd be no reason to if they were temporary. That, and I'd already been burned by one.

I'd been burned by almost everyone.

This room looked even less impressive than the other one, only slightly bigger. There were two beds. One was as plain and uncomfortable looking as I expected. The other had a brown and green crochet blanket draped at the foot. That one obviously was taken. I saw no dresser, so no win there. My clothes were meant to stay in my bag forever it seemed. But there was a chair, an uncomfortable looking fake leather armchair. It sat out of place, an eyesore. It certainly wasn't for guests. Those weren't allowed beyond the security doors.

"If there's anything you need, just let someone know."

I didn't thank him. Instead, I turned to Dr. Preble and responded with the first thing that came to mind, "Elise is hoarding rotten food in her dresser." The doctor looked baffled, he certainly wasn't expecting that. I didn't give him time to say anything in return, to accuse me of making up lies out of spite. I turned on heel and went into the room and curled up on the free bed.

EIGHT

A STRANGER THAT KNOWS ME

STARING at the same four walls of room 22N, except to go to medical check-ups, became wearing a lot faster than I thought possible. I ended up venturing out into out into the institution sooner than I anticipated. Because I paid so little attention to Carina's tour, and every time I went to a check-up I was escorted by personnel, I got lost trying to find my way around. Asking for directions from an orderly failed. Each one I approached merely rolled their eyes at me and told me I should have paid more attention, or that it wasn't their job. I didn't expect the nurses or other doctors to be helpful either. The whole staff came across as less than helpful, unless it benefited them.

Asking other patients never crossed my mind as a viable option. I didn't want to interact with people for the most part. Rare few people accepted me with open arms and open hearts out in the real world. At The Kendrick Institute I expected a lot of the same treatment I got out there, only ten fold. I gathered many of them didn't want to interact with me either, for some reason or another relating to my appearance or their own mental health reasons.

Eventually, I made it to the community room. The second I stepped into the large open area, I got a bad case of newbie syndrome once again, enhanced by the stares that I should have been accustomed to getting. That being said, the stares weren't as numerous as usual. Most of the patients were oblivious to me, too busy with their own demons to acknowledge anyone else. But, the stares coming at me unsettled me more than any other before. They didn't jeer or mock me for being some freak beneath them. No, the patients that stared were scared and confused; like they thought a ghost had just appeared in their midst.

Except for one. One man, sitting on an ugly orange chair under the farthest window on the left of the room, he watched me like a starving hawk, desperate and intense. He appeared older, maybe sixty-ish, with a mop of salt and pepper curls and sad brown eyes. My palms began to sweat and my heart rate quickened under his scrutiny. An overwhelming desire to run tingled at my feet. Every ounce of my body told me to beware this man.

I turned away from his intense stare and surveyed the other side of the room. A small book-cart on the far right end of the room caught my eye. Smiling at the idea of losing myself in a book, for the first time in what seemed like forever, I made my way over to it.

The selection on the cart consisted of twelve books at most. A meager smattering of titles, but I managed to find an interesting looking dystopian novel among the worn out pile. I grabbed it up and settled on the floor under the farthest right window in the room, as far from the staring man as possible.

The words on the page failed to stick in my head, disrupted by distraction. Scopaesthesia kept niggling with my mind. Sure enough, when I looked over, I caught the man with the peppery curls staring, watching me. He stood when he saw me looking at him, taking a tentative step before changing his mind and sitting again. I narrowed my eyes at him before going back to the book, silently letting him know that I didn't want to be messed with. The bow of his head made me think he understood.

He didn't. The feeling flared. I looked up and the man's eyes bore into me again, he was up and moving, halfway across the room coming at me. I practically heard his sneakers squeal against the linoleum when he stopped abruptly at my notice. Panicked, he shuffled back to his original spot, wringing his hands. The next time I looked up, he was even closer. Just a few steps away from being inside my personal bubble. The unease he made me feel shifted to annoyance.

"What?" I asked, flopping the book into my lap, losing my place.

The man's face crumbled, chin quivering and tears filling his eyes. "Princess. Sorry," he whimpered, turning on his heel and fleeing back to his corner, wiping his eyes furiously as he sat back down.

I felt bad for hurting his feelings with one annoyed word. I didn't mean to make him cry. I just wanted to know why he kept watching me, approaching me. I was sure I just got myself into trouble again, if he complained. Or if anyone saw. Great. Just what I needed.

"Time for afternoon meds," a female voice called out over the din of the community room. I looked for her, but didn't see her through the meandering crowd of patients that got up at her call. "Please walk in an orderly fashion to the pill line," her voice so detached she may as well have been a robot.

I lingered in my corner of the community room until most of the crowd thinned, waiting until I was certain the man left the room. I wanted to avoid being next to him in line. That would have been awkward as anything. At the same time, I made sure I left with people, so I didn't get lost again.

My plan turned out to be a huge mistake. I found myself near the end of the line, and the few patients behind me kept crowding forward; either eager to take their medicines or making sure they did what they'd been told to avoid trouble. I kept getting shoved into the person in front of me every time the patients surged behind me, earning dirty looks from the patient before me. After what seemed the billionth time, I wrapped my arms around myself protectively and stood facing outward instead, hoping it'd help. It didn't. The jostling continued, everyone involved becoming more and more annoyed as the minutes dragged by.

As I neared the front of the line, I spotted the older man from before hovering around a corner. He repeatedly crumpled and uncrumpled his water cup while chewing on what had to be his pills. He didn't seem to be paying attention to anything else. Good. I kept my eye on him while I moved up the line, making sure he remained preoccupied. The way he watched me, unnerved me to the core. It wasn't just how he had obsessively stared. Something about him made me want to hide.

"Next!" the nurse called again prompting my feet, and everyone else's, to shuffle further along the line. All the while, I kept watching the strange man. There was a tap on my shoulder, to which I apologized without looking. The tapping persisted, getting faster. Finally, having enough of the rude behavior, I turned and saw it had been the pill line nurse. She glared at me in contempt, "I said, next, Ghosty," she enunciated next extra clearly, and left her mouth hanging open to mock me further. Ouch.

I'd been so focused on the guy from the community room that I didn't notice when I reached the front of the line. "Sorry," I mumbled, holding my hands out for the little plastic cup with my pills and the paper cup filled with water. She shoved them at me instead, tapping her foot when I didn't immediately take them. I grabbed them from her and sheepishly lifted the pill cup to my mouth. Before I could drink, someone crashed into me. The resulting tumble sending my tiny water cup out of my hand and spilling onto the nurse's uniform. One might have thought I'd spilled acid on her, the way she reacted.

Wide eyed, I stuttered an apology that fell on deaf ears. Her eyes blazed, alternating between me and the person that caused the accident. I had to know who put me in this position. I followed her gaze as she shifted; the man from the community room. Of course he caused this. "Thanks a lot," I groaned, "now I have to dry swallow my pills. Can't you just leave me alone?"

"No, no, no," he repeated to himself, his eyes wide and fearful.

Rolling my eyes, I lifted the pill cup to my lips again. A hand shot out, and knocked the paper container from my hand. It and the pills pinged about on the dingy linoleum floor. I didn't have to look to know this was the work of my stalker. I spun on him, angry and shocked. Why had he singled me out like this?

The nurse groaned into her walkie-talkie, "John Doe is being disruptive in the pill line. Can I get some assistance please?" After getting a garbled response, she jammed the walkie back into her pocket, it squealed in protest at the abuse. She then turned her attention to me, "Well, hurry and pick them up."

"You want me to take them still? The floor is dirty!" her expectation completely grossed me out. I couldn't believe that a nurse wanted me to put floor pills in my mouth. She of all people knew how unsanitary that was.

"We don't want to waste it, do we?"

I narrowed my gaze on John Doe and pursed my lips tight. Thanks to him I had to stick pills in my mouth from the dirty floor and dry swallow them. I began to stoop to pick them up, and got shoved away.

"No! No! Poison!" John Doe screeched, stomping them into dust. He grinned at me, huffing and satisfied with his work. "I do good?" he asked earnestly. His pride cut short moments later when the orderlies came and dragged him away. His legs and arms flailed against their control, and his cries echoed off the bare walls as they went.

Shaking off my shock, I looked back at the nurse, dismayed and unsure of what to do. "What?" she snapped. "I don't have any more of your meds to give you. You should have held on to them better. Now you have to go see Dr. Preble and explain to him why you haven't taken your medicine."

Did she really blame me for this? Ugh. I always felt hate was a strong word, and never wanted to make snap judgments of others. My bullying played a large part in that belief. But at that moment, I truly began hating the staff of The Kendrick Institute. They didn't care about anything other than their bottom line. Truly evil. Turning on my heel, I stormed away before I did anything to land me in more hot water.

I fumed through the halls, in no mood to see the snooty doctor. I wondered how much trouble I'd get in if I didn't go see Dr. Preble. The more I thought about it the more I didn't want to go. He was creepy and talked down to me all the time. I doubted the nurse would go see him anytime soon either, since no one wanted to do their jobs. My feet stopped with a new thought. Perhaps I'd just skip my meds. That sounded like a great idea to me. They gave me headaches anyway.

My feet started back up, taking me towards room 22N instead of Dr. Preble's office.

DINNER TIME ROLLED AROUND and I still had a mountain sized chip on my shoulder. My mood dipped even lower when John Doe approached me at dinnertime, head hanging low and shuffling his feet. He looked pitiful. Still, I couldn't let go of my anger. I got in trouble because of his actions, because he had some weird vendetta against me. I wasn't about to sit there and find out what he wanted. I shoved my spoon into the gruel on my tray and started to leave.

John Doe stepped into my path. Every time I tried to go around the other way, he sidestepped back in, preventing me from leaving. Every time, my irritation flamed harder. Finally I gave up, "What do you want, John Doe?" I growled.

He sniffled, wiping his hand across his nose without looking up, "No John. Abe. Abe sorry."

"Abe? You should be. I got in a lot of trouble because of you!" I snapped.

He looked up. Big tears rolled down his cheeks, one of which had a nice bruise forming on it. Shit. The orderlies really roughed him up for his disturbance earlier, instead of just taking him away. "Abe sorry," he repeated. "Abe protect Princess. Pills bad. Abe sorry."

My heart broke, even though I was still furious. He didn't deserve to be beaten over a few smashed pills. But, I needed to remain tough.

I didn't want to encourage him to keep following me around and doing things like that. "I'm no princess, and I don't need protecting." I pushed my way past him and dumped my tray.

"Abe sorry," his pitiful moan drifted to my ears as I left the cafeteria.

John Doe, Abe, or whoever he claimed to be, weighed on my mind while I walked back to my room. My anger towards him slipped from it's dock in my heart and drifted slowly. In his delusional mind, he thought he helped me. I couldn't blame him, well I could, but it wasn't really his fault. His mind didn't work the way it should, or else he wouldn't be at the institute. I understood that all too well. He seemed genuinely concerned for me, genuinely sorry for getting me in trouble.

I decided I should probably be nicer and give him a chance instead of being rude when he approached me. He seemed just as lonely as I felt. Plus, I'd want someone to do the same for me. Give me a chance before hating me. The decision lifted some of the weight on my shoulders. Made me feel better. I wasn't prepared to apologize just then, though. I knew he'd find me sooner or later.

NINE

REWARDS OF GOOD BEHAVIOR

My first impression of the doctors and other patients turned out wrong. Well, my impression of the nurses, doctors, and orderlies had been pretty on the nose. They weren't to be trusted. The one I made about the harmlessness of most of the patients was where I went wrong. So wrong. To put it in relative terms; the drama of high school sucked, more than words could describe. Yet, it paled in comparison to life at The Kendrick Institute. If I could, I'd have gone back to those over-packed halls filled with gossips and bullies in a heartbeat. At least there I had Q, and the teachers weren't power mad masochists.

Let's just say the majority of the patients were either afraid of me, or were exactly like the kids in high school. Some were worse. Like Elise. Her personal mission seemed to be to make my life miserable by getting me into minor trouble, and to fuel the fear of the patients more wary of my appearance. Not only was she a bitch, she was a master manipulator.

A small population of the patients didn't even have me on their radar. I liked them. They left me alone, I left them alone. A mutual, unsaid and unagreed upon accord. It just happened.

Then there was Abe. It seemed every time I turned around he would be there, ready to save me from whatever he thought threatened me. Or to creep me out. Take your pick. Whichever the case, he had a persistent nature.

After our initial meeting in the community room, I thought for sure he'd give up on his delusional need to help me. I'd been less than kind, and I felt like garbage because of it. Plus, the orderlies had "taught him a lesson" that left him bruised for days.

Skittish by nature, he did become wary, for a little while anyway. He'd hover nearby, ducking out of sight when I caught his distressed stares. I could tell he warred with himself, wringing his hands and running them through his salt and pepper curls. The need to save the princess battling self preservation. His duck and cover maneuver quickly turned into hesitant approaches, only to retreat after a few steps.

This went on for weeks. Even though it irritated me to be watched that way, I let it slide. The trouble wasn't worth it. I didn't want to get him in trouble either. Despite what he'd done before, he wasn't a threat. Others were.

Then the gifts started. Simple things, mostly origami flowers. Many of the intricately folded flora looked like no flowers I'd ever seen before. His imaginary flowers were beautiful and delicate. I wished they were real. Within another few weeks, I had a gorgeous bouquet of paper flowers stuffed in a red plastic cup.

He also left me stones, buttons, bits of string, and other random trinkets. Most of those I discreetly disposed of once in my shared room in the short term wing. I began to think of him as my own Puff the Magic Dragon, but I wasn't ready to actually befriend him. Not yet.

The only thing that kept me afloat was the promise of being allowed visitors after I'd shown I could cooperate and not cause trouble. Believe me, trouble came knocking on more than one occasion, on behalf of my first roomie. Not to mention, my tongue became harder and harder to control when it came to the staff's fake niceties and heavy fists. The struggle was real. After the longest month and a half ever, and heaps of willing myself to behave even when Elise tried to provoke me, the approval came through.

The second I had the phone slip in my hand, I flew to the phone room; slapping that miraculous piece of paper on the counter topping the half door for the attendant, a short dark haired man with a friendly smile but dead eyes, to file and grant me access. When he opened the door for me, I felt as though Saint Peter had just unlocked the pearly gates for me.

"Thanks, Pete," I named him as I slid past.

"It's Todd, actually," he corrected, but I paid no mind to correcting myself or apologizing. I was on a mission.

A delayed mission, I realized the moment I looked at the bank of wooden phone booths that lined the back wall. Each one was occupied. With a defeated huff vibrating my lips, I sat on one of the hardwood chairs, grouped in the center of the room, to wait. Phone calls were limited to fifteen minutes, I knew I wouldn't have to wait too long. Still, the seconds ticked at a snail's pace surrounded by the excruciating muffled conversations of fellow patients. They felt like mocking promises of finally being able to contact someone who cared. Q.

While I waited, I planned what I would tell my best friend. So much had happened since I'd seen him last. So much, yet not much of anything at the same time. When your whole life took place within the same walls day in and out, with a set schedule of when to do things, you couldn't expect there to be too much variety.

The squeal of an accordion door opening pulled me from my planning. My head snapped to attention. Every muscle in my body twitched to move while I watched a greasy haired androgynous patient slowly exit the booth, teary eyed and pink nosed. Their obvious upset helped keep me in my seat until they were clear. I didn't want to topple over someone who'd just had an upsetting experience.

Just because I didn't make an effort to get to know anyone, didn't mean I was going to be an asshole.

I scanned over the phone instructions posted on the booth wall as I sat and closed the door. They were simple enough, I wouldn't screw it up. Finally, my fingers wrapped around the receiver and dialed Q's number. The line rang twice and hung up.

The ignored call didn't dishearten me. I expected it. It was our thing. Our code. Anytime an unknown number called Q, he hung up after two rings. When I called him from an unknown number, I immediately called him back and let it ring twice before hanging up. Then I'd call again. That was when Q would finally answer.

As the line rang for the final time, my heart jumped in anticipation. My breath caught when the line picked up. "Elle!" a sense of relief washed over me when Q's voice filled the line. I had to fight off the emotions that threatened to overtake me. It had been far too long since I'd heard a friendly voice.

"Q!" I half sobbed, "You have no idea how great it is to hear your voice. There's so much to tell you."

"Where are you? You just disappeared after you last texted me."

"The Kendrick Institute. They threw me in a psychiatric facility Q. I just got phone privileges and visitation instated. You have to come keep me from going bonkers."

"Way ahead of you Ells, headed to ask Ma." I listened to him stampede through his home, and soon heard to sound of Janice Queen humming in the background. "Hey, Ma, can I skip school tomorrow and go see Elle?"

"That's a dumb question Quentin. No."

"Ma! Come on, be cool," he argued while I listened.

"I'm cool, just not that cool. I'm happy Elle's finally back in touch with you, but no. Visiting can wait until the weekend."

Q turned his attention back to me, "Sorry, have to wait until the weekend. But I will be there as early as possible on Saturday. Not even the hottest man could keep me away."

We chatted for a few more minutes. I told him about Elise and how awful the food was, but there wasn't much time for anything else. My allotted time went by way too fast. There was still so much to tell him. It would have to wait until Saturday. "I gotta go, Q. I only get fifteen minutes. But, I'll see you Saturday?"

"I'll be there, don't worry Ells. I love you."

"Love you too."

As I reached put replace the phone on the receiver, my head began to spin and the world turned to frosted glass. The vision came on so fast, I didn't have time to react. The speed at which the hallucination came on wasn't the only thing that threw me off guard. This time the frosted world was inky dark, with dots of light. Like looking at the night sky through a dirty lens. The only sound of was of a man singing. His lyrics were muffled and warbled too much to understand a word, but the tune reminded me of a lullaby.

As quickly as the trip inside my head came on, it left. I came to with the dial tone screeching from the phone, and Todd pounding on the accordion door while pointing to his watch in irritation. A single tear slowly rolled down my cheek, and I had no idea why.

Placing the phone on its cradle, I made a hasty exit from the booth, and the phone room.

BY THE TIME Saturday rolled around, my excitement at seeing a friendly face could hardly be contained. It hadn't been hard to keep out of trouble while waiting either. The promise of seeing Q kept my mood elevated so much, nothing got to me, not even Abe's constant stalking.

That morning, to my surprise, the nurse brought me some of my confiscated clothes; a pair of ripped blue jeans and a plain black t-shirt, no real underwear though. I appreciated them, even though I suspected it wasn't for my sake. The normal clothes were a show for my visitor. They could have at least given my own underthings back, though. It was bad enough I had to go bra-less all the time, but the paper underwear were extreme torture. They chaffed when they stayed together, and every move I made was accompanied by the sound of them rustling in my pants.

I hated them.

Even though I had my own clothes for the day, I still threw the institute issued sweater on over my t-shirt. The chill from the late fall weather seeped into the walls and floors of the place. No matter how many times they heard complaints about it being too cold, the thermostat felt like it remained at a steady 70 degrees. Definitely warmer than the outside, obviously not warm enough.

As I made my way to the visitation wing I fought the urge to run. The Kendrick Institute had strict rules about running in the halls, just like everything else. It didn't surprise me they had a whole wing dedicated to visitation. Dr. Preble liked to keep the patients "safe" from outside influence, touting many were disturbed by strangers. I could buy that. Though, like the street clothes, I figured it was more for keeping up appearances than anything. What the public got to see, and what everyone else saw, were decidedly different.

I showed my visitation pass to the orderly stationed outside the double doors leading to the visitation wing. He was a far cry from Thug One and Two, small in height and slight of build with frizzy brown curls pulled back into a low ponytail and brown rimmed glasses framing his muddy eyes. I'd disturbed his riveting game of solitaire spread over the desk before him, though he barely took the time to look up from it. Just long enough to see my pass and buzz me through the secure doors. His lackadaisical view of his job didn't give me much hope that the visitation wing never got crashed by unapproved patients.

Beyond the doors sat a whole new world. One bright and colorful, and surprisingly, homey. The large space was more a converted gymnasium than an actual wing, complete with skeletons of basketball hoops hanging over each end. Beneath a modge-podge of dime store oriental rugs, bits of the colorful stripes on the hardwood floor could still be seen. Chairs and couches of various colors, and signs of wear, were spaced sporadically about; each one adorned with vibrant pillows that begged to be hugged.

In the back of the room were long tables, with lacy white table-cloths, lined with a variety of snacks. Several clear drink dispensers, and hot drink carafes sat nestled among the food; strong coffee aroma filled the air. I couldn't wait to pillage the offerings. Surely the fare was a million times better than the institute's less than mediocre cafeteria. My stomach flipped excitedly at the thought of actually edible food.

Food would have to wait, though.

Moments after entering the visitation wing my eyes were drawn to the most colorful thing in the space, a shock of aquamarine hair. Q. He stood at one of the windows, watching something outside. Immediately, my eyes welled with tears of joy and relief. Never in my life had I been so happy to see a friendly face. I tip-toed up behind him, tapping him on the shoulder.

"Ells!" he beamed as he turned, greeting me with a broad smile and eyes sparkling with the same tears I held off, and wrapped me in the bear hug to end all bear hugs.

We moved our reunion to one of the many available seats, a navy blue microfiber chair that barely had enough room for one of us, with Q taking the bulk of the chair and me draped over his lap. Immediately, a supervising nurse approached us, reminding us to keep things PG.

"It's okay, Ma'am," Q noted. "I'm gay."

"Either separate or this visit is over," she threatened, her face pinched. I maneuvered to sit on one of the chair's arms. "Thank you," she huffed, running her hands over her tightly pulled back hair as she walked away.

We erupted in quiet laughter. "Is everyone here like that?" Q asked when we composed ourselves.

"Worse."

"Yikes. Seriously?"

"Nurse PG over there is so mild compared to others," I began, ready to spill all the tea I'd experienced so far, only to be interrupted by Nurse PG shouting followed by a whimpering I knew all too well. My eyes tracked the commotion to the other side of the visitation wing. The prudish nurse was involved in a chase with Abe. A groan slipped past my lips, "Oh no."

"What is it?" Q asked looking where I did.

"That patient Nurse PG is chasing, shouldn't be here."

"You sure, he could be waiting for someone."

I shook my head, "No, he doesn't have people on the outside. Abe's a John Doe." I explained the situation to Q, including the reason why Abe was considered a John Doe, but I knew his name. As he listened his eyes dipped sympathetically while watching Abe skirt out of Nurse PG's grasp time and time again. "He's harmless really, so I don't make too much of a fuss with him following me around, even though I wish he'd leave me alone. I hope he doesn't get in too much trouble for this."

"Well, Ells, maybe he won't." Q's voice held a hint of a plan. My best friend always advocated for the little guy, case in point; me. It didn't surprise me he wanted to protect Abe too.

"What are you implying?"

"You say he's harmless, so why not just accept his friendship. You need someone in here with you. Otherwise, you're gonna really lose it," he paused, taking another moment to watch the scene across the room. "That being said, I have an idea."

Internally, I winced. But, Q was right. He almost always was. I felt reluctant to accept Abe into my exclusive circle of one. While I'd grown use to him following me from a distance, I wasn't sure I could handle him all the time. Reluctantly, I agreed, "Okay. I can do that. What's your plan?"

Q grinned from ear to ear and held a finger up to me. He maneuvered out of the chair and strode across the room to where Abe still gave Nurse PG a run for her money. As he approached he let out a loud chuckle, "Abe! Hey buddy." The older man stopped in his tracks, his salt and pepper curls bouncing wildly from the abrupt action. He looked confused, but not nearly as much as the nurse did. "Me and Ells were waiting for you to show up for our visit, come on," he gestured for Abe to join him.

Understanding, I hustled to join Q, arriving just in time to hear Nurse PG doubt Abe had a visitor. "Mr. Doe here never has visitors."

"He does today," I chimed in. Abe's face lit, making him look years younger than before.

"Yes. Abe visit Princess," he proudly declared in his broken speech to the nurse.

"Whatever," she replied, not wanting to deal with it anymore, and walked away.

Abe came back to the chair with us, happily taking a spot on the floor. I wondered what I'd just gotten myself into.

TEN

THERAPY WITH A SIDE OF BRAINS

ABE WAITED FOR ME, bouncing anxiously on his heels when I came into sight. I had my doubts about befriending the odd man, but in the end Q was right. I needed a person on the inside. Having a "me against the rest" attitude wasn't good for me. But with Abe on my side, officially, I didn't mind it being me against everyone that wasn't Abe. In fact, he mellowed me when it came to the other patients, even Elise. Her all around vileness rolled off my back rather than made me get defensive every time I was near her. It made for a much more pleasant experience at the institute, not that it changed how I felt about being there. I'd still have left in a heartbeat if I could have.

I even learned to tolerate most of the staff, saving a hefty dose of saltiness for a select few. Namely Carina, Thug One and Two, and, of course, Dr. Preble. They were like a team of super villains. They deserved all the sass they got from me. There was just something about them that brought out the degenerate in me. I couldn't help it.

"Hey Abe, you good?" I asked, stopping next to him. He seemed more agitated that usual, something had definitely upset him.

"No good. They plan. Hurt you," his eyes shifted around, making sure we weren't being listened to.

"What do you mean, they're trying to hurt me?"

"You go home," he grabbed my hand, squeezing it tight.

"I don't have a home, Abe. This is my home now." I hated those words. But they were true. After months of being stuck here, I came to accept The Kendrick Institute as my fate. I'd probably never set foot outside their grounds again.

"Home. I get you home."

Abe wasn't making any sense at all. He rarely did. But, this was different. He really seemed to think something bad threatened me. I'd grown used to his strange behavior and insistence on calling me Princess since allowing him in my personal bubble. I'd even humored him with his attempts to prevent me from being treated, from taking my medications. Honestly, he'd been good for me, he helped alleviate my aggravated state.

The nurses kept telling me I'd been good for Abe too. He livened up and began speaking for the first time since he arrived at Kendrick Institute many years ago. Not that he talked to anyone except me, and was still a little hard to understand with his broken speech.

But this insistent warning? It genuinely worried me. Not because I fully believed I was in real danger. Because it took his anxious hovering to a whole new level.

"No one is trying to hurt me," I gripped Abe's shoulder in, looking into his eyes to assure him.

"Yes, yes are. Your brain, they want it. They cut it. I send you home. Home only safe place."

What he implied shook me. Scared me even. It almost sounded like he thought they wanted to lobotomize me. Where did he get such an idea? I brushed the worry aside. "I'm sure you're mistaken, Abe. They can't do that. Are you sure you didn't just dream it?"

"No, no dreams. Real. I know plan. I know. I heard."

I patted Abe's hand, hoping it comforted him, as I mulled over my options. I could go along with his delusion and get him to settle down. Or, I could go to Dr. Preble. There were risks in both. Trying to settle

Abe by myself might have agitated him more, making a situation that was potentially dangerous. He could've ended up hurting himself in his bid to rescue me from the institute. Plus, the possibility of him hurting me with one of his "potions" was real. Dr. Preble had more ability to handle the situation.

Then again, involving the so called enemy held a whole slew of other problems, including Abe getting punished. Beaten. Also, I feared Abe would end up hating me if I involved Dr. Preble. The old man was the only person in this place that made me feel normal. Which said less than you'd think. I didn't want to lose him, even if he annoyed me half the time.

I didn't know what to do.

I did the only thing I thought of that didn't end in either of us getting hurt. "I'm sorry, Abe. I'm sorry you're scared for me. I'm going to be okay." I began to walk away, but Abe grabbed my arm. I looked back at him and saw him shaking his head furiously.

"No, no, no, no."

Yanking my arm from his grip, I apologized to him again. It's all I could do. Apologizing for his feelings was silly, I knew that, but there was nothing else to do. I yanked my arm from his grip, "I have to go."

Abe's quiet tears lingered in my head, drowning out all other noises as I walked away, "I sorry. I fail you. I fail."

His lament haunted me while I walked through the halls of the institute, just wandering aimlessly thinking about the situation. My mind and heart fought in an agonizing split of what to do. Abe was genuinely concerned for me, but did that worry have any merit? Not likely. His reality only made sense to him. He thought me a princess for crying out loud. I wanted him to stop his worrying, which he wouldn't do on his own. At the same time, Dr. Preble hadn't made my short list of reliable people. He could help, but it wasn't wanted by me.

"Elle, just the patient I'm looking for," my lace-less white sneakers squeaked on the linoleum under the abrupt stop the interruption caused. I looked up and saw the devil himself walking towards me, Dr. Preble and he looked happy to see me. That couldn't be good.

"Can't be that hard to find. There's only so many places I can go."

"Now, don't be like that," he responded to my obvious remark about being trapped here. "I thought we were past feeling glum."

My eyes rolled, "Like I can ever get used to being here against my will."

Dr. Preble clicked his tongue against his teeth. "I need to discuss some things with you about your treatment plan. Follow me to my office."

I groaned, not caring that he knew my displeasure at the order. There was only one reason he would be asking me to go to his office. The same reason for every visit. He figured out the meds weren't working, at least when I took them. It didn't matter if I took them or not. The only difference between the days I did and the days I didn't were the headaches.

I had to give it to the staff of the institute, they were a lot quicker than my old doctors. It would take them several months to figure out I'd been faking it. These guys figured it out in weeks. I was pretty sure the constant supervision clued them in. That, and the fact Abe stole my meds a lot.

My steps changed into a dragging shuffle as I fell in line behind the doctor. I was not looking forward to this.

"WE'VE NOTICED your medicine isn't working the way we hoped, again." Dr. Preble noted the moment my butt the red Naugahyde chair reserved for patients in his office. No time to try to get comfortable or admire his ghastly taste in decor hanging amongst the medical diagrams and diplomas. He needed a human touch in his office, to put it nicely.

"What gave it away?" I asked snidely. "My non-zombie status?"

His responding chuckle was insincere. "Henry found John Doe with a handful of your medications yesterday. Can you explain that?"

I shrug. "Abe," I corrected, "steals them before I can take them. I can't exactly wrestle them from him or ask for more." I hated that the staff refused to accept Abe's real name. No matter how many times I corrected them, they still called him John Doe.

"You could have reported him."

"And let your brute squad hurt him for it? No thanks. He doesn't deserve that. Abe is harmless, and he thinks he's protecting me by taking the meds."

Dr. Preble cringed. He didn't like me calling out the fact he let the nurses and orderlies handle the patients roughly. "We are here discussing you," he cleared his throat before continuing, "not John Doe. You seem to have adopted a rather devil-may-care attitude about your treatment. Don't you want to get better?"

I snorted, he knew there was no chance of me getting better. I could only attempt manage my symptoms, which never worked. Thinking on it, I hadn't had as much issue with my hallucinations since Abe started stealing my meds. The days I got to take my meds were the days I had more trouble with them.

"I hate to say it, but you have given us little choice in how we continue to treat you. Short of having an escort with you in the pill line, we can't guarantee you take your meds. When you do take them, they seem to have little affect on your condition. I think it's time we consider a less-than traditional approach."

My heart morphed into a bird, frantic to fly away. Sweat slicked my palms. My thoughts immediately jumped to Abe's warning. Was he right? "What, what do you mean?" the words stumbled out of my mouth."

"Well, I feel that we should consider the brain maps we did when you first got here. Use those as a guide for our plan of action."Dr. Preble spoke vaguely, leaving out key information.

I remembered the brain mapping, the experience was mind numbing and awful. He never shared those results with me. Almost none of my medical information had been. I shifted in my seat, which creaked in response, "What plan of action?"

"I think the best course of action is going to be altering the afflicted portion of your brain."

"Altering exactly what part of my brain, and how?" I gulped back the rainbow yawn threatening to appear.

"Your brain map was not exactly conclusive, but it pointed to the most activity in a hallucination being in the frontal lobe."

He didn't have to explain further. I knew what he was getting at. I shot out of the sticky seat. "A lobotomy!" I screeched at him, my voice nearly only audible to dogs. "You can't do that. It's illegal! I want a lawyer."

"This isn't a police station, Elle. You don't really get a choice in this. You were placed here under orders from the state, which means I decide how you are cared for. This is our last option. Our best option at this point."

"Doesn't change the fact that it is barbaric and illegal! You'll never get approval for it." I leaned across the desk and jab my finger at him in accusation.

"Not if I call it brain surgery, pure and simple. The details can be fudged."

I fell into the chair in disbelief. What the fuck? Abe was right. It wasn't one of his delusions. Frightened tears squeezed past my eyelashes and down my face at the implications of his words. Dr. Preble didn't care about legalities, he was God in his own eyes. He was going to do what he wanted by lying to bolster his success rate. Higher success rates equaled more money.

"Now, now, Elle. I know it's scary, but I am only doing what is best for you. You don't want these episodes to continue your whole life. Always fearing you're going to hurt someone again. This is the best course of action. You will see that, in time."

"If I'm not a vegetable," I spat.

Dr. Preble stood, straightening his white coat and gestured to the door. I was dismissed. Nothing else would be said on the matter. Game over.

Weak and defeated, the reality of my situation hung over my head like a dark cloud. I left Dr. Preble's office with, all things considered, a death sentence. I marched straight to my room, a zombie with no interest in anything. Once there, I flung myself onto the bed and cried myself empty.

ELEVEN

I BELIEVE IN MAGIC, OR SCIENCE

ABE WAS RIGHT.

The simple statement played over and over in my head, yet still felt unbelievable to me. The whole time I knew him, I assumed he was a simple and harmless patient, living in a world of delusions. That was obviously not the case. There was so much more to him than he let on, he seemed to know everything.

The meeting with Dr. Preble left my eyes open. My mind raced like a greyhound chasing any sort of logic behind the shocking revelation. He meant to fix me via lobotomy. How on earth could a medical professional even think of doing something so archaic? It was unthinkable. Worse, nothing could stop him. Despite his adamant assurance, his treatment plan held nothing good; it gave me a bad feeling. I tried to look at the positives of Dr. Preble's plans, the way Q would have. None existed, other than not caring bout the shitty food anymore.

The idea of Q coming to see me one day and finding me a shell of who I used to be, only made me want to cry some more. God, I missed him. His parents too. I had no clue when he'd come visit me next. By then it would probably be too late. If only Dr. Preble allowed me phone privileges today. I would have called them in a heart beat. Mr. Queen's moral medical practices would have sent them flying to the institute. They'd have saved me.

If only the opportunity to run away presented itself. I'd do what Abe wanted me to. But there was nowhere for me to go that wouldn't land the few people I cared about in a world of shit.

The more I thought about it, the more I couldn't let go of the idea of escape. I started feeling like there could be a chance. A small chance. Maybe Abe being right about the drastic treatment course Dr. Preble wanted to take meant he was right about helping me. He insisted he could send me home, or at least somewhere safe. He wanted to help me escape the cruel fate waiting for me under Dr. Preble's scalpel. Why shouts I let him help me?

I knew what I wanted to do. No, what I had to do. My self-preservation instinct had kicked in. I had to at least try to save myself, I had to find Abe. If a small chance existed that he could help me, I had to take it. I had to reach for that small glimmer at the bottom of the abyss I'd sunk into since learning my fate.

I bolted from my room, startling my current roommate, without even putting on slippers or shoes. I knew I risked get written up for running in the halls and for having bare feet outside my room, but I didn't care. Let them write me up. What did it matter at that point? I'd either be leaving, by some miracle, or I'd soon become drooling lump. Either way, getting written up seemed like small potatoes.

Searching for Abe turned into a wild goose chase. My first instinct led me astray, and he wasn't in his room. I stopped just long enough there to ascertain his presence. I moved like lightning after that, flying through the halls, only slowing to avoid colliding with other patients. I didn't even heed the venomous glares and shouted orders to stop running from nurses and orderlies. None of them tried to stop me, though. The extra work of chasing me down and writing me up was too much work.

I had to stop to catch my breath after not finding Abe in the cafeteria or the community room. The soles of my feet stung from slapping against the cool linoleum floors. I lifted them one by one, balancing on the other, to rub the sting away while I thought. The bathrooms were a no go for me. I didn't want to be the weirdo stalking the men's room. I knew for certain he wasn't in visitation. He never had visitors on his own. I hoped Q continued to visit him if I managed to escape. Or after I became a vegetable. Abe liked Q.

The only place left to look that Abe regularly visited was the garden. This time, I walked. Finding him was still urgent, but with all other possibilities eliminated I needed to slow down. At first, I didn't see him there either. Frustration built in my chest, frustration and panic. I thought that maybe those brutish orderlies did something to him as punishment for the meds they found on him yesterday.

I collapsed next to a lilac bush and gathered a handful of pebbles. I'd wait and rest for awhile, then go look again. One thing for sure, I had no intention to quit looking. I'd do it all day if I had to.

I transferred the tiny smooth stones from hand to hand while I thought of a backup plan, just in case. Maybe I could get a message to Q. Make friends with a patient getting out soon, or do the impossible and find a nurse or orderly that would help me. The sensation of the pebbles slipping past my fingers and thudding lightly into my other hand felt soothing, cathartic even. Almost as much as the old stone necklace these bastards confiscated upon my arrival. One thing for sure, I wanted that back.

A susurration in the dead lilac bush caught my attention for a moment. I figured the sound came from a rat or bird, or something, most likely a flea infested rodent than a bird. It wasn't a far reach to think beneath the shiny veneer of The Kendrick Institute lurked a kingdom of vermin as despicable as the people above. I shrugged it off and continued ruminating on possible solutions. Soon, the rustling grew louder and closer. I crouched, sticking my face next to the base of the bush, trying to view what made all the noise. The sound got louder as whatever hid in the lilac bush inched closer to bursting through the few, remaining and dead exterior leaves. The rustling stopped suddenly, leaving an unsettling hush behind. Suddenly, a dirty hand burst through the leaves and flowers just to the right of my face. I jolted back, screeching, accidentally tossing the tiny rocks into the air. They rained down on me in an annoyingly painful downpour of stone, dirt, and dust.

"Princess," Abe whispered through the foliage, "No be scared, safe. Come in."

I turned, surprised. Abe smiled at me broadly, his face half emerged from the lilac tree. "Abe! What on Earth?"

"Hiding. Brutes wanted hurt Abe. Come in, we speak."

"But, how? I'm surprised you fit in there, let alone the pair of us."

"Enter, you see." Abe's face dissolved back into the tree.

I shrugged to myself. What did I have to lose? Definitely not my dignity. That went out the window a long time ago. Worst thing I expected; getting horrifically stuck, having to be rescued by orderlies, and winding up on Dr. Preble's table.

I surveyed the garden, making sure that no one watched me. The nurses and orderlies in the garden seemed distracted by a commotion near the flower beds. I seized the opportunity to dive into the bush, even though I expected that would be as far as I got. I pushed my way past a few branches, which scratched at my arms and caught in my hair. To my surprise, the branches and leaves soon gave way to a clearing and little crawl space on the side of the building.

I squeezed through the opening into the secret space and marveled at the room I found myself in. The small space didn't hold much, with a standing sink it one corner and a table set up in the middle. The walls were lined with shelves stretching from the floor to the low ceiling, and were filled with jars and bags of what looked like colored sands. A dim bulb swung low on a chain over the table, providing the only light in the room.

"What is this place?" I gasped, still amazed at the secret place. My hands slid over the colorful jars in humble wonderment as I strolled through the room inspecting everything.

"Apothecary."

"How is it that the staff doesn't know about it?"

"Mine, only mine. No one else sees. Magic room."

"Ummm, okay." I dismissed his response. There had to be another explanation. Magic didn't exist outside of fantasies.

"You trust, you see."

I rocked on my heels, unsure of what I got myself into trusting him, "Abe, I don't understand."

"No need understand. Trust. You trust. I free Princess. I send home. Make right my bad."

I had no idea how Abe thought he had the ability to free me from Dr. Preble and his goons. There wasn't much any of us could do against them and their syringes filled with tranquilizers. But he was my one shot at it, so I rolled with it. I'd find my own solution once Abe's plan didn't pan out.

"How do you plan to do that? Are you planning on telling someone? Is that your plan?"

"No. I free you. You run. Escape. Return home." Abe skittered around the hidden room, picking up jars and examining them before putting them back. Some he kept and tucked in his arm, like a baby. "Elixirs. Elixirs get you home. Princess has no magic to return home."

"Abe," I sighed, "For the last time, I'm not a princess, and I have no home. The only way out of this shit of a treatment they have planned is telling someone who gives a damn."

Abe stopped, his eyes flaring, and slammed the jars down on the table in the center of the confined space. "Home! I send Princess home. Magic. Trust." His broken words held a fierce, almost forceful tone. If I hadn't known better, I'd have been afraid. I conceded to his whim and stepped back against the wall behind me.

Appeased, Abe grabbed an empty jar and a jug of water from another shelf and placed them next to the jars of colored powder. Then, he gestured for me to join him at the table. I took cautious steps forward, wary of his expectations. Of what he'd do when only he saw the magic results of this experiment.

"Watch, magic." Abe spooned some grayish powder from a short jar into the empty jar followed by a smaller amount of green powder and a larger amount of a pink one. He stirred them together before adding in a black liquid from a bottle and some water. I continued to watch, curious, as my old friend coated his hand with a white powder. "Watch," he repeated, pouring the gooey liquid concoction onto his powder-coated hand. In moments his hand began to smoke.

I jumped back, startled by the blue smoke slowly rising from his hand. The smoke gave way to flame. Yelping, I jumped into action and scrambled for the bottle of water. Abe stopped me with his flaming hand. I stared, amazed, at the fiery appendage wrapped around my wrist. It didn't hurt, not one bit.

Abe flashed a Cheshire grin, "Friendly Fire. Tomorrow. I distract. You escape."

My face slowly mimicked Abe's. There was a chance this would work.

TWELVE

PREP FOR SURGERY

LATER THAT NIGHT, I had a spring in my step. I practically skipped from the dining hall to my room. With Abe's "magic" help, my odds of getting out of this place definitely increased. Once out, I'd have to live on the road, which sent ice through my veins. Chances of being caught and brought back were high. But I'd at least taste freedom one last time, and I'd have the time to out Dr. Preble while I was free. That alone made the promised freedom worth it.

My mood lightened, to say the least. That is until I saw Thug One and Thug Two lurking about my room. This meant one of two things; my roommate got in trouble or I was about to be. They both eyed me, chucking as I passed between them into the room.

I did a quick inspection of my room. The room had been turned, tossed more like it, by the thug-like orderlies. The beds were unmade, blankets and pillows on the floor. The drawers in the dressers hung open unevenly, as did the drawers on the side tables. Clothes were strewn about, lying on the floor and hanging off the furniture. It looked like the place had been hit by a bomb.

My roommate was nowhere to be seen.

I knew what that meant, but I wished I didn't. That scared me.

Angered me. I wheeled around, feeling fire rage through me, and faced the brutes that stood outside the door. "What the Hell?" What is this for?" My arms flailed wildly about as I ranted. I held on to the sliver of hope this wasn't about me. I hoped my roommate had given the institute a good reason to search our room.

One of the orderlies, not sure which one really, replied with a smirk, "We was bored while waiting."

"Was bored? That's not a reason, that's not even good English. I swear they hired you because you're morons with muscles." Suddenly, the second half of their reason hit me. While waiting. For me. "What do you mean, while waiting," my ire became quieter thanks to the new, fearful lump that formed in my throat.

"Doc needs to see you."

The lump in my throat doubled in size, threatening to choke me. Dr. Preble never wanted to see patients after dinner. "Oh," I said, defeated. Just like that, I found myself shuffling behind a wall of meat-heads, heading to something I knew wouldn't be good.

We reached Dr. Preble's office in what seemed record time. He sat in his big chair looking smug with, to my surprise, a guest sitting across from him. Mrs. Wembley. Never had I been so happy to see her round, plain face.

"Mrs. Wembley, it is so good to see you," I rushed at my social worker and hugged her tight. She giggled nervously at my uncharacteristic move. "Please, I need to talk to you in private. I need help," I whispered in her ear. When I pulled back to look her in the eye, she looked concerned. Her concern, though, seemed more for herself than for me.

"Elle, dear. It's nice to see you too," she brushed off my whispered plea.

"Ah, Elle," Dr. Preble greeted me, "come and sit. I have good news."

"Really? I doubt I'll consider it good."

"Don't be like that, Elle. Dr. Preble is looking out for you," Mrs. Wembley chided.

"Have you heard what he's planning for my treatment? If you had, you wouldn't say that. He's going to lobotomize me!" I stood and flailed my arms for dramatic effect, which didn't help my case. Mrs. Wembley scooted away from me, her concern doubled.

"Oh, come now. Dr. Preble isn't going to do that. Lobotomies have been ruled out as treatment options years ago. It's just brain surgery, removing a mass he says he found and believes is what has caused your hallucinations to become stronger."

"He's lying! You can't give him consent to do this."

"The state has already approved the removal," Dr. Preble interrupted, "got the approval this morning. Mrs. Wembley is only here on formality, to sign the paperwork so we can do the surgery tomorrow."

"Tomorrow! No!" I tried to run for it, but the hulking orderlies blocked my path. They grappled their meaty hands onto my arms as I thrashed all of my limbs in an attempt to get away. I was now fighting for my life.

"Oh, dear me," Mrs. Wembley gasped. "Don't hurt her, please. She's only scared."

"I'm not scared," I huffed, "I'm trying to save myself."

"Boys, please, gently take Miss Elle to a solitary room," Dr. Preble ordered. "I was afraid of this, that she would become agitated. Her condition has gotten much worse in these few months. She has become paranoid, as you can see with her accusations."

I didn't hear Mrs. Wembley's response. I'd been dragged too far away, fighting each inch of the way. Nurses and patients we passed all stared in shock. I caught a glimpse of Abe as we passed the game room. He stood, wringing his hands. When our eyes locked, I knew his mind worked overtime, he became scared and began planning.

The orderlies tossed me into one of the solitary rooms meant for agitated patients. The white padded room had no bed, no luxury of any sort. Just four walls, a ceiling, and a floor; all covered with the same material. The door slammed at a deafening decibel, despite the padding.

Shortly after the window on the door slid open, revealing Dr.

Preble. His face wore its usual self-righteous smirk. "Do try to calm yourself, Elle. There's no reason to keep yourself in this state all night. Either way, your procedure is set for first thing in the morning. Then you'll feel much better."

Grief and anger tore through me like a beast, turning me into what they said I was. I wanted to rip his face off. I charged the door at full speed, not caring if I hurt myself or not. No satisfaction came from that. He managed to slide the window closed before I made contact with the door.

I pounded and clawed at the door repeatedly until my arms felt like porridge and all of my energy drained away. I crumbled there, too tired to even cry. All my hopes of freedom died. There had been no point in planning with Abe in his secret room. No one won against Dr. Preble, least of all me. My escape plan failed.

PART 2
MOONSHOT

THIRTEEN

ESCAPE FROM PREBLE ISLAND

SLEEP TOOK me out despite my efforts not to succumb to it. I wanted to stay alert. Chances were, in a few hours, this version of myself would be a memory. A ghost. I'd become the phantom everyone mocked me to be. With sleep came dark visions of a new kind.

The nightmare began as it always did, brush scraping at my legs. This time I was being pulled along by an unseen ally, winded and afraid. The wall of trees appeared, the fireball flew at me and deflected. The robed figure lunged for me and then the dream changed. His sharp fingers ensnared me, morphing into sharp, svelte knives designed for slicing through skin and muscle. Doctor's tools. They crept towards my head, singing for my brain. The cool metal sliced into my hairline.

My own tortured screams woke me.

I kept my eyes buried in my arm, staring at the shadows on the floor. The icy grip of the dark figure's cold fingers seemed to linger on me. I waited for the sensation to go away, for the hosts of my biggest fears to vaporize. They didn't. The nightmare gripped tighter on my arm. The tugging was real, and desperate. The touch did not belong to a ghost from my dream.

Fear crested, big as a tsunami, in my chest ready to swallow all the world. My time had come, they came for me. Too soon. I imagined myself a rock, heavy and unmoving. I wanted to be impossible to move, resist to my last breath. I prepared to fight as long as I could. The tugging increased in urgency the more I ignored it.

"Princess. Move. Hurry." My head whipped up at Abe's unmistakable speech pattern.

"Abe!" I flung my arms around him. Seeing him made me so completely happy, my personal bubble needs flew out the window. Standing, I looked to the door ready to run for it. It remained closed. We were trapped, but the question of how he got in with me remained too. As far as I knew, he didn't have a key. "Abe, how did you get in here?"

"Magic. Through door." He fumbled in his thin robe, searching for something. In moments he pulled out a small red rock with a triumphant look on his face. "Escape now. I distract. Away," he pointed towards the back of the room.

I scrambled away and he jammed the red rock against the back of the lock and shouted. Sparks shot out from the rock, sizzling against the walls and floor. Smoke rose steadily from the burns left behind, along with the with the scent of hot metal and char. The singes multiplied quickly, and I feared the room might catch fire before Abe managed to get the door open. After long minutes, the door slammed open with a bang, tearing its hinges backward. Abe scuttled out and gestured for me to follow him. After that display, I believed. Hesitation became a thing in my past regarding Abe's abilities. Especially with the horde of frantic orderlies and nurses about to descend on us.

Before we began to slink through the halls of the institute, Abe threw a white ball at the floor behind us. The ball exploded in a fine powder. I needed no explanation to what it was. It was the same fine white powder Abe had coated his hands with. He flung another ball, a black and shiny one. Glass shattered as it made contact and ignited the powder into the harmless flames. Alarms screeched to life, echoing through the halls of The Kendrick Institute. The flames fooled the fire alarms, just like they'd fool everyone else that came across them. A perfect diversion.

We hurried along the halls on quiet feet, only stopping to ensure our path stayed clear. Every time we turned a corner, Abe threw another pair of the magic fire producing balls, covering our tracks. Every time our path got blocked by a door, he used the prodigious, lock busting red rock. The last door we conquered lead outside. The most important door. The tiny explosion the rock made on the gray metal barrier sang a song in my heart. I loved it as much as food.

Like a caged bird set free, my metaphorical wings spread wide with delight the moment the frosty, late winter night air grabbed hold of me. But, we weren't home free yet. The garden wall still stood between us and the world at large. We sprinted through the damp grass into to the garden and to the last obstacle standing between me and the outside world. At the wall, he fumbled in his robe again, this time producing two vials. He handed me one, a silvery blue liquid sloshed against its glass walls. The other was a clear vial, which he smashed against the rough bricks as he whispered something to himself. The space where Abe broke the vial rolled open in moments, making a door.

Frantic shouts and screams pulled my attention from the magicked door. Patients, nurses, and orderlies streamed from the doors of the institute and into the garden, evacuating to safety from the flames dancing in the hallways. I almost wanted to see their faces when the fire ghosted away, leaving no trace it had ever been there. The aftermath of my escape being regaled as mass hysteria and everyone began taking shiny new pills. Patients and staff alike.

Despite the erupting chaos, the orderlies spotted us loitering at the new hole in the brick wall surrounding the garden. They became bulls, making us the red capes. Several of the larger orderlies, including my favorite two goons, shoved through the panicked crowd amassing on the lawns. Patients tumbled to the cold, wet grass in their wake.

"Go," Abe shoved me through the door without warning.

"Come with me." I feared being alone would be the death of freedom. I didn't think I could do this without him. I didn't want to. His life at The Kendrck Institute held nothing but pain and sadness. I worried what would become of him. Would he become the shell of a man he once was, like before I came along?

I reached for him through the gap. Shoving my hands away, he shook his head. "Can't go home. I did bad. Too dangerous. Go. Run. Find river. Follow. Island in river, big tree. Enter tree. Drink vial. Sleep. Home."

"Please," I sobbed lightly, watching the orderlies that rapidly approached us.

As if he knew what I thought, he replied again, tears that matched mine ran down his ruddy cheeks, "Abe be fine. Happy for Princess." With those words, Abe smashed a pair of balls against his chest and whispered to himself again. Flames quickly engulfed his body just as the first of the orderlies reached him and screamed in fear. They didn't dare grab him. The other orderlies scrambled towards the gap in the wall, which began to close up faster than it had opened, they too hesitated at the strange happenings. Moments before the wall fully repaired itself I saw Abe toss one more thing through the narrowing gap. The small object landed at my feet.

My necklace. The one thing that connected me to my past. The one I wore daily until taking up residence at the institute. He had gotten it back for me. I scooped it up and fastened it back where it belonged, feeling instantly more whole.

By the time I looked back up, the door was completely gone. The garden wall stood intact, keeping me from thanking Abe for everything. Keeping me from helping him. I knew the nurses and orderlies were going to punish him severely for this, once everything died down. The poor man deserved nothing less than the best care. I kissed my fingertips then pressed them on the cool, rough bricks, sending Abe a silent thank you. A prayer to whoever listened to watch out for him. A promise that Abe's effort to free me wouldn't have been in vain.

I turned and ran, vial in hand, following Abe's broken instructions. I planned to find the river, the tree, and drink the vial. After everything Abe showed me, after all the miracles he performed, how could I not? He proved his magic worked. I hoped he was right about it sending me home.

MY LUNGS BURNED. I wanted to stop, but I couldn't. I tried that briefly, and nearly froze. Moving kept me warm, and safe. With no idea what happened back at the institute, no idea if there were men looking for me already, I had to run. I ran because Abe told me to. I ran because I didn't want to go back. I ran because I desperately hoped for the home Abe promised lay at the end of his plan.

I figured I couldn't be far from the river, unless I'd run in the wrong direction. I hoped not. That would've been just my luck, running all that way for nothing. Turning back wasn't an option either way. If I didn't reach a river by sun-up, I decided to give up on Abe's plan and keep running. I'd scrounge up some cash and call Q, just so he knew I was fine, and then get as far away as possible. Cross state lines. Hell, I even considered heading to Canada. Even if I had to enter illegally, I'd do it. There weren't very many options. Magical tree or Canada.

I pushed myself to keep going, and, after a few minutes, my persistence rewarded me. The distinct sound of water flowing and splashing greeted my ears. Dampness filled the air, well a different dampness than the constant fresh spring air of the Pacific North West. The sensations invigorated me, motivated me to push harder. My escape was almost at an end. Before I knew it, I stood on the silt and rock beach of a narrow river, watching the hypnotic current as it tumbled over rocks and fallen logs. The tranquil moment had to be the most beautiful thing I'd seen since I'd been hospitalized. Mostly because it represented freedom.

I figured I had a lead on any search party, so I slowed. But, I kept my pace brisk while I walked along the river bank, the gritty earth grinding under the soles of my thin hospital shoes. As I traveled along, I began to feel more relaxed and the desperation clogging my head dissipated. After some time, I found myself thinking about the incredible events of the past day. The best part, learning real magic existed in the world. No question about it. Others might have argued what Abe did counted as cool science that looked like magic. I knew better. Science didn't explain that door appearing in the middle of a brick wall.

No matter how relaxed I felt, how big a lead I thought I might have, I couldn't fully calm down. Every strange sound coming from the dark surroundings made me skip a step, nervously laughing at myself when I realized it couldn't be the meat heads from the institute.

I began thinking about prison break stories; escapees stealing through the night with cops and bloodhounds on their tails. That thought lingered in my head, messing with the little confidence I had. Worry rooted deeper and stronger in my mind. Someone out there possibly tracked me like the criminals in those stories. The probability of The Kendrick Institute having bloodhounds registered as slim, but police did. More than likely they'd been alerted the moment things calmed down back at the institute.

I needed to do more to make sure I got away. I needed to do what criminals would do in this situation. What survivalists said to do to cover one's tracks. I had to walk in the river. I took a deep, bracing breath and stepped into the frigid water. My teeth clamped and my jaws locked to prevent me from yelping as the frigid water seeped into my shoes, socks, and the hems of my thin pants. Worried that ankle deep wouldn't be enough, I waded out further so the water came up to my knees; which knocked together with every step I took.

"This is stupid," I whispered to myself. I knew wading through the river, in the dark, wasn't the safest idea. I could easily lose my footing on slippery rocks, or get swept away in a strong current. I quashed down any worries about hypothermia for the moment. I'd worry about that later. The more I had occupying my mind, the more likely I'd get hurt. I had to do my best to keep my mind on my footing, stay alert, and move closer to shore if I sensed any danger. I may not have wanted to go back to that Hell-hole, but I didn't want to die either.

Hours passed. Night began to fade and the gray-blue skies of morning started to brighten with the rising sun. My time spent alternating walking in the water and along the shore did little to alleviate anything. Every ounce of me felt frozen and stiff and I wanted to cry from exhaustion. Yet, stopping was an option I wouldn't entertain. I had to keep going until I found the tree on the island.

"ARE YOU FREAKING KIDDING ME!" I screamed into the vast empty valley beneath me. "A waterfall!"

Abe said nothing about the island with the big tree being in a lake beneath a waterfall. He was kind of in a hurry, and didn't have the best communication skills, but it would have been nice to know that I had to jump off a waterfall to get to it. I groaned to the sky. My flight to freedom kept getting harder and harder.

As I stared over the edge of the small cliff, the fuzzy feeling of a vision began crawling up my spine and invaded my head. My mind had the worst sense of timing, this had to be the worst place for a hallucination to take over. I tried pushing against it taking me from reality, and failed.

Strange, warbling bird song filled my ears as the world glazed over. Every way I turned, greenery and flowers took over. Ferns larger than a man surrounded a large white monument. I couldn't tell what the monument depicted, thanks to the cloudiness my visions took on. Despite the haze, the scene stole my breath.

Moments later, the scene gave way to the waterfall's edge and the surrounding forest. I sucked in a relieved breath. The hallucination had been short, thankfully. There'd been no time for anything bad to happen; like falling.

Back in the real world, the time came to continue my journey. I studied the cliff and waterfall, looking for a way to climb down. In my mind, climbing was safest. If one existed, I didn't see it. I had no choice but to jump. Joy.

I paced back from the edge and readied myself. My eyes closed against the breeze. Deep breaths filled my lungs as I tried to find the courage to leap off of the small waterfall. One last pat over the vial I'd tucked away. This was it. Opening my eyes, and sending out a prayer for the water to be deep, I began the short run to the edge. Water splashed up my legs with each stride that took me closer to the edge. On the last step, my legs pushed off harder, lifting me into the air.

The short dive was far from graceful, with my limbs flailing and a Wilhelm scream echoing behind me. At least I didn't belly flop when my body broke the surface of the lake. The cold water sucked the breath from my lungs. A few kicks and I surfaced, got my bearings, and headed off on the long swim to the island.

The swim pushed my body to its limits once more. All of my muscles screamed for rest by the time I reached the little island. Mostly because I'd been on the move since before the sun came up. I pulled myself onto the grassy beach, soaked, frozen and exhausted, and flopped onto my back. A few strands of my pale hair clung to my cheek. I swooped them back into place, leaving my hands tucked behind my head. I never wanted to move again. I only let myself rest under the green canopy for just a few minutes, though. The Kendrick Institute and the cops were possibly minutes behind me.

I rolled onto my stomach, to get a better view of the tree, but didn't see the opening Abe told me to look for. I'm forced to get up to inspect the rest of it. Walking slowly around, my hand trailed over the rough bark almost reverently. I'd been stuck inside so long that this moment felt nearly sacred. Just as Abe sort of said there would be, I found a large crevice in the tree. Well, more of a tall crack that stretched from the ground up into the thick foliage where it disappeared from sight.

My mouth screwed to the side while I inspected the crack. It didn't look like I would fit through it. Maybe if I didn't have boobs or hips. I tilted my head to the side and then to the other trying to see another angle.

Something odd caught my attention. When I looked at the tree from a certain angle the crack looked smaller. I hopped to the side to look from the opposite direction. The crack looked bigger. In fact it almost looked like one side of the crack pointed in towards the other, like sliding doors. Weird.

Despite the weirdness, from this angle I could tell that I'd easily fit between the jagged edges of the opening. I slid in, amazed to find the tree completely hollowed out. The spacious interior of the tree grew noticeably warmer, like the season changed from winter to spring in a breath. The fear I'd freeze to death in my damp clothes lessened because of it.

I settled onto the ground, curling my knees up against my chest and dug the vial of silvery liquid from my pocket. The bottle passed between my two hands while I pondered the reality of my situation. I'm was an escaped mental patient, and authorities were looking for me. Despite all of the amazing things Abe had been able to do with his magic in these past 24 hours, I doubted this little vial would magically give me a new home. I knew I'd drink it, I owed that much to Abe. But, I also needed to come up with my next plan of action. Figure out how I'd survive.

But first, I had to keep my promise. Or at least try to.

The top of the vial came off with an audible pop. A pleasant aroma filled my senses, it almost smelled like baking bread. I shrugged to myself and tipped it over my open mouth.

The potion tasted nothing like its aroma. Minty instead of like baked bread. Not the good mint though, like liquid antacid mint. Resisting the urge to gag, I swallowed the potion and waited. Nothing happened. I shrugged again. Like I said, the chance of it working was slim. Then again, I may have misunderstood Abe's intention for the potion. Maybe he meant it would nourish me somehow, and that I should rest in the tree before finding my own way to a new home.

Not, Likely. He was pretty insistent about him needing to send me home.

I lay down, knees bent into the air, and drummed my fingers on my belly. Soon, a heavy sleep began to take hold as I relaxed inside my hideout. A heavy sleep, and that all too familiar fuzzy feeling began to trace the edges of my mind. I didn't panic. Nobody could get hurt now. Instead, an odd thought struck over having two episodes so close together. That never happened. The tingly sensation increased more and more as the seconds ticked by. My exhausted body felt every inch of the journey it made, heavy and knotted. My eyes struggled to stay open, leaving me to wonder what would come first; sleep or hallucination.

Sleep won.

FOURTEEN

A NEW WORLD

THE WARM SUN dappled over me, reminding me that I'd left the sterile confines of The Kendrick Institute, reminding me that my brain remained intact. That comfort allowed me to keep my eyes closed and enjoy the peace. I stretched, my arm gliding along the cool, smooth ground beneath me. Breathed in the crisp verdant air.

The serene moment scratched to a halt. Dirt and grass wasn't smooth.

My eyes shut tighter against the unexpected find, struck by the realization that perhaps I wasn't free. That I didn't escape. Was my escape, the incredible feats of magic by Abe, all in my head? A strange new hallucination? A side effect of Dr. Preble's inhumane plans for me?

No. It couldn't be. I wouldn't be aware of it. Or would I?

The sudden thunder of hooves rumbled towards me, accompanied by a horse nickering. "Whoa, Zenobi. Whoa, girl," A deep masculine voice cut through the air.

Definitely not in the institute. My eyes flew open. Lush green canopies and vibrant flowers greeted my sight. Definitely not in the tree either. Near trees, but not in the tree. A few turns of my head let me know that I lay on a smooth white platform made of some sort of stone. Marble perhaps. That explained the lack of grass and dirt. But, how did I end up on top of it? More importantly, where was I? How did I get here?

I flopped over on my belly and maneuvered in the direction the voice and horse nickering came from. Trying to stay out of sight, just in case, I peeked over the edge. Whatever I lay on top of is pretty tall, at least nine feet. Good thing I had no fear of heights. Nothing like puking from fear to reveal your location.

All I saw was the horse, Zenobi, a stunning Gypsy Vanner mare, so deep black she almost looked blue. She had a long white star running from the tip of her nose and disappearing into her overgrown mane; which was also white with some black strands woven through it. I imagined her tail to be the same. I briefly locked eyes with the beautiful creature, she chuffed and shook her head.

There was no sign of her rider, though. I wondered where the man went to. As if to answer, snapping twigs drew my attention to my left. Ah, there he was.

"This is decidedly where the portal opened," the man said to himself, "but there is no sign of anyone having been here." He came into view moments later, though I didn't see much of him. He wore a long gray cloak that covered him from neck to ankle. I all I saw was the back of his head, long golden brown waves pulled into a half ponytail. He ambled with a confident grace back to Zenobi and pet her muzzle. She nudged him in response, her eyes closing with affection. "Maybe we should investigate further in the woods. What do you think?"

Zenobi shook her head.

"No? Do not tell me you are too tired," he chuckled. I watched, amazed at the exchange between the man and his horse. I'd heard of people being able to understand their animals but had never witnessed it first hand.

Zenobi whinnied and stomped a hoof while lifting her head repeatedly. Did the horse just rat me out?

"What is it, girl?" The man turned, looking up. His mossy green eyes met mine and his face contorted sternly. I slunk back, gasping, even though I knew it was useless. He saw me. Stupid horse. "You there, come down this instant. You are on sacred ground."

"Yeah, um, I don't think I will. Have a nice day," I called back and instantly regretted it. Have a nice day? Really? My dorkiness knew no bounds.

"Under the authority of Vale's King and Queen, I order you to come down."

Vale? This kept getting weirder and weirder. First, I woke up not where I fell asleep and then this guy's talking about royalty and giving me orders. "And are you a leader or something?"

He scoffed, "No, I am a guard, and I am ordering you to come down from the monument before I make you come down."

I weighed my options. I stayed up on the monument and continued this exchange, maybe get arrested; or I got down and tried to explain this whole mess in hopes he'd help me figure out where I had landed. Maybe how I had ended up there too. The latter made the most logical option, for sure. I doubted he'd feel helpful if I continued to defy him. "All right, fine. I'll consider coming down. But you need to answer something first."

"What is your query?"

Query? Ha. What was with this guy being so formal? I mean, who talks like that? "First, are you with The Kendrick Institute?"

"The what?" he replied. The question in his voice sounded genuine.

Good. That answered that. A relieved sigh escaped my chest. "So, no then. Great. Second, you need to promise you aren't going to hurt me or turn me in to the institute."

"Miss, I have no idea what this Institution of Kendrick you speak of is. Therefore, I cannot turn you in to them. I can promise you this, no harm will come to you as long as you have no ill intent."

"Cool, I can get on board with that. I'll come down, but I might need a little help."

"I will assist you, should you require it."

I took a minute to study the edge of the monument and decided a backwards approach would be best. Making sure I didn't go over the edge, I scooted into position and braced my weight with my arms as I slowly lowered my legs over the side. My body, sore and stiff from my run to freedom, protested at the exertion and my arms threatened to give out. I slipped, in a moment that demonstrated my complete unathleticness. Luckily, I steadied myself before plummeting off the monument.

Apparently, my moment of clumsiness counted as a call for assistance from the strange man. His hands grasped my waist to steady me, his touch felt comforting and secure. I didn't fear falling anymore.

My feet secure on the ground, I took a moment to brace myself. I knew he'd react to my appearance. After all, everyone did. "Thank you," I turned to face the self proclaimed guard, getting a good look at him and feeling intimidated by his well-over-six-foot height. I forced a smile, hoping to hide my hesitation. Trying to appear normal.

He stepped back, eyes wide with shock, bumping into Zenobi who nickered in annoyance. My heart sank to my knees, even though I expected nothing less revealing my face to him. But, I didn't want to be rude, or show my hurt feelings. He was the only person able help me right now.

"I'm Elle," I offered an hand in greeting.

"Elle?" His eyes almost misted over as he stammered out my name. He continued to stare at me with his deep green eyes darting across my face. I fidgeted under his scrutiny, different from the gaping stared my albino-like looks got. It almost seemed like he couldn't believe I stood before him. Like he knew me.

Saying I didn't feel something along the same vein, would have been a lie. A vague familiarity settled into me as I took him in, from his sandy hair to his intense green eyes and golden walnut skin. I squinted and angled my head, examining him closer. He was probably one of the most attractive men I'd been this close to. I guessed his age somewhere in his twenties, definitely not a high school boy. He almost looked dangerous due to the obvious bend in the bridge of his nose and the scars in his left eyebrow and lip. Not to mention the rugged facial hair. His appearance screamed tough guy, but his eyes were soft and warm.

I tapped my hand on my leg nervously "So, yeah. I know. I'm pale. Now that we have that out of the way, can you help me figure out where I am?"

The dude continued to stare, dumbfounded.

"Hello? Earth to you?" I waved my hands in front of his face.

"Sorry, I... What were you doing on top of the monument?," he snapped out of his daze. "It's forbidden, everyone in Vale knows this."

Looking behind me at the monument for a moment brought me a moment of surreal-ness. The monument, surrounded by lush forest and flowers, looked just like the hallucination I had on top of the water fall. I shook it off and turned back to the man.

I let out a breath. This was going to be fun. "Look, dude, I can kind of explain that, but not really. It's complicated. And kind of unbelievable. A really long story. But, I really need your help. So, I need you to stop staring at me like I have three heads."

"I am sorry, I don't mean to be rude. How can I help?"

"Start with a name?"

"I am Daric Monroe," he bowed. "You are Elle?"

"Yeah, I've established that." I wondered if he'd be much help, that maybe he was more pretty and strong than anything else. I hoped not. Those looks would be wasted if there wasn't anything behind them. "Listen, if you can't help me. If my oddness is too much for you, can you point me in the direction of someone that can help me."

"No, I can help," he insisted. "Can you tell me how you got up there?"

"Well, like I said, it's complicated. You see, I was at The Kendrick Institute and..." I broke off, realizing I didn't want to reveal too much. Letting Daric know about my illness seemed like a bad idea. I didn't want to make him even more uncomfortable. "They were going to hurt me, so I ran away. I drank this stuff one of the pa.., my friend gave me. I fell asleep and woke up on top of your monument. I have no idea how I got there, I promise. I wasn't meaning to disrespect anyone by being on it."

Daric scratched his bearded chin in thought, "So, you were the one that opened the portal?"

"Portal?"

"You truly have no idea, do you?"

"No, I don't. Like so much in my life, I have no clue."

"What do you mean?" Daric's eyes brimmed with concern and curiosity.

I felt a little hesitant about revealing personal details, details that made most people run from me. But, something about him warranted trust, despite just meeting him. I figured the truth would come out eventually, so I summarized my earliest memory, "I don't know who I really am. I've been suffering from amnesia for most of my life. At this point, I don't think I'll ever remember who I really am or where I come from."

"That is tough, I am sorry to hear it." Daric fell quiet for a minute while he processed what I told him. "I think, Elle, that I know someone who can help you. Queen Neala and King Carradoc, the rulers of Vale."

FIFTEEN

JOURNEY TO VALE

I rode on Zenobi as we traveled through the forest. Daric walked along side, leading the way. I kept looking to him, wanting to say something; though words failed me every time. Each time, I caught him staring at me. Each time, he quickly looked away. Needless to say, an awkward tension built between us.

After about an hour of this repeated behavior, I had enough. "Do you have to keep staring? I get it, I'm weird looking. I'm used to it. Doesn't mean it doesn't hurt when people stare."

"I do not mean to cause you any discomfort, Elle. Your appearance is not bothersome in the least. I know many in Vale with similar attributes. I am just amazed and curious."

His statement surprised me. He didn't find my looks to be any weirder than anyone else's. To him, I looked normal. I considered this for a while, finding happiness in the possibility I wouldn't be a freak here. At least not for my looks. "Why do I make you curious?"

"You seem to have been through a lot, but I know you are leaving out details. I am just trying to understand you better. I cannot fully help you if you are not honest."

"I can't exactly be completely honest if I don't understand this myself, can I?"

"I guess not. Perhaps I can help if you tell me what you do understand. Tell me everything that led to you entering Vale."

"That's one thing I'm lost on. You mentioned portals, and say things like entering Vale. Where am I, exactly."

Daric halted Zenobi. "As hard as it may be to believe, you have somehow managed to travel through a portal into another realm. Vale to be precise."

Another realm? Why not? I'd seen too much to argue. "Maybe not as hard to believe as you think. I'm recently converted to the belief that magic is real."

He gave me a crooked smile and raised his scarred eyebrow in response. Daric didn't look so scary when he smiled. He looked downright jolly. "Is that so? Well, that makes explaining where you are so much easier. There are many realms all connected to each other, accessible only by portal. Most of these realms are completely unaware of this, most do not have naturally occurring magic." Daric's eyes appraised me, "From your dress and manner of speech, I would say you are from either what we call Reta or Biva. Since you said you recently discovered magic is real, Reta would be the realm you came from. It is likely, though, that this is not the name you know it by."

"Earth. I would say I'm from Earth."

Daric smiled again, warm and friendly. I couldn't help but smile back.

The remainder of the trip, we talked casually. I filled him in on everything that happened leading up to him finding me, leaving out only the small detail of The Kendrick Institute being a psychiatric hospital and my mental illness. Those details were not ones I felt ready to divulge. Daric shared a few essential bits of knowledge about Vale, names of important people and what-not. He answered all of my questions about the flora and fauna we encountered.

I'm enthralled by it all. I practically squealed with delight when a little yellow bird with a blue face and blue tipped wings lighted on

Zenobi's head. Its long blue tail feathers cascaded down the side of the horse's neck. The curious little bird hopped closer to me slowly and decided I wasn't scary. The bird trilled and flitted onto my shoulder, only landing briefly before flying off again.

"I feel like a princess!" I exclaimed, delighted by the brief moment with the creature. Daric smiled and shook his head, stifling a laugh. I knew he had no clue what I meant, but there is something in his eyes that sparked at my statement.

Out of nowhere, a chilled wind swept through the trees, sending a chill down my spine. Hospital issue pj's weren't exactly meant for even the slightest bit of cold. At least the climate here made them a little more weather appropriate than the chilled weather I left behind.

"You are cold," Daric observed and stopped Zenobi again. In one smooth motion, he removed his long gray cloak and handed it up to me, "Here, take my cloak."

"Don't you need it?"

"Not so much, the cloak is a formality rather than a necessity for me."

"Are you sure. I feel so bad taking away any more comfort from you. I've already taken your ride, I'd hate to take more from you."

"I will be fine, truly. Do not worry about me." The wind howled through once more, this time Daric shivered.

"Really?" I arched an eyebrow at my traveling companion.

"I may be a slight bit cold, but I insist you take the cloak. My uniform is much warmer than what you wear. But, if it is all right with you, we can double up. Ride together, as it were. Borrow a little warmth from one another."

"Whatever works for you, Daric."

Daric easily mounted Zenobi behind me. Wordlessly he took the cloak from me and wrapped it around my shoulders, fastening the clasp and placing the hood on my head. "Be warm, Elle," he half whispered as he settled closer against my back. "It will not be long now before we reach the kingdom." My cheeks flushed at the intimate closeness with the man that I knew little about. My heart warmed as a secure feeling eased over me. He felt like an old friend, like Q.

The warmth in my heart melted into sadness at the thought of my old friend. What was he going to think when he tried to visit at the institute? The sadness lingered over me until we reached the edge of the forest and I got my first glimpse of the kingdom of Vale.

The village lying outside the royal villa was quaint. The tightly packed homes and buildings are all painted up in bright sherbet colors with white trimming. It reminded me of pictures of Venice one of my old fosters had, only without water filled canals and gondolas. Cobblestone pathways and carts took their places. The streets were free of litter, cleaner than any I'd seen before. The whole place felt safe and pure, like nothing bad could happen. I certainly wouldn't mind calling this place home. Perhaps this would be a good place to lay low for a while. Heck, if I really traveled through a portal, I'd never be found by Dr. Preble.

The people bustled about with cheer. Everyone seemed so friendly as they greeted one another while going about their business. As we walked Zenobi through the streets, a few folk stopped and greeted Daric, eying me with great curiosity. Daric greeted them in return, some by name. I noticed, as Daric had mentioned, some of the villagers had hair or skin as pale as mine. My heart swelled knowing I didn't look strange to them.

We stopped in the center of the village at a large fountain. The fountain itself surrounded a large statue of a man and woman wearing crowns. King Carradoc and Queen Neala, I assumed. Standing in front of the royal pair stood a little girl.

I began to feel off, hallucination off. Worried I'd spiral down into one of my visions, I stiffened and clenched my fists. The last thing I needed was a vision to happen. If that happened, Daric might have rescinded his offer of help and carted me to their version of the insti-tute. Or jail. I shook my head vehemently, whispering for it to go away. Slowly, the sensation dissipated. I breathed a sigh of relief. Disaster averted, somehow.

Daric pulled a package wrapped in white fabric and tied with twine from the saddle bag. "I have a quick stop to make. Do you mind? I will not be but a minute."

"I don't mind. I'll wait here if that's okay."

"Please, do not go wandering."

"Trust me, I'm gonna be glued to the fountain. I have no desire to get lost."

"Good." Daric tied Zenobi to a post nearby and entered a sherbet green building with no sign hanging from the eaves.

I sat on the edge of the fountain, careful not to accidentally dip the hem of Daric's cloak in the clear bubbling water, to wait. It didn't take long for the sun to make the cloak uncomfortable. I chuckled to myself. Even in parallel worlds it's warmer where there are more people out in the open. That was science for you, working no matter where you were. I slid the hood from my head and decided to do what I did best, people watch.

I'm enjoying the quiet moment. At no time in my memory had there been a moment like this, where I sat in public and no one gawked or teased. I fit in. My eyes fell on a small group of boys playing nearby, tossing a small brown ball back and forth between the three of them. The ball flew way over one of the head of the boy who was closest to me. The boy, who couldn't have been more than seven, ran backwards, hands stretched in the air to catch the wayward ball. His heel caught on an askew cobblestone, sending the poor kid tumbling onto the hard ground. He skidded to a halt in front of me.

I jumped from my seat to help him, wanting to make sure he hadn't gotten hurt. I began helping him to his feet as a woman with hair nearly as light as mine rushed up, in full on mom mode. The boy obviously belonged to her.

Her eyes followed the boy as he stood, and continued past his head up to me, "Thank you, miss..." Her words faltered when her gaze settled on me, her face surprised. She shook off her surprised look and thanked me again as she ushered her child away.

The woman's reaction hurt. I didn't expect it, Daric had said I didn't look so strange. Others I'd seen have similar features. Even the mother. Her surprised reaction chipped away at the tiny bit of confidence I felt. Perhaps I did look strange to them. Maybe only Daric didn't think so, or maybe he was being nice. Either way, I felt deflated and offended when I sat back on the fountain edge.

Everyone near me seemed to be watching me after that. My comfort level dropped rapidly. Soon, the feeling became too big to hold back and a few silent tears escaped my eyes. I adverted my gaze to the ground to avoid everyone's eyes.

Daric returned shortly after, startling me with a tough on my shoulder. "What is the matter, Elle?"

I looked up and sniffled, "It's nothing, silly. I just get uncomfortable when people stare."

He looked around the area, noticing the way the people were looking at me now, whispering to each other, "Perhaps, you should wear the hood," he said with understanding. "You will also need to wear the hood when we meet with the Queen and King, until I say not to. Just as a precaution."

Baffled at his new instruction, I asked, "Wouldn't that be disrespectful?"

"Unusual, yes. Disrespectful, in other situations. Your case, a necessity for your own comfort. It will keep prying eyes from making you upset. That is all. But, know this, I do not think anyone means any harm with their stares. You are merely a stranger."

"Oh," I replied meekly, pulling the hood over my head. Something about his explanation didn't hold water. There was more to it, but I didn't want to fight. My position with him, with his help, relied on me being cooperative.

Daric helped me back on Zenobi and mounted behind me again. The time to go see King Carradoc and Queen Neala had come. Hopefully soon I'd have some help, or some answers to why Abe sent me here.

SIXTEEN

MEET THE ROYALS

ONCE IN THE ROYAL VILLA, Daric handed Zenobi off to a young stable-hand. She nickered excitedly when they offered her a piece of fruit. I watched, mildly jealous, as she trotted happily next to him flicking her tail to and fro. Jealous of her snack, I grumbled to myself. I hadn't eaten anything since the institute. Nothing decent since before then. My stomach growled in agreement. I needed food, before I decided to eat my arm.

I turned to ask Daric if there was any chance of getting food before meeting the King and Queen, when a petite dark haired woman approached us. She carried a tray with two cups, one a tall glass with water and the other a mug that steam rose out of. The tray also held some fruit and biscuits.

"Ah, thank you, Veena. I can always count on you." Daric grabbed the tall glass and one of the large, flaky biscuits from the tray.

Veena turned to me, "A tea for you, Miss, just how you like it. You are hungry after such a long journey, please take as much food as you like." I hesitantly took the mug and a piece of fruit. I didn't want to look greedy. "Go on, do not be shy. You can take more." I gave in and snatched another piece of fruit and a biscuit as well.

When I brought the tea to my lips I was pleasantly surprised. The tea was identical to the ginger turmeric tea I ordered regularly. My eyes widened at Veena. "How did you know?"

She smiled back, "It is my job, Miss."

"She's a psychic," Daric explained.

"Yeah, okay." I didn't know what else to say. My mind reeled with all of the unexplainable things I'd experienced just in the past few days. Magic, potions, parallel worlds, and now psychics. I took a bite of the biscuit, the extraordinary flavor burst in my mouth. It was flaky, savory, and buttery, and practically melted in my mouth. "Thank you."

"You are welcome." Veena walked away when she felt satisfied we had all we need.

We ate and walked across a red bridge over a pond filled with lily pads and a few large fish. They weren't koi. They more resembled beta fish, stunning iridescent blues and purples with long tails. Gorgeous. I had to stop, leaning over the railing of the bridge and watched them swim gracefully before continuing on the path with Daric.

"Where are we going?" I asked between bites and sips.

"I am taking you to the grand hall," he pointed to the large cream colored building directly across from the pond. Green ivy dotted with white and blue flowers climbed the outside. The building looked simple, not what I expected for a royal building. I wasn't exactly expecting a villa either. Most people think of castles or palaces when it came to kings and queens.

"Are they nice?" nerves settled over me when I realized what came next.

"I can assure you, Queen Neala and King Carradoc are going to love you. They are wonderful people." His assurance did little to calm my nerves. I didn't fully understand why I felt so nervous about it, I had nothing to prove to these people. No reason to impress them. All I wanted was a little help, maybe a home. Nothing more.

But I couldn't shake the feeling that kept hanging over me; the feeling of familiarity. The feeling that something big waited just a few feet away. A humming in my chest, a song I wanted to sing, but the words keep slipping from my tongue.

A pair of guards stood tall at the doors of the grand hall. They eyed me curiously, likely because I wore Daric's cloak. The same cloak they wore over their uniforms.

"Greetings, Karrah, Rollan," Daric greeted his fellow guards.

"Daric," the female guard nodded in return, a few wisps of auburn hair escaped from her braids. "You missed muster, Captain Seylah is none too happy."

"She will live. I had something important to tend to."

The male guard snickered, and glances between me and Daric. He thought Daric meant me. He wasn't wrong, in a sense. Just not in the sense he meant.

Daric didn't miss this assumption either. "You git, Rollan," he smacked him on the ear in jest, "that is not the reason. I sensed an unauthorized portal opening and investigated."

"I assume she is the responsible party?" Karrah asked, her dark eyes scanned over me. I shuddered under her scrutiny. She came across as all business compared to Rollan's jovial demeanor.

"Sort of. It is complicated." Both guards gave Daric confused looks. "I need to see the King and Queen to straighten this matter out."

"They are not in the grand hall today. King Carradoc is not well, he's having a bad day. High Counselor Drem is standing in for them." Rollan said, a hint of disgust in his voice.

Daric groaned, wiping his hand down his face. From their tone, I guessed this Drem guy wasn't well liked. "I guess he will have to do, for the time being." After another minute of hesitating, he said, "Fine, announce me."

"Um, Daric," I interrupted. "What do I do with this?" I held up the mug in my hand. I didn't think it would look good if I met this High Counselor guy holding a cup. First impressions and all.

"Oh, right." He turned to Karrah and Rollan, "Would you mind? I'm sure Veena or someone will be along shortly to gather them."

Karrah rolled her eyes, not pleased with the request. Rollan happily agreed to it and took the mug and Daric's glass. Karrah entered the grand hall to announce Daric.

Daric faced me, putting his hands on my shoulders, "When we get in there, let me do all the talking. High Counselor Drem is, well, he likes the rules. A lot. And one has to know how to talk to him to assuage him to their side. Just keep your hood on and follow my lead."

"And he can help me?"

"I hope so. If not, I will go above his head."

Karrah reappeared from within the grand hall, "The High Counselor will see you now," she says, unenthusiastically.

"Good luck," Rollan winked. I liked him. He reminded me of Q, enthusiastic and fun.

The grand hall's simple yet luxurious interior embodied the overall feeling of the villa. The large space's Italian plaster walls stood bare save for tapestries in rich jewel tones. The gleaming cedar floor added its aromatic nature to the room. In the center of the floor sat a raised platform decorated with ferns and flowers in tall vases, and two heavy looking wooden seats. The one thing about the grand hall that impressed me was the lighting. Soft glowing orbs hovered at various levels in the air, no sign of connection to electricity. Those amazed me to no end.

As we approached the platform in the center, the man sitting there stiffened his back and squared his shoulders. High Counselor Drem. He appeared to be near 60 with large, hooded blue eyes and a joker-like mouth. His mostly gray hair was slicked against his skull and hanging behind his ears. The chilled look in his eyes gave me sent a shiver down my spine. He creeped me out more than a little, he was clown living in the sewer level creepy. I didn't know why, but I wanted nothing more than to hide. I stepped back and to the side, hiding partially behind Daric.

"Daric," Drem drawled out, his nasal voice low and haughty. "I'm told you have a matter of importance you need help with." Every word came out like molasses, deliberately slow.

"I seek assistance with a young woman I came across early today. She needs help. It is my belief she has accidentally came through a portal from Reta."

"The people of Reta have no magic, they cannot open portals."

"Are you questioning my portal detection competency?"

Drem sneered, "No. Of course not, Daric. Your skill at detecting portals is above any I know of."

"Then consider that I am not wrong," a mild threat lingered in Daric's voice.

"Fine. Girl, remove the cloak you wear."

I looked at Daric. His instruction to keep it on clear in my mind. He nodded, giving me the go ahead. Unclasping the cloak, my fingers shook. I didn't like the cold and judging way Drem studied me, like I was something beneath him. I had a feeling he'd already made up his mind about me. He didn't seem to like me, or Daric very much. Daric took the cloak from my shoulders the moment I finished unclasping it. I looked up.

Drem's eyes widened and he leaned back. His mouth snarled in disgust. He almost looked horrified. He quickly cleared the distaste from his face, "It is obvious to me that she has fooled you, Daric. She is of Vale, obviously a child born in the time of the Frost Moon. I am afraid you have been duped. She is likely conning you."

"And I tell you, she is not conning me. You are obviously no help, seeing only things in black and white. I have no choice but to take this over your head, immediately." He handed me the cloak back, which I placed back on along with the hood.

"You will do no such thing! Queen Neala was very specific that she and King Carradoc are not to be bothered today. You know how important the healing ritual is for him. They must remain alone in their garden. No exceptions."

"Trust me, Drem, they will make exception for this. If you stand in my way, you will regret it." Daric grabbed my hand and pulled me out of the grand hall, defiant and boiling.

LATE DAY SUNLIGHT peeked through the dense leaves of the tall trees that seem to wall in the extravagant garden. Fragrant flowers, many which I couldn't identify, bloomed all over the place. Fountains and statues adorned the well manicured lawns between the cobbled pathways. I wanted to stop and drink in the beautiful place, but Daric pulled me along urgent and unrelenting.

We rounded a bend in the path and stopped. My breath tightened in my chest. There before us sat a very frail looking man and a woman that radiated love and kindness. They had to be the King and Queen. But it wasn't the pair that caused my breath to seize. It was the beautiful statue they sat in front of. It reminded me of the one I often saw in my visions, it had the same shape and color. I shook the thought from my head, it couldn't be the same one from my visions. My visions weren't real, they existed only in my head.

"I told you," a harsh whispering voice came up behind us, "you have to wait and see them properly. Barging in on their privacy is not going to win you any favors."

Daric whipped us around, and once again I found myself face to face with the large eyed man that made my skin crawl and my blood run with ice. "And I told you, Drem, that this will not wait." Daric stared the older man down, towering over him and challenging his authority, "You will not interfere."

Drem grabbed Daric's wrist, "You cannot tell me what to do, boy. And you will not take this insignificant wretch to beg in front of the Queen and King."

"Just watch me," he yanked his arm out of Drem's grasp and turned to continue his urgent pace, dragging me along with him. Drem huffed loudly as he followed behind us.

From behind my escort, I caught glimpses of King Carradoc and

Queen Neala. Their eyes watched us, full of interest. No doubt, the spat with Drem caught their attention. I stayed half hidden behind Daric after we stopped in front of them, but Drem continued past us, sneering with discontent as he did. He settled a few paces ahead of us, asserting his status over Daric.

"My apologies, Queen Neala, King Carradoc. I told Daric you were not to be disturbed, but he did not listen. He is out of his head."

"I find that hard to believe, Drem. Daric is one of my most level headed and loyal men," the Queen replied. "If he has a reason to do something, there is always a good reason."

Something in the Queen's voice triggered a reaction in me, I felt the tell-tale fuzziness of a vision developing in my head. I braced myself for the onslaught, but hoped that I'd be able to fight it off. I balled my hands into fists, digging my nails into my palms to keep me grounded in reality; a tactic I used before. It never worked, but I had to try.

"Your Majesties," Drem spoke up before Daric had the chance, "I assure you his mission is not important. He merely wants to let this miscreant he found in the woods beg you for something."

"Drem, so help me if you keep interrupting I will strike you. I do not care about consequences. Not this time. Not for this." Daric stepped towards Drem, venom in his words.

"Calm yourself, Daric," Queen Neala commanded. "Now tell me, what is so important that it could not wait?"

Daric pursed his lips and stepped back, hanging his head for a moment to collect himself. "I was on patrol in the woods and I sensed a dissipating portal. I followed the scent to investigate, knowing that portal travel is severely regulated. That is when I found this girl."

"As I said," Drem interrupted again, "he found some girl in the woods. No reason to interrupt your day."

Daric tensed, holding himself back. "Yes, she was in the woods; but Drem rejected my request when he heard that and did not let me finish. If he had let me finish he would have found out that she was not just anywhere in the woods. She was on the monument."

"She was on Elloe's monument?" The Queen's voice faltered. The fuzziness of a vision surged higher and I dug my nails deeper into my palms.

Drem piped up, "More reason for this conversation to end this moment. She has broken a law. The monument is sacred ground, she needs to be jailed not helped."

"No," Daric shook his head fervently. "She had no idea she was in the wrong. She seemed confused; had no idea how she got on the monument and no recollection of entering a portal. She must have come through from Reta without knowing it. Someone else is responsible for her being there."

"I see, so you have brought her to me to send her back to the other realm. This could have waited, Daric," Queen Neala chided. Every time she spoke the fuzzy sensation grew deeper, more intense. I had to hold out.

"Respectfully, no, Your Majesties. She does not want to be sent back, she was in a bad place. They were going to hurt her. But that is besides the point. The point is she belongs here. I know she does."

"Is that so? Maybe it is about time I hear a few words from the girl?"

My body shook with nerves. I wasn't sure I could do this. Just hearing the few words she spoke to Daric and Drem had nearly pulled me out of this reality and into a hallucination. I felt certain a conversation with her would send me completely under and be ruined by it. Memories of that fateful day that began this adventure assailed my mind. How I'd accidentally pushed Amanda down a flight of stairs. What if something similar happened with Queen Neala? I buried my head in my hands at the thought.

Daric gently held my shoulder, "It will be all right."

"No, no it won't. Something is happening and I can't explain it to you. It's complicated," my voice muffled through my hands.

"Queen Neala wants to speak to you, girl. You will step forward and do so," Drem commanded in his slow harsh tone.

"Quiet, Drem. Can you not see this is hard for her?" Daric

responded to Drem in an equally harsh tone. He softened his voice before speaking to me again, "What is wrong?"

"I'm sick," I stumbled over my words.

"She admits she is not well. She should not be so close to King Carradoc. He could be at risk." My illness gave Drem another reason to argue against our being there.

"I'm sick, not contagious," I defended.

Daric ignored Drem's warning, "Just take a minute and breathe slowly." I followed his suggestion, and after a few minutes I felt calm enough to remove my hands from my face. "You good, Elle?"

"Elle?" a weak new voice entered the conversation, King Carradoc's.

Daric turned his attention back to the King, "Yes, that is what she says her name is. But, well, I will let you talk with her now, if she is ready?" he looked back at me, I gave a meek nod in response.

I felt nowhere near ready, but didn't want to give them any more reason to not trust me. Drem already did a good job of that. I stepped out from behind Daric and moved forward, keeping my head down. I was too nervous to look them in the face just yet. Thankfully, Daric's warm hooded cloak helped to hide me and my nervous state.

"You are called Elle?" Queen Neala asked, curious trepidation laced her words.

"Yes, Your Majesty, I am."

"Would you remove your hood, please?"

My hands trembled as I lifted them to the hood. I closed my eyes and took a deep breath to build a sliver of courage. I wished I had half of Q's confidence just then. He'd sass Drem and proudly fling off his hood to shock the royals with his bright hair. But I wasn't Q. I timidly pushed the fabric from my head and looked up.

A small gasp escaped from Queen Neala. Both of the royals before me wore shocked, tearful masks. I spun around, looking for another possible reason they could be reacting that way. I only saw Drem, looking annoyed, and Daric, who wore a beaming smile. No dragons or massive silent explosions. I sighed, heartbroken and crestfallen, and dropped my head as I turned back around. Yet again, my odd looks offended someone.

I found myself face to face with Queen Neala. While I had my back turned, she had come up and stood behind me. Her dark eyes searched over me, glinting with sadness and hope all at once. Her eyes fell to my necklace and she let out a small crying gasp, her elegant hands fluttering to her lips. When she looked up again, tears gathered in the corners of her eyes.

"Elloe?" She whispered as she brushed a strand of hair away from my face. Her arms wrapped around me in a tight embrace, which was warm and comforting and real. But, I didn't understand what was happening. Was she saying I was hers? I wanted to accept it to believe it, but my built up defenses told me not to trust it. I'd been hurt so many times.

Over her shoulder I saw King Carradoc struggling to stand, but determined in his movements. Daric's large form passed in my peripheral vision, rushing to his side. He helped him stand and assisted him walking over to us. Up close I saw King Carradoc's eyes were the exact same shade of gray as the peppering in his brown close cut curls. He smiled weakly, sighing tearfully, "Elloe, you have come back to us. It is a miracle."

SEVENTEEN

MOTHER KNOWS

It was a surreal moment, surrounded by strangers and being unexpectedly loved. A *"who were these people, and why did they hug me?"* moment. My head warred between accepting it, and rejecting it. Relishing in the warm embraces, or running from the garden before they had the chance to reject me.

"My name is Elle. You have me confused with someone else," in my head I added *I think, maybe.* In truth, the idea tickled me. It would be amazing to have a real family to call my own, the stuff of dreams for any kid that's been in the foster system. Especially those who were in it as long as they could remember. Like me. Not to mention the fantasy of being a long lost princess that so many little girls dreamt about.

Thinking about it, was it really that far-fetched? Considering everything I knew? It was. But, at the same time, it wasn't. No one ever came forward to claim me. No one. Abe insisted the potion he gave me would send me home. I drank it and woke up in a parallel world. And all those times he called me Princess. He never called me Elle, always Princess. If he knew me from here... I couldn't even finish the idea. It felt too much to hope for. Yet, it was happening.

Reality crashed into me.

Abe wasn't crazy. I mean, he proved to me his sanity remained intact. I saw his magic work first hand at the institute. Now, his claims about me began to pan out. It made me wonder why he had been hospitalized in the first place. Was it self punishment for the "bad" he said he had done?

"I recognized her the moment she came down off of her monument," Daric said behind me. "She does not remember her life here, I did not want to overwhelm her by telling her."

"She does not remember?" Neala whispered, pulling back to look me in the eyes. Heartbreak swam in her eyes, pained that I had no memory of her or home."Is it true? You do not remember who you are?"

I shook my head, "No, I don't. I don't know if I'm your daughter. I think I'd like to be, but. . . I just don't know." I looked at the people surrounding me, all wore hopeful and expectant expressions. Except for Drem, he looked like he just opened a can of fermented fish. "How can you be so sure?"

"There is no proof we can offer you immediately, only our word. That stone around your neck, we gave that to you when you were a little girl. That is how I'm so sure. For your proof? There are ways to test it, if you are willing," she replied.

Fear gripped my heart. The idea of belonging somewhere felt so tempting, and too good to be true. But, what if, despite Neala's confidence in the matter, I wasn't who they thought? I couldn't bear the disappointment if whatever test they had for me said otherwise. What happened then? Would they send me back? Would they be mad at me? Where would I go?

At the same time a flicker of hope fired in my heart. Hope for answers. Hope for belonging. A hope that I'd done the impossible and stumbled my way home. My true home. Thoughts of sitting in the lavish garden with Neala by my side, or snuggling up to Carradoc as he told me tales of Vale filled my head. I wanted that more than anything.

My desire to fit somewhere, to have a home, won over my fear, "Yes."

Queen Neala clapped excitedly, the smile on her face brighter than a million super novas. "Drem, do you think you can get everything needed for a spirit match?"

"My Queen, you know I can get anything for you. I can administer the test as soon as tomorrow."

"Thank you, Drem, but I will be administering the test myself. This is something I want to do."

The High Counselor's eyes darkened a little with the queen's words. He dipped low, "If that is your will, My Queen." He scuttled away, taking the chill of his attitude with him. I had no idea what I'd done to make him dislike me so much, but his feelings about me were very clear.

King Carradoc began to cough, his chest heaving in violent spasms. Daric and Queen Neala jumped into action, trying to help him. He waved them off as the coughing ceased. The fit left him looking weak and tired, on the verge of falling over.

"Do you need to sit down?" I asked, touching his hand gently. He looked like he'd break under the slightest amount of weight.

His eyes filled with loving delight, "Yes, I think I should."

"Here, let me assist you?" Daric began to help the fragile king.

"May I?" I jumped in, feeling compelled to care for the man.

"I would like that, very much, my dear." His weak smile brightened his pale face, filling my heart with warmth.

I looped an arm around him and walked him to the bench. He eased down, pulling me with him, refusing to let go of my hand. I couldn't either, not wanting to break his heart. I saw Queen Neala and Daric watching us. Tears danced in the queen's eyes and they both wore huge smiles.

Looking back to King Carradoc, he still beamed. A smile I couldn't help return as he patted my hand lovingly, as a father would. It didn't take long for my eyes to brim over too.

I really wanted to belong here.

❄

THAT EVENING, Queen Neala escorted me to my room after inviting me to join them for dinner. Even though my stomach rumbled, I declined the meal. I needed time to think, and rest. The day had been exhausting both mentally and physically. She opened the large wooden door, inlaid with intricate, silver filigree moons to a darkened room. "Illuminate," she said into the dark. Slowly, the room began to light as soft glowing orbs appeared across the ceiling.

The room had the same elegant simplicity I'd seen throughout Vale. Pale blue satin finished walls and the same cedar floor from the grand hall made up the bones of the space. A four poster bed larger than a California King took center stage, made of rich cherry wood and adorned with fluffy white pillows and matching blanket. A matching wardrobe and vanity sat against opposing walls. A large window, dressed in white curtains, opened to a small balcony closed off by silver metal railings that matched the filigree on the door. The balcony looked over the courtyard Daric and I rushed through when we first arrived.

It was nicer than any room I'd had in foster care for sure.

"This is my room?" the question came out in a whisper as I drank in the room. I held back from diving onto the bed. Instead I sat reverently, running my hands over the tall wood post at the foot of the bed.

"It sure is. Since you were a babe. We had a team streamline it for you this afternoon, but you can change it if you want."

"No, it's perfect."

She clasped her hands under her chin, a wistful expression lay in her dark eyes. She watched me for some time before breaking her gaze. "I will leave you then, let you rest. If you need anything, anything at all, a guard will be right outside your door. Veena, or one of her girls, will bring you something from the kitchen if you change your mind." She hesitated leaving, looked like she never wanted to leave my side.

Alone, I flopped back on the bed, relishing in its luxurious softness. I couldn't remember every lying in a bed so comfortable. My body eased into the downy bed as relaxation seeped into every pore. A drowsy calm settled over me and my eyes began to droop. As I fell asleep, my mind whispered dreams to me. Dreams about Vale and how much I wanted Neala to be right.

I FELT OVEREXPOSED STANDING on the riser sitting in the middle of Drem's apothecary. His lab, a huge room with vaulted, glass and iron ceilings rigged to open out with pulleys. Half of the room looked like a run-of-the-mill, low-tech lab, much like Abe's hidden room back at The Kendrick Institute. The other half, in stark contrast, grew extensive gardens brimming with plants and flowers, filling the air with their sweet and savory scents.

Despite the open and lush atmosphere, the lab felt cold and cramped. An extension of the displeasure that rolled off of Drem every time I came near him, as if the room didn't like me either. At least, that was my impression of the two. Everyone else seems completely at ease with Drem and in his space.

Neala stood next to me, holding my hand. Carradoc, accompanied by a handmaid, sat in what looked like an old fashioned wheel chair; although fancier. Drem loomed over his work table, an array of ingredients and tools sitting before him. A handful of guards stood scattered about the room, vigilant and curious. I recognized a few of them; Karrah and Rollan, the guards from outside of the grand hall the day I arrived. Karrah looked as serious as I remembered, and Rollan practically buzzed from excitement. Daric was there too, standing tall and proud on official duty.

A lot rode on the outcome of this spirit match. Not just for me. At the end of it, I might get a family of my own. Not a foster family being paid by the state to care for me and love me. My own flesh and blood family. Neala and Carradoc would get a daughter back, one they thought dead until I came stumbling into their world. Even

Daric had something on the line, his reputation; validation for defying rules. I knew I wouldn't mind rubbing that bit in Drem's face too.

"Shall we begin?" Drem's droll voice cut the anticipation laden air. He mixed together powders and herbs with barely any glances at what he grabbed or taking any measurements. His dexterity in handling his ingredients fascinated me. It was like a dance, smooth and fluid. My mind drifted to when I watched Abe mix things in his little apothecary under the institute. I practically saw a ghosted image of him moving in time with Drem, clumsily shuffling into Drem's fluidity.

"My Queen," Drem's addressed Neala, breaking me from the mesmerized state watching him put me in, "I am ready for the final ingredient."

Neala left my side, seemingly floated to the other side of the table to join Drem. As she inspected his work, I noticed how familiar Drem's potion looked. A jar of white powder and another filled with a thick, dark liquid. I smiled remembering the Friendly Fire Abe made. This couldn't have been that, or so I thought.

Neala dipped a delicate finger into the white substance and frowned. "Drem, it seems you are slipping in all the excitement. This stabilizer seems off," she said, rubbing her fingers together, "too grainy."

Drem grumbled an apology, "I am sorry, my Queen. I will make another batch right away."

"No need, Drem. Allow me," she replied and began to make another batch of stabilizer herself. Drem stood back, unhappy, and glowered at the rest of the room. It was obvious he didn't like being told he made a mistake.

"There we go," Neala announced, brushing her hands together as she finished up. "Now, just the final ingredient to this," she popped the lid out of the jar containing the dark liquid. Taking a long pin from the table, she pricked the end of her finger, letting drop of blood fall into the mixture. She held her pricked finger out to Drem, who rubbed a green goo on it. The small wound healed over immediately. With her free hand, she replaced the lid on the jar and gave it a shake. The dark liquid shifted in color, taking on a very slight reddish hue.

Deja vu filled my senses, yet again taking me back to Abe's apothecary, as Neala poured the white powder over her right hand. She rubbed the powder, coating the hand completely while she circled back around the table to me. Drem followed behind her with the other jar.

"Now, this may look frightening, but it's nothing to fear. No harm will come to you no matter how it looks." Neala smiled sweetly at me, but I couldn't help but feel a twinge of nervousness. Not from fear of the test, but from failing the test. I wanted so badly to belong here with her. With Carradoc. "Are you ready?"

I nodded, swallowing hard. This was it.

Drem opened the other jar and poured the liquid over Neala's powder coated hand. A blue smoke began to rise from her hand right before it burst into flame. I smiled, it was just like Abe's concoction. My eyebrows drew together, and I whispered, "Friendly Fire?"

Neala and Drem both shot me surprised looks. "You know about Friendly Fire?" Neala asked, looking somewhat hopeful. "You remember it?"

I watched the flames dance on Neala's hand, "Well, not from too long ago. Not from here. The man from the institute that helped me escape, Abe. He made this, used it to convince me magic existed and to enable my escape. But how will it tell you if we are related or not?"

Neala wore a serious face for a moment, taking in what I told her. She looked over to Carradoc and then to Drem, both wore similar serious face, only more concerned. Some silent communication passed between the three of them. When she turned back to me, she shook off the moment and a soft smile took over her face again. "I want to come back to this man later, but for now, I will answer your question. The key to this particular brand of Friendly Fire is blood. You see when I put in the drop of my blood, the mixture changed ever so slightly. A marker of sorts was introduced. Now, when the

Friendly Fire touches you, it will detect if we carry the same genetics. If we do, the fire will react. If not, it will stay the same."

My mouth formed an *o* and I nodded in understanding. "I'm ready," I said after a moment passed. My arm stretched out to Neala, ready for her to take my hand. But, I couldn't look. I shut my eyes tight in anticipation.

Her hand took mine, gentle and firm at the same time. My heart spiked, waiting for some audible reaction. I didn't have to wait long. Gasps from all over the room floated to my ears, prompting me to open my eyes. The flames of the Friendly Fire danced in iridescent rainbows. They changed.

A hopeful warmth settled in my heart, "Does this mean," I paused looking to Neala with hope, "I'm home?"

Neala's arms wrapping around me became the only answer I needed. Her body shook with happy sobs. In moments, a hand on my shoulder pulled my attention. Rollan had wheeled Carradoc closer and helped him stand. With tears in his eyes, he wrapped his thin arms around Neala and me.

Over Neala's shoulder I caught glimpses of the guards, who all wore smiles. I swear I even saw tears on Karrah's face. I didn't see Drem, however. He vanished from the room sometime after my eyes closed and before my eyes opened again, not that I cared. I had too much to be happy about to worry about him. My emotions spilled over. Tears fell merrily down my cheeks as the truth settled in. This was my home. I'd found my family.

AFTER THE SPIRIT MATCH, a maid came to wheel Carradoc away. He needed rest after all the excitement wore him out. I went with Neala to the library, which had to be the grandest room I'd seen since arriving in Vale. Along with the vast collection of books that climbed near to the ceiling, the library held exquisite works of art. Scenic paintings hung in any empty space not taken up by the grand bookshelves, and statues dotted the floor plan. We sat in a warm corner, near an empty fireplace, where a small table waited with a small assortment of butter cookies, fruits, and tea.

Neala poured two cups of tea while we settled in to the sunset colored cushioned arm chairs. I took one of the butter cookies, pleasantly surprised by the unexpected hint of honey that washed over my tongue. The tea, once again the brew tasted so similar to my favorite ginger tea. Perhaps my love of the flavor came from the childhood I didn't remember.

"I'm sure there is much you want to know, Elle. Elloe." Neala chuckled softly, smiling as my real name passed her lips. "I never thought I would be talking to you again, sharing tea." She wiped the mist from her eyes, "You will have to excuse me. I am going to be emotional."

"No, I get it. This is a huge deal for me too, with a capital H." I reached out and touch her shoulder with a little hesitation and quickly dropped it back into my lap, still feeling a little strange about the whole situation. "I guess what I want to know most is what happened."

Neala sipped her tea and placed the cup on the table, her eyes misty and compassionate. "There is not much I can tell you, other than a trusted member of our staff kidnapped you and faked your death. Now that we have you back, we have even more questions to why. Questions likely never to be answered. You do not remember anything?"

"No, to be honest I'm still very confused about all of this. I'm still not sure this isn't a dream made up by my brain; an after effect of what the doctors wanted to do to me to cure me."

"What do you mean?"

I sighed. How do I tell her that there is something wrong with me? That I've hurt people I cared about, that I might hurt them? "I'm sick. I have been for as long as I can remember."

Panic crossed Neala's face, "Sick?" Her hand fluttered to her chest. I could tell what she thought, she got the same look when Carradoc grew weaker than usual.

"How long has he been sick?"

"He fell ill a few years ago. We are not sure what is causing it. Drem is doing all he can for Carradoc, but nothing seems to work." Neala grew quiet, her mind obviously loitering on her husband, my father. The words floated strangely in my mind, my father. She shook her head and came out of her sad haze, "So, what about you? There must be something Drem can do for you as well."

My insides churned, disgusted. I didn't like Drem; didn't trust him. Even more than Dr. Preble. He didn't like me either. He fought like Hell to keep Daric from bringing me to Neala and Carradoc. I'm sure he had no idea who I was at the time, of course neither did I. Nevertheless, his actions were still insulting.

"I don't think there is anything anyone can do. Treatments have never worked for me. I got good at faking it, just to keep people off my back about it."

"We have different methods of treatment here than in Reta. Perhaps there is something that can be done here. What exactly is wrong with you?"

"There's something wrong with my brain, it causes me to see and hear things that aren't there. Doctors never were able to give me a firm diagnosis on it. I also have PTSD from some traumatic event I can't even remember. Both have made my life a lot more complicated, and cause a lot of heartache." I hesitated telling her the rest. What would she think of me if I told her everything? I knew I had to be honest with her, though, completely honest. I took a deep breath and continued, "Before I came here, I had been hospitalized because a hallucination caused me to hurt someone. They decided I'm too dangerous to others and myself to be unsupervised. Like I said before, treatments did not work the way they should. They only made them out of focus."

Neala looked thoughtful, the corner of her mouth curved up and her eyes lit as her thoughts came together. "Elloe, my dear girl, I have a feeling that the reason treatments never worked for you is because there may be nothing wrong with you to begin with. I do not think you need to worry about having any more hallucinations."

I'm confused, "What do you mean?"

"It has to do with how you got to Reta. I know you do not remember anything about that night, but I do know you must have been taken through a portal to get there.

You see, that night when we lost you, we had found what we now know was a glamored body disguised as yours. There was no sign of Abban, the man who took you. We sent parties through a portal to try to bring him to justice, but we never found him. He is good at disappearing. Because we had found a body we never suspected that he might have taken you through the portal with him."

"What does that have to do with my visions?"

"Even before that night we regulated portal travel fiercely. One steadfast rule was that children could not pass thorough portals; doing so caused them to lose part of themselves for the time they were in the other realm. You could say a piece of their spirit would be torn from them and left behind."

"Like a horcrux?"

"A what?"

"Nevermind." I chuckled awkwardly to myself. Of course she wouldn't know what I referred to. I didn't think blockbuster movies based off of wildly popular books were cross-dimensionally famous. I supposed most of what I was familiar with made little sense to anyone here. That would take some getting used to, not being able to make the references I used to.

Neala paused, very likely wondering what I meant. "Anyway, dear, when the children would return they would once again become whole, although it took time before their magic was restored. The timeframe seems to correlate to the length of time they were in other realms. They would report that while in the other realm they felt different, incomplete, and would be able to see and hear things that their left behind spirit could. Sometimes they seemed haunted by the experience, they would have nightmares about not being whole. This is why portal traveling was banned for anyone under 16."

Her theory intrigued me, delighted me. Could it really be possible that I was never sick? Neala's story explained so much of what I experienced all these years; the visions, the auditory hallucinations, and the feelings of being not quite right. None of the treatments really working.

I stopped and thought about what she said, and it dawned on me. I hadn't had an episode since coming here. Yes, I had a couple close calls, but then again I never had close calls before. Only full on episodes. A broad grin stretched over my face. I wasn't sick, or dangerous.

"I wish to discuss something you mentioned in the spirit match," Neala interrupted the quiet celebration happening in my head. "You mentioned a man helped you escape with Friendly Fire."

"Yeah, Abe. He's an interesting fellow. I thought for sure he was off his rocker when I first met him. He was hard to understand, you see, he never spoke in full sentences. Only fragments. But, he was fiercely loyal."

"Abe?" she tapped her chin in thought before excusing herself for a moment. She returned with a book. When she opened it on the table I saw it was some sort of ledger or census record. There were illustrations of people with names and dates under them. She rifled through the pages, "Is this Abe?" she asked stopping and pointing to one of the drawings.

I peeked to the image she pointed to. It was Abe, younger, but him for sure. "Yeah, that's Abe," the corner of my mouth turned up. I actually kind of missed the guy. "The picture is younger, but it's definitely him." Panic bloomed on Neala's face. "What's wrong?"

Her finger slid to the right, revealing the name under the picture of Abe. Abban. What? Didn't she name Abban as the guy responsible for, well, everything I'd gone through. In my mind, it was not even possible. Not Abe. Abe was not malicious in any way. "I think we need to bolster security for you for a while, Elloe. If this man is the one that you say helped you, you could still be in danger. He might come back too."

I swung my head vehemently, refusing to believe Abe to be the bad guy. "No, I don't buy it, Neala. Abe is gentle and kind. He'd never hurt a fly, let alone me. Like I said, he is loyal. He protected me from the doctor and stayed behind so I could get away."

"We all thought he was all those things too, until he turned. We cannot be too careful with him out there."

My escape played in my mind, to how I begged him to come with me. He refused. "I have to disagree still. He's not coming back. He won't. I think he's punishing himself for failing me. He often told me that he failed me, that he's sorry." I paused, thinking, "He said he did something bad and can never go home."

"He's fooled you, dear. He fooled us all. Yes, he did something bad. Even though he admits to it, claims to be sorry, he's deceitful. I'm not taking any chances. We will not lose you again."

I sipped my tea, deep in thought. It had turned cold, much like our pleasant conversation. Neala was wrong, I wanted to prove it. I had no way to. Abe may have taken me from my home and sent me to another world, but I just couldn't see him as the villain. Whatever he did had to have been to protect me, just the way he did at the institute. I needed to figure out just what he tried to protect me from.

EIGHTEEN

STRANGE ADJUSTMENTS

I scowled at the wardrobe full of lace, ruffles, silk sashes, and flowering brocade. Dresses in nearly every color, each one fancier than the last. No pants or shirt in sight. All dresses. I didn't do dresses. Groaning, I flopped on the bed backwards. My ghostly hair pooled around my head, adding to my annoyed expression.

"Is there a problem, Princess Elloe?" the handmaid asked.

"Elle."

"Pardon?"

"Call me Elle, please. Not Princess, not Elloe. I'm Elle."

"As you wish," she replied. "Now, have you decided on a dress to wear?"

"No. I need pants and a comfy shirt, preferably geeky." I tugged at the Institute issued shirt I still wore and thought about all the great shirts that cesspool took from me. Shirts I'd never see again. I turned my attention back to the handmaid. She looked puzzled.

"It is not customary for women to wear trousers in Vale."

"But you can get me some, right?"

"I do not think it would be appropriate. I am certain you will look lovely in one of the dresses." Her unwillingness to help me, irked me.

I just wanted clean pants and a shirt, that weren't from the institute. I needed to change, badly. She was no help. "If I may make a suggestion though," she added cautiously.

"Sure," my reply came out half-hearted. I was ready to just close my eyes and pick one at random.

"King Carradoc has requested a visit, has he not?" I nodded, aprehensive flutters filled me at the thought. He had requested I spend some time with him today. I was nervous about it. Nervous and excited. I wanted to get to know him, and Neala, very much. So far, I'd been shown nothing but love and patience from them. Still, I didn't want to disappoint them. " Well, if I were you, I would pick a green dress. A light shade of green. King Carradoc has always been fond of green. I think it would make him happy to see you in his favorite color."

I considered her suggestion. I knew Carradoc would be happy to see me no matter what I wore. But, I did like the idea of showing up in his favorite color. It might help foster conversation, because I certainly had no clue what to talk about. Standing, I walked over to the wardrobe, carefully looking at each dress with the handmaid's suggestion in mind. My eyes landed on a pearly, pale sea green dress with elbow length sleeves.

"Thanks," I appreciated the handmaid's suggestion, and I pulled the dress from the wardrobe to get a closer look. It looked simple enough, not frilly or poufy, and had a scoop neck and empire waist. Yes, the dress fit the bill. Best of all it was clean.

"Happy to be of help, Elloe." I grimaced at the name I wasn't used to yet. I'd get there but felt, deep down, I'd always prefer Elle. "Sorry," she said noticing my wince, "Elle. Do you need help dressing?"

"No, thanks. I got this." She smiled and curtsied before leaving me. There was a lot I'd have to get used to. I dressed quickly and ran a brush through my hair before setting out, barely glancing at the mirror above the vanity. My appearance, while always on my mind, never landed high on my priority list.

A pair of guards fell in step behind me the moment I began

walking through the halls of the villa. Guards have been shadowing nearly every step I took ever since Neala learned it was Abe, Abban, that sent me back. She feared he'd decide to follow any moment, and finish what he started years ago. I knew that would never happen. As cemented in her belief in Abe's guilt Neala felt, I felt just as certain of his innocence. So, I was stuck under protection. Under constant watch. It was already getting old.

They followed me to the royal bedroom, but didn't show any sign of going in with me. They flanked the door as I stepped up preparing to knock. All the excitement since my arrival took its toll on Carradoc. On strict orders to stay on bed rest for a few days, I visited him there.

My hand trembled against the light wood of door to Neala and Carradoc's room. I still had so many questions, and so many new, unexpected fears. When I was little, I fantasized about this, finding my real family. In those fantasies everything immediately fell into place. Every ounce of self-doubt and worry melted away to instant love and feeling complete. Now that my dream had come true, I realized how silly I'd been thinking my life would magically be fixed when I found where I belonged. I had a long way to go to get there.

The dress I wore didn't make things any easier. The dress fit nicely, comfortably. It didn't have a single flaw. The flaw, once again, came from me. I was more uncomfortable than a cat in clothes. I kept fidgeting with the fabric of the skirt and the ends of the sleeves.

After too long hesitating with my hand resting against the warm wood, I gently knocked. Moments later, a sweet faced maid with peaches and cream skin and vibrant golden hair answered the door. Wordlessly, she motioned for me to enter.

Carradoc sat up when he noticed me. The bright smile I received almost erased the grayish pallor his skin had taken on. His gray eyes twinkled, despite the dull glaze onset from illness. For a moment I could almost see the man he was before the illness depleted him. I wished I could remember him that way. I wished I could remember him at all.

Despite the obvious love pouring from him, I felt awkward. The love wasn't there for me, yet. The guilt welling in my chest taunted me, told me I didn't deserve the love he gave. Anyone's love for that matter. I knew they had no expectation for me to feel an instant connection. That I would develop one in time. The love would come. Still, the guilt ate at me.

I stopped at the foot of the four poster bed draped in heavy curtains. Carradoc looked all that more frail lying against the sumptuous pillows resting against the massive headboard. "Hey," my hands fidgeted with the fabric of my dress some more.

"Hey," he returned my informal greeting like it's nothing, like he always spoke that way. Maybe he did, maybe he didn't. It made me smile, though; released a bit of the tension I carried. "You look," he tilted his head, studying me, "uncomfortable. Nice, but not quite right for you."

His assessment surprised me. Most people wouldn't think to mention something so truthful. They'd focus on flattering words. His honesty was refreshing and lifted the corners of my mouth. "Yeah. I'm not big on dresses," I chuckled. "I kinda feel like a kid playing dress-up. I had help picking this one. "

"You never were. More than not, you would shed your skirts and run about in pantaloons, your beautiful hair in tangles while you ran like a devil through the grounds. Your mother and I gave up eventually, only making you wear them on formal occasions. I am sure we can make your wardrobe more your style, if you would like."

His recollection of me as a child sure sounded like me. "That would be great." Unsure of what else to say, I fidgeted with the dress some more and chuckle nervously.

"You can sit, if you would like. I do not mind," Carradoc gestured meekly to a blank area on the grand bed. What if I did carry a disease like Drem said? I could compromise his health even more. I didn't want to be responsible for him deteriorating. I looked at my father, unsure of what to do. He stared back, his frail face filled with earnest hope. Another worry was born in my head. The worry of disappointing him. I didn't want to disappoint him more than I worried about hurting him.

I hesitated long enough to raise his concern, "It is all right, my little moon girl, you will not hurt me. I am sick and frail, but not made of glass," Carradoc chuckled with a sparkle in his eyes. His reference made me cringe, despite knowing he didn't mean it to hurt me. He merely called me a term he found endearing. Likely a name he called me as I bounced on his knee years ago. He couldn't have known the similar way others teased me with similar terms. Carradoc didn't fail to notice the hurt that crossed over my face."Did I say something wrong, Elloe?"

Not wanting to upset him, I lied, "No."

"Be honest, dear. I will not be upset if I did. I just want to know."

"Well," I started as I finally sat on the edge of the bed, "back on Reta, I didn't look like others. People there can be wary and mean to anyone different. Especially young people like me. I've lost count of how many times I've been called names because of how I look. Sometimes they'd call me Moony or Moon Face. I guess I'm a little sensitive to it, even though I know you mean well." I kept my eyes on my lap, afraid of how much my admission might bother him. Not wanting him to see the tear that hung to the corner of my eye at the painful memory.

Carradoc's cool hand brushing the side of my face brought my gaze up to meet his. He wiped the errant tear away as it rolled down my cheek."Oh, Elloe. I am truly sorry you had bear the brunt of such prejudices. They are awful things, that are an unfortunate part of any world. In time you will see some here, though it is looked down on by most. No matter how hard any world tries; no matter how much light there is, there will always be shadow. It is up to all of us to keep those shadows at bay by becoming beacons of light.

If you like, if it will make you more comfortable, I shall refrain from calling you as I just did."

Carradoc's wisdom and kindness were stunning, touching. Rare. I'd never met anyone so thoughtful. It brought new tears to my eyes.

Inspired tears of joy. Wiping them away, not wanting to lose control and release a flood of them, all I could answer with was a nod. Carradoc's warm, thin arms wrapped me into a hug filled with all the comfort I'd hoped for. He opened something in me that felt a little like trust and a lot like daughterly love.

I knew in that moment I needed him more than I thought I needed anyone. I couldn't lose him just when I met him. He had to get better. He had to.

NINETEEN

MY OWN PERSONAL BABYSITTERS CLUB

After a week of being home, I felt more adjusted than I anticipated. It didn't take me long to get used to the flow of daily life around the villa, or to grow fond of my parents. The awkwardness I felt after just arriving came around less and less.

A large part of my new found comfort were the tunics and leggings Carradoc promised me. Piles of them were brought to me the day after my talk with him. They weren't the t-shirts and jeans I really wanted, but were much better than having to wear dresses every day. Neala offered to send a seamstress to alter the tunics to something more my style, an offer I planned on taking her up on. I kept a few of the dresses in my wardrobe, for special and official occasions. After all , that's how it was before, or so I'd been told.

And then there was the food. The food was amazing, easily one of my favorite things. Veena and her staff, became some of my favorite people. Not only for their abilities and talents. Each and every one of them were genuinely nice, and infinitely patient. I thought for sure they'd hate me, or at least find me annoying with how often I thought of food.

The only thing I couldn't get used to was the guards constantly with me. I really hated being followed around. I tried my best, at least once a day, to lose them. I knew I didn't need them. Abe was not a threat. I just couldn't convince Neala of that.

To save my sanity, I tried not wandering when I didn't have to. My heart felt restless, though. It wanted to know everything it could about my home. So I wandered, and explored. Often stealing to the library and taking a book, then finding a hiding spot to read in until I'd been found.

This day was no different. The villa grounds called to me and I heeded that call. For the moment, I'd shaken the pair of sentry assigned to me for the day. It was easy when both your guards were male and you needed to use the bathroom. Just slip out a window, classic sitcom style.

Outside the window sat a tiny alcove next to a narrow strip of grass and a large dirt patch. Across the dirt patch were hitching posts and racks that held wooden weapons. Thick wooden posts, padded in leather, jutted from sporadic spots of the dirt yard. Training posts. Of course I'd slip away right next to the training yard. Lucky for me, no one trained at the moment. But that didn't mean they weren't just beyond my sight headed for it.

I estimated I had only a few more minutes before the guards realized I ditched them. I needed to get out of there, and fast. I crept across the yard and along the racks of wooden training weapons, my hand running over them as I passed. Their worn handles threatened to leave splinters in my fingers, but I didn't care. What were a few splinters compared to sweet, sweet alone time? At the end of the racks I came to an opening to another yard. I peered around the edge of it. All clear.

I gave the training yard one last glance, making sure I hadn't been found yet, then rounded the corner of the opening. I found myself staring right into the chest of a guard. Sweet freedom didn't last as long as I hoped.

Following the uniform up, I prepared to bat my eyes and laugh off my escape from my security detail to some irate soldier. Instead of a random guard with an angry face, I saw Daric's wickedly charming grin. My cheeks flushed, half embarrassed. I hadn't seen Daric since the spirit match. Despite being validated, he was still suspended from duty for a while. Seeing him again felt really good.

"Whoa there, why the rush?" He smiled down at me. "What happened to your guards?" of course he knew about my constant babysitters. He'd end up on that duty eventually. Though, I wouldn't mind. My journey with him, and his role in reuniting me with my parents, endeared him to me more than the rest of the guards. Plus, I couldn't shake the connection I felt, like I knew him as well as I knew Q. Maybe I had, once upon a time.

"Daric, you're back on duty?" I tried changing the subject. He crooked his scarred eyebrow at me, a silent scolding for trying to evade his question. I had a feeling he knew what happened to my guards too.

"Fine. I slipped away. I needed room to breathe. I feel smothered having babysitters all the time."

"I heard you have been doing a lot of slipping away," he chuckled.

"So?"

"Elle, they are for your protection. Your mother explained how dangerous Abban is, yes?"

"Yes, she has," I rolled my eyes. "But he's not. I don't know why no one believes me. Abe is no threat, even if he were to come back. Which he won't. He's afraid to; ashamed."

He nodded, but I knew he was just being polite. He didn't believe me. "Come on then, I will walk with you. Unless you rather would give me the slip as well," he winked causing me to flush all over again.

"You'll let me take off, home free? No escorts?"

He leaned down to my ear, "I will offer you a head start at least, before pointing guards in your direction." A mischievous glint entered his eye. He had to be the coolest guard in Vale. I knew we would get along like gangbusters.

"You mean it?" he nodded once in response. "You are awesome! I owe you big time," I said hopping away.

"I will hold you to it," Daric called after me. I waved a thank you without turning, taking advantage of the probably short lived freedom.

MY BABYSITTERS FOUND me seventeen minutes later. To be fair, I'd stopped on the bridge over the pond to watch the fish swim and became entranced by their hypnotic movements. Unfortunately they weren't alone. Close on their heels marched Drem, his robes flowing behind him. He didn't look pleased, but when did he ever.

"Ah, Princess," he dragged the word like a snake's hiss, sending the sensation of the slithering beasts writhing under my skin. "Your guards told me of your insubordination, sneaking away. I dare say you are rather cavalier about your safety. Abban could return any time now."

"He won't. He's not the bad guy." I replied staring back at the fish pond.

"Yes, you keep on saying that. But what evidence do you have? Have you recovered some memory you have not shared?"

"No. I just know," I turned finding myself face to face with the slimy adviser. "Having spent most of my life on everyone else's back burner, I've gotten pretty good at judging a person's character."

He arched his dark bushy eyebrow accusingly. Of course he didn't think I did. "Tell me, have you been doing memory exercises like you are supposed to?"

"You know, I'm a little confused about that. How exactly am I supposed to remember things if I'm not allowed to be reminded?" Drem gave strict orders to everyone to not help me gain my memory back with, well, memories. No pictures, no stories, no little clues. I was supposed to meditate and clear my mind for the memories to strengthen and come back. Personally, I thought his method to be horse shit, and so did Carradoc. He more than once had already told me things about my past with a mischievous twinkle in his eyes.

"Questioning the method will only hinder success, Princess. Now, if I hear of you ditching your guards again I will have no choice but to inform your mother and father. I do not think you want to cause more worry for them, do you?" he clearly threatened under the guise of it looking like a favor to me. The more I interacted with him the more I loathed him.

"Fine," I huffed and slumped back over the bridge rail to watch the fish.

"Good girl," he gloated as he left me with my guards and a sour taste in my mouth. I mocked his words to the water and wondered if he could actually hear himself talk. How he got the job as royal counselor, too. Everything that came out of his mouth sounded like hogwash.

At the same time his words hurt. Made me feel defective. Staring at my watery reflection the feeling festered. Soon, all I saw staring back at me was a failure. I'd been home for some time now, long enough that just day to day things should trigger some memories. Still I had none.

Not to mention the sympathy in a lot of people's eyes when they saw me. That hurt as much as the disgust I'd gotten before. Sometimes it seemed I'd traded being treated like a freak to being treated like a china doll. Poor, broken Elle must be protected. Poor Elle's fragile mind must've been damaged in her trauma, or else she'd remember and have her magic back by now.

I wished I had something, anything, to throw at my reflection. Instead I stuck my tongue out at myself and headed back to my room.

TWENTY

RETURN OF THE NIGHTMARES

I woke crying and shaking. It'd been weeks since I had a nightmare, let alone one related to the visions. Blissful weeks free from the torment of my, literally, torn soul. This nightmare felt different, though. Stronger, more vivid. It lingered in my quickened heart beat that slowly calmed as the night shadows morphed into the familiar shapes of the things in my room.

As my eyes adjusted, I realized one shadow still looked all too wrong. Too near, too human. It seemed to stretch towards me, wispy fingers clawing. My eyes slammed tight against the dark room, sure my mind still dreamed. I had to be.

Something cold brushed my cheek, and my eyes re-opened. The shadow loomed closer, right next to me. It's human form more defined than before. This was no usual shadow. A scream froze in my throat, and fear paralyzed me. I couldn't move, no matter how hard I willed myself to. The shadow lunged towards me, and an earth shattering scream finally broke free from my throat. The scream dissolved into frightened and uncontrollable sobs.

"Lights!" the unmistakable sound of Daric's voice boomed over my cries. The lights slowly began to illuminate the room, chasing away the darkness. The humanoid shadow zipped away in a cloud of smoke. The unexplainable paralysis ebbed away, freeing me. My body crumbled against the headrest of my bed, shaking with fear and tears.

"Are you alright, Princess?" Daric asked, placing a gentle hand on my back. I peeked out from the ball I lay in, noticing there other guards in the room as well. They inspected everything methodically. I managed a nod.

"Clear," they called in succession. "No sign of intruders."

"I swear I saw something," Daric barked at the others. "Check the yards and gardens beyond Elloe's windows." The other guards gave their compliance and left my room in a flurry of gray.

"You saw it too?" my voice quavered. "The shadow?"

"I thought I saw something. Your distress was real enough, and there was something very off when I came in. You were so rigid and how your body just collapsed when the lights came on was not natural. Something was definitely influencing you." He lifted my chin and looked right into me, "Are you certain you are unharmed?"

"I'm fine. Scared out of my mind, but fine. It's really weird."

"What do you mean?"

"It's like the shadow came right out of my nightmare."

"Nightmare?" Daric sat on the edge of the bed, settling in to hear my tale.

"I've had this recurring nightmare forever, being dragged through the woods by someone unseen and chased by something dark, a shadow. Only this time I saw who was dragging me. It was Abe. Abban," I corrected.

"Your abduction?"

"No," I sighed in exasperation. I was getting sick of everyone being down on Abe. "Abe didn't abduct me. He was pulling me along, away from the shadow. He tried to defend me from it, blocking a fireball it threw. I woke up then and saw the shadow hovering near me."

Daric didn't reply for a long time. "I do not know what to tell you, Elle. To me, it still sounds like Abban placed some influence over you, to jumble your memories. He dealt in shadows a long time ago, or so I heard. Got himself in some trouble in his youth. Drem would know better of what to make of what happened here tonight." At the mention of his name, I couldn't help show my feelings on the High Counselor, making a face. "But," Daric added, "seeing how he seems to have a thorn in his side these days, it may be best to avoid him."

"He doesn't seem to like me much, or you."

"No, he does not. What can I say, he does not have good taste."

I stifled a chuckle. Daric sitting and talking with me made me feel much better. I really enjoyed his company, and it didn't hurt that he was absolutely gorgeous. Q would be drooling over him.

Daric stood, "I need to go back to my post. Should you need anything, I will be right outside your door."

My heart kicked up at the thought of Daric leaving, I didn't want him to. His presence soothed me, like a security blanket. Plus, I knew sleep would be impossible alone. I already saw my mind wandering a trillion miles an hour, making things up. Seeing the shadow in every corner and jumping at every noise. "Could you stay, just a little longer. I'm still completely wired. I don't want to be alone yet."

He ran his hand over his beard and eyed the door. Conflict etched in every centimeter of his face. Duty or compassion. "Elle, it would be highly irregular, improper even."

"You'd still be doing your job, guarding me. Just a little closer. Theres nothing improper going on. Door's open. There can't be anything against you keeping me company while my nerves settle, right?" He still looked hesitant, although a hint of his jolly nature began to peek through his business face. "Look at it this way, you won't be bored. It has to be dull as anything standing outside of my door all night. Hang out with me for a bit, be entertained by my weird," I flashed a goofy grin at Daric.

His resolve crumbled, "Fine," the mischievous grin spreading across his face said he was more than fine with it. "Scoot over." He dropped his staff on the floor and parked himself on the edge of the bed.

Daric stayed for a long time, just talking about our lives. He did most of the talking, telling me things about Reta that I hadn't learned yet. Next to him, all I felt was calm and peace. I ended up falling asleep a little before dawn, his deep voice soothing my active brain. I practically forgot my nightmare and all about the shadow.

TWENTY-ONE

THE BEST SURPRISE

I LOOKED up from my book and saw two guards approaching, one being Daric. My heart fluttered as I smiled and waved at him. I saw him smile in return, but he remained steady in his actions; he was on duty. As I moved my eyes back towards my book I caught a glimpse of something unusual peeking out from behind Daric's head; a violet tuft of hair bobbing in and out of view. I recognized it immediately.

"No way," laughter bubbled from me as I rushed to my feet, knocking the book in my lap to the ground. Breaking into a sprint, I crossed the distance between me and the guards in seconds. I pushed through the guards and tackled Q with an enthusiastic hug and planted a kiss on his lips. I had never been so happy to see someone in my life.

"I love the purple!" I said through happy tears.

"Girl, these eyes are so happy to see your face. You have no idea."

"I know! I didn't think I'd ever see you again. How are you even here?"

"Well..."

"Princess." Daric's voice snapped me out of the happy mood seeing Q caused. One look at his face and I saw his clear irritation; I felt a little bad for it. My excitement seeing Q made me forget him for a moment. He'd been my closest friend and ally since my arrival. "You seem to know this interloper we found slinking around the edge of the villa." He bit every word.

Q broke into a fit of giggles, I knew my being called Princess had caused it, but it brought my laughter back too. Q would never laugh at me in a mean way. "Yes, Daric. This is Q. My dearest friend."

His green eyes frosted over, "If you were expecting guests you needed to inform us. We are on alert for a reason."

"I didn't know. How would I know? I don't have magic. Neither does Q. I have no idea how or why he's here. I'm just glad he is." I berated. I didn't like this Daric and wondered what had gotten into him.

"Next time, know better." Daric and his companion turned back the way they came, leaving me with Q. We head off the opposite direction. Looking back, I glimpsed Daric looking back as well, his expression still sour, though I swore he looked a hurt as well.

"What's with Officer Man Candy?" Q wiggled his eyebrows.

"I don't know. He's not usually like that."

"Shame. A whole ass snack like that is wasted on anger."

I shook off the bad feelings and focused on Q. I could figure Daric out later, I wanted to enjoy this unexpected reunion with my best friend as much as possible. I couldn't do that worrying about Daric's odd behavior. "Anyway, how did you get to Vale?"

"That, sweetie, is a long story. Any chance we can do this over coffee? I am exhausted."

"There's no coffee here."

"Sacrilege!"

"I'm sure we can find something you like." I hooked elbows with Q and walked him to the bench I sat on before he arrived.

As we sat, he stooped and picked up my dropped book. He carefully unfolded the few pages that crumpled when it hit the ground. He'd always been super respectful to books. Both of us were. Books were sacred doorways to far off places that kept the real world from devouring us whole. He glanced at the cover and grinned, "Is this a magic book?"

"Yup. I'm hoping reading it will help me out when my magic comes back."

"Comes back?"

"Apparently Vale born are all magical on some level."

"Cool."

"You want to see cool?" He nodded with enthusiasm. "Veena, I'd like a tea and a dark flower brew, please."

"Who are you talking to? Is Veena like a smart device or something?"

Moments later, Veena waltzed in with the drinks I just asked for. I took the cups from her, handing the dark flower brew to Q. "Will that be all Your Highness?"

"Yes, thank you Veena."

Q stared in wonder as he watched her walk away. "Whoa. How did you do that? I mean, you just asked for a drink and a few minutes later she arrived."

This time, I grinned. I knew he'd get a kick out of this, "I didn't have to ask. She was probably already on the way. I only asked to freak you out. Veena's a little on the psychic side, she knows what people need and when. Although she ignores me half the time because I always feel like I need food."

"Still a raging food demon then?"

"You know it."

"So, what is this dark flower brew?" He sniffed the drink and pulled away with a disgusted look. I knew exactly why. The first time I was offered a dark flower brew, I made the same face. The bitterly sour scent of the drink stung the eyes, and was strong enough to singe even the sturdiest of nose hairs.

"It's the closest thing to coffee in Vale. It tastes better than it smells, kind of the opposite of coffee. They make it from these black flowers that grow in a certain part of the forest. I even like it, but I still prefer my tea."

Q blew on the drink before taking a hesitant sip, bracing for a horrible taste. His eyes lit when the sweet drink washed over his tongue and he greedily downed half of the glass. "Wow! That is better than coffee, it's like a spicy hot chocolate, with a fruity aftertaste."

"With a kick; gives you more of a buzz than coffee too."

"Oooo. I can't wait." He downed more of the energizing drink, this time savoring the flavor.

Watching Q, I sipped on my own drink. He slowly spun around, taking in the beauty of the garden with his mouth shifting between smiles and awe-filled gapes. Child like wonder radiated from him just as it had from me when I saw the gardens for the second time. The first time I'd been too rushed, and anxious, to appreciate it fully.

"So, are you going to tell me this long story?" I asked.

He turned to face me, grinning and his eyes full of excitement, "You are going to love this, it's the stuff of insanity." He pulled another mouthful of brew and wiped his mouth. "A few weeks ago I got this call from The Kendrick Institute telling me a patient I knew had passed away. I got pissed, called the lady on the other end every name in the book. You'd been dead, or so I thought, for over a month. When I brought up your name, she apologized and told me you weren't dead as far as she knew. You had disappeared months ago, run away during a strange mass hysteria event. She was calling because Abe had passed and had left me his things."

The sad news stabbed at my heart, "Abe's dead?" I missed him and his insane antics. Though he never wanted to return, this meant he actually never would. Part of me had hoped I could clear his name and he'd be free to come home too.

"Yeah, I'm sorry. Abe was a good guy," Q stopped and finished the brew in his cup. He stood up and began to pace, his hands flipping about as they tended to do when he was talking. "Anyway, I was confused. I couldn't think why Abe would leave things to me. The last time I saw him, I'd punched him, hard." His hands flew at a million miles and hour. The brew had kicked in.

"You hit Abe? Why?"

"I went to visit you and you weren't there. Abe told me you'd gone to Vale. I interpreted that as that you had passed through the veil; that you had died. Then he kept rambling about how he was sure you were happier and felt better being there. That made me so mad. I hit him."

"I can see how that was all miscommunication. Abe wasn't always the best at conversation."

"Right? Anyway, I go there and I get this box and take it home. In the box there is a whole bunch of stuff, I didn't really look through it, though. I was really confused and kind of mad at you at that point. I couldn't believe that you had run away and not come to me.

But there was a letter on top, from Abe, that I opened. I had to know why he gave me all this stuff even though I barely knew him. In the letter, which was extremely eloquently written by any standard, he told me he wasn't mad at me, he knew what I did came from a place of hurt. He offered me a way to see you again. He said in the box I could find some jars of mashed up medicines and chemicals he stole from the institute and dyed with food so they just looked like colored sand to the nurses."

Q stopped again and looked longingly at his empty cup. On cue, Veena entered the garden with another cup, grapes, and lacy almond biscuits dusted in sugar. "Oh, God, I love this girl! Thank you, what's your name again?"

"Veena."

"Thank you, Veena. I could marry you."

Veena blushed, laughing, "Already married."

Q clicked his tongue against his teeth, "Probably for the best, love. It would never work. You'd make me fat and I'd constantly be chasing all the hot guards."

"You are most welcome, sir. You are correct, our love could never be. My wife will be thankful for that."

"Oh snap!" Q rushed the tiny girl, wrapping her in his lanky arms for a quick hug. "I knew I liked you."

Veena laughed and bowed out. Q swallowed down his new cup of brew in seconds. "Now, where was I?"

"Ummm, colored sand."

"Right! He said the contents of the jars could be combined to create spells; more importantly, a spell to open a portal to Vale.

So, of course I thought he was nuts. He was in a mental hospital, after all."

"Hey!" I threw a biscuit at his head, "So was I."

"No offense! You know you're the best kind of crazy," Q winked and I blew a kiss in return. I missed this so much, the easy camaraderie between us picked up like it'd never been separated. "I tucked the box away and forgot about it. A week later I'm bored out of my mind on a rainy day, still moping that my best friend abandoned me. I found the box while rearranging my room and decided to dig through it. My spirits lifted when I found a bottle of rum. I popped the cork took a huge swig. It was heaven.

I'm drinking and dancing around my room in my boxers, doing a marvelous impression of Justin Timberlake when Abe showed up in my room. Of course, I screamed like the queen I am."

"Of course," I laughed. I could see the scene play in my mind.

"I'm flipping out. When I stopped he's just starin' at me and he asked if I'm finished being a baby. I realized then I wasn't having an alcohol induced hallucination. He was there, speaking as clearly as any other person rather than the broken speech he'd adopted at the institute.

He told me he figured I wouldn't believe the letter so he put the bottle of rum in the box. He'd just been sitting around waiting for me to drink it; kinda thought I'd do it sooner. He'd been watching me for a week! Creepy. He'd mumbo-jumboed the liquor so I'd see him when I drank it, you do not want to know what was in it for it to work. Eww.

Anyway, I began to believe his story, he walked me through a few spells for practice and I made the potion to open the portal. I drank it, went to sleep and woke up in the forest. After that, I found my way here when Officer Man Candy and company found me."

"That is quite the story. Almost as good as my escape from The Kendrick Institute. I'll tell it to you sometime."

"Seriously." He sat back down, taking my hand in his. "Enough about me, though. Are you good here?"

"Yeah, things are different here. No one cares about my monochromatic theme for one. A lot of people share some of my features. My mother has my hair. My father has my eyes. There are even one or two other people I've seen that share my paleness. Still, having all three is uncommon. It's something that happens when a child is born under a certain moon, showing their connection to the moon."

"Awesome. So no more feeling like you look like a freak."

"Not as much," I smiled at him. "I'm learning to accept myself. Want to know the best part?"

"Of course!"

"I haven't had a single hallucination in the time I've been here."

"That is epic! They cure you or something?"

"No, I never had any diagnosable condition to begin with. It all had to do with me being too young to go through the portal and part of my spirit being left behind. When I came back, I became whole again. Soon, my magic should return."

"You're magic too? Seriously epic. I always knew you were the coolest girl in the world."

TWENTY-TWO

THOSE PESKY FEELINGS

"Princess or not, I'll crush you!" Feathers floated in the air, creating an indoor flurry. An epic pillow fight for the ages raged on for nearly thirty minutes. It was definitely one for the books, even though I was losing.

Q smashed his weapon of choice into my head and knocking me ass over end onto the floor where I erupted into more laughter. My face hurt from the permanent smile I'd worn since his arrival. Life felt nearly perfect for the first time in my memory. Every box in my happiness meter had been ticked. I had good health, a home, a family, and more than one friend. The happiness that encompassed me reached insane levels.

"Cease-fire?" Q asked, reaching his hand out to help me up.

I playfully eyed his offered hand, sure he had something up his sleeve. I knew the offer meant to keep me from attacking while he helped me stand. This wouldn't be the first time he'd played that tactic. "Truce," I grinned, taking his hand.

Just as I suspected, the cease-fire didn't hold longer than a few seconds. The moment I was upright, Q's pillow slammed into me again sending another flurry of goose down into the air. He would so pay for that one. I flung my pillow at him and missed, hitting the wardrobe instead.

"You missed," Q teased.

"I won't next time," the boast held no water. I knew I'd probably miss. I dashed across the room and snatched up my pillow. My arms wound back, and I prepared to attack. Just as I began to swing a knocking on the door interrupted the fun. The pillow flopped limply onto the floor. "Time out," I welcomed the interruption, just a little. It gave me a few moments to recoup. I hopped over the pillow and trotted to the door to answer it. Inches from the door a pillow hit me in the head, "Hey!"

I pulled the door open, feathers still flying around my head, revealing Daric. I swatted at a feather that crossed my vision, "Hey, what's up?"

"Guard change," he smiled as he plucked a feather from my hair. "Why are there..," Daric's smile faltered into a scowl, "Oh, I see. What is he doing here?"

I looked over my shoulder to see Q, awkwardly waiving. "Uh, beating my ass in a pillow fight?"

"You understand what I mean. What is this male doing in your room with the door closed? It is not proper."

"Q," I emphasized, "is hanging out, we're catching up. You can join us." Daric scoffed, rolling his eyes. "What?" I stepped forward, defending myself and Q.

"I'm going to go for a walk," Q interrupted the tension.

My hand pushed against Q's chest, stopping his exit. "No, you can stay. Daric is mistaken." My eyes narrowed onto Daric. His attitude toward my friend began to truly grate on my nerves.

"No, I'm gonna walk. Let you two work out whatever this is," Q motioned between Daric and myself . "Be prepared to meet your feathery doom when I get back," he kissed the top of my head as he passed, earning a poisonous glare from Daric.

Once Q disappeared down the hall, I lay into my unusually surly friend, "What the Hell, Daric? What has gotten into you?"

"One could ask you the same question, Princess. Having a male guest in your room at this hour."

"You come in here almost every night and talk until I'm ready to sleep."

"With the door open," he retorted between gritting teeth.

"I have no idea what your problem with Q is, but he is my friend. My only friend from my life before, when the world thought I was a dangerous lunatic. The only person to stay by my side no matter how weird I look or how many voices I heard. He's my friend."

"What am I, then? If he's your only friend?"

I turned around, pulling my fingers through my hair. I couldn't believe he could act like such a dick. I turned back, "You're my friend too! I swear you are only hearing what you want to hear, that whatever grudge you have against Q is clouding your hearing."

"And you're thinking straight? What do you think your parents would say if they knew he was in your room?"

"They know. They love Q and understand the situation completely. You are the only one, besides Drem, who doesn't count because he hates almost everyone, that seems to have an issue with him here. An issue that came from nowhere." Comparing my friend with the vile High Counselor felt gross, wrong even. They were nothing alike at all. I knew Drem's issue with Q was all about me. Q being from Reta and being my friend solidified his pond scum position in Drem's eyes. As for Daric? I had no idea what his beef with Q was. He got along with every decent person I knew of in Vale.

Daric ran his hand over his face, frustrated. For a minute I thought I'd won this stupid and unnecessary argument. "They'd feel differently if they knew your intimate relationship with him," he retorted, speaking to the ceiling instead of me.

"Intimate relationship?" I laughed. The idea that Q and I were anything but friends was completely preposterous. "With Q?"

"I saw you kissing him, do not try to deny it."

"I won't, it's not a big deal. Q and I kiss platonically. So what?" Daric let loose a sarcastic laugh, pissing me off even more. "Right. A friendly kiss. It's not like he's jamming his tongue down my throat and feeling me up. It's not like that at all."

"Right."

His disbelief infuriated me. How could it be so hard for him to see the truth that was plain as day to everyone else that met Q today? I inched a little closer, "Yeah. That's right. I love Q, with all my heart. As. A. Friend. We kiss, as friends. Neither of would enjoy kissing each other THAT way."

Daric scoffed again, crossing his arms over his chest. He arched his scarred eyebrow, stubborn and unbelieving. "Somehow, I doubt that."

"You sound exactly like my last foster parents. Which is so ridiculous. I'd never think you'd fall into the category of people that think boys and girls can't just be friends. That affection can't be shared between friends unless it's romantic."

"Do not try to turn this on me. I know what I saw, and that was not just a friendly kiss," Daric growled low.

"Get off your high horse, Daric. You're mistaking excitement to see each other as something else. Trust me, we'd both rather be kissing you." The second the words left my mouth, I regretted them. I slapped my hand over my mouth, as if it could take them back. I was horrified. More than horrified, I was mortified beyond compare.

Daric's face mirrored how I felt inside. He looked horrifically puzzled, like the idea of kissing me was completely alien. "What did you say?"

"Nothing. I think you need to leave. You can switch duty with someone else until Q leaves," I blurted as I shoved his tall frame with all my might, ushering him from my room.

I closed the door in his face and leaned up against it for a moment before flinging myself headlong on my bed. What had I said? I wanted to become one with the bed, melt into it and fade away. Never in a million years would I ever admitted the small crush I'd developed on Daric. That just wasn't something I did. My usual M.O. was drooling from afar until I lost interest, or gave up because I didn't have a snowball's chance in Hell. I could only blame the heated conversation. There was no way I'd be able to face him again.

The bed shifted under added weight, but I don't look up. I knew it had to be Q back from his walk. Daric's terrified face all but confirmed he'd never set foot in my room again. I guessed it was better that way. Keeping our interactions professional meant no guilt about breaking rules on his part, and I could focus on recovering everything I'd lost. I would not be distracted by crooked smiles, mischievous forest green eyes, or deep rumbling laughs. Who was I fooling? The unrequited crush would disable me for weeks, if not months.

My friend patted my back, comforting me. "Oh, Q," I lifted my head just enough to talk, " I really screwed up this time. I just monumentally messed up the best friendship I've had since meeting you. I'll never be able to face Daric again."

I turned my face, hoping for some Q-ism of cheer. Instead, I'm greeted by Daric staring down at me with that crooked half smile of his that made me feel like my insides were molten, and made my brain go all gooey. I groaned back into the bed, "Go away. There is nothing more to say, I've made a big enough fool of myself. Go gloat somewhere else."

"Elle, look at me please," he pleaded low and quiet.

I didn't want to. Well, I did but I couldn't bring myself to. I'd embarrassed myself enough.

The thought hit me. I had the power. I could make him go away, pull the princess card. He had to do what I told him to do. "Just go. You know you have to listen to my orders, and this is an order."

"No."

I groaned internally. Why did he have to be so stubborn? I was going to have to woman up and face him. After taking a few moments, and deep breaths, I sat up and faced Daric, "Are you defying a direct order?" I asked , mustering all the authority possible. The waiver in my voice didn't make the order all that convincing.

His soft expression held a glint of mischief, "Yeah, I am." His cupped my face with his large hands and pulled me in, kissing me delicately. My body exhaled and the world quieted.

When he pulled away, I was left dumbfounded and staring at him feeling a little like one of those old cartoon characters that just got kissed. My heart drummed like sneakers in a dryer, my skin felt like fire, and I felt lighter than air. I wasn't entirely sure my head still sat on my shoulders. I wanted to melt away into an Elle puddle, all soupy and warm from the buzz his kiss gave me.

"You did mean what you said, didn't you?" Daric asked, concerned when I didn't respond with a smile. His dejection snapped me out of the blissful haze.

"Yeah," I blushed, tucking my pale hair behind my ear and gazing down at my lap. He just kissed me and I still shied away. What the heck was wrong with me? I forced myself to look up again. Daric beamed, his crooked smile bright and his eyes glowing. "I'm just nervous."

"Me too. I am sorry for acting as I was."

"Like a dick."

Daric chuckled, "Yes. I was jealous. You were right. I only heard what I wanted to, looking for validation in hating Q. He made you so happy with one glimpse. Then you kissed him. I saw red, plain and simple. There is no excuse for being mean to you, though. I let my feelings get in the way of my job. I should not have done that. I am truly sorry."

"You could've asked instead of getting so mad. I would have told you Q's gay, but I didn't think I had to. It's pretty obvious."

"It is now. I feel like a fool. Am I forgiven?" The way he looked at me shows me everything he felt. His sadness at hurting me in even the smallest way, his affection for me, and the hope in his heart all reflected in his eyes. Something about them sent heated shivers through me.

I nodded, overwhelmed by everything. Daric kissed me again, thrilled with my silent answer. "I should get back to my post before I get in trouble," he said afterward. "I'll be right outside if you, or Q, need anything."

As I walked him to the door, I noticed that he had closed it when he came in. I chuckled in my head, after all a closed door is what brought all this about. Daric pulled me to him by my waist when he noticed the smirk on my face. "Door," I tilted my head towards it.

"Quiet," he jested, kissing me one more time. This time the kiss was slower, deeper. My toes curled and I lost myself in it. My head swam with his scent, verdant and manly, as our lips explored one another's. It was heavenly.

Behind us, he door swung open, breaking our kiss. We jumped apart quickly. I feared we'd been caught by another guard that by chance noticed my room unguarded and came to check on me. Worse yet, by Neala coming by to say goodnight.

Thankfully, only Q stood in the door frame, grinning like the cat who got the canary. "Who's being inappropriate now?" he wiggled his eyebrows at us.

"Shut up, Q," I playfully shoved his arm. He stuck his tongue out at me, I reciprocated.

"I will take my leave and stand watch now," before he left, Daric offered a hand out to Q, wrapping him in a one armed bro-hug when he took it. "Thank you for caring for Elle, watching out for her when she felt alone."

"My pleasure, man. She's my best friend, she holds me up as much I as do her." Q replied, mildly confused by Daric's change of heart.

Daric left us to our antics, closing the door behind him.

"Big change in Officer Man Candy," he elbowed me when we sat side by side on the floor next to the bed. "I take it you won that one?"

"Yeah," I bit my lip. A rush of warmth filled me as I recalled the kiss. I grabbed a stray pillow from the floor and hugged it to my chest. "He was jealous of you. He saw me kiss you and got the wrong impression."

Q burst out laughing, "That's a first! So," he paused for dramatic effect, "is he a good kisser?"

I blushed into the pillow, just before smashing it into Q's face to continue our pillow fight. I had a good feeling about beating him this time. Or it could've just been the cloud of happiness Daric's lips left me floating on.

TWENTY-THREE

THE GENIUS THAT IS Q

I'm certain Q fell in love with Vale. I'd never seen him so energized before. His curiosity exploded from him, asking everyone a million questions. The people at the villa seemed to accept him as if he were one of them. The only one person that failed to adore him was Drem. But, like I told Daric, he didn't count. Drem had terrible taste in people.

"When I get home, I think I might continue to tinker with some of the potions Abe left me. See if I can make my own magic, do some wild experiments. I was thinking I can combine technology from there with the magic from here. Who knows, maybe I can rig a cell phone to work cross-dimensionally so we can stay in touch all the time."

"That would be amazing. If anyone can do it, it's you. I'll pull a few books from the library that might help." I swung his hand in mine, picturing him working like some mad scientist, mixing technology and magic. This venture landed right up his alley, especially with his upbringing. Mrs. Queen practiced holistic and spiritual healing, and his dad practiced more traditional medicine, Dr. Queen. One might have said Q was made for doing what he proposed.

The time for him to return home approached faster than either of us liked. I didn't want him to go at all. I'd miss him too much. Our separation would be different this time, less final. He no longer mourned me, knowing I lived just a portal away. A portal he had the know-how to open and pop through to visit any time he wished. His idea about the phones would make staying in touch even easier than that. If it worked.

"You know, Elle, I've been thinking about your dad too. It blows that he's so sick, and they can't help him. You'd think that magic could cure anything, ya know."

"It's magic, not a miracle. Everything has its limitations. I guess it's one of those *"grass is greener"* things."

"When did you get so wise?"

"Probably when I stopped living in fear of myself." I held myself back for so long because of thinking there was something wrong with me. I was broken and unbalanced. Now, that constant fear of my own mind faded to memory and I opened myself up to life. "Anyway, I'm sure our science would be just as astounding to anyone here that relies on magic. They'd feel it was all powerful too."

Q stopped mid step, dropped my hand, slapping my arm with the back of his hand, "Elle, that's genius. Why didn't I think if that? I mean, I did, but for something else."

"Ummm. What? Why?" Q was on to something, I wasn't sure what though.

"The cell phone thing. Mixing magic and science."

"Yeah, I agree about the phones. It'd be great to be able to talk to you all the time."

"No, not the cell phones. Carradoc. What if the magic isn't good enough? What if he needs our science? Heck, I know Ma and Dad would love a chance to solve a mystery like this using their combined powers of medicine. That makes three forces of healing fighting for your dad. Don't you see?"

I saw it in my head as he explained excitedly. Magic and medicine working together to save Carradoc. Was it possible? A slow smile crept across my face. This was brilliant, and I was down for it. Would it actually work? I had no clue, but we had to at least try. And I had to be part of it. "Q, I think you may be on to something." I clutched his arm, "Come on, let's go have a chat with my parents, see what they think of your idea."

NEALA AND CARRADOC were in the grand hall. For the first time since my arrival, Carradoc actively participated in attending to kingdom matters. My heart leapt seeing him feeling so well. He'd been feeling good, and looking better for a couple of days now. Drem hadn't needed to treat him, or force sleep on him to help his body rest and heal. Despite the upswing, worry still lurked in the corners of Neala's eyes. She didn't hold hope that this healthy spell would last long. He'd had days like this before, only to relapse further into his illness.

Still, it gave me hope. Hope, strengthened by Q's brilliant idea, that this would be how I saw my father more often than not.

Watching them run their kingdom together was, for lack of a better word, beautiful. Together they seemed an unstoppable force of good. Their silent teamwork, knowing what each other thought, and seeing all the love they held for not only each other but their people astounded me. Inspired me. I didn't mind waiting because of it. I relished watching, like looking into a window at what I should have been seeing my whole life.

Despite enjoying seeing the scene before me, I itched with impatience. My feet fidgeted and my fingers flexed at my sides in anticipation of sharing Q's idea. The excitement I felt became almost too big to contain. Waiting for them to be finished was torture. After long minutes the meeting dispersed, and Q and I finally got the chance to make his proposal.

A noticeable bounce added to my step as I approached my parents. I swooped on them, giving each of them a hug. This time I didn't feel cautious about embracing Carradoc. His recent run of good days made me less worried that I'd break him.

"Elloe, what a wonderful surprise," Carradoc sighed into my ear, his coarse whisper a small reminder he was in fact still ill. "We thought we would not see you today. With your wonderful friend leaving tonight, we were sure you would be occupied all day."

"Honestly, Mr. C, you didn't think I wouldn't need to say goodbye to my new surrogate parents, did you?" the nearby guards shifted uncomfortably at Q's informality. Personally, I loved it. I love that Q felt so accepted here. That Neala and Carradoc made him feel so comfortable. That he saw my family as his, just as I dreamed of his as mine for so long.

"Goodbyes are not the only thing that brings you here though, are they?" As usual, Neala intuitive nature clued her in to the underlying issue. That, or the excited energy that radiated from me.

"No, they aren't," my jubilation bubbled over at the admission. "We wanted to talk to you about Q's return to Reta, the possibility of him not going alone."

"You wish to return to Reta?" a ghost of disappointment crossed Neala's, and Carradoc's face. They thought I wanted to leave them.

"Oh, not forever, of course. I mean, I want to return there. I miss so much there. More things there than people, mostly Q and his family. But I belong here, I know that. I love it here. I love you guys. I could never leave you willingly now that I've found you." I clasped Neala's hand to reassure her.

"I do not see why you cannot accompany Q home, under guard of course."

I groaned internally. Their overprotective stance on me stretched across dimensions now. Even though they knew of Abe's passing, they still saw him as a threat. He wasn't. The unknown threat resided in Vale. I'd be safer on Reta than I was in Vale. "I'll only agree to a guard if it's Daric." I threw in my own stipulation to theirs.

Neala arched a perfect brow at me. "You certainly have become fast friends with the guard that found you." She hinted she suspected the truth of my relationship with Daric, but I didn't confirm it. I wasn't not ready for that. Mostly, out of fear that we'd be forced apart.

"He's been a great friend, helped me adjust so much. But, I'm not the one I was asking about going with Q. I was asking about Carradoc." Daric loved Carradoc as much as anyone. I trusted him most with my father.

"Elloe..."

I caught Neala's hesitant tone and cut her off, "Wait. Hear me out. Q thinks that since your medicine and magic aren't working, there may be something on Reta that will. Everyone on Reta always thinks that magic would be the most amazing thing capable of doing things not possible. I'm sure that some of the technological and scientific wonders of Reta would make Vale citizens feel the same. Why not try it? And Q's parents represent both ends of medicine there. His dad is a very talented doctor, and his mom is a spiritual healer, she uses energies and holistic medicines. Q really thinks they can help. Q wants to help. I do too."

They looked at each other with a sad questioning while they considered my words. Hesitation took over their appearances. Hesitation and a lot of pride. At least I hoped it was, pride that I've stepped up to do my part in helping my father get better. The silent words between them hung heavy in the air.

"Sweetheart, I think your friend has noble vision. But, it is just not possible for me to portal travel, It's too risky."

"That is more than true, children," Neala added. "Even though he has had a wonderful week of better health, it is not wise for Carradoc to do any sort of travel. Let alone between worlds."

The delicate thread of hope I clung to frayed into nothing. This may have been our last shot at saving him. I wanted to cry and scream, run away from the grand hall in childlike defiance. I didn't want to accept their answer.

"Understood," Q spoke up when my words failed.

"No," I said. "That can't be it. There has to be a way that Q can see if his theory is right. He has to. I know it'll work. I don't know how, I just do." My mind raced over possible solutions until it landed on a perfect idea. "What if we took a sample of his blood?" I asked excitedly.

"Won't work, girl. Blood has to be stored at a pretty low temp if not used within a few hours of being drawn." Q shot down my brilliance with his real medical knowledge.

I flopped in defeat onto the steps next to Carradoc's seat, feeling defeated. "I guess that's that. Do not pass go, do not collect 200 dollars."

"I would not say that," Neala chimed in. "I do believe that the first step in your journey is a perfect way to have our magic and your science work in our favor."

"What do you mean?"

"You will see," she replied with a smile before calling for a maid.

TWENTY-FOUR

VALE TO EARTH

"Ma, I'm home." Q called, tossing his jacket onto the standing coat rack with enough style to be called superhuman. He made most things look effortless.

The light stringy music that filled the air stopped. "You're home sooner than you said you'd be," she called back. She bounded down the stairs, tying her silk kimono around her. The little pink and yellow butterflies on it seemingly fluttered around her in a shiny tornado. "You caught me in meditation, Quentin," she paused when she saw me and Daric with her son. "Oh, you have guests." Mrs. Queen smiled sweetly at me and embraced me, "I was so sorry to hear you died, Elle. But now here you are, fresh as a daisy. And there's something different about your aura, so much brighter.

"I'm in a better place," I poked fun at my supposed death, earning a round of laughter. I hadn't realized until then how much I actually missed Mrs. Queen. Mr. Queen too. They were more family to me than anyone before all this happened. Janice always had a keen wit, and you never knew what would come out of her mouth. She always said what was on her mind.

Mrs. Queen eyed Daric, "And who is this handsome boy?"

"Daric," he introduced himself, bowing slightly.

"Pleased to meet you, Daric. I'm Janice Queen, Quentin's mom."

Daric shot a puzzled look at Q, "You did not mention you are royalty in this realm."

Mrs. Queen laughed, "Aren't you sweet?"

"Queen is their surname, Daric," I explained. "Not her title."

"The pleasure is all mine, Janice Queen. Your son is a good man and friend. He has kindly offered us lodging in your home while we are in this realm."

Q's mom blushed slightly at Daric's charm. "I guess that means you're staying for dinner. Yay! I'll whip up something extra special." Janice, aside from being a talented spiritual healer, made the best food. Better than Nikki McIntyre even. Once, after tasting some homemade wonton soup she made me when I was sick, Nikki tried offering her a job in her cafe. Janice declined, of course, declaring that cooking from the heart was better than cooking for money. Her fancy way of saying if it was her job to cook, it'd lose all the joy it brought her.

"Can we have pizza?" Q suggested.

"Really, pizza? It's a special occasion. How often does your best friend come back from the dead?" she whined at the less than stellar request. Part of her love language was food and being told she couldn't cook didn't sit well with her.

"She wasn't dead, Mom, just missing."

"I know that, can't I be funny too."

Q rolled his eyes at his mom. "Please. Elle hasn't had pizza in months, which is practically forever in teen years."

"Fine, fine. I'll order from Vinnie's. Why don't you take your friends to settle in and I'll call you when it's here." Suddenly, I was ravenous at the mention of Vinnie's. They had the biggest variety of pizzas, not to mention the best Mediterranean inspired veggie pizza. No other pizza place had the magic to make broccoli appealing on pizza.

. . .

FORTY MINUTES later we were all gathered around the Queens' kitchen table diving into delivery box lain before us. The cheesy goodness dripped in long strings from the hot slice of pizza as I took my first bite. The flavor exploded in my mouth. Heavenly. I had to teach Veena how to make pizza when we got back to Vale. I looked at Daric who eyed his slice suspiciously.

"Take a bite, trust me," I coaxed, taking another, larger than I should have, bite.

Daric tentatively bit into his slice. His eyes widened with delight and he chomped down the remainder of the slice and grabbed two more.

"He's never had pizza before?" Mrs. Queen asked in disbelief.

"Pizza virgin!" Q exclaimed, pumping his fists into the air.

"There isn't pizza where we live. But I plan on changing that. I've just realized that I can't live without it." I took a huge bite, exaggerating expressions of pleasure as my teeth ripped through the crust and cheese.

"Sounds like an," she paused to think, "interesting place. Is it some sort of progressive treatment facility?"

"Mom! Rude!"

"Sorry, didn't mean to be. Just curious," she pouted. The room fell silent, except for the sound of chewing, and the air hung with an awkward tension. "So, what's new with you, Elle? I haven't seen you since just before, you know. It seems like whatever treatment they put you in is working well."

"No, actually. The Kendrick Institute didn't work out. Their treatment plan was a little too aggressive for me and I ended up going somewhere else that confirmed I'd been misdiagnosed." I said carefully, not wanting to reveal too much. As progressive and understanding Mrs. Queen could be, I didn't think she would buy that I lived in another world.

"Really? The Kendrick Institute just let you decide their plan wasn't right and leave. Sounds more progressive than I thought."

"No, Ma. Elle ran away from that place. They were gonna cut her brain up."

"No! Really? I'm gonna tell your father about that. Those poor people there," she pouted her lip for a moment. "Anyway, back to you, Elle. You said this new place said you've been misdiagnosed?"

"Yes. The hallucinations were not really hallucinations. My mind was showing me memories, things from my past and things that caused my amnesia. I just wasn't understanding them." The lie was slight, but, again, I couldn't see her buying the whole truth about what my visions were. Not many people would accept the answer of, "Oh my soul was split in two."

"Are you a patient at this place too, Daric."

"Patient?" Daric asked.

"No," I cut him off. "Daric's not a patient, neither am I. I'm actually with my parents now."

"New fosters?"

"No, my real parents. I remembered them and sought them out," the lies kept racking up. "Daric works for them."

"That's wonderful to hear Elle. No wonder you're so bright now. So you have your memories back?"

"Not all of them, not yet. I'm working on it though. Daric's been a good help in that." I leaned over and planted a kiss on his cheek.

"Well that answers what else I have been curious about," Mrs. Queen laughed. "Whether or not I need to set up the other guest room or not. I guess I don't. Unless you two aren't comfortable sharing a room, then I will."

"If you do not think it improper, I would prefer to be with Elle." Daric replied.

"Ma doesn't care."

"As long as you're safe," she pointed at Daric and me with a stern motherly look that made me blush.

"It is my job to keep Elle safe, you can be sure of it."

Q burst out laughing, "Dude, not what Ma means."

"I do not think I follow." Q leaned over, whispering to Daric. His furrowed brow smoothed and his eyes lit as Mrs. Queen's meaning was translated to him. "Oh." He grinned, grabbed another slice, and chomped it; a dollop of pizza sauce stuck to the upturned corner of his mouth. We didn't have to hide our relationship, or be afraid of being caught. My heart fluttered in my chest nervously. I was not sure the implied sex was something I was ready for.

Mrs. Queen jumped right back into more conversation. I was thankful for the detour back to another topic, "So, what are you parents like?"

"They're really nice, good people. My mom, Neala, is wise and strong. Beautiful. I have her hair. My dad, Carradoc, is funny and kind. He's sick though, really sick. No one can figure out why. That's why we're here. Q and I were hoping between your spiritual healing knowledge and Mr. Queen's specialized medical training we can find some answers."

"Dad's on call tonight, but I think we can lend a hand. I'd love to meet them. Are they nearby?"

"No, they live pretty far away and Carradoc is in no condition to travel."

Mrs. Queen stood, tossing her napkin on the table, an uncharacteristic outburst. "Okay, that's enough kids. I'm done being patient, hoping you'll start telling me the whole truth. Not these half-truths you've fed me since you got here. What is really going on?"

We looked back and forth at one another, unsure of what to do or say. "I'm not sure," I started, but Janice interrupted me.

"Don't give me that. You have had murky pink in your aura all afternoon, and it flares when you answer my questions. You too, Quentin. The only one not lying is Daric, but he keeps saying weird things that don't make sense. So, what is going on?"

"Ma, I don't think you will understand this. It's complicated."

"Nope. If you want our help, you will tell me the truth. Even if it's complicated or hard to believe."

I sighed. "Sit down. It might be easier to take if you sit down." I waited for her to settle in her seat, fighting the desire to run away.

When she was ready I began, "Daric and I are from a place called Vale. It's not here."

"You're being vague again, Elle."

"I'm choosing my words carefully," I corrected. "Think of it as a parallel world, except it's not. It's a tiny bubble compared to Earth. There are lots of these parallel worlds, all of them connected with Earth being the largest. Each different parallel world is an alternate of sorts to specific parts of this world.

My parents are the rulers of Vale, the King and Queen. Daric is one of their guards. Years ago, I was kidnapped and when someone helped me escape, the only way to get away was through a portal here. The trauma gave me amnesia. I was too young to portal travel, causing my soul to split, which caused my hallucinations."

Mrs. Queen sat silent for a long time. I worried she thought I lied to her again. Just when I thought she would start fuming, a smile broke her stern expression. "There, that wasn't so hard. What can we do to help your father?"

"Blood tests. Whatever tests they do in Vale aren't good enough. They're missing something, I know it. As much as I love it, magic can only do so much."

"Magic, huh? Well, it's going to be hard to do blood tests without samples. How do you propose we do that?"

"Q?" At my one worded request, he went and retrieved the sample we brought with us.

Q's mom looked at the sample in his hands when he comes back. "I'm sorry, that won't be viable. You know that, Q. Blood needs to be refrigerated if not used in four hours of being drawn. I'm sure it's been more than four hours."

"No, it's cool, Ma. Queen Neala magicked it for us. It's at 4 degrees Celsius until opened."

"Very cool," she reached for the vial with excitement in her eyes. "You guys have no idea how cool. I love mixing my way of healing with what your dad does, Q. Love it. Now I get to see real magic and modern medicine work together. Real magic. It's unheard of. Total medical nerd goals."

"Ma, don't," he shook his head with a hand over his eyes. "Don't try to be cool."

CRICKETS CHIRPED LOUDLY outside the guest bedroom window. It felt like it'd been ages since I'd heard their night song. I realized I miss them too. There was nothing quite like them in Vale. Sure, there were insects that sung at night, sweet and dulcet songs that could have been composed by any of the classical greats. But they held nothing to the simple trilling music of the crickets I remembered.

I wished I could relax. So much weighed on my mind. Right after dinner Janice rushed off to meet with her husband, sample in hand and ready to solve the mystery. Searching for answers to save a man they didn't know. All for me. I doubted I'd sleep with the anticipation prickling at me all night.

Not to mention the other thing weighing on my mind.

I was sharing a room with Daric. For real. Just us, door closed, no guards.

It was scary; exciting. This wasn't me in my room and him right outside the door, keeping me safe. Or him simply coming in to soothe me after a nightmare. This was him and me in the same room. Alone. All night.

I didn't expect anything, or planned on acting on hormonal impulses. Not doing the one thing that Mrs. McIntyre always insinuated would happen if I spent the night at Q's. Thinking of Nikki's fear suddenly made this situation hilarious. An unexpected laugh danced from me.

"What is so humorous?" Daric asked when he came in the room, finding me laughing to myself. He'd been with Q cleaning up after dinner.

"Before. The foster family I was with right before all of this happened. They never let me sleep at Q's, worried that Q and I would be sleeping in the same room."

"Did they not know of his preference?"

"Yes, they did. But still, it wasn't right for a girl to sleep at a boy's. They were certain our hormones would take over and we'd, you know."

"I have a general idea." He chuckled. "Now here you are, sleeping at Q's."

"Only, I'm not sharing a room with him. I'm with you."

"And there is reason for Janice Queen to tell you to be safe?"

I bit my lip, almost afraid of the implication. Almost happy about it. "Yeah, maybe."

He slid onto the bed next to me, wrapping an arm around my shoulders. "Elle, I am not expecting anything of you. We are here to help your father, not trying to sneak around rules of propriety." He rubbed my arm with his free hand, comforting me.

I turned my face up to see his. His eyes sparked and his mouth turned up in a half crooked smile that made him dangerously attractive. "You're awesome, you know."

"I am not all that awesome, as you say."

"Why do you say that?"

"Well, I would be lying if I said it did not cross my mind. Stealing in during my watch and laying with you. Kissing you as much as I want. Holding you against me and tracing every inch of your skin. Entwining my body with yours until the morning breaks Vale's night mists." My skin tingled as I imagined his words coming to life.

"But, there is more to loving you than wanting you. It is more important to keep you safe and happy. That is more meaningful, to me, than a night of secret passion. No matter how tempting. That can wait until you are ready. I do not want to pressure you. There is so much on you already with trying to remember your life before you disappeared, and trying to get your magic back. So, I'll wait, patiently. Until you tell me you are ready."

I stared at him, my jaw hanging. Could he be any more perfect? It almost made me want to hate him. It definitely made me want him. My crazy teenage hormones were activated. Somewhere deep in my mind, Dot's virgin alarm blared.

"What, did I say something wrong?" Daric's genuine look of concern filled his face when I didn't respond.

"You can't say things like that," I exasperated. "You just can't. Real people don't say things that perfect. I just," I paused at a loss for words. "You can't be so perfect. It's a surefire way to seduce a girl."

He reached around my neck, entwining his fingers with my hair, "Well, we certainly do not want that." He flashed a crooked smile and pulled me to him, kissing me. His lips moved hungrily, nipping at my own playfully with light growls. My body shivered against his hands, which gently stroked my cheek, my neck.

I deliquesced in that kiss, slowly becoming a pool of ecstatic light. I burned with aching in my core for more of him. I had a hard time catching my breath when he pulled away, "I thought you said. . ."

"No pressure? I will not pressure you, or take advantage. But, I did not say I would not make the most of the situation."

Warmth spread through me as I smiled back at Daric. "I can live with that," I pressed my lips to his again.

"EVERYBODY BETTER BE DECENT," Q called, entering the guest room after knocking once. He stumbled about, hand over his eyes even though he could clearly see through the gaps in between his fingers, trying to catch a glimpse of whatever he thought happened.

"You missed the show by about a minute." I teased.

"Really?" Q's face lit mischievously as he pulled his hand away. He rocked on his feet at the end of the bed, waiting eagerly for details.

"No, not really." I threw a pillow at him. "I'm not ready for that. Daric's understanding."

His face fell, "Really? I was so looking forward to living vicariously through you. It's not every day a man of that hotness waltzes into my life, even if he's with my bestie." He plopped next to me, "So you're telling me absolutely nothing happened. That Daric proved to be the most perfect and patient gentleman ever made in any realm?"

"I didn't say that." I blushed.

"Dish, please."

I opened my mouth, ready to tell Q about my night but got interrupted. Daric stepped through the guest bathroom door in his dark blue guard uniform pants, towel in hand. Steam from the shower still wisped from his chest. I lost track of what I was saying. I'd gone derpy.

Q's eyes grew to the size of saucers, "Are you sure you're not ready? Because, damn. If that was mine, I'd be ready."

"Shut up," I shoved Q playfully with my shoulder. Of course, Daric seemed oblivious to our conversation, busy drying his sandy hair.

"Anyway," Q yawned, "Ma and Pop are up, and they want to talk to you some more about Carradoc. And there's breakfast," he added as an afterthought. As if I needed more incentive to get ready for the day. Good food and possible answers.

"Already? Your parents are the best." I leaned against Q in gratitude. "Give me a few minutes to shower and dress, I'll be right down."

"Daric, dude," Q turned his attention to the elephant in the room, "you coming or waiting."

Daric pulled his tunic over his head, "Do you want me to wait, Elle?"

"No, no need. Go eat. Trust me, I won't be long. I need food."

Daric planted a quick kiss on my lips and headed out the door with Q. I made a mad dash for the bathroom, eager to get downstairs as quick as possible. Answers and food. What more could a girl ask for?

❄

Q AND DARIC sat behind mountains of pancakes and corned beef hash. Not that canned stuff either. The home-made corned beef hash with real potatoes, onions, and meat. A nearly empty pitcher of orange juice sat front and center. The pair shoveled forkfuls of food into their mouths with gusto. There didn't appear to be much of anything left. Maybe I should have forgone the shower.

I plopped in an empty seat between Q and his dad, watching the boys shove gobs of food dripping with rich, buttery maple syrup with a pout. I felt like Oliver, denied more when I hadn't even had any. In moments, a plate of golden pancakes dripping with syrup and a pile of corned beef hash appeared before me along with a big glass of orange juice. "You didn't think I forgot about you, did you?" Janice winked. "I know your love affair with food runs deep." Happy, I wiggled into my seat and dug in to the fluffy golden cakes.

As I ate, the scene sent aching waves through me. I wanted this all the time. Don't get me wrong, every day with Neala and Carradoc came wrapped in a big bow. I was happier in Vale than anywhere. But, family meals like that couldn't happen as long as Carradoc's health remained fragile.

After breakfast, we all gathered in the sitting room to discuss Carradoc's ailing health. "You were absolutely right about your father, Elle. There is definitely something amiss with his blood. But it doesn't appear viral or infection," Mr. Queen stated.

"No?"

"It's a toxin, something we haven't seen. And we've thrown every-thing we can think of at it already, except a designer antidote. We don't have enough of his blood sample left to make one and test it."

My heart sank. Our last ditch plan fizzled. I didn't think I could get another sample without raising a lot of questions. "Does that mean we're done?"

"Well, there is a way we can continue today. We would like to test your blood to see if it is a match with your father's. If it is we can design an antidote with your blood and try it against the toxin in Carradoc's. With it, and some detox treatments we can possibly start the healing process. But there is one more thing we think you should know."

"What is that?" I leaned across the table, a worrisome rock forming in my throat.

"This is the hard part. This toxin we've found in his blood, like I said, is nothing we have seen. We have reason to suspect it isn't something he came across accidentally. This toxin is so smart, it was very hard to detect it from the blood sample. Like it was made specifically for him. Our professional opinion is that someone is poisoning him."

TWENTY-FIVE

THE BEST OF PLANS FAIL TOO

Owen Queen had a private lab at the hospital. The state-of-the-art equipment made it ideal for the tests we were running. A one stop shop, no need to send anything out to other labs. But, the small space hardly had enough room for two people, Mr. Queen and an assistant. Janice acted as his second, and I had to be there. There was no way we'd get anything done in the time we needed to with Daric and Q hanging around too.

The boys were left to their own devices, with a pocket full of cash, in the hospital. Owen tried offering Q the keys to his hybrid sport utility vehicle. Something I knew Q would usually jump at. He loved his father's car. They were refused though. Both of them wanted to stay close. Everyone felt invested in the outcome of what we were trying to do.

The pocket of cash probably wasn't necessary, there wasn't much to do in the hospital. Although, I imagined they could put quite a dent in the funds in the cafeteria alone.

After my initial blood draw, the Queens' offered to let me loose with my friends. No point in me remaining in the lab while they poured over samples and theories. Knowing myself better, as tempting as hospital food could be, I wanted to stay in the cramped lab until we had what we needed. I'd have been a mess doing anything else worrying about what was happening in the lab. How much progress had been made.

It took nearly all day, hours glued to test tubes, centrifuges, and microscopes before any progress was made. Hours more before Owen declared, "Eureka!". The turnaround time, in the grand scheme of things was impressive. Unbelievably fast. Not because of Owen Queen's medical genius alone. No. We employed Abe's books and powders bequeathed to Q. Magic and medicine, working together just like we planned. Janice was beside herself, a little girl given a pony.

"Elle, I think we got it," Owen clapped a hand on my shoulder, his eyes sparkled with excitement. "Do you want to go get the boys? I'm sure they'll want to be here for the big test."

Wordlessly, I bounded out of the lab. The faster I found Q and Daric, the sooner the test got performed. The sooner we could head home to save my father.

I spied a familiar face sitting at a table with Daric when as I got to the cafeteria. A familiar face, blatantly flirting. Amanda. I backpedaled out into the hallway again and plastered myself against the wall around the corner. She was the last person I needed seeing my face.

"What's with being Secret Squirrel?" Q snuck up on me, making me jump.

"It's Amanda. She's flirting with Daric," I seethed, annoyed by the false laughter coming from her mouth.

"Ew. Leave a guy alone for three minutes and the hoes descend. What is she doing here?"

"I don't know! I haven't exactly been keeping tabs on her, Q."

"Right. Well, go get in there and stop her."

"I can't! If she sees me there will be all kinds of trouble, I'm sure.

For all she knows I'm an escaped mental patient. You get in there, and keep Daric from saying anything about me."

"I need a pretty floral bonnet, I'm about to end this." Q adjusted his imaginary hat and plastered a grin on his face before setting out into the mall. "Daric! There you are," he said a little too loudly, making sure Amanda's attention fell on him. "I swear I can't do anything with you."

"You know this guy, Q?" Amanda accused, matching his voice level. I understood why he practically yelled, he wanted her to match his tone so I could hear too.

"Yeah, we're good pals. What bring you here Amanda?"

"Not that it's any of your business, but physical therapy for my leg. Duh. After that psycho pushed me down the stairs, I'm going to need it for a long time." Their conversation dropped for a few beats. I didn't have to be at the table to sense the awkward tension hanging over it. "Anyway, Q, you didn't answer how you know Daric here." Man she was bossy.

"Elle introduced us," Daric informed her. I slapped myself in the forehead. Shit. Not good.

"Elle?"

"Not that Elle, obviously," Q fumbled. "My cousin, Elenore."

"Oh, well, that's cool then. He was about to lose some serious hot points. Anyone friends with that Elle has got to be seriously messed up."

"Ouch, rude."

"Not sorry. Elle's so deranged."

"God. Don't be such a bitch, Amanda. Elle didn't mean to hurt you. Lighten up."

Amanda scoffs, "That's not what I heard. Winnie Daniels told me that Harper Tafoya told Gerard Nichols that Ann Marie Smith overheard Elle saying how much she wanted something bad to happen to me. Then she 'accidentally' pushed me down the stairs, and now she's on the loose. I can't be too careful. She is a raging psycho."

"A woman who believes hearsay over facts, surely has her own issues," Daric jabbed having caught on to Amanda's true nature.

"Ugh, whatever. You're probably a freak anyways, hanging out with this loser."

The conversation died. I waited a few minutes before peeking around the corner. I barely caught a glimpse of Amanda's golden ponytail going through the exit on the other side of the hospital cafeteria. Coast clear. I wasted no time joining my friends at their table. "I thought she'd never leave."

"Who was that awful girl?" Daric asked.

"My ex-foster sister. The one I accidentally hurt." Amanda's words were hurtful. I knew she didn't like me in the time I'd been in her home, but I can't believe she thought that I'd hurt her, or anyone, on purpose.

"Hey," Q changed the subject, looking at his phone. "let's get out of here and go to the lab. Ma says they're ready to test the antidote and wants us there." In the stress of encountering Amanda, I'd almost forgotten the reason I'd sought out Q and Daric in the first place. The antidote.

We hurried to the lab.

WITH THE ANTIDOTE ALL READY, and working the time for Daric and I to leave had come. The Queen's weren't about to let us take off without a proper goodbye this time. They wanted to send us off with a celebration of our success in the lab. If the results from testing the antidote made with my blood on the small sample of Carradoc's blood were that good in the lab, Carradoc would be on the mend shortly after we returned to Vale.

Janice Queen, ever the doting mom figure, made sure I got all my favorite meals I couldn't get at home. She blew the roof off and went all out, ordering a multi-cultural feast: shrimp in lobster sauce, lumpia, carne asada, ratatouille, and pickled avocado slices. The spread looked like food heaven. The list of things I needed to teach to Veena grew.

"Janice, I was quite impressed with your candor over pizza. You have quite the ability in reading auras. Can you, perchance, tell me if your family has always been in this region of Reta?" Daric asked between samplings of dishes.

"I assume Reta means..."

"Earth," I finished her assumption, to which she nodded.

"Well, Daric, as far as I know, yes. Why?"

"I am simply curious if you could be of Vale descent."

The rest of the table exchanged curious glances at one another. As far as we knew, from what we'd been told, Earth had no innate magic. Anything magical that happened came directly or indirectly from visitors from other realms. "Is that even possible?" I asked.

"Indeed. Just as Abban continued to use his magic when he came here, there have been others who relocated to Reta from other magical realms, for one reason or another. Naturally, they live their lives, have children. Any descendant of theirs would inherit some degree of their ancestors natural abilities."

"So you're saying, Janice's aura reading might be inherited magic from Vale?" Owen questioned Daric's revelation, to which he nodded once in response. "That makes me wonder, was Quentin able to make the potion to go to Vale because of his genetics, or can it be taught to anyone."

That was a good question. I had no idea if I'd have been able to recreate Abe's potions on my own before returning to Vale, and have them work; or if it was a tiny spark of magic left in me that allowed the potion to work. Before I could ask, a knocking at the door interrupted our magical discussion.

Q's dad excused himself to answer it. Moments after he disappeared from the kitchen I heard him greet whoever knocked, " Good evening, Officers. How can I help you?"

My heart pounded in my ears and the world slowed. Why were the police at the Queens' door? Their words floated back to the kitchen all muffled, only bits and pieces were clear enough to hear. Words that in any other home would be seemingly random: evening, complaint, escaped, safety, look, warrant.

I felt sick. Ice ran through my veins and my stomach roiled with nausea. Amanda must've seen me after all, or she read between the lines better than I thought she could. I shoved away from the table, jumping out of my seat and knocking over the pitcher of water. "Shit, shit, shit," the string of expletives flew from me. I paced back and forth, my dinner companions all watching with worry. An overwhelming desire to run gripped every cell in me, "I have to get out of here. I can't go back to The Kendrick Institute. I can't. I'm not dangerous and I'm not sick. I have people now. I can't go back there."

Daric was suddenly at my side, trying to calm me. But he had no idea what to say. Yes, he had become a large part of my life. He knew all about what I went through before returning to Vale. But, he was not part of my life when being sick ruled my life. When my life wasn't my own. When I was the crazy girl. He didn't know that Elle. "I will protect you, as is my duty," his promise fell flat against the panic rising. He couldn't protect me from the laws governing in this world.

The officers appeared at the entrance to the dining room. Their faces said it all. They readied themselves for the violence they were told I had in me. I begged, backed into a corner. "Please, let me be. Don't send me back there. They'll kill me."

"Calm down Miss. No one is going to kill you. We just want to help you," an officer with black hair and a stereotypical mustache inched closer, hands up in a non threatening gesture. He feared me, the twitch in his voice and the tremble in his fingers gave that away. His fear coiled him tight, he'd be quick to respond if I lashed out like he expected me to.

His partner, a gray haired older man, watched and waited. His dark eyes darted between me and Daric, staying on my larger than life partner longer than on me. Daric glared at the approaching officer, muscles tensing and hands clenching. He was ready too.

The older officer sensed, correctly, that Daric posed the bigger threat. He moved his hand to hover over his weapon. The air between the four of us hung thick with fear and fight. Someone was bound to get hurt if anybody made any sort of defensive move. I knew I had to do something to diffuse it before it exploded. I knew what I needed to do.

I stepped out from the corner and in front of Daric, hands up. I trembled so hard I felt I might collapse, tears streamed down my face. "I'll go," my voice came out as a squeak as I took another timid step towards the dark haired officer. He stepped forward, mirroring my movement, while reaching behind his back to bring out his cuffs. Out of the corner of my eye I caught Daric lunging, his arm aimed like a missile at the officer.

"No!," the word flew out of my mouth. I turned and push against Daric's chest in time to stop his attack. It took a moment for me to realize I didn't stop him on my own. Q held him back with me. As always, he and I were on the same page. Daric couldn't be allowed to assault a police officer in my defense. If he were jailed there would be a world of complications that we didn't have the time to deal with. That Carradoc didn't have the time for. Heck, we didn't have time for me to go back to the institute either. But, dealing with one would take up far less time than dealing with both. "You have to let me do this, Daric. Let them take me in. Q and his parents will figure this out too. I know they will." At least I hoped so.

"We got this Elle," Q confirmed with a curt nod, looking Daric in the eye, serious as death, "We got this."

Daric conceded, his body relaxed. His emerald eyes filled with worry and he cupped my face in his large hands. "I will see you soon, I promise." He sealed the promise with a chaste kiss, soft and tender. I nodded, sniffling. His sweet gesture felt uncertain, causing my eyes too well over even more. Deep down, I knew going with the officers was only temporary, but part of me feared an imagined doom that threatened to stifle my heart. A darkness that said something would go wrong and this would be the last I'd see anyone I cared about.

After I surrendered again, the dark haired officer cuffed me, despite the insistence that they weren't necessary. I didn't blame him. He only did what he was trained to do. As he led me out of the Queen household, Q began to bark the order for his parents to get on their phones. They had calls to make. An institution to bring down.

TWENTY-SIX

HELLO PREBLE, MY OLD ENEMY

Back at The Kendrick Institute. A phrase I never hoped to have running through my head. At least this time I had some hope glimmering in the back of my sound mind. On the other hand, this time, I didn't have Abe to keep me occupied. To keep me from spiraling into depression.

That train of thought may have been over dramatic, given that I'd only been back for a few hours, but I already felt the walls closing in. Already I was dreading meeting with Dr. Preble. I already felt his steely desire to cut into my brain to fix me.

The thought festered into something even more horrible since I knew there was nothing wrong with me. He'd be repairing the unbroken. I had to hold onto the fact that Q, his parents, and Daric knew exactly what was going on with me and the institute. Surely they'd ride in to save the day before a scalpel met my brain. Otherwise, it'd be buh-bye gray matter and hello veggie town for me.

That would kill my parents. Probably literally in Carradoc's case.

Dr. Preble had to be the devil, he seemed to appear every time my mind settled on him. I half-expected him to sprout horns and conjure a contract for my soul. Brain, soul, what was the difference?

The air in the room crackled with his arrogant energy when he strode in, his white coat perfectly starched and a smugness set in his eyes. It didn't take a genius to tell how pleased he felt having me back in his clutches.

"Well, look what the piggies dragged in. I must admit you're looking very well considering you've likely been off your meds all this time. Very normal." He brought templed fingers up to his lips, "But, knowing you as I do, looks can be very deceptive. You're an incredible little actress, that can fool almost everyone. Almost." He leaned forward, "So let's get back to where we left off. Help you as quickly as possible."

"No, you won't be. I have people now, real people that have my back. They know all about why I ran away from this place too. They're going to come for me. And you can bet that if you cut into me, they'll expose you. Heck, they're probably alerting the media right now. You're fucked."

A flicker of distress intruded on his creepy calm demeanor, replaced quickly with his usual hubris, "Still clinging to the delusional idea that I'm the bad guy, I see."

My eyes rolled. *That's because you are,* I thought to myself. No point in saying it out loud. He'd never accept it as truth. In his eyes, his actions and thoughts were heroic. His little brain surgery would save me from a lifetime of confusion and pain. Save society from me. There would be no convincing him otherwise. I could almost see his self-image; a superhero in a white cape wielding a magical scalpel. Like most egotistical people who saw themselves heroes, he failed to realize he was the villain in someone else's story.

We sat in silent standoff, eying each other. The only sounds in the room were the drumming of Dr. Preble's fingers on his ultra polished desk, and the ticking of the analog clock nestled between the diplomas displayed above his desk. The ticking clock I could handle. The repeated thrumming of his fingers taunted me. I wanted to slam my hand on his, stopping the noise. But that would be giving him what he wanted, a rise. A reason to drug me into submission. There would be no fight against his illegal plans for me if I gave in to that urge.

A knock on the office door stopped the stalemate of glares and drumming fingers. At first, I hoped relief had come. Janice, Owen, Q, and Daric would burst through the door and set me free, the media behind them flashing their bulbs and asking questions faster than lightning. Then the door opened, revealing my other three nightmares; Thug One, Tung Two, and Carina. Preble called them in for my inevitable, made-up *"code gray"*. My eyes flicked to the small black button labeled so, next to the door frame.

Chills spread through me at the sight of the impish grins the thug orderlies wore. I knew those grins. Those grins were reserved for when they got to have their kind of fun. In other words, when the hands on approach was expected to get rough.

A flash of a syringe being pulled from Carina's pocket turned those chills into tremors. My ass readied to fly out of the seat with nowhere to go. The sadistic trio blocked the door, cornering me. That didn't mean I'd make it easy for them.

At the first flinch of my muscles it began. "Code gray!" Carina lied loudly, flinging her small arm up and hitting the button. The alarm blared and I sprang into survival mode. The Naugahyde chair threatened to hold me down for them with it's evil sticky covering. I was certain I'd left bits of skin when I pried myself out of it. I barely managed to get it between me and Carina, shoving it into her, before she could get to me. She stumbled back, losing her grip on the syringe and it clattered against the floor. But it didn't shatter, stupid plastic thing. Instead, Thug One snatched it up with surprising speed. I had no idea he could move that fast.

I enlisted the matching chair, promoting it to my second ally against Thug One's advance. The move didn't slow him as it did Carina, he shoved it aside like it was made of air and lunged at me. His hand wrapped fast around my wrist, squeezing tight enough to send a shock of electric pain up my arm. Without thought, I swung my head low and bit into his hand, rewarded with freedom from his grip and a satisfying, girly scream from his lips. Who knew he was a soprano?

My eyes shot to Dr. Preble, who still sat behind his desk, unwilling to get his hands dirty. His face, on the other hand, suggested he enjoyed the melee before him. His eyes glazed with childlike delight emphasized by a joker's grin stretching across his face. That chomp on Thug One's hand gave him what he hoped for. Violence. Proof his plan was the right thing to do.

Shit.

The momentary distraction allowed the thugs to recover and reach me with little warning. I twisted and bucked against their sweaty hands. Thug One handed the syringe off to Carina, steadying his grip on me. Thug Two, positioned behind me, snaked his beefy arm across my chest. Despite losing most of my mobility, I continued to fight against them, fruitlessly, as Carina inched the syringe closer and closer to me. Having already blew my chance to do this peacefully, I gnashed and kicked in an attempt to keep her away.

"Restrain her head you idiot," she barked at Thug Two. His arm slid upwards, resting against my throat and he grabbed a fistful of my hair with his free hand. My own guttural scream echoed off the walls from the harsh way he pulled my head into submission. I couldn't bring myself to witness any more of the assault on me. My eyes clamped shut, releasing the welling tears. My body stilled, knowing I could be severely injured when the needle entered my flesh if I continued jerking around. I braced myself.

The needle's pinch felt amplified a million times; its exit from my flesh drawn out. The sedative etched a burning course through my veins, tormenting and slow. An inferno of blood and chemicals threatening to destroy me from the inside. My eyes didn't open until I felt hands and limbs lifting.

Once released, the instinct to flee kicked in. No one tried to stop me as I bolted from Dr. Preble's office. I knew it was no use to run, and they knew they'd have me where they wanted me at any moment. I'd been drugged and would pass out soon enough. Then they'd collect me and lock me away until they're ready to cut into me, keeping me heavily sedated until they did. I didn't care that it was useless. I still ran as fast as I could through the hall of the institute, tears trailing wherever I turned. I needed this farce of an escape to feel in control one last time. It was all I could do, fueled by the hope that the Queens and Daric would free me from this place in time to save me from becoming a drooling mess of a meat popsicle.

It took all of five minutes for the drugs to steal the strength from my limbs. My vision fogged as the floor rose to meet me. Unconsciousness enveloped me.

My dreams were a dark void filled with sounds; commotions, arguments, and the soothing voices of my friends. I cried, desperate to wake and know if I was still whole. But no matter how hard I tried, I couldn't seem to get back to reality. In the darkness of my mind, fear developed. Fear that I was lost forever to the real world. That I'd become stuck in this inky dream world where nothing existed outside of sound. Mostly, I feared Dr. Preble had won.

TWENTY-SEVEN

NOT A MEAT POPSCICLE

I'D BEEN LOST in the desert for ages, I became ancient, dusty, brittle. At least that's what it felt like. Confusion accompanied the too bright light assailing my eyelids. The last thing I remembered clearly was passing out in the halls of The Kendrick Institute. My eyes refused to open, afraid of the nightmare that waited beyond. The only glimmer of hope: I thought clearly, though actual speaking and mobility might have been different. Those would be tested later. In that moment, I silently reveled that the surgery didn't take my mind away from me. That, or that it hadn't happened yet.

I tested my theories, searched for evidence. I felt no pain, or the fogginess of pain killers. One point for no surgery. My hands moved, another point, finding my face and then inching up to the crown of my head. No bandages. Relief eased my nerves and a deep sigh escaped me. I remained whole and myself.

"Hey there Sleeping Beauty," Q's laughter jolted my eyes open. Soft yellow walls illuminated by afternoon sun greeted me. Sheer curtains billowed with a cool breeze coming in through the window. I was back in the guest room at the Queen residence. Q's bright violet hair plastered messily to his head, not his usual perfectly coiffed do.

Worry laced his eyes, though it faded with the smile creeping across his cheeks.

"Q!" my voice came out in a hoarse cheer, the effect of the sedative still lingering there. I'd never been so happy to hear my own voice. My arms flung around my oldest friend, squeezing him tight and not wanting to ever let go. "You saved me."

"Just call me the violet knight!" he laughed, pulling back from the hug. "It wasn't just me, you know." He turned his head, looking down on the floor. "D, man, wake up." A heavy grunt rose from the floor that warmed me to the core. "D, Elle's up. She's okay."

Daric popped into view, at my side in an instant with his hands cupping my face. Green eyes searched mine, relieved and full of love. "Elle," he sighed as his hand stroked my hair. His lips met mine, magnetized with a sweet urgency. Everything melted away when his arms enveloped me, becoming a sanctuary from the storms I'd faced. Warm and secure, the drugged cloud and uncertain lingering effects of my latest brush with Dr. Preble became nothing more than memory.

The kiss deepened, love tipped with promises of protection. Daric slowly made his way further onto the bed with me, his arms drawing me in closer to him. His body pressed against mine, a shield against all the bad I'd just gone through. Every inch of me sang his praises, wanted to reward his bravery. The world just beyond our bodies twinkled away in dancing lights.

I could've stayed in the safety of his arms forever. I wanted to. I wanted him. If Q hadn't subtly reminded us of his presence, I don't think we'd have ever come up for air.

"Sorry, Q," I blushed.

"I guess nearly losing your mind makes a girl needy," he teased back, wiggling his eyebrows.

❄

IF Q WAS to be believed, my rescue from The Kendrick Institute had been an epic adventure, rivaling the best action movies. I wasn't entirely sold it had been that exciting. Daric had, in fact, taken down both Thug One and Thug Two, on top of knocking Dr. Preble into next week. I wished I had seen that part. The rest, I have Mrs. Queen to thank for. Without her, I would probably have been lost in my own brain.

The down side to my narrow rescue: the public attention it garnered.

The Queen house was under constant watch. Buzzards from news agencies across the state camped out on the lawn in hopes of a glimpse of me, dying for an interview. I didn't have time for them, or to wait around for the growing trial against The Kendrick Institute and Dr. Preble. Daric and I had to get home. Every minute wasted counted as another minute that Carradoc's life hung in the balance. These morons made it difficult to get away to an optimal location to open a portal. The ideal location would be where we came in, a clearing in the woods about a mile and a half west of the high school. That location opened directly into the villa. Leaving Q's house meant getting followed and the media seeing us open a portal. I didn't even want to think of the ramifications the Queens would face then. The hysteria the magic would create in wake of our leaving.

This world, for the most part, didn't know they were but one bubble in a network of parallel worlds. Not secret information by any means, but knowledge its inhabitant weren't ready to know about. They barely got along with each other, and most feared those they didn't understand. The hate and fear alone that followed us being exposed could be devastating. When this world was ready, both worlds would benefit greatly from one another.

The days it took for us to catch our break were excruciating. Long hours of doing nothing, with worry about Carradoc growing in my belly. Every time the front door as much as creaked, the media frenzy flared. It affected everyone. Owen braved their rabid infatuation, diplomatically dealing with them when he left for and returned from work. Janice's clients shied away from their spiritual sessions. Not even delivery drivers were immune to the onslaught of questioning. Then, as it always went, they caught wind of something better and placed me and the institute on the back burner. While we were grateful for the breathing space, I wouldn't wish that experience on anyone.

We wasted no time moving into action. We grabbed our waiting bags and the antidote, and squeezed into Janice's small car.

We made the short drive to the drop-off point in complete silence. No one wanted to break it, as if speaking would draw the attention back onto us and delay our trip even longer. Even then, we would have kept going. Too much time had been wasted already.

Janice pulled the car to a stop on the side of a road lined with coniferous trees. The stadium lights from the football field in the distance were the only landmark to be seen. Before I even stepped out of the car, an electric excitement traveled over my skin, creating goosebumps, and a melodic hum called to me. "What's that humming?" my voice called out over the noise.

"What humming?" Q asked, cocking an ear to the sky. "I can't hear anything, except the teacher's whistles over at the school."

"Nor would you, Q," Daric chimed in. "It is the song of Vale, calling travelers home. All from Vale can hear it, feel it, when they near where portals have successfully been opened."

"But I thought portal sensing wasn't a magic everyone had." I remembered Neala mentioning something about Daric's valuable skill sensing portals. If everyone could sense them, that wouldn't make sense.

"What I can do is different. At home it is different. Portals are regulated, as you know. We do not need to be reminded of where the portals are. Beyond our world, everyone needs it rather than a few people, in order to get home."

"But, I couldn't hear it before?"

"Do not quote me on it, but I believe that was because of your torn spirit. Your magic being stripped away after passing through."

I slung my pack over one shoulder, "I guess that's a good sign then. If I can hear it, it must mean I have some magic coming back, ya think?"

"You got a built in homing system now Elle, cool." Q's fascination with the magic of Vale had no end. "Speaking of home," he dug into his ragged messenger bag and pulled out an old slide phone that'd been altered. The standard backing had been replaced with a clear one and filled with a clear pink liquid with silver flecks floating in it. "I call it D.C., dimensional communicator. It's filled with a portal potion mixed with quartz and sterling silver. The silver and quartz changes the way portals work, only allowing vibrational tones through and not actually opening a portal. Abe said it should work."

"Abban? I thought death had taken him."

"Yeah, Abe died," I agreed with Daric while flipping the phone over and over in my hands. It'd a true marvel of technology and magic, if it worked.

"I kind of summoned him with more of the rum he left me."

"What rum?" Janice shot a mom glare at her son. She may have been a free thinker, but she still had rules. Underage drinking definitely fell on her radar as being not something to be done, ever.

Rubbing his neck, and keeping his eyes off of his mother replied, "Not a lot of rum. I needed help. I'm not that big of a genius, yet," he added sheepishly. Somehow it made sense Q turned to the dead for help with something he didn't understand. He never liked asking for help with anything academic. He never needed much help for that matter, being one of the smartest people I knew. Admitting ignorance fell right up there with going to school naked in his book. At least asking for help from a dead guy from another world held the benefit of being really interesting.

"Can I see that," Janice asked, pointing at the phone. Seeing her examine the piece of magic infused technology was like watching a dance. Her slender fingers turned it over, caressing the edges in awe. She was as in love with it as Q. "This is beautiful kid. Absolutely cool." Q finally looked his mother in the eyes again, beaming. "But, we're still having a conversation about this rum when we get home." She handed the phone back to me, and I pocketed it.

The pleasure dropped a few notches from his smile, "Aw, come on Ma." Another stern glare from Janice and he conceded, "Yes, ma'am."

"We will be sure to test it when we arrive in Vale," Daric chuckled at Q being humbled by his mother.

"I'm sure it works," I patted the outside of my pocket. One thing I always counted on was his Q's genius. "We'll know for sure soon." I reached in to the car for the last thing we needed before leaving. The cooler bag holding the antidote. With it securely braced under my arm, the time to part ways had come.

Even though I knew this goodbye had no permanence, my eyes misted over when I turned to face Janice and Q. "I guess this is it."

"Hey now, no crying darlin'," Janice toed up to me with her arms wide, clouds forming in her eyes too. I accepted her embrace and tried to listen to her command. "You start crying and I'm gonna cry too." She backed away, wiping her eyes. "You be sure to let us know how that antidote works."

"We will, Janice," I said patting Q's D.C. again. I turned to Q, "I'm gonna miss you."

"No you won't," he winked, pointing at Daric and my pocket holding his invention. "We'll be talking real soon. D, my man. Take care of her," he ordered while giving Daric a bro-hug.

"Count on it," Daric replied, wrapping me into their hug.

As soon as Daric opened the portal, we stepped through.

TWENTY-EIGHT

A LITTLE TOO LATE

The halls of the villa sat darkened when the portal spat us out. Flickering candles replaced the brilliant magical orbs that usually lit every corner. I didn't like the dreary atmosphere clinging to the usually joyous and love filled dwelling.

"No," Daric whispered, a hint of dismay hanging in his voice.

"What is it?"

"The candles," he took off at a run down the hall. I chased after him, calling out for answers he never gave. He only ran, his sandy tangles flying behind him. He stopped abruptly at Neala and Carradoc's room. In moments his form stilled, his head hung low. Worry slowed my pace. Daric's body language sent icy fingers into my heart. Every step became twenty, or so it seemed. My worry climaxed as I reached him and dreadful knowing seeped in before I looked into the room before him.

Like a withered leaf, my hand landed on Daric's broad, drooping shoulder. Peering around his hunched frame, my stomach dropped at the bad dream that met my eyes. Black, sheer fabric swathed the room, which was lit by the same candles adorning the halls. Handmaids dressed in gray, sprinkled flowers on the floor and fragrant oils on the furniture. Drem stood stoic near the bed, where Carradoc lie motionless, his fingertips gingerly caressing Neala's shoulder, her shuddering body draped over that of her departed husband's. Nothing could be heard except her mournful sobs.

My hand slid off of Daric, falling limp to my side.

No.

No.

We were too late, too slow. Carradoc succumbed to the disease. Not the disease, the poison. The world around me muted. My vision blurred. Every muscle in my body filled with the instinct of flight.

I ran.

My feet carried me fast and far from the horrific scene. It was my turn to ignore the calls dogging me every step of the way. Nothing stopped me. I kept going, out of the living quarters and through the gardens until I reached the stables, locking myself Zenobi's stall and curling up in the pile of hay in the corner. Tears streamed down my face, so much so I thought I might drown in them. I thought that might be okay, seeing how on some level this was my fault.

Zenobi nudged my shoulder, nickering softly. I didn't want her comfort either. I didn't deserve it. I pushed her muzzle away, but she persisted. Stubborn horse. There was no pushing her away. Finally, I turned my face to hers and she leaned her muzzle onto my forehead. I couldn't help but stroke her silky cheeks and allow her to comfort me.

"It was all for nothing, Zenobi. Pointless," I commiserated, mostly with myself. Zenobi couldn't answer or give advice. But she did listen, in her own way. The way she and Daric communicated proved that. I pulled away and swiped my sleeve across my nose. "I'm cursed, cursed to not have a real family. Cursed to be alone."

"There is no curse on you," Daric appeared over the stall gate, grief etching every feature, every word. "All of the misfortune in your life can be traced to one person, and that is not you. You are good and wonderful. It is in no way your fault that a monster lurks in the shadows, causing grief and pain."

I sniffled, "You sound like him, like Carradoc." Fresh tears welled in my eyes and my throat tightened against saying my father's name, like it'd become a sacred word not to be uttered.

"I have spent my whole life in his service. Something had to have worn off." He pulled the gate open and joined me in the hay on the stall floor, his long legs sprawled before him.

"It's not fair," I turned to Daric, burying my face in his chest. My tears marked his shirt, like badges of grief.

"No, it is not. But, I promise you I will help you make this right. We can find whoever did this and they will pay for everything they have done to you. For stealing your life and taking your father from you."

"We were so close, though," I groaned, looking up into Daric's face. "The Queens were so amazing, and worked so hard to find an antidote to the poison they discovered in Carradoc's blood. We could have saved him if we hadn't been delayed. I can't help feel this is my fault."

Daric lifted his hand and brushed the tears from my cheek. "I know how you feel, and it is not the fault of anyone but the person who administered the toxins. But, we have an antidote now and can use it if it is needed. If the scoundrel who created the poison decided to use it on you, or even Neala. Since Janice and Owen crafted it from your blood, it should work for either of you."

"In theory." Daric rolled his eyes at me incredulously, he knew it would work. I knew it would. I saw the antidote's results in a petri dish for myself, killing off the poison in what little of Carradoc's blood we had left. It was the best magic I'd ever seen. "Okay, fine. The Queens are geniuses and we have nothing to worry about there. I just feel so defeated."

He stood and brushed the hay bits from his pants before offering me a hand. "Come on," he coaxed, "it is not time to be alone. You need to be with Neala as much as she needs to be with you. You have each other, and that is everything in times like this."

I nodded, wiped away the tears staining my cheeks, and took his hand. He was right. I shouldn't have run off like I did. Hiding to wallow in grief as I had to before. That was stupid. Unnecessary. I had people now, more than I could ever dream of. My mother needed me. We shouldn't face this alone, and we didn't have to.

We walked side by side, hand in hand back through the garden. Our pace slowed to match our somber moods. I didn't care if anyone saw us. Most would write it off as my guard comforting me, as he would Neala as well. There was no one to see us anyway. The whole villa mourned. The whole of Vale mourned. There wasn't a soul I knew of that didn't adore Carradoc.

A knot, a twisted mess of emotion, lodged into my throat as we approached my parents' door once again. How I wanted to ignore what lay in there. I wanted it to be just another nightmare. To go back in time and come back sooner, avoid being taken by the police and ultimately delayed. I could've saved my father then. All that was impossible. So I swallowed the lump and forced myself to step across the threshold.

The darkness enshrouding the room seeped into my heart as I tiptoed in to be with Neala. My grief deepened in acceptance, became more real. I would not run this time. Facing the harsh reality was the only thing to do. Carradoc died. My father was dead.

My arms wound around Neala's waist the second I reached her side. She responded in kind, her arms wrapped around me as she placed her head against mine. Our sadness and love combined into one. Together we silently mourned the loss of the man we loved; her husband, my father. In that moment, I knew a kind of comfort I never understood before. One of family. It surprised and humbled me. My foolish attempt to run away from my feelings felt all that more ridiculous.

Time ceased to exist. Our daily agendas pushed aside, they no longer mattered. We spent the day sitting vigil over Carradoc, denying ourselves anything more than simple tea and scarce moments outside of the room. That's how death was met in Vale. Vigilance and fasting. Somehow, I didn't need to be told this. It just came to me, without thought. Somewhere deep inside, I knew. Tragedy unlocked the tradition from my missing memories without me realizing it.

TWENTY-NINE

UNDER THE DOME TREE

Carradoc's death still felt like lead in my chest weeks after his internment in the royal mausoleum. Life went on without his sparkling eyes and constant wisdom. While I hadn't let the sadness consume me again, I had little reason to smile since that day. I spent too much time wishing I had more memories of my father, not just the ones recently made. Memories of him being healthy and strong, instead of being sick. I wondered more and more about what kind of dad he had been, what we did together when I was a child. The lack of knowing only made me sadder.

The one thing that brought me even the smallest sliver of happiness was walking through the gardens that he'd loved fiercely. Still under constant guard, these walks were never made on my own. With the revelation that Carradoc's death was not as simple as succumbing to an illness, Neala was doubly worried about my safety. Admittedly, I didn't mind the guards anymore. I didn't want to be alone. Plus, more often than not, Daric was on my guard detail.

"I hate my brain."

Daric chuckled, "There is nothing about you to hate, Love. But, I understand your frustrations."

"No, you don't. You think you do, but you don't. You can't. Your brain has never locked your entire life away from you."

"No, it has not. I know you wish for your memories to return. It cannot be rushed. Drem still insists the best way to help you remember is to not interfere with genuine memory coming to you. Look how naturally our funeral tradition came back to you."

"Ugh, Drem. Why are we listening to him anyway? That has to be the stupidest drivel about memory recovery ever. Those traditions aren't personal, I don't think that counts the same way." Trying to recover my memories on my own exhausted me. I was tired of it. In the months since my return, my memory had barely grown. "Can't we just bend the rules?"

My escort stopped, rubbing his bearded chin in thought. After a minute his eyes lit with an excited gleam, "I thought you'd never ask."

"What?" I asked, hoping he meant it. That he was up for some trouble.

"I think it is about time I show you something," Daric grabbed me by the hand and started to run.

"Where are we going?"

"You will see. I promise you will like it."

He led me outside the fortified walls of the villa, following the outer walls to the back. We veered off, taking a well hidden, thin dirt path hidden behind some towering shrubbery. I never would have known it was there just by looking. We traveled through a dense thicket which gradually thinned out into a wide clearing occupied by thick, lush grass and what appeared to be a dome made entirely of large white blossoms. This was where Daric stopped.

"You brought me to see a giant ball of flowers?"

"Come on," he tugged my hand again, this time walking straight for the dome. With one hand he pushed aside a row of flowers as if they were nothing more than a fragrant curtain. It didn't take much urging from Daric for me to trail into the space behind him. Inside, the little world he introduced me to stunned me. The dome of flowers was actually a fat, stumpy tree with branches that drooped to the ground under the combined weight of the blooms hanging from them and it' natural shape. They formed a natural tent, perfect for hiding away from the world. I wished I'd known about it sooner.

While I marveled at the gorgeous setting, Daric lay down in the plush grass. He beamed up at me, enjoying my reaction.

"This is amazing."

"I knew you would like it. Join me?" he offered a hand up.

I eased down in the grass next to him and stared up at the bits of sky visible through the dense branches. He took my hand, interlocking his fingers with mine and placed our joined hands on his chest. We lay in silence, taking in the beauty of the moment.

After a few minutes, I couldn't shake the feeling that something was off, or missing. The more I thought about it, the more I was sure that the feeling was right. I sat up, looking around.

"What is it?"

"I don't know. I can't place my finger on it. I feel like something is missing." No sooner than I had said the words aloud, my mind flashed with images of low branches weaved together and fashioned into a seat, no a swing. A swing made from vines, branches, and a rectangle of wood. I saw a burrow filled with baby bunnies. Another flash showed me a tea set, with pile of lace cookies. Thousands of twinkling lights, like fireflies. There was a boy with wide green eyes and an explosion of freckles across his nose. An innocent kiss.

A memory. My insides tingled, warm and happy, at the realization. I remembered something.

"I remember this place, sort of. Bits and pieces. There was a, a, um," I looked around and my eyes fell on the base of the tree, "a burrow!" I crawled over and inspected it. Empty. "There used to be bunnies in this burrow. And there was a swing and tea parties, and fireflies that weren't fireflies?" I wondered aloud.

"Yeah, there was."

"Wait. What?" The boy flashed in my mind again, a mischievous half smile on his face as he pulled me into the branches. I knew that smile.

"You. We were friends, before I mean. We played here as kids, a lot. Why didn't you tell me?"

"Trust me, I wanted to. The minute I recognized you on the monument my mind came back here, to long afternoons hiding from your tutors. But, I thought it would be better to see if you remembered first. Not because of Drem, but because I wanted to see your face when you did. I was not disappointed."

"Thank you for the surprise then," I planted a quick kiss on the corner of his lips, loving the feel of the smile beneath mine. "So, I have a couple of questions."

"Fire away."

"What were those firefly things?"

"You made them with magic. You said they completed our secret place."

I lay back down next to Daric and closed my eyes. "I wish I could remember how. I wish I could remember more."

"You will, do not worry. I am certain you will," he took my hand again, this time kissing it before setting our hands on his chest. "You said you had a couple of questions. What else did you want to ask?"

"Well, it's more of an observation. I remembered that you kissed me." I turned my head so I could look him in the eyes.

"I adored you, even then." Something in his response, in his eyes, seemed sad. The kiss held a deeper memory for him.

"What happened?"

"I only kissed you once before today in this place. You disappeared that night. Abban somehow found our hideout, he found us right as I kissed you. It was all innocent, of course. We were kids. I just knew I wanted to kiss you because I loved you, and that is what you did. You kissed the people you loved.

He dragged you out of here so fast, scolding you. Threatening me. I was scared. Being a stable boy I thought I was in for really harsh punishments for kissing the princess. I stayed behind, terrified of what might happen. It took me a few minutes to realize my concern for you was greater than getting in trouble. I mustered up and dashed off to defend you. Only, when I had caught up enough to see you...," Daric paused, putting his face in his hands.

"What?"

"I saw you struggling to break away from Abban. He pulled a tube of something out of his robe and poured some on your face. Immediately, you fell still and silent. He picked you up and took another tube from his robes. This time he waived it over your head and his as well. Just like that, the pair of you vanished. When your body, what we saw as your body, turned up days later, I decided then and there I was going to become a guard someday. I felt your disappearance, your death, was my fault. If I hadn't been so scared, I could have saved you. I felt becoming a guard would make up for that."

"There's no way any of that was your fault. You were a kid, like you said. You couldn't have taken on a grown man on your own. Let alone a grown man capable of the kind of magic he was."

"I know that, now. But as a kid, it did not seem like it."

"I get it now, though, your hesitation about Abe. Why you don't understand why I defend him."

"I saw him take you."

"Yeah, that's why you have such a hard time believing me that he wasn't the bad guy. He abducted me, sure, I'll believe you there. But it couldn't have been his will. Otherwise, who did he save me from by pushing me through that portal? Or, why would he have sent me back instead of letting those doctors drill into my head? It doesn't make sense, unless he wasn't the orchestrator."

He contemplated my theory, sitting up as he did. I could see the struggle in his mind. Challenging what you always knew as true was never easy. For years, he and everyone else thought of Abe as the bad guy. Only with the revelation of Carradoc's poisoning did people begin to question whether or not he worked alone. "Okay," he agreed after a few minutes, "I can believe that. Abban did not work alone, that we know now. With what you so adamantly say about him protecting you, perhaps he was just the pawn."

"Exactly!" finally someone willingly listened. Perhaps, if I could gain more memories back I could get everyone else to listen too. Or even figure out who was behind this whole thing. But, that meant really trying to remember my past. That meant turning to the one person I didn't want to. Drem. My face twisted at the thought.

"What is it?"

"I need my memories back, now. That means working with Drem, doesn't it?"

"I am afraid so, if you want quick results."

"I don't want to." I whined as I pull myself into a sitting position.

"I do not blame you. Drem is, well there is just something about him I do not like. Ever since Carradoc became ill he has become very involved with much more than he used to be. There is nothing that happens that he does not hold back his opinion on. I hate to imagine the liberties he'll take now that Carradoc is gone."

"He just seems so slimy. Can't we just hide here all day, every day?" I leaned onto Daric's shoulder.

Daric stands first and helps me to my feet. "Come on, I will at least walk you to Drem's lair to let him know you are ready to take your memory 'seriously'," he slowed his voice to mimic Drem on the last word. Drem often accused me of not taking my recovery serious enough since I refused what he deemed acceptable help to remember. I didn't know what that was, per se, but it didn't seem pleasant or like it'd be normal.

"Lair? Sounds like Q rubbed off on you a bit," I laughed.

"What? It is fitting of that place he works out of."

"The huge, well lit room with an extensive garden filled with gorgeous flowers and plants is a lair?"

"Yes."

"Well, superheroes beware."

THIRTY

IN THE GARDEN OF EVIL

MY NERVES JANGLED when we got to Drem's lair. I really didn't want to be doing this. He looked all too delighted that I'd finally agreed to his help. Now that the time had actually come to use it, I was seriously thinking of backing out. I didn't know what it was about the man; every time I saw him, I threw up in my mouth a little.

"I change my mind. I can't do this. His ick is gonna infect me and I'll have nightmares."

"His ick?"

"Yeah, his ick. You know that thing that makes his so, I dunno," I wiggled about like I'd seen something disgustingly horrible.

Daric's eyes crinkled with his laughter, "It will be fine, Elle. Ick, as you call it, is not contagious." He looked about, making sure no one would see, and wrapped me in his arms. "If it will make you feel better, I know of a great place to swim I can take you after your lesson."

"Another secret hideout?"

"Yeah."

"Have I been there before?"

"Yeah."

"Cool. I'm looking forward to it." I kissed his cheek in thanks, and as a promise that I'd go. The moment my lips left his face, the door opened and clanged against the wall.

"You are late," Drem drawled in his haughty way.

"Only by a few seconds, sheesh."

"Mind your tone with me, Princess." Drem turned on his heel and stomped further into his lair, his robes flying behind him.

"I wish I didn't have to do this."

"I know. I will be right out here waiting for you."

With a pout, I followed Drem into his lair to be tortured.

Drem waited near a long wooden table covered in potted plants and various jars filled with liquids and powders. A solitary stool sat next to him. It reminded me of a grander version of Abe's secret room back at the institute. "Take a seat, Princess."

I plodded over and slumped onto the stool. "What now?"

"First, I suggest you adjust your attitude and show me some respect. Unless you wish for your mother to learn of your inappropriate relationship with that guard?"

Shit. "I don't think I know what you're referring to, Drem," I tried playing it off.

"You think I did not see that little display of affection at my door?" Drem narrowed his eyes.

I cringed inwardly. I had hoped he hadn't seen that. "Whatever, can we just get this over with? Neither of us really want to be doing this."

"Nonsense, Princess. Your memories are important to me too. They're important to us all." Chills rippled through me at his reply. His worlds felt like snake oil, completely twisted to his own benefit. Then again there was something about him that screamed evil. Granted, that was probably my opinion that made everything he said seem that way. His speech pattern, slow, colder than an iceberg, and haughtily nasal, didn't help. "Now, close your eyes and clear your mind," Drem instructed. "Keep your breathing even and deep."

I rolled my eyes as I closed them. Bottles clinked together and papers rustled as I heard Drem shuffling things around on the table. A sulfur-like smell filled the air, followed by the scent of burning sage. My nose crinkled in offense. "Is this really all necessary? The leaf burning and the deep breathing? Are we going to chant next?"

"No talking. Your mind is not clear if you are talking," he ordered. I released a sigh. This was going to be impossible. I found keeping my mind clear to be harder in silence than when it wasn't quiet. After what seems like forever, Drem finally instructed me to open my eyes. When I did, he shoved a vial of thick yellow liquid into my face. "Drink."

My lip curled in a wonderful Billy Idol impersonation as I took the vial from Drem's knobby hand. I lifted the vial to my nose, its smell assaulted my senses; like a skunk fell into a vat of moldy cheese and tried washing itself in cat pee.it smelled like it would eat away my insides if I drank it. "What is it?" I gagged.

"A potion that will help with the memories."

"It smells."

"So? Do you want to get this over with or not? Stop being such a child."

Pinching my nose, I brought the vial to my lips and said an unanswered prayer. Tasting worse than it smelled, the gooey liquid was like swallowing a slug, it's mucus trail coating my throat as it went. My stomach protested against the foul potion and threatened to send it back where it came from. "You know, if this stuff gives me more memories back, I'll gladly drink it every day," I said between big gulps of air, trying more to convince myself than Drem.

"More memories?" Drem asked, looking a little bothered.

"Yeah, I, uh, remembered something the other day. Daric says it was even from the day I disappeared."

"Daric says," Drem scoffed, mocking me. "You mean Daric told you. Your memories do not mean anything if they are coerced by things told to you." His reasoning, like always, felt off to me. It simply made no sense in my mind. I felt the need to defend myself, and

Daric, constantly in Drem's presence. No matter what, he thought I was out to sabotage my recovery.

"He didn't tell me. I remem..." a sudden, sharp headache stopped my words. My head began to feel fuzzy, weird. I shook it off. "I remembered a, something about a," the memory thinned into vapor. My mind became slush and needles.

"Is there something wrong, Princess?" His molasses voice added an edge of indifference to the question.

"I'm not feeling very well all of the sudden. I think I need to go."

"The drink can have that affect, but you should try to work through it."

"No, I can't. Something feels really wrong." I hopped off of the stool and the room spun. I steadied myself and took a shaky step towards the door. My head pounded harder with each step and the room became a tornado, spinning wildly out of control. I could barely see. There was no way I was making it to the door. No way this was normal. I turned and screamed at Drem, "What the Hell did you give me?" I collapsed to the floor, sobbing. Never in my life had I felt this bad; not even at my lowest at The Kendrick Institute.

"What did you do?" I heard Daric growl as he came up behind me. "She came to you for help, not for this! Queen Neala will be hearing about this." He swept me into his arms, "Come on, Elle, I will get you out of here."

VEENA'S spicy willow and chamomile tea soothed me, easing the massive headache brought on by whatever Drem gave me during our session. After the experience, I knew Drem would not help me recover my memory. It'd been a mistake going to him. I would just keep doing it my way, with Daric's helpful field trips. Screw that old creep.

I sipped the last few drops from the cup and placed it on the tray beside me. My head fell back against the fluffed pillows me and I closed my eyes against the light. I drifted towards sleep, towards relief, when a light knocking on my door pulled me back. Not feeling well enough to get up and answer the knock, I called out instead for my guest to enter.

Neala peeked her silvery head in before entering completely, a sympathetic smile highlighting the concern in her eyes. "Elloe, dear one, I am not disturbing you I hope?"

"No," I pushed myself more upright at her appearance, "I'm just resting."

"Are you feeling any better?" she asked as she settled next to the bed.

Daric went to her immediately after settling me in my bed after the session with Drem. Neala became livid over my falling ill, no doubt becoming filled with worry that my reaction to the medicine would start me down the same path that claimed Carradoc. She vowed to have strict words with Drem. After time passed, she was much calmer, her fears smoothed away, possibly from reassurances her trusted adviser fed her. That didn't sit well with me.

"Some."

My mother smoothed my hair, "Good. I am glad to hear it."

"Did you speak with Drem?"

"I did, a little. He assured me the reaction you had was normal. In time your body will not react so violently."

My insides soured. That hadn't been normal at all. "If it's all the same, I'd rather not. I'd rather keep trying on my own, my own way. I don't think what he gave me would help, even if I get used to it."

"What do you mean?" Neala's head tilted, curious.

"Well, it's still fuzzy, but I know I was about to tell Drem about something I remembered right after he gave me that stuff. In moments I couldn't remember it. I still can't, like it's just out of reach. It's as if his concoction did just the opposite of what he promised, like it made me forget."

Her eyebrows furrowed delicately in thought, "I will speak to Drem again. Perhaps he made an error in crafting the elixir, though it is not like him to do so."

"Do I have to go again?"

"Not if you are uncomfortable doing so, dear one. Maybe in time, if you have not recovered, you can try again."

Maybe when pigs flew. "Sure," I respond off-handed. I wouldn't. She knew that too, deep down.

Her warm hand patted mine, "I will leave you to rest. Come and see me when you are up to it."

I returned her invitation with a smile, "I will, I promise."

After Neala left me, I fell back to my pillows with a sense of uneasy relief. I didn't have to continue with Drem's lessons. But, I couldn't shake the off feelings that he gave me. His carefully chosen words every time he spoke seemed to hide something, unlike the obvious disdain he held for me. It left me unsettled.

The pit in my stomach grew into a gaping black hole inside of me the more I thought about Drem and his unusual behavior. Thoughts of the nasty tonic swirled in my head with every strange interaction I had with him since coming home. These thoughts morphed into grotesque and distorted images as I drifted into an uneasy sleep.

THE NIGHTMARE ROLLED BACKWARDS.

The dark figure moved away, his arms stretching out towards me, his fireball absorbing back into his hands. Trees disappeared into the ground. I ran in reverse with the darkened forest zooming ahead of me. Abe seemed to throw to me the ground as the bad dream continued to move in reverse, instead of pulling me to my feet. I cowered in a ball on the cold, dirty ground. The dark figure loomed before me, back turned.

The dream righted itself, playing as it should.

I heard muffled voices. "You did not say we were going to kill her, only take her."

"You daft fool, I did not think it needed to be said. You honestly do not think merely taking the princess away is going to get me what I need. What I want."

"It could. You never know."

Flesh hitting flesh thudded out and one of the men unleashed a small grunting cry.

"You truly are an idiot, Abban. That girl is the reason Neala and Carradoc are still together. Do you not recall their tumultuous relationship the few years before she was born? They were on the brink of divorce. It was only when Neala found out she was with child that their bond was repaired. Once the brat came in the picture all my work to have Neala for myself shattered."

"I still do not see the need to kill the girl," Abban squeaked.

"Exactly what do you think will happen if we return her once my goal is accomplished? She'll rat us out, and once again my love will not have me. She must be killed, it is the only way."

"You don't have to kill her."

"Oh, poor simple Abban, I am not killing her. You are."

The dream lulled, but minute details in the two men's body movements suggested it started rewind again. My suspicion was confirmed when the dark figure marched backwards and turned on his heel, stooping down into my face. The shadows receded from his hooded face.

He was revealed. The hooded figure that haunted me for years was Drem.

The breath in my lungs froze with fear at the revelation. I sputtered awake, desperate for air; trembling and terrified. With this dream ,all of the pieces fell together. Drem had been the one responsible for my abduction. His plan to kill me failed when Abe defied him and saved me by shoving me through that portal.

It could only mean that it was Drem that poisoned and killed Carradoc. The hateful way he talked about my father proved it.

This enlightening memory jolted me from my bed. Hastily I put on my robe, forgoing the slippers that protected my feet from the cold floor. There was no time to search for them. I didn't want to waste anytime getting to my mother and revealing what I knew.

Drem had to be outed. He had to be punished for his crimes.

THIRTY-ONE

THIS WORLD MUST HATE ME TOO

ROLLAN CAUGHT me as I stumbled again. Another flash of memory stalled my rush to get to my mother and let her know what has happened. Ever since waking from the nightmare, my memories kept flooding in at random, rapid intervals. Each one triggered by little things my eyes swept over as I charged through the moonlit halls; a vase, a painting, the curvature of the hall. Or like this one, the stumble I took.

I ran through the halls screeching in joy. Carradoc roared behind me when his gentle hands caught my wait. He swung me through the air, making my long white hair whip like a flag, and wrapped me in his great arms. When he placed my feet on the floor he tweaked my nose. "My little moon girl," he sighed with a smile, "do you think you can catch me?"

The memory faded. I wriggled my way out of Rollan's hands, found my footing and sprinted off again. I heard the guard sigh behind me, his feet picking up pace to keep up. Rollan had infinite patience with me, not questioning my actions. The moment he saw me in my panicked state he stayed by my side. I knew he sensed that my unsaid mission was important. I often thought his nature was too easy going for the job he held. Daric assured me Rollan's easy demeanor contrasted his fierceness in a fight.

When I reached my mother's room, I flung the door open without knocking. I didn't care about whether it was proper or not. Telling Neala the news held more weight than anything else. I knew deep down she wouldn't mind, once all was said and done.

The room sat dark, darker than the day Carradoc died. The curtains still shut the room away from light. The gauzy black fabric still hung over mirrors. The air smelled faintly of the oils the maids had sprinkled about. It was as if time had frozen there, preserving the sadness in a three dimensional image. Apart from the candles, nothing had changed at all. My insides twisted, the pain of loss renewing itself.

"She's not here," I groaned in defeat, coming to terms with finding the room emptier than it should have been.

"I could have saved you the effort, Princess, if you had let me," I jumped at Rollan's response. I'd forgotten he was steps behind me.

"Do you know where she is?"

"I am sorry, Princess, I do not know where Queen Neala is. But, I will help you find her."

THE GARDENS WERE the next logical place to look. Like me, Neala had spent more and more time in her and Carradoc's garden. His spirit, his energy, felt the strongest there. It was easy to connect with a sense of him while wandering among the flowers and ferns. I flew there as fast as my feet would carry me. The pebbles along the path scattered under my frantic steps, the occasional rock fighting back and gnawing angrily at the soles of my feet. Rollan puffed behind me, determined to keep up. My pace never slowed, only quickened with each passing moment, in my search for Neala. I desperately needed to see her.

When I spied her sitting in the exact spot as when I met her, my chest clenched in contradiction to the relief of finding her. Suddenly,

I was back in that moment. Daric dragging me through the villa with Drem on our heels replayed in my mind. There'd been so much love there. So much. Seeing her alone, her graceful fingers lingering on the cool stone bench and lost in thought, only reminded me of how empty she must've felt inside with her best friend gone.

I thanked Rollan for his escort and dismissed him before approaching her. He left with a promise to let Daric know I had gone to Neala with important information. That he would send him to me as soon as he could.

"I have to talk to you, it's important." I skid to a stop in front of her, finally allowing myself to take a real breath. It was only then I realized she wasn't alone. Drem, the man of the hour himself, stood a few feet away, slightly hidden behind one of the large ferns that flanked the statue behind the bench. I hoped she had been in the middle of setting him straight once more about the results of the failed memory session earlier.

"What is it?" she asked, looking up at me. Her dark eyes were glossed over, like she'd been emotional recently.

"In private," I looked from Neala to Drem and back again, imploring with my eyes. This wouldn't, couldn't, be said with him around.

"Of course, dear." Neala turned to Drem, "Would you give us a minute?"

He dipped into a low bow, keeping his eyes on me. The way he glared unnerved me; like a warning wrapped in a smirk. A message. I wanted to throw up.

Once he was out of sight, my news burst from lips as though if I held it in another moment longer, I'd explode. "It's Drem."

"What about Drem?"

"He's the one that kidnapped me. He killed Carradoc. I know it."

"Now, Elloe, that is a mighty accusation to make against Drem. He has been nothing but supportive to the crown."

"No! He's not. He's a snake, mother. He stole me from you to ruin your marriage and when that didn't work he began to poison Carradoc. You have to believe me!"

"There's no need to raise your voice at me, young lady. And frankly, I am appalled that you would accuse Drem of this. He loved your father as much as I did. After all he has done for this family, for you. He offered his valuable time to help you recover your memories."

"He made me violently ill!"

"A normal side effect from the elixer, he assured me. He thinks that, perhaps, it is your dislike of him that clouds your ability to advance in your healing. That you subconsciously are refusing to be helped by him."

"I don't trust him. Even before I knew the truth about him, my intuition told me not to."

"Like it or not, Elloe, Drem is an important part of Vale, my most trusted counsel. You must learn to accept that and him. He is not going anywhere. I need him now more than ever."

I stared down my mother. Though I hadn't known her long, I knew this was not like her. In the months that I'd been in Vale, she never doubted me. She'd been patient and kind. Never argumentative when I came to her with anything. Everything in me shouted that there was something different, something wrong with her. I couldn't place it and it bothered me.

"I hate to interrupt," Drem's slow drawl cut the silence. My head turned and my body instinctively prepared to defend itself as I watched him pass by. Something cold and knowing glinted in his eyes as he passed me.

My gaze followed him then moved on to Neala's face. She lit warmly in his presence, opening her arms to welcome her to him. They met in an embrace, a kiss planted on Neala's outstretched cheek.

Hell no.

A tunnel formed in my vision, blocking out all other things in the garden. All I saw was them, the stomach churning exchange, my mother wrapped in Drem's arms. They were too close to each other, too intimate for Queen and adviser. It was wrong.

Small details I missed before, jumped out at me. The ever prevalent light in Neala's eyes had gone out. Her eyes had been cold, almost dead, since the beginning of our conversation. The air about her lost its comforting warmth. She felt distant. The pieces added together to one thing; she'd been spelled. Enchanted. Brain washed.

Drem had her right where he wanted her. In his arms. In love with him. It churned my stomach.

My feet stumbled backwards and my head turned fervently back and forth.

No.

All words are lost to the resounding disbelief playing over and over in my head like a skipping record.

No.

"Is there something wrong, Princess?" Drem sneered in victory. He knew I figured it out. He knew I had no way to prove it.

Tears began to spill as I turned to sprint away from the grotesque scene.

I ran to my childhood hideout. More memories swirled in my head with the fresh memory of Neala's forced betrayal. By the time I hid away under the flowered branches, I felt like I might explode from the onslaught of emotions. I wanted to.

I wanted to shatter like my new world had. Fall into a million pieces so jagged and small that they would never be put back together again. That would be better than living in a world where the bad guy, the man who kidnapped me and killed my father, won. It wasn't fair.

Life never was in my experience.

I began to think that I might be cursed to not have a happy home life once more. Every home I had ever known got ripped away from me in some fashion or another. But this had to be the worst. Coming back home and regaining my memories was supposed to be my happily ever after, or at least a turning point in my life. It wasn't supposed to be just more misery and heartbreak.

I'd almost rather be a drooling mess at The Kendrick Institute.

Picking up a rock from near the base of the tree, I screamed into the still air and threw it with all my strength. I picked up another and another, throwing each stone with all of my frustration tied to them. All of my heartache. But my feelings didn't ebb with the release. They only intensified to the point that my tears blurred my vision completely and I crumbled into a heap with an unthrown stone still in my hand.

With one last screech, I tossed the rock feebly through the branches that created the walls of the little grotto. Moments after it left my hand, I heard it hit something, someone, and a grunt of mild pain. I knew it was Daric before he passed through the branches. Only he would look for me there. I hoisted myself up, emotionally spent, and ran to greet him before he entered through the hanging leaves.

His arms wrapped around me the moment I crashed into him. He placed a gentle kiss on the top of my head, leaving his lips there as he soothed me, letting me finish crying before speaking. "Rollan told me about your rush through the villa in search of Queen Neala, and how you left the gardens in utter distress. What happened?"

"I remembered, I am remembering still. I'm seeing flashes of my life before I was taken."

"That is wonderful news, Elle. Does that mean you remember that night?"

The pain of Neala's dismissal grew fresh thinking about it. "Yeah," I managed to sniffle out after a moment of choking on my emotions. I looked up into Daric's rugged face, his eyes full of question and concern. He didn't have to ask, I knew what he wanted to know. "Drem."

A fire storm flared to life behind his eyes. I knew what he was too angry to ask,"Yes, he killed my father too."

A low growl resonated in Daric's chest. "We have to do something. Your mother surely must be doing something as we speak."

"No, she's not. She won't."

"What do you mean, she will not?"

"Drem has taken her from me as well," my tears started up again.

"She's dead?" Daric exhaled, tears mingling into his anger.

"Worse, Drem has made her love him. He's won, he's gotten all he wanted." We settled near the trunk of the tree, leaning against it. I told Daric everything I remembered from that night and regaled him with how Neala had dismissed me not long before. "I don't know what to do, Daric. I feel like I'm lost, like coming home was pointless. What are we going to do now Drem's won?"

Daric's eyes narrowed, his lips turned down in a grim expression. "He has not won, Elle. Not yet. He will not, not as long as we know the truth. I promise you with my life that I will not give up on this. We will find a way to save Queen Neala and we will defeat Drem."

"How? He's so powerful."

"No one is powerful enough to be unbeaten. We will find a way. It may take time, it may seem hopeless, but there is always hope. He will not win."

PART 3

MOONLIGHT

THIRTY-TWO

STUDY UNTIL YOU DROP

My eyes ached. The words in the book before me blurred into a jumbled mess. I couldn't concentrate any more. I shoved the thick book away from me, accidentally causing an avalanche of tomes to tumble off the table.

I'd spent the past week with my nose buried in books in the library, learning all I could about Vale and magic. Trying desperately to trigger memories involving using magic, in hopes it'd jump start mine into returning. Obsessed to the point of exhaustion and unable to control my reeling mind. All I'd succeeding in so far had been triggering memories as I learned about Vale through books. Years of long forgotten moments of time. Sure, part of me rejoiced about it. But mostly, they served as reminders of how shattered my life had become. Kidnapped, memory severed, jostled from home to home, forcibly hospitalized, nearly lobotomized, transported to a world I didn't know, and both of my parents stolen from me just as I regained them. One by death. One by betrayal. Sure, Neala technically was part of my life, but she wasn't the mother I'd grown to know and love.

All of this occupied my mind all of the time. It made the good memories all that more bittersweet. Reminded me I'd lost more than I'd gained.

Some days I struggled seeing the light that flickered weakly at the end of the tunnel. I wanted to throw in the towel and return to Reta; live with Q and his family. It was a real possibility now that the threat of The Kendirck Institute had been eliminated. I wouldn't have to live as a hermit or be on constant lookout. Plus, now that I was legally an adult, I could pick where I wanted to live if I did return to Reta.

The added bonus of me being of age to portal without consequence meant I wouldn't be subject to hallucinations anymore.

Daric would very likely have gone with me, if I asked. There didn't seem to be anything he wasn't willing to do for me. He became and instant and constant rock for me. A bright spot in my graying reality. But, I wouldn't ask that of him unless my fight was lost. I didn't plan on that happening any time soon.

I wasn't just going to roll with the punches anymore. That was the old me.

Fighting for my mother and my new home outweighed any of my desire to give in. Too long I dreamed of having a real home, with a real family. There was no way I'd let slimy old Drem completely take it away from me without a fight. Neala would do the same for me, and I couldn't let Carradoc's death go unpunished. Having failed to save him, I owed him at least that much.

I just needed to figure out how I could go against Drem. As little magic he had naturally, magic not coming from potions and drafts, he still had loads more than I did. There in lay the crux of the depression I fought against daily. I was powerless. I didn't even know what I could do in the long run, other than make "fire flies". Children were limited magically, not having their full abilities until, well, sixteen. Magical maturity seemed closely tied to soul splitting in children using portals. According to Daric, what I could do as a kid was small potatoes compared to where I should have been at my age.

I got up and tidied the mess I'd made, my back creaking from spending hours hunched over books. It was little moments like that where I wished I still had guards babysitting me constantly. Where I once despised being under constant guard, I now loathed even the briefest moments of not being able to keep my surroundings in view. Having guards would ensure my safety when my back was turned. Danger still roamed the halls of the villa. Freely.

Neala pulled the 24/7 guard duty shortly after my "little tantrum" as she called it. With Abe confirmed dead she deemed the service no longer necessary. She even pulled Daric from my service, saying our budding relationship was a distraction from his job. She probably had a good point there. Anytime I was with him, I couldn't help but feel my teenage hormones raging.

"You are lucky your mother does not fire him from the guard," Drem drolled at me when I refuted the order. "But, she is a believer in love after all." He smirked knowingly, reminding me he currently had her enthralled to him with some spell. She'd never have turned her back on me or the memory of her husband so easily. "Besides, with you two being young, it will not last, so there is no real cause for concern. Real love blooms over years."

Years, or brainwashing magic.

I never had a violent nature, but it took all my willpower to not clock the scumbag's smug face then and there. He made me that mad, all the time. Though, I'd probably only manage to bruise my alabaster skin. I had little to no fighting skill.

The door to the library creaked, stiffening the hairs on my neck. Forgoing the mess, I bolted up to survey my surroundings and waited. Soft footsteps drew closer with every moment that passed. My palms slicked and my heart morphed into a million little butterflies flitting erratically against my ribs. Even though I knew the chances of this person being Drem was low, it was all I could imagine, being cornered in my favorite nook in the library by him. The veiled threats he liked to sling at me coming into fruition. His large eyes glistening with gleeful hatred as he overpowered me, forcing some horrible concoction down my throat, and turning me into some mindless follower. Another zombie follower.

"Princess," Rollan's tenor voice broke the nightmare unraveling in my head and made me jump. I'd been so rapt in it I'd partially forgotten someone entered the library.

"Rollan," I stammered as I regained my composure, brushing my hands through my hair, "you need something?"

"Yes, sorry for startling you," he fumbled in the folds of his cloak. His hand came out holding Q's D.C., which buzzed repeatedly in his grasp. "You left this in the garden. I just happened by when it began to go off. Thought I would find you here and return it."

I took the device from him, cupping it between my hands. I hadn't realized I'd left it behind when I took a break in the garden for tea. The ground-breaking device never left my side, usually. It was my life line to Q, to a large chunk of what sanity I had left in my life. Although, I hadn't heard from him since the first time he called me on it.

We were thrilled his idea worked, for the most part. It worked as advertised on his end, he was able to make calls no problem. I tried calling him on it several times the day after Daric and I returned to Vale, to let him know what happened. Every time it failed to connect, assailing my ears with something not unlike an old-fashioned modem dial tone. He finally called late in the night. He'd wanted to give me time to be with Carradoc as the antidote to Drem's poison healed him. I broke down in tears and revealed we'd been too late. I'd been waiting desperately since to hear from him. So much else had happened in that short time; I needed him desperately.

"Thank you, Rollan. I've been dying to hear from Q."

"Tell him hello from me," he winked a smoky blue eye and left me to take the call. If they weren't worlds apart, I would've shipped it. Hell, I shipped it anyway. Q certainly thought the muscular guard was hot. Hot enough to learn his actual name rather than give a silly moniker to, like his name for Daric; Officer Man Candy.

As soon as Rollan was out of earshot I flipped open the device and brought it to my ear. "Q!"

"Hey Dollface. How are things?"

"Where have you been Q? I've needed you."

"Grounded, for drinking that rum from Abe. Again," I could practically hear his eyes rolling. "Sorry. So what's the tea?"

Finally being able to speak to Q unleashed something in me. The keystone holding me up suddenly vanished and my emotions came tumbling out. "Q, it's all falling apart," I wailed.

His naturally flirty tone immediately shifted to concern, "What's wrong, hon?"

I dove into a sob filled re-cap of the night my memories began to flood back. He listened quietly to my story, only interrupting with occasional gasps and one word comments. "So now, I'm doubling my efforts to try to get my magic back. It's the only way I can have a chance at getting my mother back from Drem. I'm buried in a mound of magic and Vale history books as we speak."

"Are you sure that's the best idea?"

"What do you mean? Of course it is," I replied, taken aback by the question. It crushed me, to be honest. Made me feel like I was even more alone in this that I thought. I never would have thought Q wouldn't agree with me. My breath stumbled over a sob that threatened to come out, "Fixing Neala and stopping Drem seems like the right thing to do to me." I snapped through tears.

"Oh, Ells. Chill. I didn't mean it that way. Listen, Dad always says that sometimes the best answer doesn't come from a defense. You need an offense. Learn all about what you're up against before fighting it." I mulled over Mr. Queen's advice in silence, letting it truly sink in.

He was right. I'd poured over every history book and magic book I could lay my hands on with no real solutions, at least not until I got some ability back. All I accomplished so far amounted to torturing myself, driving myself near mad.

True, I learned a ton about the different magic abilities of the people in Vale. There were conjurers, psychics, trackers, alchemists, and dozens of other classifications of magical use. Every one had an important role in the realm. Then there was me, with only the memory of being able to do anything. A kid's trick at that.

"I need to learn all I can about Drem," I answered slowly, as the pieces fell together. That task alone seemed insurmountable. Drem wrapped himself in secrecy. I didn't think anyone knew all that much about him personally, except maybe Neala. My choices were minimal, do some research in records; or swallow my pride and call a truce. Acquiesce to Neala's request, or pretend to, in order to get some answers. "Thanks."

"No problem, love. Glad I could help."

"Don't go so long between calls ever again, okay?" I ordered. Those few minutes on the device with him proved how much I needed his genius. Even if he gave his dad the credit.

"Sure thing, Mom," he teased. "I gotta go, I'm technically still grounded-ish. I'm in the slave labor phase of punishment."

"Ok. Thanks again. Oh, and Q?" I quickly added before he could hang up. "Rollan says hi."

THIRTY-THREE

TEA, LIES, AND OTHER THINGS HARD TO SWALLOW

I HATED LYING to my mother. Even if the reasons were good. One thing for sure, I'd need some good old fashioned comfort food afterward. Something from my other life. Fried, covered in cheese, and dripping with salty brown gravy. The idea of a hot plate of poutine sounded much more appealing than sitting to tea with Neala and plying information out of her with fake compliance. It would've been so easy to turn heel and march my happy ass to the kitchen and eat away my nerves, send some excuse to her. Even more lies. That thought made me feel slimier than Drem. I just couldn't do it.

I paused outside the garden entrance, nausea welling inside me like a pot readying to boil over. Crossing the threshold proved harder than it should have been. After a minute of frozen anxiety, my feet continued reluctantly along the garden path to find Neala. She sat at the wicker tea table just off the path from the bench and statue where I first met her on my return to Vale. Backed by the lush green ferns and drooping purple wisteria like flowers hanging from the towering trees, she looked as beautiful as ever. As if Drem's poisoned words and potions hadn't infected her with an emptiness that stole away her light. Her silvery blonde hair was pulled into a loose braid that began at one side of her head and swirled around to the other, a few errant wisps tickled at her cheek. Her dark eyes drifted lovingly onto the tip of the statue, barely visible over the tops of the thick bushes that encircled it, and a sigh escaped her lips.

In that moment I knew there still lay a spark of herself somewhere deep inside. A spark untarnished by Drem, that still longed for Carradoc's sweetness and believed in her daughter more than false words. It made me hopeful that beating Drem existed in the realm of possibilities.

"Hey," I announced my arrival, breaking her reverie. Her dark eyes turned to me, and my heart leapt at seeing the light in them for the first time in long weeks. That joy quickly fizzled as they morphed back into the dull orbs I'd grown accustomed to seeing lately. I'd hoped it would've lasted for the conversation I needed to have with her. Her answers probably would have been less influenced by her magically induced twitterpation.

"Elloe, dear. It is poor form to be late when it is your request to have tea together." The coldness of her answer stung, as did most of the things she said to me lately. Before, she would have teased me playfully about it. Since I discovered her brainwashing, her tone had become increasingly arctic as more time passed. I barely recognized her and missed the warmth of her true nature. A piece of me died every time she opened her mouth and Drem's words came tumbling forth.

"I'm sorry, Neala. There's not excuse for it, and won't happen again," I eased into the chair across her already plying her with honey. I desperately needed her to be forthcoming. It would be some time before I'd be able to look in records for anything about Drem. Access was by appointment only, and luckily didn't need authorization from anyone other than the keeper. I couldn't get in for another week, hence going to Neala first.

At first, I didn't want to consider asking her; even though I knew she'd be a fountain of information. Information that'd likely be tainted by bias. Daric convinced me otherwise. "It will be fine Elle, I promise. She may not be herself at the moment, but it does not change her factual knowledge. It is her emotional knowledge that appears to be encapsulated in magic. Besides, despite what is going on with her, Neala is still your mother. That relationship still needs fostering, even if it seems one sided at the moment. She is in there, in some form. Maybe she knows it too. We will get her back, and abandoning her might leave scars she does not understand." He'd demonstrated the sage Carradoc had more and more since his demise, filling the need of dealer of wizened advice. He may have only been a handful of years older than me, but at times he seemed much older than that. There weren't many young men I knew of that were as mature as him.

In all the turmoil that surrounded my life in Vale, at least I had Daric to lean on. He'd steadily proved to be the most loyal and understanding boyfriend a girl could ask for. His devastatingly rugged looks were the cherry on top. I had to pinch myself more than once to believe he was real. Before Vale, I was too much of a freak in both looks and oddities that no one even gave me a second glance.

"See it does not," my mother lifted her robin egg blue tea cup to her lips, a smile touching the corner of them. Another thing that hadn't been affected by the brainwashing, her love of tea, or what tea she preferred. Just like me, she loved a spicy ginger turmeric blend with honey, except she preferred a pinch of cinnamon instead of lemon. I liked to think there was some memory tied to it. Lazy afternoons in the garden with my father perhaps. Maybe in those memories she became herself again, even for just that moment when the tea sat on her tongue.

I lifted my own matching cup, pretending, as the steam delivered the aroma to my nose, we shared that moment. Like nothing was wrong. We were just mother and daughter sharing tea, and untroubled by the evil in our lives.

"What did you want to speak to me about?" she asked, her dark eyes settling on my own icy ones.

"Well, I've been thinking that maybe I need to give Drem another chance," I began my lie with a large sigh. It felt wrong, like a pair of shoes two sizes too small. "I was childish, and wanted to blame someone for my grief. I'm sorry."

"I am glad you are coming to your senses. Drem has only the best intentions for Vale," her words sounded robotic, rehearsed. Not her own. I wondered if she sensed it too. The far way look that crossed her eyes seemed to confirm it. Daric may have been right there.

"I thought, maybe if I knew more about him, it would be easier to understand him. Since my relationship with him has been rocky from the start, I didn't think it would be smart to ask him first. So, I come to you, and maybe in time, I'll be able turn to him." Turn him into a toad more like it, or a distant and unpleasant memory.

"That is a wonderful idea," an empty light flickered in her happiness of my surrender, nothing like the real light she used to have. "Now, I cannot tell you as much as he could. I know little of his life before he came to the palace. Only he does, and maybe records might have something on his family." Family? I'd never considered him to have one. He sure didn't act like he did. I assumed he'd sprung from a bog.

"What else?"

"He has been an invaluable asset to Vale, and a loyal friend and confidant." She offered nothing more, merely sipped on her tea and stared blankly at me.

"And?" I prodded after minutes of awkward silence. Surely she had more to say about him personally than that.

"And nothing. That is all you need to know about him. The most important thing. Oh, and he cares deeply for our family. What more could you want to know?" her head cocked sweetly to the side, empty of any real thought about my question.

Chills ran the length of my whole body. Despite the small glimmers of hope I'd seen, she was worse off than I thought. I had to bite my tongue, leash the rampaging concern and anger dying to escape and let Neala know exactly what else I needed to know. What else I already knew. My fingers dug into the arms of the woven chair I sat in. I fought against the tears that wanted to flow. This whole set up had been pointless. I needed to get out of there before I ruined the frail connection we had left.

"Oh, yeah. Nothing really, now that you mention it," I offered a disheartened chuckle. I gulped my tea, slurping the rest down as quickly as possible. My favorite flavor had grown bitter, like my mood because of the fruitless investigation. Awkwardness blanketed the area, and there'd be no recovery from it. "Well, this was nice," I stammered out, "we should do it again."

"That will be lovely, dear. Perhaps next time Drem may join us." I swallowed hard and nodded quickly at her suggestion, instead of unleashing my churning mind on her.

"I'm gonna go, I have more studying to do if I'm ever going to get my magic back." I stood, gave my goodbye, and walked away as calmly as possible. The calm shattered the minute I rounded the bend. Once out of Neala's sight, I broke into a sprint. Pebbles flew from beneath my feet. My eyes pricked with the tears that ran down my cheeks. That tea had been the most painful thing since Carradoc's death. Seeing a ghost of my mother drowning in dark magic, was too much for my cracked heart. Even though I said I'd do it again, I didn't think I actually could.

With every step, my pace increased until my feet were at a full run. In my haste to escape from new wounds I ended up barreling right into Veena, who waited just beyond the end of the garden path. My momentum sent us both stumbling without falling. "I'm sorry, Veena. I didn't see you."

"Is everything all right, Princess?" she asked as she helped steady me.

"Yeah," I sniffled and prepared to lie again. My hate for Drem sprouted deeper roots with every lie I had to tell because of him. I didn't want to lie to my family or friends. I had to. "The garden just makes me miss Carradoc is all."

"Me as well. His departure has left a huge hole in everyone's hearts." *Everyone except Drem,* I scoffed inwardly at her sympathy, even though I knew she meant well. She didn't know everything. She adjusted her dark tresses and wiped her hands over her apron. "I know exactly what will make you feel better. I saw it earlier in your mind. Now, I need to know what it is and how to make it." Her slim fingers wrapped around mine and she pulled me along with her to the kitchen.

THIRTY-FOUR

HE MAKES SENSE

I SPENT the rest of the day in the kitchen with Veena, teaching her many of my favorite foods from my old life. There were, of course some ingredients that she didn't have. We ended up making do with substitutes that were as close as we could get either by me trying them or describing the flavor I wanted. The distraction from everything else gave me much needed rest in my mind. Focusing on one of my favorite things rather than Carradoc, missing magic, and Drem, became the healthy dose of therapy I sorely needed. By the time I left the kitchen, Veena knew how to make pizza, pickled avocado, fries, poutine, and a few other old favorites. I felt like I'd just spent my life savings on therapy, only ten times better.

I was also ravenous. My stomach grumbled in anticipation of the deliciousness I carried with me. The walk back to my room tested my willpower. It took everything in me to not sample the goods we'd made while I walked.

Daric waited outside my room, leaning against the door frame. He'd pulled his coppery brown hair away from his face in a half pony tail. His guard uniform replaced with a pair of dark jeans he'd brought back from Reta and a loose white tunic. It warmed my heart to see the combination, his embracing of my two homes. The moment he saw me approaching, his green eyes lit; though it could've been from the steaming white sauce cheese pizza I'd brought back from the kitchen with me, along with a hot and gooey pile of poutine. He'd been dreaming of pizza since we returned from our antidote making trip. I was surprised he hadn't bugged the kitchen about it already.

"You'll never guess what I've been doing."

"Looks like you were teaching Veena a thing or two," he nodded to the food in my hands. "About time." Again, the clarity of his words came off as ambiguous to me. Did he mean my arrival or the introduction of pizza to Vale? Either way, I was glad to see him. Like always.

"Been waiting long?"

"No, not too long," he swept up next to me, his crooked smile reaching his eyes with slight mischief. He took the over-sized tray from me one handed, leaving a kiss on my cheek in the process. "Come on, tell me of your afternoon with Neala."

Just like that, a gray cloud crept back into my head and heart. The tea had been a disaster, and Daric could see it written all over my face. "It was bad," I said, defeat heavy in my voice as I opened up my door and called for the lights. In moments the room lit in a soft magical glow. I kicked my simple black flats off, sending them flying across the room, one landed under the bed. I wanted to follow it, hide under my bed for eternity. Instead, I flopped onto the mattress.

The mattress on my bed had to be the best in all existence. Three seconds on it and the tension in my body seemed to melt away, the plushness of it hugging onto me. I often wondered if it had been infused with magic, like so many things here had. It wouldn't surprise me if it had.

Daric slid the tray onto the sideboard table, nabbing a slice of the pizza and picking the poutine up with his free hand. He swooped onto the bed next to me presenting the food. He knew me so well, despite all the years we'd been apart. Sometimes I felt guilty about how little I knew about him in comparison. My young childhood memories were still filtering back to me, through a deluge of trauma and time. Something told me that wouldn't make a difference in how well I knew Daric, or anyone for that matter. Time and distance had a way of making loved ones feel like strangers to anyone, not just to amnesia sufferers like me.

My fingers dug right into the gooey mess of cheese and gravy, not caring how messy I got. The flavor exploded across my mouth, resulting in a delicious moan. The poutine was the best I'd ever tasted. Veena had some kind of magic in the kitchen for sure, even though that actually didn't fall in her wheelhouse of magical ability. She was just that good a chef. Daric nodded in the direction of the platter of fries as he claimed the slice of pizza for himself, "What is that anyway. It sounds like it may threaten my status with you."

I choked out a laugh. Poutine definitely ranked high on my list of things I loved, but not quite as high as Daric. "It's poutine, and it's pretty close to it," I teased, lifting another pinch of dripping fries into my mouth with an exaggerated moan and a cheeky grin.

"I see how it is," he teased right back. His emerald eyes glinted with a playful, amorous challenge. "I think I will have to reclaim my place." He snatched the platter from me, holding it high over my head, and leaned to press his lips against mine. One arm snaked around my back, pulling me in closer as his tongue teased at my lower lip. I responded, deepening the kiss, desperate for more of the warmth spreading through me. "How about now?" he asked as he pulled away.

"Still thinking about it," I stuck my tongue out, a little irritated he ended the kiss. Food may be delicious, but not as delicious as his lips.

"So, are you going to tell me about tea with Neala?" he ran his thumb over my lip.

I didn't want to regale him with what happened. I didn't even want to think about it. Instead, I closed the gap between us again, devouring his mouth with mine. I craved the warmth and security of his arms around me, the happiness that invaded the sadness and frustration inside me whenever he touched me. It was like a drug that kept me afloat. I needed it. I wanted more. Forget drowning my sorrows in comfort food. Daric was all I needed; wanted.

The need for anything other than reliving the nightmare of tea time propelled me forward, climbing onto Daric's lap. My hands tangled into his sun-lightened hair then traveled down his neck onto his chest, crumpling his tunic beneath them. Urgency rose in my kisses. They deepened, begged for more.

Daric pulled away, his face something other than delighted by my advance. I tried to move in again, but his hands held me back. "What are you doing, Elle?"

"Don't you want this? Want more?"

"Not like this, sweetheart. I appreciate the enthusiasm. I really, really do," he gently kissed the end of my nose and slid me off his lap. "But, not as a diversion from talking about things you do not want to. I know everything going on hurts, but do not rush into something you are not ready for to numb the pain."

"Who says I'm not ready?"

He looked at me stern and compassionate at the same time, "You do. The place your life is in right now. Me. Take your pick. Trust me, you'll regret it if we do this now, because it will be tainted with that numbness you're looking for with it."

Rejected, and feeling sheepish, all I could do was stare into the empty hands in my lap. Even though he was right, I wanted to be nothing but angry at him. At everything. But, my emotions swirled; anger, sadness, confusion, defeat, and awe. Once again, he proved more than perfect and that he knew me through and through. Better than I thought. Better than I knew myself. I couldn't fight the tears that dripped down into my open hands.

"Hey," he soothed, wiping a tear away from my down-turned cheek before lifting my chin with his fingers. "It is okay. This is not changing, me and you. I am in this with you, here for you. I love you." I had no words, he'd stolen them all with three of his own. They broke me and healed me all the same; became the gold to my broken pottery to turn us into Kintsugi. My arms flung around him in wordless response. He kissed the top of my head and chuckled lightly. "So," he said pulling away and offering the platter of fries to me again, "tell me about your afternoon. Did you learn anything useful?"

He knew the reason I had tea with my mother in the first place, that Q gave me the idea to learn my enemy to know the best attack. He'd been impressed with the strategy, never assuming advice like that would come from Q. Even correcting him, letting him know it was advice Mr. Queen had passed down before, he thought higher of our vibrant friend for it.

"Nothing. You should have seen her, Daric. She looked as empty as her answer."

"Which was?" he prodded with concern.

"That Drem is a good man and loyal and blah blah blah. Nothing useful or truthful." He had no words to respond with, just shaking his head in disbelief. The change in my mother was just as hard on him as it was me. He'd known my parents his whole life, they looked after him after my abduction. They'd taken my best friend under their wing and encouraged his passions. Neala's compassion was a large part in how successful he'd been in his career as a guard. " I really, really hope records pans out with more I can use. Until then, I'm hitting the books again. I have nothing better to do."

"Are you sure you want to do that? It does no good when it only stresses you out."

"What choice do I have? If I sit around here all day, I'll go crazy. My thoughts will eat away at me, and stress me worse than studying does."

My D.C. buzzed then, interrupting my small rant. I groaned. Any other time I'd love to talk to Q, but I had nothing good to tell him. That wasn't a good enough reason to ignore the call, though. I dug it out of my top, earning a strange glance from Daric, "What, I don't have pockets in this outfit."

"You mind if I talk to him? You do not seem to want to." Shrugging, I tossed him the device. He could tell Q the news and save me from having to rehash it yet again.

Daric flipped open the device and held it to his ear as he stood, "Q?" He walked to the door, opening it and propping it with his foot, "Sure, sure. Hang on."

"Where are you going?" I followed Daric to the door. I may not have been in the mood to talk to Q, but that didn't mean I didn't want to try to hear what was said between my two favorite guys.

"I am going to talk to Q, get his insight for myself. I will bring this back in the morning," he wiggled the device in his hand. I opened my mouth to protest, but he silenced it with a kiss before nabbing a few more slices of pizza with his free hand and making a hasty exit.

I didn't like it. Something about Daric insisting he spoke with Q alone made me feel like he was plotting against me.

THIRTY-FIVE

BANNED FROM THE LIBRARY

Daric banned me from the library. Not that he had the power to do that. He went to Neala, telling her I overworked myself trying to regain some semblance of my magic and needed a break. A break I wouldn't take. I wasn't happy about it either. The library had become a refuge, and I had planned on using it to help the week pass by quickly. Apparently, Q had helped him come up with the idea too. My boys betrayed me.

"What am I supposed to do now, Daric? Studying was the only thing that was going to get me through this week," I fumed at my boyfriend. I wished I could rail at Q too.

"The only thing? Really?" he stood defiantly in the library door, arms crossed over his chest and eyebrow arched. "As I see it, this incessant studying only contributes to your stress right now. It's tied to fixing Neala and defeating Drem, and you know it. You need a break."

"I need my mother," I seethed back. Anger clouded my mind, all I could see was red. Instead of waiting for his, likely logical, response I stormed away. What he did felt like a betrayal, and I didn't want stick around just to continue to feel bad.

Daric's footsteps echoed behind my own. Yet, his footsteps remained as steady and patient. Even when I quickened my pace, his did not change. There wasn't anywhere I could go that he wouldn't figure I'd seek solitude in. He knew all of my refuges, all of my happy places. There was no hiding from him. Not to mention, he could out pace me easily just walking. He gave me the space I thought I needed, for the time being.

I wandered the villa in my tantrum, no real destination in mind. The goal was to tire Daric of his pursuit. When I paused at the bridged pond in the courtyard, and at the training field, he paused too. Several times, I thought of turning on my heel and giving him another piece of my mind, but I never did. Mostly because I didn't want to talk to him, or look at his face. Both of those actions would crumble the resolve I had to be angry with him. He had that affect of me.

An hour in, I tired of the chase before he did. The flame burned out of my ire, and somehow we'd ended up right where we started. I was still angry, just less so. Leaning up against the wall, I slid down to a sitting position and hugged my knees. Minutes later, Daric's shadow loomed over me. I could feel his easy, amused smirk without even looking. I wasn't going to either.

"Still being stubborn."

"No."

"I was making an observation, not asking, Elle." Daric mused. "This exemplifies how badly you need to have a break. You are fraying, overwhelmed."

"I'm not overwhelmed. Don't you want Neala back and Drem gone? I need my magic to do it."

"Yes, and yes. If you keep going like you are, it will not be pretty. You need a break, before you do," he nudged my toes with his. When I didn't respond immediately he offered more, "I promise, to keep you so busy that the week will be up before you know it."

"What about guard duty?"

"I have leave for the week. Captain Seylah approved it yesterday."

A whole week with Daric sounded a million times better than spending it with my nose buried in books. Just me and him spending real time together, like before Drem poisoned Neala's mind. Still, I couldn't shake the feeling that it would be like giving up on her. Like giving up on trying to become whole again.

I had no choice but to give in though. I'd already been banned from the library. "Okay. I give. Only," I added to ease the self imposed guilt I felt over it, "if we can still spend a little time working on magic." I looked up at him, eyes set in the ultimatum I gave. If he wouldn't give me that one thing, I wouldn't agree to it. I'd be stubborn, as he said, and spend every day doing exactly what I already was.

"As you command, Princess," he winked as he bowed playfully.

AS PROMISED, Daric kept me busy the week leading up to my appointment in records.

We had long, lazy picnics under our inflorescenced dome tree. The whole day spent under the heavy eaves with a basket laden with treats from Veena's kitchen; both from Vale and Reta recipes I'd taught her. Jars of pickled delights that she taken to experimenting with after our lessons, bottles magicked to keep warm teas warm and cool, fruity water cold, loaves of savory and sweet bread, and the makings of a decadent charcuterie board; grapes, cheeses, spreads, and meats in several varieties.

Daric also brought along a book of Vale fairy tales that he read aloud as we feasted. The tales were beautiful renditions of familiar stories told across the dimensions. Tales of fair maidens, heroes, and love triumphant over evil. He read until our eyes grew heavy. We napped safely under the dappling light and fragrant air in our hideaway.

Another day he took me riding through the forest, past the monument where this life began. Both of us on Zenobi's graceful back as she galloped along the path through the trees. It felt like flying.

The ride ended in another secret place Daric promised to take me to before everything fell apart. A stream that bubbled with the clearest water, the bed it ran over paved with a rainbow of stones that glittered in the light streaming through the trees. Along the bed, a flurry of tiny, purple and pink shrimp-like creatures crawled in groups looking for bits of food.

We followed the stream into the mouth of a cave and to a cavern that echoed the sound of the water. Daric called for lights, as we did in the villa. As the light grew brighter they reflected off a large pond, sending dancing beams of light around the whole cavern. The white stone walls and floor sparkled like precious gems. Our swimming hideout. We splashed the day away, arriving home well after nightfall.

Every day was filled with adventures like those, and between adventures he did his best to teach me some symbol magic since it could be used by anyone. Before I knew it, it was the evening before my appointment. Neala had sent an invitation for me to join her for some dessert and tea in her garden. Because I intended to keep up the charade of trying to accept Drem, I decided to ply her further by dressing in a long, blush colored day dress. The look only added to my ghostly appearance, but at the time it pleased Neala to see me be more lady-like. Though, I knew her new insistence on my feminine attire came from Drem's influence. He never approved of my wearing trousers.

"Are you sure you do not want me to come with you, Elle?"

"Of course I want you to come with me, Daric. But, I think it's best I do this alone again." I didn't really need to see Neala alone. She'd invited Daric too, but I didn't want to share yet, despite how painful seeing her slip further and further away from reality. But those moments when she went quiet, I saw her. Those moments were what I wanted all for myself. I was being selfish, and I didn't care.

I stepped out from behind the dressing screen next to my wardrobe, turning my back to Daric. "Help with the buttons?" I asked, brushing my pale hair over my shoulder so he could access the tiny pearled closures that ran up the back of the dress. Wordless, he stepped up behind me and began fastening them. His fingers brushing against my bare back with every movement, sending heated shivers through every centimeter of my body. It felt like sweet torture. When he finished the last button, his lips brushed against the nape of my neck before his arms spun and encircled me in one smooth motion. "Are you trying to keep me from going? Because that is how you do it."

"Just attempting to send you off with a smile on your face. Make tea more bearable, and perhaps entice you to hasten back," he punctuated his words with a deep kiss that left me breathless. I nodded dizzily when he broke the kiss. "Meet me in our place."

"You got it," I slipped from his arms and headed out to meet Neala.

The weather had turned by the time I reached the entrance to Neala's garden. A downpour of rain threatened to drown out my evening with my mother. One of her maids waited at the garden entrance for me, a young, plump girl with blazing red hair and sprite-like blue eyes that turned green toward the centers. "Good evening, Princess," she chirped. "Her Majesty is waiting for you in her rooms instead, with the weather and all. Would you like me to walk with you?" her eyes sparkled with hope. Even though I didn't particularly want company, I didn't want disappoint her. Her pure vibe was hard to resist.

"That would be cool."

"Cool," she tested the word like a child learning something new and exciting. A pleased smile crept across her face. She repeated, "Cool. Come with me." Her skirts flounced as she turned and walked with me; there was a clear thrilled bounce in her step.

"Are you new here?" I attempted small talk. Her face wasn't familiar to me, and her enthusiasm meeting me suggested she'd been waiting to do so. I'd met pretty much everyone working as the villa since arriving home.

"This is my first week. My name is Genasia. It is a pleasure to meet you, Princess."

"Elle, please."

She giggled, like a child caught breaking a rule, "Can I ask you a question, Elle?" she giggled again.

"Um, sure."

"What is it like on Reta?" From her question, I suddenly understood what she wanted. I'd heard reports from the village of an uptick in interest in all things Reta in young adults, especially those too young to portal still. No question the popularity came from having a princess that lived there for nearly a decade. Surely, Genaisa's popularity among her friends would rocket skyward once they found out she met me.

"It's different, for sure," I smiled at her endearing eagerness. My experience on the other side in no way resembled normal. People treated me differently, often horribly. How could I dash her dreams with the truth of how awful it was, when it wasn't like that for everyone. "Bigger, more people, and no magic. Most of them would give their left arm to experience the magic we have here."

"Oh," her statement more of a let down than anything.

"Sorry, I can't tell you more. Truth is it sucked for me there. I'd take being here over being there in a fat minute."

"No, it is my mistake, Prin.. Elle. I did not realize your life was not good there. I should not have pried." Her gaze went to the floor. We'd reached Neala's door by then. I didn't want to leave the sweet maid with her feeling guilty for being curious about my world.

"Totally cool, Genasia. Don't even worry about it. But if you want I can teach you some of the fun things another time."

"Perhaps some of the colloquialisms?" her blue-green eyes lit as she suggested it.

"Sure," I laughed, "I can do that." I began opening the door to my mother's room as Genasia excused herself. A sudden brilliant idea struck me, one that would make the girl's day. I turned and called out to her, "Oh, hey, Gen. Catch ya later."

"Gen," she murmured to herself. "I like it. Yeah, catch ya later," she mimicked me and turned to head away. I heard her practicing the phrase to herself as she disappeared around a corner. My head still shook in amusement as I entered the room.

THIRTY-SIX

BLINDED BY THE DARKSIDE

It was the first time I'd entered Neala's room in weeks, and like before seemed an extension of my mother. It too had become a shadow of the warm and inviting place it once was, despite the fact it hadn't physically changed much. The only notable change; nothing of Carradoc remained. My father had been erased. With him, all the joy and love vanished from the room. Drem had seen to that, as if he feared anything that reminded my mother of my father.

I noted to myself to bring something to Neala to fix the absence of Carradoc, and to test if small things that linked to memories of her husband would break through the brainwashed fog she lived in. As I planned what to bring a thought occurred to me. I wondered if words would do the same. I decided to test that immediately.

Switching gears, my mind stumbled through possible ways I could casually bring up Carradoc during tea. The last thing I wanted to do was upset her. There had to be some roundabout way to do it, something indirect. I passed a sideboard sitting under a large gilded mirror with a trio of polished stones set in the top panel that matched the stone in my favorite necklace. I was surprised it hadn't been taken away yet, since the stones were symbols of my family. My hand fluttered to my chest, touching the stone that hung there, as a cloudy memory rolled into my head.

I squirmed around Carradoc, trying to climb him in an attempt to get a better look at the mirror. He lifted me into his arms and touched the tip of my nose with his. My cloud colored hair engulfed us, a mess from a day of playing. After getting my hair under control and out of our faces, he held me close. Together, we challenged our reflections with silly faces until we rolled with laughter. I watched, eyes dancing with love and happiness, as Neala approached over Carradoc's shoulder and joined in.

"Mama, Mama!" I said, spying the pretty stone that hung around her neck on a delicate silver chain. "Can I wear your pretty necklace?"

"Of course, baby girl. It is yours, after all." She took the necklace from her neck, placing it around mine instead.

"Really, Mama? I love it. It is just like the ones in your mirror."

"It is. They are special moonstones for our family, a reminder of our love. As long as we have them, we have each other."

The memory faded into reality. I had my answer, and suddenly I didn't dread this evening so much. I'd bring up the mirror, and I wore the necklace. Two birds with one stone, or four. Literally. I couldn't believe my luck in finding a way to fight against Drem's hold on her without magic. That sliver of hope energized my steps as I ventured further into Neala's room to find her.

The plan fizzled, like a sparkler reaching the end of its life, the moment I rounded the entrance room corner into the sitting area. Neala wasn't alone. Drem sat next to her at the little dinette table, he'd doffed his usual dark robes in favor of trousers and a fitted tunic under a buttoned gray vest. While the uninformed passer-by might see a dapper looking man, his new look couldn't hide his true nature from me. He still looked ugly and vile to me. My spirit groaned. I didn't know if I'd be able to bring up my father with him in the room.

His large, sleepy, eyes met mine and his lip curled into a satisfied sneering smile. "Princess," his molasses like voice slithered from him, "so glad you could join us."

"Drem. I didn't know you'd be joining us." I turned my attention to Neala, "I'm sorry if I'm a little late, I didn't know the weather changed and went to the garden as planned. Genasia was kind enough to escort me after delivering your message."

"Not at all, dear. I'm surprised Daric is not with you. We did invite him, after all." She swept her hand over the side of her head, brushing back an errant silvery lock. "I understand he took some leave. I hope he is not unwell." A shadow of fear fleeted across her face, as if remembering the tragic illness that took Carradoc, and was gone as quick as it came.

"He's fine. He took the time to make sure I took time away from my studies; like he discussed with you." I took the chair across from the pair, keeping it a little further away from the table. I wanted distance between Drem and myself. "I wanted to come alone."

"Trouble in paradise already?" Drem hummed, a hint of satisfaction in his tone. He wished.

"No, we're happy, good. More than good." I defended, "I'm just selfish about spending time with my mother. I've got a lot of lost time to make up for." Neala liked that answer, her dark eyes sparkled with motherly adoration.

I scanned the offerings on the table. A tower of decadent tea cakes with clotted cream and sweet glazed fruit tarts took center stage, next to a bowl spilling over with golden and red raspberries, blackberries, and some tiny pink plum-like berries native only to Vale called dewberries. I plucked one and popped it in my mouth, delighted in the sweet and tart, pineapple-like flavor.

Along with the sweets and fruits, a steaming china pot painted with bright blue flowers sat on the dinette. The steam rising had the distinct strange scent of dark flower brew. I knew the chocolate-like flavor of the drink sharply contrasted the smell, except when it got cold. Then it tasted like it smelled. Still, the brew didn't appeal to me when hot. Not wanting to cause any issue, though, I poured myself a cup anyway; but I didn't drink.

Drem lifted his cup to his lips and too a long sip. "Your mother tells me you are ready to stop with your misguided protests against me." In his eyes I saw a glimmer of triumph. I wanted to smash his face with the teapot. He made me have violent thoughts more than I'd like. Another thing that made me despise him even more. I abhorred violence, especially the idea of it coming from me. All it did was bring back the feelings of guilt from Amanda's accident.

I narrowed my eyes briefly. The way he worded the jab felt like an attack, which it definitely had been. "Yes, well, you know how over-dramatic teens can be. I had a lot going on, and in the crazy turn my life took I lashed out in the wrong direction. Sorry," I ended the fake excuse with a half-hearted apology, hoping it played of as typical teenage behavior here.

Neala seemed to buy it. The jury was out on Drem's opinion on my new attitude.

We nibbled on treats and sipped our drinks in silence, my consternation keeping me from speaking up too much. I still wanted to test my theory on Neala. Drem's presence made that harder to do. Fortunately, I didn't have to wait long for an opening to present itself.

"Oh, Elloe!" she exclaimed. "You still wear your necklace." Neala got up and came around the table, lifting the stone in her fingers delicately. Her eyes sparkled with elation, adoration.

The smile spreading across my face couldn't be stopped by anything. Thank you, Mom. "I hardly take it off. It was my comfort in Reta, and now that I'm home it's all that more special. Do you remember the day you gave it to me, at the mirror?" I motioned back towards where the mirror lay out of sight.

"You remember that?" she asked, tearing a little. She seemed touched that my memories still grew. At least Drem hadn't taken her compassion for my recovery from her.

"I just did, as I passed the mirror coming in. Remember all those silly faces we all used to pull in it?"

"Yes, I do," she said wistfully, going somewhere, sometime long gone. Her dark eyes misted over more, "Carradoc was such a light," she sniffled.

"I miss him too." I wrapped my arms around her tight, comforting her. Inside I celebrated that I'd gotten through. It was the first time in a long time she'd said his name.

"Neala, dear," Drem called. His two, simple, drawn out words acted as a trigger for his brainwashing. She pulled from my arms instantly, her face once again robotic and dull.

"I must apologize," she said passively, "I need to excuse myself. I have a sudden headache, and must lie down." Without another word, Neala disappeared deeper into her room. I was crestfallen. Two words. It only took two words for Drem to ruin the evening. To ruin my hope. The seething anger inside me bubbled to the surface. My eyes shot hotly at him.

"Ah, yes. There you are," he drawled haughtily.

"Excuse me?"

"No need to continue this farce, Princess. You may have your mother fooled, she is so susceptible to suggestion, but I am not so easily thrown off." Drem left his chair and coolly strode up to me, "do not mess with me. I will win, every time."

I stood, meeting his gaze. "I will get my mother back."

"I would love to see you try, little girl. Now, if you will excuse me, I need to go check on my love," he emphasized "*my*" to drive home his perceived possession of her.

Like I said, I abhorred violence, and didn't have an inherently violent bone in my body. That being said, it took everything in my power not to leap onto his back as he walked away. I could see myself doing it, taking him down and strangling the life out of him. It nauseated me.

I watched, embers igniting in my heart, as he slowly sauntered after Neala. The moment he was out of sight, I bolted up from the chair I sat in, nearly knocking the table over in my haste. I dashed from Neala's room, vowing I'd never return as long as Drem was at her side.

As I passed the stone crested mirror once more, I held onto the pinprick of light it had offered me. Neala was in there, buried deep in layers of hostage making magic masking itself as Drem's love. I'd hold onto that as long as I could.

THIRTY-SEVEN

RECORDS SAY WHAT?

DREM upset me deeper than ever. Every ounce of me screamed silently for the kind of solitude I had forced on myself for years. I didn't want to see anyone. Instead of keeping my promise to meet Daric in our place, I ran straight to my room and threw myself onto my bed. I wished I could have slammed the door, but the sturdy doors in the villa proved too heavy to be dramatic.

Daric came to my door some time later. I turned him away. I wanted to be alone, even though I knew refusing company, an ally, was incredibly stupid. Being alone meant wallowing; allowing Drem a minor win. Still, I spent the night in darkness. Seething in anger, and crying. Sleep became a hesitant friend.

The next morning, my vision was still rimmed crimson. My fitful night left me exhausted and my mood became worse for it. If it hadn't been for my appointment in records, I would've hidden away in my room for the rest of the day; tucked away under my downy blanket, only emerging to let Veena or another kitchen maid deliver food and drink. I longed to pretend, for even just a fraction of a moment, that the world still spun as it should.

But it wasn't in me to give up anymore. I'd had my moment to wallow. What I needed was to stoke the fires in me again. Most of my life I'd been bullied and pushed out. I was tired of it. Now that I had a real home, a real family, I wouldn't let Drem tear it away from me.

I forced myself from bed. Frustration and ire fueling my movements I stormed around my room, getting ready for a long day surrounded by Vale's archives. Comfort would be key today, comfort and an endless supply of tea. I picked out a pair of loose leg pants and a black t-shirt I'd brought back with me. Not bothering to brush my hair, I threw it up in a messy bun, I didn't care it looked like cloud landed on my head, or that my rough night was evident on my face.

After throwing on a pair of flats, I dashed out the door and headed off to records; making sure to send a mental note to Veena to meet me there with my breakfast. I intended to make the most of my appointment and spend all day there if necessary. I didn't want to waste anytime and possibly have to schedule a second appointment for records.

The records office was located on the top floor of the library, under a dazzling, domed, frosted glass roof supported by iron framework. Lin, the records keeper also ran both libraries in Vale; the one in the village and the one in the villa. Since many of the records were old, and delicate, he had to divvy out time for appointments to make sure every visitor knew proper handling techniques, and was properly sanitized before entering. So he could keep a close eye on the precious information he protected. His rules were strict, if you so much as had the sniffles, you were denied entry. He only allowed specific foods and drinks inside. Nothing that could damage the precious papers filed away there.

When I reached the top of the stairs leading to the records office, the records keeper stood waiting. Lin embodied the look of an elven mage with his short cropped, ink black hair and almond shaped, mist colored eyes. He was tall, lean, and clean-cut; and wore the color of storm clouds which made his bronzed skin look even warmer. He laughed with Veena, who held a tray laden with fruits, scones, hard cheeses, and two tall, sealed cylinders that held drinks. They noticed me at the same time.

"Good afternoon, Princess," Lin greeted with a slight bow, his voice melodious and even. "From the looks of the tray Veena has brought for you, you plan on quite the day here."

"That sounds like the Elle I know, Lin. Insatiable." Lin gave her a shocked look at her informal referral. "Oh, do not be so alarmed Lin. The Princess prefers it, I only saved you her usual speech. Trust me, old friend, Neala has approved our addressing Elle as she wishes."

"What she said."

"In that case, Elle, Veena, follow me." Lin led us to the large, intricately carved, wooden door to the records office. He placed his left hand on a carving of the large beta-like fish that lived in the courtyard pond, swirling around a lotus blossom. The door unlocked under his touch, and his touch alone.

The scent of paper, binding glue, and aged ink drafted through the door as it opened. The welcoming smell lifted my lips in a soft smile. It was the smell of hope. Somewhere in there were the answers I sought.

Lin stopped me just as I passed the threshold. Off to the side of the doorway sat shell shaped sink set in a counter. Veena continued past me, I watched her slight figure go around a corner. After moments, she reappeared empty handed. "Good luck today," she smiled at me before leaving.

Lin wasted no time getting to business once she left. "First off, before we start you need to scrub your hands and up two inches on your wrists. Scrub for at least two minutes. Dry them thoroughly. We do not want the oils from your skin transferring to any of the documents you read today. Once you have done that, I will apply a coating of protection." He pulled a vial of purple liquid from his vest pocket. "This potion serves two purposes. It makes an invisible barrier, like gloves, to keep new oils you may produce from getting on my documents. It also will prevent your hands from drying out."

While I washed up, he continued on with his list of handling rules. Most were handling instructions, such as keep documents flat, don't let them hang off the edge of the table, no licking fingers, lay books in a book rest, and turn pages carefully. He also instructed me to cover my sneezes if need be, don't spill, keep foods and drinks at a separate table from the one I worked at, and use a fork to eat when need I needed to. The most important rule, or so it seemed, Lin was the only one allowed to search within the records. I had to let him know what I needed, and he would retrieve it.

When he applied the protection potion, he told me to rub it into my hands like I would lotion. The liquid was cool and smelled like antiseptic. As I rubbed it over my hands and wrists, I sensed a fine layer forming over my skin. It truly felt like I wore latex gloves. I couldn't help but think of Mrs. Queen and how she'd marvel at the magic. All the uses she'd think for it, medical grade protection with none of the waste. She'd insist on Q learning this potion for Owen to use at work.

We walked around the corner. The nook was cozy, warmly lit by the sun filtering in through the high glass ceiling. Two tables were situated on either side of the nook. One was larger and wooden with a book rest built in to one end. The other one was a smaller circular table with a tiled top, the tiles depicted a lotus blossom like the ones on the door. The smaller table held the tray Veena left behind. A chair sat between the two tables so it could be used for either.

Lin motioned for me to sit, "What is it you are looking for today?"

"Any and all information on Drem," my answer came out resolute. I didn't want to leave any question about what I looked for.

"Interesting choice of subject. May I ask why?" he eyed me with some suspicion. Suddenly, I wondered if Lin bought into Drem's facade.

To be safe I fed him the lie I'd given to Neala, the desire to give Drem a chance and get to know him. "The man isn't exactly an open book. Neala wasn't much help either. So I thought I'd look here."

"You observation of Drem is impeccable, Elle. I can tell you upfront, there is little information here on the man who would be

King," a hint of disdain laced his statement. He noticed I didn't miss the sour note in his voice and studied me for a moment, "you are not surprised I noticed his aspirations. Not that his are for power. The man has been obviously in love with Neala for decades. For me anyway, I do tend to notice those sorts of things. People's feelings of others. Like I can tell, you adore Veena, would do anything for your mother, are head over heels for the guard Daric, are growing fond of me, and loathe Drem."

"Oh but, I...," I began to protest before Lin cut me off.

"No, no. You do. Do not worry, though. Your secret hate is safe with me. I find the man repugnant myself," he winked. "I will, however, get what I do have on his career here. That is all I have. Nothing personal. He's been careful not to allow any to be recorded. Why, I think the only person who would, would be his mentor."

"Drem's mentor?" the thought never occurred to me before. The slime-ball seemed so comfortable in his place here, like he just popped out of nowhere and declared himself adviser to the crown. The role of apprentice didn't seem to fit him.

"Yes, Drem was apprentice to Eisele, King Tor's, your grandfather's, adviser. She was a force herself in her day. Why, I remember Drem being quite envious of her as well, she had so much power. In comparison, he still is weak."

"If she was so powerful, why isn't she still the adviser to the crown? What happened to her?"

"She failed to serve the crown. King Tor died under her watch and Neala never forgave her. Eisele was let go, and exiled once Neala took the throne."

"What do you mean? She killed him?"

"Not purposely," Lin sighed. He dove into telling me about King Tor's death. Eisele had been treating him for debilitating joint pain all through his body. She came up with an unorthodox treatment when nothing else seemed to work. Friendly fire. Eisele adapted the potion for the harmless flames into something medicinal. The potion had been adjusted to create mild levels of heat and mixed with a pain killer, then injected into King Tor's joints. Over time she needed to make the potion stronger to keep it working. A mistake was made in crafting a dose and the treatment turned deadly. The potion heated too much and essentially burned King Tor from the inside.

When Lin disclosed that detail, my hand fluttered to my throat. I could almost feel the flames surging through my own veins. "How awful. No wonder Neala was so devastated."

"The kingdom was shocked. Eisele was meticulous in her work, she'd never made a mistake like that before. Everything she did was perfection." Lin sighed again, he obviously held a lot of admiration for the old adviser's genius.

The wheels in my head screeched into overdrive, shifting directions. Suspicion tickled its way into my train of thought. Drem conveniently wormed his way into his position with the death of my grandfather. With his mentor suddenly out of the picture, he became closer to Neala. The only obstacle to having her left had been Carradoc. What were the odds he'd been poisoning Neala's mind for much longer than I thought? Playing a very long game. The only thing in his path had been love, and the grief of losing it became the final piece in his poison finally taking hold. Convenient wasn't the definition of how he got the job. To me, that had been planned.

It began to look like my long day would be a lot shorter than expected

"Forget Lord Drem. I need two things," I my eyes steeled with purpose fell on Lin, "where I can find Eisele, and any records of her treatments for King Tor."

THIRTY-EIGHT

DIVING DEEP INTO DREM WORLD

Lin, being an intuitive man, understood track I was on. With a knowing glint in his stormy eyes, he dashed off into the stacks of records to get the requested documents. While he was away, I helped myself to some of the fruits and cheeses Veena left, and washed them down with ice cold water from one of the canisters. The food and drink hit my hollow stomach roughly, leaving it in knots. I couldn't be sure if it was because I hadn't eaten yet, or if nerves were upsetting me.

I looked up, out of the domes glass above and watched the clouds wisping overhead. Their aeolian dance cast shadows that darkened the bright morning sky for brief moments at a time. As I watched, I prayed that whatever information Lin brought back to me proved to be more fruitful than everything else I'd looked at so far. The weeks in the library and that disastrous tea with Neala marred my quest. The excitement that what Lin presented might be perfect, resonated through me in tandem with the fear that it wasn't.

This research had to pan out. If it didn't, I would be back at square one. I hated the idea that this could have been a dead end. As I saw it, all of my eggs were in this particular basket now. On my own, with no way to fight against Drem, the odds against me were immeasurable. I didn't think I'd have the time to save Neala before she completely disappeared without some sort of inside information.

When Lin returned, he had less documentation than I'd expected; a singular thin book and a rolled parchment. My disappointment was immediate. How could such a small amount of material possibly tell me anything?

He laid book and parchment on the reading table. "Be sure to roll the map out laying down, and use some of the page weights in the drawer to hold it down," he motioned to a drawer built into the underside of the table. "I hope you find what you need, if you need more just call for me. I will be in my office in the back."

"Gotcha," I swiveled the chair about, the child in me sending it in a full circle before pulling it up to the reading table. After he disappeared into the stacks once more, I turned my attention to the book on the table. The book was bound in thick dark leather and was no thicker than a basic composition note-book. Ribbons wrapped around a brass toggle held the thin tome closed. Carefully, a lifted it and transferred it to the book rest. After rummaging in the table drawer for a couple of page weights, I opened it up and began to pour through the contents.

The first page held just a title; *Treatment log, King Tor, experimental healing fire for debilitating joint pain.* The page confirmed what Lin told me. Eisele created a treatment for King Tor. I turned the page, finding a log of treatments; when, how much, and effectiveness. As the list lengthened, the doses and strength of the treatments increased. Some were entered in standard black ink, a few in blue. Reading further would enlighten to the differences there. My eyes ran over the list again and again, trying to memorize it in vain. If only I'd been blessed with a photographic memory.

Eisele's concoction worked for what appeared to be months before the list ended with King Tor's death marked in red ink. My throat prickled with oncoming tears as I stared at those red letters. The death of my grandfather felt all too familiar. Is that what

Carradoc's treatment record looked like? Did Drem even keep one? I doubted it. Drem was slippery that way.

I pushed my emotions down, choking on them, as I turned another page just to get the log out of my sight. With a deep breath, I continued on. The remainder of the pages were as expected, Eisele's personal notes on her treatments. Details on how it was created, administered, and the full effects with King Tor's testimony noted. Most entries were the same, and followed a basic pattern. The healing fire would work for a few weeks, then the pain began seeping back in and she'd change the formula; the first time the new formula was used led to the change in log color.

The search for useful information looked fruitless. Every entry seemed cloned from others and nothing at all stood out. With every page turned, I felt more and more like I chased an ice cream truck only to find it sold out. My time in records suddenly looked like a great big waste of time. Until I got to the final entry.

The log held no detailed record of the final treatment that took King Tor's life. Instead, the last detailed entry had been the prior day's entry:

Healing fire treatment day 273. Dosage: 50ml.

King Tor notes: The healing fire does little to chase the ice from his bones. There is a splintering sensation with most movements.

I worry for my King. The healing fire treatments are yet again weakening. His face pictured no relief after the administration this time. Though, he put on a brave front, I know he suffers. I can not help but feel it is my fault. This treatment plan has me feeling like a neophyte, even though I have plenty of experience in my field. I am not sure how much stronger I can make them and keep them safe, though I do not believe we are at that threshold yet. For that, I am grateful. There is still time to explore other treatment avenues. I hope I can find one that will be a more permanent fix.

Tomorrow I must leave the villa for a supply run. I do not trust Drem fully to not drive away suppliers with his prickly demeanor, so I must go myself. At least I can trust my assistant to follow my direc-

tions here and administer King Tor's treatment. Tonight, I draw up a new batch of healing fire, stronger to keep the dosage lower. I am taking a risk increasing both the pain relieving and the fire elements of the treatment, but that is what I feel I must do. Otherwise, there might not be any relief for the king.

I sunk back in the chair, knowing the outcome of the last entry. There was little to go on, not enough to say whether or not King Tor's untimely death was Eisele's fault, or Drem's. The fault, logically could be seen as both of theirs. I needed more information. Carefully, I turned the pages back to the log page and looked at the last entry again.

Day 274, dosage 50ml, increased strength by ten percent, result: Death

The handwriting clearly belonged to Drem, chicken scratches compared to Eisele's flowing penmanship. He'd have been the only one with access to the log, being her assistant and all. No matter how I analyzed it, there were no more clues. I needed more to get to the bottom of this. My gut feeling said Drem was behind it, and revealing him would help save Neala. The only way I could see doing that, was talking to Eisele herself. She would be my last long shot. I had to locate her.

There was only one problem immediately stopping me from doing that. Lin only left me with the map, but with no information on Eisele's location. How did he expect me to find her with a map, but no coordinates? I stood and walked to the edge of the nook, calling for Lin. He appeared in minutes.

"How fares your research?" he slipped a hand in his vest pocket and rocked on his heels.

"The treatment log's a dead end."

"So sorry to hear that. How about the map, was that useful?"

"Well, I need more than just a map to tell me where I can find Eisele."

He cocked his head, confusion on his face for a moment, like he didn't understand what I was asking. "Did I give you the wrong map? I could have sworn I grabbed the right one."

It was my turn to be confused, "Ummm, as long as it's a map of Vale it should be the right one. Right? I mean, that's how maps work."

Together we went back to the table. Lin picked up the rolled map, examining the markings on the outer edge. "No, I gave you the right map."

"So where do I find her?"

"The map will tell you," he said calmly.

I, on the other hand, grew frustrated with the back and forth. I threw my hands up, exasperated. "Where on the map? Maps don't magically tell you where to find things."

A light went off in Lin's mind, his expression changed from being baffled by the deranged princess, to being amused by the clueless princess. At least he didn't look at me like an idiot for not knowing what he did. "They do when they are maps linked to track specific people." Grabbing a pair of long page weights from the drawer, he began to gently unroll the map until it lay flat on the table as he explained. "When one is exiled, they are tracked to keep their whereabouts known. To make sure they aren't violating their mandate. That tracker is linked to two maps and an alarm the Captain monitors. One map is kept here in archive, an individual map that logs all movements of the exiled," he pointed to a list of locations on the left hand side of the map. "Like a key on a traditional map, you see. The other map is kept in the guard's keep and has the location of all exiled of Vale.

Back to the key," he motioned for me to look closer, "if you notice on Eisele's map her general location has not changed in years. Small movements in her area is all. Now, watch this," he gently tapped the last coordinates in the key. As soon as he did, a red mark began to pulsate on the map. Eisele's location was revealed, at the far northern border of Vale.

"Amazing. Do you have something I can write this down on?"

"You plan to go to her?" he quizzed.

"You won't tell on me will you," I bit my lip, worried Lin would do just that and ruin my chance to learn more about Drem.

He rolled the map back up, and disappeared around the corner. My heart sank. There went my chance, or so I thought. A minute later he came back and handed me the map, and a container of the liquid gloves. "Young lady, your secret is safe with me. Just return this when you get back, okay. Be sure to use the protective barrier when handling it."

"Thank you, Lin. I will. You've no idea how much this means to me."

JUST SO WE'RE CLEAR, I HATE CAMPING

By the time evening rolled around I felt more impatient than anything. I hadn't been able to sit still for more than a few minutes at a time all day. I tried keeping myself busy, venturing to mine and Daric's place, wandering the gardens, and even in the library reading more magic books.

I'd even gone to the kitchen several times to see if Veena was free for more lessons in Reta food. She'd been too busy every time for anything more than a few words of conversation.

I paced by my door, waiting for Daric's knock at the end of his shift. The knocking came at the same time every day. The moment I heard it, I rushed opening the door and grabbed him by his hand. I led him to my bed and instructed him to sit, then wasted no time diving into what I needed to tell him.

Daric sat rapt on the edge of my bed while I paced the cold floor, regaling everything I'd learned in records that morning. His emotions ran the same gamut mine had, everything from disappointment to excitement sent his mossy eyes on a roller coaster ride.

When I finished explaining about wanting to go find Eisele and talk to her myself, he only had one question, "What do you need from me?"

"You're coming with me, of course. I need you to help me plan the trip, and come up with an excuse for us to leave for an extended amount of time." I had no idea how long it would take to get to her, or how long it would take to learn everything we could from her. I had a feeling it wasn't going to be a short trip.

"Okay. Let me see the map."

Following Lin's instructions I poured the protective barrier stuff onto my hands and rubbed it in until I felt it begin to work. Then I instructed Daric to do the same while I retrieved the map from the drawer in the sideboard. I handled the map like it would explode at any given moment. Lin would kill me if I as much as dog-eared a corner. Carefully, I rolled it open on the floor, using heavy trinkets from around my room to hold the corners down. Daric knelt next to me on the floor, leaning over the parchment. His intense gaze studied the map for a mere minute before learning what he needed to know.

"This shouldn't take more than a day, day and a half to get to on Zenobi. She, and the other guards' horses can make distances like that faster than the average horse."

"Could we just portal?" I didn't want to waste time on travel if we could avoid it. The sooner we got to Eisele's the better I'd feel. The sooner I'd have answers. I hoped.

"I am afraid not, sweetheart. Every portal is regulated, remember? There would be no way we would get approval to open one to a destination so close, let alone to a location of a person who has been exiled."

"Oh, yeah," I slumped into a pout. Why did portals have to be so restricted? I understood the safety aspect. I knew first hand the awful effects of portaling too young, though mine were compounded by traumatic amnesia. Still, it sucked. But, if traveling was what we had to do, so be it. At least the trip there wouldn't take more than what Daric estimated. "Then how do we get permission to leave the villa for an indefinite length of time?"

He sat back on his heels, rubbing his hand over his mouth in thought. I loved the stern, serious look he got when thinking, his lips would purse just a little and his brow furrowed. There was just something about it that toyed with my heart. He distracted me from doing what I should have been, which was thinking of ideas myself. I could honestly watch him all day.

After a minute or two of thought Daric had an idea. A devious smirk settled on his lips accented by his signature crooked eyebrow, "How do you feel about camping?"

Camping. The idea terrified me, even though I knew what he proposed was a cover. As long as I could recall, which wasn't all that long even with old memories coming back daily, camping made my palms sweat and my heart race. Something about it sent me into full blown panic attacks. I'd had a few fosters that were extremely outdoorsy, and had real problems with me not wanting to camp. One even tried forcing me. That only led to a meltdown and a severe episode of the visions I used to suffer.

Knowing what I did now about my abduction many years ago, the exact reason why camping made me feel that way was clear. The woods, unbeknown to me at the time, were a severe PTSD trigger. The idea still set a tremor in my hands that I had trouble controlling.

"Hey, hey," Daric noticed my distress at fake camping, and gathered me in his arms. His embrace warmed me like the sun on a warm spring day, chasing the fearful chill settling in my bones away. "What is bothering you?"

"Camping, just the idea of it, scares me to death. My abduction caused that for sure."

"Even if you know we are not really camping?" he questioned, one hand rubbing my back in comfort.

"Yup. It's pathetic, I know."

"No, not pathetic. It was traumatic. We can come up with a different excuse if it will make you more comfortable."

For a brief moment I considered eloping as an excuse, even though I wasn't anywhere near being ready for that. I loved Daric, I did. I hardly knew him, considering my memory loss. I did know, however, I wouldn't mind spending the rest of my life wrapped in his arms. He made me happy, and I felt safe with him. At home. I only considered the idea because I knew it would cause a real stir. I pushed the idea aside, "No, camping is fine. I just need to remind myself we aren't actually doing it, just saying we are."

"You sure?" I nodded in response. "Okay, camping it is. I assume you want to leave as soon as possible?"

"You know it. How long before Captain Seylah will give you more leave?" this trip would be a lot easier to plan if Daric were allowed to be on my service still. He wouldn't have to ask for leave because going where I went was part of the job.

"I am certain she will allow it as I need it. She is sympathetic to you. To us. She may be a tough warrior but her heart is soft. A sucker for love. I will ask her in the morning."

"Would it be too hard to leave the next day, if she approves that is?"

He chuckled at my eagerness, his easy smile lighting my world, "I do not see why it would be, my impatient girl. If we can pack up quickly enough that is."

"I am an expert at speed packing." It was true. Years in foster care saw to that. My head spun with how fast I was in and out of homes over the years. It got to a point where packing became second nature.

The villa bells chimed, sending me groaning internally. The hour grew late. Which meant he needed to leave. Even though Neala was okay with my seeing him, she'd set limits to how late he could be in my room. He also had duty early in the morning. A good thing, considering the talk he needed to have with Captain Seylah. Still, I hated him leaving anytime we were together. I missed the days he had the night shift on my service and he could spend those hours with me, talking into the night.

"Time to go," he leaned down for a quick goodbye kiss. It only made me want him to stay more.

"I know," my pout came out full force. Daric chuckled at my insolence and rubbed his thumb over my lip. "I'll see you tomorrow. Don't forget to ask about more leave."

"As if I could forget. A fake vacation with my girl, taking down an evil usurper, that is what every soldier dreams of. I cannot wait."

After Daric left, I milled in my room with much on my mind. I readied for bed. I showered and then called for a cup of calming tea, like I usually did. I thought my usual routine would knock me into dreamland, as it often did.

When Veena arrived with my night time drink, I told her about my plans to camp with Daric, "Do you think you can make a weeks worth of provisions for us?"

"I can do that, sure. When do you need them by?"

"We hope to leave the day after tomorrow. Daric needs permission for leave first."

Her face scrunched at the demanding time line, "That is a little last minute, but I should be able to handle it. As long as you don't mind simple fare. I am not going to give myself a headache trying to figure out how to make your Reta foods suitable for travel."

"I wouldn't expect anything other than easy stuff." Satisfied with my answer she left, promising to have the provisions ready when we needed them.

After Veena left, my night dragged on and on. Sleep was held at bay by the acrobatic feats of my anxious mind. My thoughts cartwheeled and tumbled over everything I'd learned visiting records. Granted, it wasn't much, not much that had the potential to be immensely useful anyway. The location of Drem's old mentor had been the best of it all. If anyone had information on the man, it would be her.

The rest had been fuel for my already raging fire. Especially the eerily parallel deaths of my grandfather and Carradoc. Both had died being treated for ailments by Drem. Technically, King Tor had been under Eisele's care, but Drem had been the last to treat him before he died. For me, that, along with the poison Dr. and Janice Queen found in Carradoc's blood, proved his guilt in both deaths. I didn't need any more evidence. Although I had plenty brewing in my own returning memories.

All of this ran through my mind, keeping the sandman away. Finally, as the sun broke through the morning mists, my body gave in to rest. It was a good thing I had no major plans planned that day. Neala needed to be informed that I'd be leaving on a trip with Daric. That could be done anytime really, even just before we left if I wanted. Packing would be a cinch for me, so it wouldn't take too long to do.

FORTY

DAMMIT DREM

THE NEXT MORNING, Neala surprised me with an invitation to dinner. Me and Daric, whom she insisted I set aside my selfishness for and bring along this time. The dinner would be formal, which came off as strange itself since there was no reason I knew of for one. It wasn't a holiday, or birthday that I knew of. No call for celebration for anything had been announced. Just an out of the blue formal dinner. Fancy dress and all.

She hadn't been joining me for actual meals since Drem's fingers gripped her senses. Her invitation hadn't been necessary, most of my meals were already taken in the dining hall with Daric joining me half of the time. Dinners were pretty lonely when he didn't. Just me, alone, sitting at a long ass table with only my internal monologue for company. The invite only told me she'd be joining me for once and I had to dress up.

Fancy dinners weren't my thing. I was already sweating from nerves by the time evening rolled around.

Daric arrived at my door wearing his dress uniform, a white fitted tunic paired with charcoal trousers and waist coat. The waist coat lapels were adorned with the ribbons and medals honoring his service. His sun-lightened locks were pulled back from his face, in a half-braid. He looked even more dashing than usual, the wolf-whistle hidden in his smile only made him more so. "You look fantastic, Elle."

"Ya think? I feel so silly." I'd picked out something different than anything I'd ever worn before. There were so many dresses in my wardrobe already, but none of them felt right. With this dinner being the last one I'd have in the villa for an unforeseen time, and the first one with my mother in a long time, I wanted it to make a subtle statement. No, I needed it to. One more little reminder of Carradoc before I left. No one else would do that for her.

Almost as soon as I got the invitation, I called for a dress maker from the village to come to me with some new dresses. Different dresses. They arrived an hour later with more dresses than I could count. After pouring over gowns for the better part of the afternoon, I fell in love with only one. Ironically, the dress I chose was also a deep charcoal, cold-shoulder dress with a v-neck and fitted bodice. From the bodice, the dress became layers of airy chiffon in different shades of charcoal.

Despite loving the dress, it still wasn't perfect. It needed that little hint of my father. My mind went to the first time Carradoc called for me and the sea green dress I'd worn when I learned he loved the color green. The idea that formed brought tears to my eyes. I'd take the wide sash from that dress and use it on the charcoal one. At first the dressmaker hated the idea. If looks could kill. Then, when the idea came together, she changed her tune. Mostly, I thought she worried I wanted extensive alterations in a short time and was relieved when it ended up being just adding a sash.

"Yes, you look stunning, Elle." He swept me into his arms for a quick kiss, "And, we match."

"Not quite," I slid one of the small, sea green, daisy-like flowers from adorning my sleek, straight, white blonde hair and placed it behind one of the pins on his uniform.

"Not exactly uniform standards, but for the night it can slide." He ran his fingers over my hair, gently caressing the remaining flowers. "Your father's favorite," he smiled.

"A little reminder for Neala before we go find Eisele. I don't know how long we'll be gone, and I want to make sure she doesn't forget him completely." We'd had a brief discussion earlier about my plan. He'd dropped by while the dressmaker was with me to see how I was doing. He knew me too well, and figured I hadn't had a restful night. With the limited interaction we decided to plan on a week of being gone at least. He left me to the torture of picking a dress with a sympathetic look for the dressmaker. "I'm afraid to leave her alone with him, Daric. That she'll be gone completely when we get back and trying to save her will be for nothing. Just like with Carradoc."

"That is an understandable fear, after all you have been through. But, I think the only way Neala will fully disappear, be beyond saving, is if she dies." My hand fluttered to my mouth at the idea, horrified he'd even brought it up. I couldn't bear it if she died too. Then I'd really be an orphaned child with no immediate family to enjoy. Daric took my shivering hand and kissed it, "Do not worry. That will not happen. Drem has worked too hard to get her to let her do that."

I nodded, shaking away those worries, "Well, then let's go get this night over with. The sooner we do, the sooner we leave, and the sooner we save her. You got leave again, right?" I had to double and triple check that he did.

"Like I said earlier, I was able to swing it, but at a cost. I will be at Captain Seylah's beck and call for a month, and she'll likely use that power on the most menial tasks no one else wants." His captain would too. She was fair, and gave her men all the time they needed. As he said, it came at a cost every time. Not in the same way either. While I hated the idea of coming back and needing to take on Drem alone, I understood.

"Then we best make haste," he offered his arm. Sliding my hand through the space his elbow made, we headed off to dinner with my mother. My heart fluttered with excitement for the day ahead of us. Soon enough we'd, hopefully, be better armed against our foe.

THE DINING HALL glowed with soft light. The usually minimal space had been decorated as if prepared for a grand banquet rather than an intimate dinner with family. Rich, golden edged burgundy banners hung from the stuccoed walls, connected by garlands of deep red and purple flowers and ivy. Every window hid behind lush, thick burgundy curtains.The impossibly high-backed chairs were all adorned with golden ribbons and ivy colored fabric. The long table had hardly a bare space showing. Between platters of amuse bouche appetizers, fresh and candied fruits, roasted vegetables, cheeses, and a variety of meats were massive bouquets made of the same flowers and ivy that hung on the walls.

As I walked in on Daric's arm, I almost expected to learn more people were expected to attend. That dinner was more than just an intimate affair, which would have made the formality of it less out of place. At the same time, the dinner would be less panic inducing.

I knew beforehand that Drem would be there. After the last encounter with him, it became clear he saw through my charade of wanting to be nicer to him. That didn't mean we couldn't be civil to one another. Being nice to people who weren't as nice to me kind of became another special skill of mine growing up. All the bullying and harsh treatment because of my strangeness gave me the ability to give myself a sugar coating. Being nice kept me safe. I only fought back if I had to, or in Doctor Preble's case because I had no reason to be nice.

Daric, on the other hand, didn't suffer Drem lightly. Drem didn't tolerate Daric well either. They were straight up antagonistic with each other, and everyone knew it. There was no way around it, if they were in the same room there would be an argument of some sort. With everything going on, Daric certainly became a ticking time bomb around the creep. I knew it was only a matter of time before that bomb exploded. Before words became physical. I hoped it didn't happen anytime soon.

Neala stood waiting near the head of the table, dressed in a white silk, boat-necked dress that cinched at her waist before belling outward to the floor. A blood-red sash draped across her torso, landing on her left hip where it cascaded down in a flurry of ribbons from a knot of matching roses and black lilies. On her collar bone sat a necklace of black diamonds and rubies that gave the appearance that her graceful neck had been wounded. Her ultra light hair was pulled back severely, into a tight up-do also adorned with roses, black lilies, rubies, and black diamonds. The look was beautiful, severe, and nothing like her. Harsh where she was usually soft. A visual representation of Drem's darkness taking over her. A dark bride even. To be honest, it sent a chill through my core. Not nearly as much as seeing Drem.

Drem sat at the head of the table, in the chair once meant for my father. The chair, that up until then had remained empty. Seeing him sitting there, sent ice through my veins and fire in my sight. I simmered, the sensations combining to keep me from losing it. Daric tensed at the sight as well, and I squeezed his hand to send my calm to him. He squeezed in return, but did not relax. An uneasy, nauseated feeling formed in my stomach. It was not going to be a good night.

"Elloe, Daric," Neala approached us, "we are so glad you are joining us tonight." She opened her arms to me, taking me in an empty hug. She glanced over to Daric before pulling away from me, "We have something of the utmost importance to discuss. I cannot wait." She motioned for us to sit as she flitted around the table to take her place to the right of Drem, her full skirt swishing as she went.

Her hand slid over Drem's as she passed him. His eyes lovingly followed her. "Neala, dear, we must not ruin our surprise," his slow speech came out laced with an eagerness that surged my nausea and put a knot in my throat. Her responding giggle sickened me further. Once again, Neala's white dress and his matching black silk suit with red and white details looked menacingly like garish wedding attire. I felt my eyes go wide and jaw slacken at the thought. My expression didn't go unnoticed by Drem, who smiled gleefully at my distressed appearance. It was like he knew what I thought.

We took chairs to Drem's left, leaving one space between him and myself. Once we were all seated, kitchen servants poured deep purple wine into our glasses. "No thanks," I tried to decline my cup, "I'm too young."

"Nonsense," Neala chirped. "It is a special night. I think we can overlook age just this once." The server filled the wineglass in front of me. Despite her approval, I ignored the glass in favor of the water already there. I drained the cup, though it did little to ease my stomach and throat. No one made any immediate move to fill their plates.

The awkward silence was deafening.

"Shall we get down to business then?" Drem drolled after a few minutes of lull. He turned his attention to Neala, cupping her chin in his hand, "I am here for you, if you need."

She looked like a puppy being praised, hanging on his words like they were life, as she gave a slight nod. She turned to me, her dark eyes serious. "Elloe, we need to discuss the seriousness of your relationship," her eyes shifted to Daric again. I didn't like they way they scanned over him like he was something undesirable.

"Oh, we aren't too serious yet. I mean, I'm crazy for him and couldn't imagine life here without him. But, we've just started out and it's too soon to be thinking serious. You know?"

"Yes, I care deeply for your daughter, Your Majesty, but I agree with her. To get too serious now would be the wrong thing to do," the double meaning of his words weren't lost on me. My focus was on Neala for the time being, though.

"Good," Neala let out a deep breath. "That makes this much easier." Daric and I exchanged uneasy glances. She was making both of us nervous. "Oh, Drem. Could you? I am feeling all flustered."

"Of course, my dear," he smirked, his large blue eyes glinting in the low light, "it will be my, pleasure." The look in his eyes when he faced Daric and I again could've skinned a cat. Too much glee, satisfaction, and wickedness lived in his face then. Whatever he was up to, he looked forward to it.

I didn't like it.

"Your mother has asked you here to let you know the time has come to let go of this dead-end relationship you have." He templed his fingers under his chin and settled his victorious gaze on Daric.

"Wait. What?" I glared an accusation at my mother. "You invited me and Daric to a formal dinner to tell us to break up?" I could feel Daric's restless anger growing next to me, keeping up with my own.

"Yes," she replied calmly, as if the reason held validation.

"Why? That makes no sense, Neala. None."

"Sure it does, darling."

When she didn't offer her reasoning, I prompted, "And that would be?"

"A nice formal dinner makes it pleasant," she batted her dark lashes around her widened eyes. I saw she truly believed what she said, thanks to her newly warped mind. All reason and logic were slowly seeping away the longer she stayed under Drem's influence. Heartbreak seeded with anger twined through me. "So after dinner, that is that."

"I'm not doing that. You can't tell me to break up with Daric just because it isn't serious yet. I won't." I stood to leave, ready to get away from the farce of a dinner.

"You will not leave, nor will you defy my orders," Neala's voice boomed with queenly authority for the first time in ages. I sat, more from shock than wanting to listen to her. "I will explain. Drem came to me with the concern that perhaps Daric was at fault for your lack of progress, and is behind your initial disdain for him. The logic he brought to me on this matter is flawless."

There it was. Drem masterminded this. The revelation wasn't lost of Daric either. In seconds he flew from his chair and stormed over to Drem, whose eyes went wide with horror as my boyfriend barreled into him. That fear only lasted moments before glee replaced it with a toothy, sneering, grin.

"Daric, no!" my cry fell on rage deafened ears. His hand gathered Drem's shirt front into a knot and he lifted him from his chair. He swung the adviser around, slamming him on the table and sending food and drink spilling across the stone floor. Daric's fists found purchase in Drem's long face. Instead of wailing, begging the raging guard to stop, Drem cackled with every punch. Neala screamed and cried for the guards, tearing at her hair.

When the shock wore off, I sprang into action. I had to pull Daric off of Drem. We needed to get out of there; try to make a run for Eisele's before they came to stop the assault. My attempts were too weak. No matter how hard I pulled on him, he continued to wail on the older man. Too much rage boiled through Daric's veins, he was a volcano erupting after a long sleep.

It took three guards, plus Captain Seylah to pull him off of his target. He looked terrifying, as uncontrollable as Mr. Hyde. His hair fell from the half-braid and hung over his face, which was red and sweaty. Anger contorted his features and poisoned his emerald eyes as he huffed and fought against the men holding him.

Drem acted as though nothing had happened, as though he hadn't just been beaten to a pulp. He stood straight, chuckling while he fixed his clothes. "You see, Neala dear, just like I warned. Violent, and no good for *our* Elloe."

"Arrest him," she ordered Captain Seylah. She moved to Drem, fussing over him like a mother would an injured child.

I made to follow as the guards dragged Daric away, but the Captain Seylah stopped me, "Give him time to cool. You may visit later."

"No, she may not. Elloe is forbidden to see Daric ever again," my mother interjected. Those words put the final nail in me. My face crumpled into my hands and a storm unleashed itself from my eyes. I didn't have to look up to know it was Neala who rested a hand on my shoulder, "I am sorry, my daughter. I know it does not seem it now, but this is for the best. Someday, you will thank Drem for being so good to us." She excused herself, claiming a headache from all the fuss.

"You may go as well, Captain," Drem ordered. "I will see that the Princess is comforted." I heard Captain Seylah respond, and march away without closing the doors to the dining hall behind her. No sooner had she left I felt Drem's presence waft next to me. I couldn't bring myself to look at him. To respond to him, accuse him of plotting against me and hurting my mother. I felt too broken. "Nice touch, wearing the favorite color and flowers of dear, old, dead Carradoc. Thought it clever to remind your mother what she lost, did you? Well, your feeble attempts are no good anymore. She is mine, fully," he boasted.

He left me alone, standing in a mess of spilled wine and food, broken plates and scattered silver, with only my compounded grief for company. I was alone.

FORTY-ONE

THE SHOW MUST GO ON

I'ᴅ ʟᴏsᴛ all sense of time and location, traveled as a ghost through the villa without any feeling left. Eventually, I ended up in my room completely drained and dumbfounded. My familiar surroundings looked alien to me. I made no move to crawl into my soft bed to seek comfort for my grief there. No. It held too many memories that only dug at my wounded heart. The first time Daric kissed me. Daric comforting me during those first months here when nightmares still plagued me. Talking the night away when sleep evaded me.

Thinking about him led to thinking of Neala too, and Carradoc. Drem had stolen too much from me. I hated him with every fiber of my being, deeper than I'd hated anyone else. The grief fog in my head lifted, evaporated away with the rising heat of fury and I became resolved. Dinner's events wouldn't delay my plans. I would go through with my plan and head to Eisele's in the morning. I just had to recruit a new escort. One I trusted. I knew I wouldn't be allowed to leave without one.

I also needed a plan to explain my long planned absence to Neala. Before, we planned the excuse that I still needed more rest, but away from the villa this time. A camping trip to rejuvenate my soul. That plan fell through the moment Daric had been wrongly arrested. Luckily, I had all night to figure out a new excuse. All I needed to do before trying to get some rest was secure a new guard and pack.

There was no doubt in my mind who I'd ask to go with me. Rollan. Through everything since I'd arrived he'd proved himself a good friend to myself and Daric. Loyal to a fault. That loyalty lay with Neala as well, but I didn't think that would be a problem at all. I'd seen the concerned looks he had lately when with her. He'd have no problem with the ultimate plan when I told him it was to help her.

The only mystery left was the why I had to leave. I had to consider the situation. They expected me to be heartbroken, which I did feel on some level. I couldn't go gallivanting through strange forests alone to abate my sadness. That made no sense. I needed to pretend to treat this like a real break-up. The answer came to me the moment I began to think like that.

Q.

If I led my mother to think I couldn't bear being in Vale for a while, that I needed to ease my aching heart with a friend, she'd likely understand. I'd tell her I needed my best friend on Reta to overcome the "breakup". He provided the perfect cover; even better than camping.

Visiting Q became the perfect lie. After all, a girl always relied on the shoulder of her best friend when their life fell apart. I wouldn't really be going to Reta, and for once I didn't feel bad about the lie I'd tell to my mother.

I had so much to do, in a matter of hours. I had to pack, gather supplies, and enlist Rollan to my trip. Wasting no time, I searched under my bed for a travel bag, which held a few outfits from Reta. The old habit of keeping one nearby, from my years of being bounced around foster homes, stayed with me. There was a comfort in it, even though I no longer lived that life. A morsel of something familiar and the knowledge I didn't need to be ready to move at a moments notice warmed a fraction of my heart. Yet, there I was, frantically packing once more. This time it wasn't because I had to go to a new home. This time, I was leaving to save the people I cared for.

I'd already let Veena in on our fake camping plans and she'd promised a delivery of camp-friendly foods first thing in the morning. I didn't have to worry in that regards to having enough to survive a few days. Those supplies would be bagged off and hitched to Zenobi, along with whatever I managed to remember to pack.

Throwing open my wardrobe, I began throwing trousers and tunics onto my bed. Soon, I had a pile adequate enough to last for at least a week. I shoved those into my bag not caring if they wrinkled. There was no one to impress in the wilds of Vale. I doubted Eisele would care if my clothes were rumpled.

Before moving on to packing the other various things I'd need, I called for the guard standing duty at my door. "What can I help you with Princess Elloe?" Marlow, the young guard who opened the door had only been on my service since Daric had been excused from it. I liked him well enough, his platinum cropped hair and honey eyes made him appear cold, but he was far from it. He was sensitive. My biggest issue with him came from his being a stickler for rules. Including entering my room. Most male guards would not enter my room on their own. Daric and Rollan were the exceptions. Daric because he was a rule breaker, Rollan because of his preferences. The rest were too afraid to be seen as doing something untoward. Marlow, took it a step further and wouldn't cross the threshold, ever.

"Yes, Marlow. I need Rollan. To talk to him about something important. Now."

"The hour is late, Princess. Perhaps it should wait until morning? I would hate to trouble him, or for you to get into trouble."

"It kinda has to be now, Marlow. It's urgent. I don't care what trouble it causes, go get him now," the demand came in full bitch mode, harsh and mean for no reason. I just felt irritated by my swirling emotions and exhaustion. I recognized the mistake too late by the hint of fear in Marlow's eyes and the slight quiver in his chin as he turned to leave. I vowed to apologize when he came back.

Guilt proved to be one thing too much for my ravaged brain. My carefully tucked away feelings tumbled out and spilled everywhere. I crumpled into the mess I'd made packing as they overtook me, body shaking with the sobs that sounded like a dying cat. That was how Rollan found me, lying fetal in a pile of clothes spotted with tears.

"Princess," his concerned voice soothed in my ear as he stooped next to me. He came alone. Marlow must not have had the courage to face me again, which made me feel even more awful. The kid didn't deserve the misdirected anger I threw at him. "I heard about Daric being arrested. It is not right. He should not have struck Lord Drem, but that is not saying he did not deserve it. My friend can be a passionate and brash man, but never strikes without reason."

His words comforted me. Knowing he stood by Daric meant he didn't stand with Drem, and I could trust him. I'd feed him the lie of going to Q's until the time came for him to learn the truth about what I planned to do. I wasn't about to reveal my real plans too early. Couldn't have anyone overhear it by accident. "Thanks, Rollan. That means a lot to me."

"What do you need?" he joined me on the floor, pushing aside a shirt in his way to stretch out his long legs. His dark hair flopped over his eyes as he situated himself.

"I need to get away," I sniffled. "I want to go visit Q, and recuperate my broken heart."

"Broken heart?" he questioned. I explained how Neala had declared we were no longer able to see each other at all. That was what ultimately led to Daric's arrest. "I am sorry. That is awful and complete shit. Anyone that knows you, knows your mind is your own. No matter how much you care for my friend, he could never influence your thoughts. I am guessing you need me to go with as an escort?" a hint of hope hung in his question.

There were two reasons I thought of Rollan as my backup. I knew

Daric trusted him completely, and I did too. Also, I wanted to bring up Q, to test his reaction at the possibility of seeing my friend. Based on the interest in his voice, he liked the idea.

"Yup," a knot of guilt formed. He was going to be very disappointed when we didn't actually go through a portal to Reta. I would, however make sure to take my D.C. so they could chat at least. Hopefully, that would make up for the deception in the end.

He smiled sympathetically, "No problem. I do not blame you for needing to get away. Do you need me to let your mother know?"

"That would be great. I don't think I can face her right now."

"I will approach her first thing. When do we leave, and how long are we staying?"

"As soon as she knows, and I don't know. Prepare for a long stay just in case."

Rollan stood, brushing his uniform off. Only then did I notice how hastily put together he looked and I knew I'd interrupted his off time. "Well then, Princess, I will see you with the morning birds. Get some rest," he ordered, offering me a hand up, "we may not be going far, but I am sure you remember how much portal travel can take out of you."

I nodded, wondering if I should have told him what we were actually doing. Since I'd already gotten enough coming from Veena for two people, he wouldn't be under-prepared; so maybe not. "Can you see Daric before we go? I'm not allowed and I want him to know I'm leaving to see Q. I don't want him to worry about me."

"Sure thing. Want me to give him a message or kiss, or something?" his thick eyebrows wiggled with his joke. I'd have given almost anything to see Rollan deliver my message to Daric.

"Why not?" I planted a kiss on his cheek, playing along. He snickered playfully and left me to finish up on my own. Everything I needed I'd managed to pack up before my meltdown, minus a few things I'd need in the morning. From experience, though, I knew better than to leave it at thinking I was prepared.

I double checked everything, making sure my D.C. and the map were kept out and where I'd remember them. After a quick survey of the room, I decided against cleaning it up. Weariness began to settle in my bones. I crashed on the mountain of clothes on the bed, sleep coming almost instantly.

FORTY-TWO

TRAVEL BUDDIES

Morning came too early with a knock on the door. That bone weary, brain fog feeling of high emotions and late nights made it sound like a battering ram attempting to splinter apart the wooden barrier. I eased myself off the bed and shuffled toward the knocking, still in the formal gown from the night before. Falling asleep before changing might not have been the best idea. The small rip on the hemline agreed. The wrinkles and damage had me completely regretting it.

My tired body exerted in heaving the heavy door open. On the other side waited Veena, holding a large mug of dark flower brew. Her intelligent eyes widened at my appearance as she handed me the drink. "Elle, you look like you have had better nights."

"You could say that," I leaned against the door frame, blowing on the brew to cool it before taking a long sip. The chocolate and fruity flavor instantly sent a jolt of energy through me. It wasn't my favorite beverage, but I needed it desperately. I even hoped she packed more in a thermos.

" I wanted to double check your plans, with everything and all," she avoided saying what actually happened, I think to spare my feelings.

"Still going," I had to choke down the tears that threatened to spill at the fresh reminder that Drem scored another point in alienating me. "I'm taking Rollan instead. I really need to get away."

Veena shifted her weight uneasily, "I will send the provisions to the stables then and have the hand prepare two horses. You would prefer Zenobi, I presume?"

"Yes. Thank you. I don't think Daric would mind my using her." In truth, I adored Zenobi. She held a place in my heart over all the other steeds in the stables. Her big personality, and gentle gait had a lot to do with that.

She prepared to leave, but turned back on hesitant heel, "You know, Elle, you can confide in me. I am psychic you know, and try not to pry. Rollan puts off very readable energy, and he is excited. More excited than just a camping trip would make him. If you are not truly camping, you can tell me."

I'd forgotten to count her abilities in my math. Most psychics of Vale and specified ability, only being psychic in certain areas. Veena's skill was a little broader than normal, she could read energies as well as anticipate needs. She mainly used her psychic ability for her job, so I didn't factor it in that she'd see through lies on some level. Although I trusted she wouldn't out my real plan to anyone, I didn't want her implicated. I lied more, even though I knew she likely would deduce that and the reason why. "We are camping with Q in Reta."

"We are?" Rollan appeared over Veena's shoulder, an excited smile reached his eyes. Guilt doubled in my chest. Crap. Any more lies and I'd be completely buried in them.

"Sure are," I swallowed away the lie. Veena eyed me with concern as she excused herself. I mouthed an apology to her, hoping she understood both my reasons and the pain it caused to create all the lies I had. I couldn't seem to stop these days.

"We are all set to go anytime you are ready, Princess," Rollan pulled my attention back to him. "Neala is on board with your plans, and wishes you a pleasant respite from your woes. She hopes you return soon."

"Great," I feigned excitement. "I just need to change at put together a few last things. I'll meet you in the stables. Veena's already sending supplies for us and having the horses readied."

"Very good," he bowed out and left me to get ready.

It could have been the dark flower brew kicking in or the excitement of what lay ahead, I felt wide awake and ready to spring into action. After taking a quick shower, I dressed in a pair of jeans with a t-shirt under a tunic. Without brushing it, I threw my damp hair up into a messy bun. I'd regret it later when my hair became a tangled mess, but time was of the essence. I drained my now cold drink while putting a few last minute things in my travel bag, then shoved my D.C. into my jeans pocket.

As I surveyed the room, making sure there wasn't a thing forgotten, unease gnawed at me. The mountain of clothes that became my bed the night before mocked me with accusation. I grumbled at the delay, but took the time to at least shove them all back in the wardrobe. The maids would likely still end up cleaning up and reorganizing it while I was away, but at least the mess would be left contained. It eased my guilt just a hair.

Finally, I felt ready to get on with the day. With one last look at my room, a bolted out the door and made my way to the stables. I couldn't wait to get the journey started. More hung in the balance of defeating Drem since last night. Not only would I save my mother, I'd get Daric back.

MY PULSE RACED FASTER as we approached the portal site. That meant Rollan would learn the truth soon. I worried he'd be angry at the deception.

We'd been riding at an easy pace for an hour since leaving the villa. Soon, we'd need to stop and rest the horses. Ourselves as well.

Our journey wouldn't be done for hours, likely well into the evening hours or possibly the next day. The northern border of Vale sat furthest from the villa than any of the others. The ride wasn't long in the grand scheme of things, but we would be taking our time thanks to my lack of experience in horseback riding solo.

Q had offered to take me riding many times through our friend-ship, but I always declined. I'd been too afraid of a vision derailing the fun. The worst scenario played in my mind at every invitation. I feared a vision would creep in over a crisp beautiful sky, turning the trees into something else. The illusion would hide obstacles and dangers, and I'd end up hurt or dead because I didn't know better. There was a lot I used to avoid doing because I thought I was sick.

Ahead of me, Rollan began to slow his horse, Fehr. Fehr could've been Zenobi's twin save his mane and tail were sold black instead of black and white. That, and he was a few hands taller. "Whoa boy," Rollan called for Fehr to stop. He'd already begun his dismount as I passed him up with no intention of stopping for more than a moment or two.

I planned to just keep going, and hoped he'd follow until I stopped ten minutes away. Admittedly, the plan was terrible. I should have been honest with him from the get go. But, the plans were better shared away from the walls where Drem roamed.

"Hold up! This is our portal site, Princess," I heard him call out, but didn't hear hoof-beats coming up behind me. Dammit.

I turned Zenobi half a turn and looked back at Rollan. The confusion on his face twisted my heart. With a nudge from the reins Zenobi finished the turn and I led her back to where the guard and his horse waited. "I'm sorry, Rollan," I said with a heavy sigh, "I lied. We aren't taking a portal to Reta, or seeing Q." My head hung low, I couldn't meet his hurt gaze for long.

"What?" his voice was filled with disappointment.

"I didn't like lying to you, but I needed to."

"Then what are we doing? Why the deception?" he sounded hurt, and not just at not seeing Q.

"Daric and I were planning this trip before he was arrested, to seek out Eisele, the former adviser to King Tor. To get information on Drem, seek help to take him out of the equation and save Neala from him. Getting her back is the most important thing to me. Drem took Carradoc, he can't keep Neala.

I couldn't tell you before because I didn't know who would overhear. I created the ruse of visiting Q to get Neala to approve your coming with me so I could still go."

His mouth went hard while he considered what I had to say. He didn't look happy in the least. The sounds of the forest were deafening in the absence of words. Tortuous even. The longer I waited for him to respond, the more my nerves grew. It seemed like ages before he did. "I do not like it, Princess. I do not like being used and lied to when there is no reason for it. That being said, I understand why."

"So, you'll still escort me?" I asked hopefully.

"You owe me."

"I really do." My heart sang, beyond thrilled that Rollan didn't have it in him to hold a grudge. In my head I made plans on how to make it up to him. The next time I went to Reta, he would definitely be going. Every time Q called, Rollan would get the chance to talk to him too. The next time Daric and I were together and had one of our Reta style feasts, I'd invite Rollan to join. "We just need to do one thing though. Open a portal so it looks like we went through."

I could only imagine what would happen if we didn't. We'd petitioned for a portal, so one was expected to be opened. If we didn't, it was very likely that a search team would be out looking for us by the end of day. That couldn't happen.

"Yeah, that would be best if we do not want to raise any red flags."

AFTER RIDING another forty minutes we stopped to rest. The horses, and our butts, were grateful for the down time. The forest thickened around us, with trees towering higher than any I'd personally seen before. Their greedy branches blocked most of the sunlight from reaching the mossy ground, which benefited us fine. Just the right amount of light remained to keep us from stumbling in the dark, and kept us cool.

The smell was different too. Like the darkness concentrated the earthiness of the soil and the verdant scent of foliage. Something about the deep aroma granted a sense of closeness and safety. Like the trees wouldn't let anything bad happen under their shade.

I dismounted Zenobi with all the grace of a toddler on an obstacle course, falling into a thick patch of large red ferns. From my position in the leaves I heard Rollan grunt as he hopped off Fehr and rushed towards me. "I'm good!" I called, shooting a hand up in the air to signal I didn't need help. I jumped up and brushed the dirt from my legs, repeating myself. Aside from minor scrapes and bruises that inevitably would appear in minutes, the only thing truly injured was my ego.

I pushed back through the ferns to Zenobi's side, who looked less than amused by my ineptness. She missed Daric. "Me too, girl," I patted her neck and moved on to search through the provisions Veena had packed for us. I couldn't help but chuckle at what I found.

"What is it?"

"Veena. She's rationed the provisions with notes," I picked up a pack to show him. The beeswax container had a label on it, likely written a food safe ink, saying it contained some lemon jerkied fish, dehydrated fruits, some hard cheese, and soft crackers. What followed that label had me giggling. *Eat only one rationed pack per meal.* All of the packs were labeled similarly. She didn't have to use her magic to foresee me eating my way through the rations too fast. She knew me and my voracious appetite well.

"It looks like Veena's looking out for us," Rollan chuckled along with me as he settled on the forest floor. He got the joke too. There probably wasn't a soul in the villa that didn't know how much I loved food. "We cannot have you eating everything in one go. Toss me one of those, would you?"

I grabbed another beeswax container, this one holding veggie chips, beef jerky, cheese, biscuits and jam, and tossed it to him. I pulled out two sealed cool bottles of water and joined him. "So, Rollan," I cracked the eco-friendly canister and popped a dried apricot in my mouth, "I am really sorry about lying before."

"No need to keep apologizing," he chided, chewing on his own mouthful of food. "Like I said, you owe me a trip to Reta."

"And time with Q," I teased. Blush crept across his olive toned cheeks. I knew he crushed on Q, though it didn't take a rocket scientist to figure that out.

"Not that it would matter in the long run, but yes."

"Why wouldn't it matter? People make it work long distance all the time."

"It would be more than long distance, as you say. Cross-dimensional. Different worlds, let alone lives."

"I'm sure it's happened before. It can happen again," I refused to think otherwise. I needed something hopeful in my life. Something other than my loved ones being torn away; brainwashed, arrested, and murdered all by the same man. As unlikely a real relationship would bloom for Rollan and Q, I needed to believe in it.

"Can you explain something else to me, Princess?"

"Elle, please." No matter how many times I corrected Rollan, he wouldn't budge on calling me Princess. He was more for rules than Daric, but not a complete stick in the mud like Marlow. "What do you mean?"

"Earlier, you said Drem took Carradoc from you. What does that imply?"

I turned and looked Rollan square in the eyes, "It means exactly what it sounds like. Drem is responsible for Carradoc's death. He poisoned him."

My companion's eyes went wide, "What?" While we finished our meal, I filled Rollan in on everything Drem related, including my suspicion of his involvement of King Tor's death. The information rendered him speechless for a long time. When he found his words, they were laced with anger. "I cannot believe it."

"Truth, I swear."

"No, I believe it, I do. Just, I cannot believe he has not been foiled yet."

"That my friend, is what I'm doing."

FORTY-THREE

I WAS NOT EXPECTING THAT

Our journey continued through the day. The scenery remained green and bright, the only thing changing was the density of the forest as we went. Vale had little in the way of geographic diversity. The village and the villa were surrounded by almost nothing but forest and minor rock formations. Other than that the forested land stretched on to the boundaries of Vale, where at last some mountains changed the scenery.

We caught our first glimpse of them after long hours of riding as the sun began to descend towards the land, with a few breaks thrown in here and there. After my revelation about Drem, Rollan became quiet for most of the ride, occasionally remarking on something that made sense because he knew the truth, or to ask questions about the whole situation. I tried my best to respond, but sometimes the answers were too painful for me. Too fresh.

I found I appreciated having another person fully in the loop. A new ally. It's not like I expected him to remain in the dark forever either. There would be no avoiding it once Eisele came in the picture. His whole acceptance merely made me wonder why I'd kept everything so close to the chest. If Daric and I had more allies in the beginning, would the trip have even ever had to happen?

The surrounding forest began to thin significantly soon after the mountains were visible above the canopy. The sun, despite beginning to go down, shone brighter on us. When we burst through the final copse of trees, the brightness of the dying light blinded me momentarily, making me shield my eyes until they adjusted. I gasped when my vision finally corrected.

"Gorgeous, is it not?" Rollan commented at my surprise. "I only came out this way a few time before, once during training. The canvas of the land here always leaves me awestruck."

The beauty of the borderlands were like nothing I'd ever seen in real life. The scene reminded me of a picturesque snapshot, heavily photo shopped for the purpose of posting on social media. An ideal place that only sort of existed to inspire millions with beauty and maybe jealousy. An unattainable place. Everything on those platforms were geared to make others guilty of envy or desire. I really hadn't missed it, or thought about it much since coming to Vale. Probably because I didn't really use it much. Outcast me had little need for social media since I had no social life outside of Q.

I had, at one point, signed up for a few of the platforms. My lesson was learned quickly, though, with an onslaught of hurtful comments. My profiles were deleted faster than they were made and I hadn't looked back aside from watching funny videos or looking at witty memes Q had to share with me.

Half a mile before us lay an impressively tall cliff face, its top dusted with remnants of winter. A waterfall tumbled over a sliver of the gray stone face, splashing over boulders that jutted from the rocky face and down into a large river that ran westward. The water itself sparkled in a rainbow of colors as it fell to earth.

The fantasy came full circle with the stone and wood cottage complete with a waterwheel sitting on the edge of the river, a few hundred feet from where the waterfall met it. The chimney wafted a thin stream of smoke into the air. A simple garden rose feet away from the river bank, accompanied by a small chicken coop. A small stable sat some yards away from the garden and coop. Soft animal sounds carried on the wind from the stable and coop. Eisele at least had animals for company out here.

One lone, massive oak tree offered the cabin some shade when the cliff didn't. The look of the whole place contrasted with the soft candy colored homes and buildings that surrounded the villa miles and miles away. Simpler and rustic, straight out of a fairy tale. "I'd live here, no bribe needed," I commented.

If this was where Eisele had been exiled, I didn't feel that bad for her in that matter. Not a bad place to be exiled in my opinion. I pulled out Lin's map to confirm my guess. I eyed the beacon flashing on the map. It too sat right where a river met the mountains, a key symbol for a waterfall in the right spot. Yes, this was where Eisele would be found. "Looks like we found what we're looking for."

"Not a moment too soon," Rollan commented on the slowly setting sun. "We could camp, if need be, but when the opportunity for a real roof presents itself camping does not seem appealing. Not to me anyways."

"Yet, you were ready to go camping with Q just hours ago."

"Well...," he winked rather than finishing his statement. I understood that on a whole level of my being. I liked having a roof over my head that I could count on.

My gaze went back to the cabin in the distance, and excitement tingled over my skin. Answers and possible help sat within reach for real this time. I just hoped she would be willing to talk to me.

Suddenly, worry crept in to the excitement I felt. What if she didn't want to talk to me? What if she saw Rollan's uniform and clammed up? I could see that happening, especially if people tended to leave her alone. Usually, there wouldn't be a reason for someone from the villa to pay her a visit unless she was in trouble.

"Uh, Rollan, did you happen to bring any non-uniform clothes with you?" I asked without taking my gaze off of the cabin.

"No. I assumed I would be on duty the whole trip. Why?"

Explaining my theory, I slid off Zenobi and got into my travel bag. I hoped I'd packed a shirt he could wear with his uniform pants. That it would be enough to ease Eisele's mind when we approached her door. All of the tunics I packed were too small for his tall frame, but I happened on one of the shirts I brought back from Reta; an over sized t-shirt with a skull and flowers on it that I'd tie-dyed one boring afternoon. Technically it was the shirt I'd planned on using for bed. I figured it better than nothing. "Change into this, and pack up any uniform items you can."

He looked at the swirling pink, purple, and blue pattern on the shirt like I'd asked him to go naked. "Interesting," he dismounted his horse and did as asked despite being unsure of the fashion choice. There wasn't much else we could do to not arouse Eisele's suspicion. I didn't even know if it'd work. For all I knew, she watched us from the window of her cabin laughing at our feeble attempt to appear as ordinary travelers. As ordinary as someone in Vale wearing tie-dye could be.

When he got back on Fehr, he looked out of place. A little silly even. His stiff and disciplined posture contrasted with the swirling colors of the t-shirt, which barely contained his arm muscles. He looked nearly cartoonish. I couldn't help but giggle.

"No laughing. This," he gestured to his torso, "is your doing."

"It's a good look for you," I snickered one final time.

"Damn right it is, I make everything look good," he pretended to preen. He really was perfect for Q. They'd make a dashing and deservedly vain pair. "Are you ready, Princess?" he nodded towards the cabin.

"No, and yes," I let out a breath that vibrated my lips. It was a strange sensation, being ready and not at the same time. "No point letting my nerves stop what needs to be done, right?"

"Right, and if she does not like me for my job it will not matter. You will charm her like everyone else."

"Except Drem."

"That man has no taste," he laughed. "Well, good taste in some women, but we will not even address that. Come on, time to go." He was right, I didn't even want to think about him and Neala. My mother had to be the most incredible woman I'd met, ever. Any man would have had to been a fool to not be snared by her charms.

The half-mile ride to the river's edge passed in no time. Too soon for my growing anxiety, which triggered all my old insecurities to surface too. Anxiety did that, no matter how well I knew otherwise. No matter how well life went. One thing, seemingly completely unrelated to past worries, brought everything back. They'd haunt me forever, as would having people taken from me.

Rollan hitched the horses to the tree next to the garden and helped me down from Zenobi. Normally, I wouldn't accept the help, being too stubborn for my own good. My legs were weak enough from a long day of riding, add in the butterflies storming in my belly, I knew trying to wouldn't be pretty. I wanted to make a good impression on Eisele. I couldn't do that limping from falling off a horse; again.

Up close the cabin looked even more picturesque. Planter boxes lined the front and hung under windows, each one brimming with gorgeous combinations of flowers; cataseta orchids, midnight hyacinth, purple pansies, pink dahlias, and white lilies. Rows of black cherry and white sunflowers grew high along the path to the door. A simple wind chime hung from the eaves, its soft music blended with the roar of the waterfall and the scent of wet earth to create a peaceful feeling. On the front door hung, over a door knocker, a dried bunch of lavender and eucalyptus. From all appearances of her home, Eisele lived in peace.

With a shaky hand, I used the bird shaped knocker to knock on the simple wooden door and waited. With every second that passed, I prayed harder and harder that this would be everything I hoped for. A place with answers. It wasn't long before I heard feet coming up on the other side of the door. The door handle creaked and my breath hitched with anticipation.

When the door finally opened, there stood a middle aged woman with short dark hair in pin curls. She wore a simple white tunic tucked into black wide legged, high waisted trousers. My jaw dropped when I first saw her, not because she was younger than I anticipated. I thought for sure she'd be much older than Drem, since he had been her assistant. To my surprise there, she seemed younger, but not by much. Her large blue eyes were what caught my attention, though. They were the spitting image of Drem's.

I looked to Rollan who was just as shocked as me, then back to the woman. Swallowing hard to compose myself, I finally managed to stammer, "Eisele?"

She looked between Rollan and myself a few times and jut out her hip as she rested her hand on it, "Oh Hell, what has my brother done now?"

FORTY-FOUR

FINALLY, SOMEONE HAS ANSWERS

"Brother?" we asked at the same time, completely shocked by her candor.

"Well, yes. My brother, the almighty Drem," sarcasm dripped from her lips in almost the same slow speech her brother used. She knew we were there about Drem, which weirded me out even more than her similarity to him. But how?

"What makes you say we're here because of Drem?"

The corner of her mouth twitched with amusement. "Not an ally of his then?" she questioned while looking between Rollan and I. "For starters, the two of you are from the royal villa. Those horses you tied under my tree are royal bloodline horses. This one here," she gestured to Rollan, "despite his strange shirt, wears the pants of a guard's uniform. He carries himself like one too. And you, well you look like Queen Neala; although I thought her daughter long dead. She may have had another, that aged rather quickly. Unlikely, but possible."

"No, I'm the long not-so-dead kid." I replied quickly, which made her rub her chin in interest.

"Second," she continued without missing a beat, "the only time anyone looks at a stranger with such abject horror and trepidation is when they're extremely offended, or that person looks like someone who has wronged them. I bear an unfortunate resemblance to my brother, and I know he has bound to hurt some of Vale and the villa just by his cruel nature."

"She is good," Rollan half-whispered to me.

"Not as good as you think," regret sat in her voice. Did it come from her failure with King Tor? "I also know no one would come here for me unless it had to do with him. That is how it worked back then too. Drem screws up and I am asked how to fix it. There was this one time when he turned Neala's skin green trying to impress her with some unpracticed spell. As punishment, I turned his skin green for a month. Did not teach him a damn thing though." I stifled a snicker at the thought of Drem, sulking about like a wicked witch, greener than Chicago on St. Patrick's Day.

"Well, I am done fixing his messes. It is not my job anymore." She began to close the door on us, we were losing her.

I had to think fast. What would change her mind? The conversation rewound in my head and settled on the regret that laced her words earlier. Regret likely tied to King Tor, and maybe Neala.

"He's got his hooks in my mother!" I blurted in hopes I was right about her regret.

The door began to slowly creak back open. Eisele stuck her head out, the alarm on her face didn't lie. I'd been right. "What do you mean?"

"Let us in, and Princess Elloe will tell you everything," Rollan stepped in when I froze. I didn't just want to blurt everything else while standing on her porch. I needed to lay it all out slowly, thoughtfully. There wasn't a detail I wanted to leave out. Every little bit would help my cause.

Without another word, she let us in.

In the entrance to her cabin we were immediately enveloped in the heady aroma of flowers and greenery. A few steps in and I could see why. Her home, much like Drem's lair, had hardly any space that hadn't been decorated with live plants. Many I recognized from both

Reta and Vale. Some I did not. A love of flora must've also ran in the family, aside from the use of it in their lives.

She led us to a small sitting area with two chairs and a cushioned bench seat under a window lined with fern-like plants with dripping purple and yellow flowers. In the corner next to the window sat a large brass cage containing a pair of white birds with long pale blue tail feathers and blue crests. They chirped excitedly as Eisele passed the cage.

"Those are beautiful birds," Rollan mentioned. He took a seat on the bench next to the cage. "Valian long-tail doves?"

"They are, they were a gift from Queen Neala, to keep me company." It seemed strange Neala would've given Eisele a gift like that when Lin mentioned she had yet to forgive the woman for King Tor's death. I filed it away as something to ask about later. Eisele settled in one of the chairs, "Now, tell me what, precisely, brings you here."

I dove in to my tale. I told it as I knew it, beginning with being found in the streets. I didn't leave out any detail that pertained to the situation at hand. Her interest peaked when I spoke of my time at The Kendrick Institute and Abe. When the tale jumped from Reta to Vale, I decided to skim over most of it to focus on when I got memories back. To realizing it was Drem behind it all, including King Carradoc's death.

Eisele squirmed in her seat, her gaze looking distant then. I didn't have to be a mind reader to know her mind went straight to the death of King Tor. That she compared it to what happened to Carradoc. She didn't remain in her head long, and her attention came back to me.

I continued with Neala's strange behaviors since my father's death. How Drem brainwashed her to gain her adoration. How the longer she remained under his spell, the stranger she acted. Finally, I finished with Daric's arrest, another of Drem's schemes to alienate me so I'd have no one left. That I suspected he wanted to take all my allies from me so I would leave. So there wouldn't be anyone else to take an ounce of Neala's love from him.

When I finished, Eisele fell back in her seat and rested her cheek on her open palm. Defeat featured heavily on her face, aging her years in an instant. "I am so sorry. This is all my fault, following my hubris and thinking I could cure King Tor. If I had not been so hot headed about it, mistakes would not have been made. Drem never would have gotten a position of power that allowed all this heartache to happen. I just assumed that since the test of the healing fire on myself went fine..."

"You tested it?" I interrupted, getting a nod in response. "On yourself?"

"Every new batch, just for safety not for practical use. I may be good, but I lack the complete bovarism of my brother."

"Bovarism?" I wasn't sure what the word meant. For all I knew, she just called Drem a cow.

"Over-inflated sense of self," she explained. "Anyway, I was confident in the new potion's ability to lessen his pain. That final batch I made seemed foolproof."

This revelation went hand in hand with the suspicions that grew in my mind when I first read the treatment log. The possibility that Drem had been playing the game longer than anyone thought. "What if it wasn't your fault?"

"Princess Elloe, you are sweet to think so. It was my fault."

"Then answer me this, Eisele," I sat forward in my seat, "if the last test of your treatment for King Tor didn't hurt you, but burned him from the inside out, doesn't that raise suspicion in your mind? Especially since you were not the one to administer it to him?"

"Side effects are different for different people."

"Not that different, especially when they'd all worked fine before. With that being said, answer me one more thing. Did Drem have any reason to seek revenge on King Tor then?"

"Not King Tor. He always had it in for Carradoc, because of your mother. He did not think it right, someone so low on the ladder, a philosopher's son, had been granted the Princess's hand.

Drem crushed on Neala since day one, and she was so sweet to him when many were not. His natural magic is very weak you know, pretty much non-existent. What he could do all came from potions and gifted magic. Others saw him as less than whole life because of it, tormented him. I think it was pity on my part that made him my assistant over Abban."

I logged what she said away as useful. I knew before that Drem relied heavily on potions. What I didn't know was his powers were entirely artificial. He took from others or made potions for temporary gifts. That's how he'd been able to throw fireballs all those years ago. How his shadow stole into my room. He'd stand no chance if those were taken away.

"You do not think he would have seen it differently? That the problem was in King Tor's granting of their relationship on some level?" Rollan made my next point for me. I pointed at him in agreement.

Eisele stood and began to pace, fighting against the truths we laid before her. She didn't want it to be true. No one wanted to believe a family member could do such a thing on purpose. She'd rather she were the accidental monster than her brother be one for real. It was a harsh reality she had to come to face if we were to gain her help. She needed to accept her brother's crimes began under her watch before this went any further.

"Damn him," she stopped her pacing and slammed her fists onto the wall. The impact sent a wave of energy rippling out, rustling the leaves and petals of her plants. The pair of doves squawked nervously. "If I knew then, if my grief had not blinded me, I never would have left. I could kill that bastard." She sat with a huff, her perfectly coiffed pin curls mussed and eyes blazing.

"I thought you were exiled?" Rollan asked hesitantly. Her accidental display of power had him intimidated. Me too.

"That is the official story," she smoothed her hair, composing herself. "In reality I chose to leave. The exile, the map and tracker are all fake. A show put on by Neala to cover my leaving. Which I should not have done. I should have given myself time to grieve properly and look into the matter further. Dammit," she cursed again. She was being entirely too hard on herself.

"We all want to see the best in our families. I can't blame you for missing it then. But now, you can do something about it. You can help me stop him."

She set her mouth in a hard line, looking stern and resolute, "If I do this, I have a stipulation. Killing Drem is a last resort." I nodded in agreement there. I hated the man. Everything about him was dangerous. That being said, I couldn't kill him. I'm no killer. "Also, there needs to be more than the three of us. Drem may not be powerful, but he's clever enough."

"We have people in the villa we can trust, other guards and staff," Rollan offered. My brain ticked the boxes on who I knew them to be; Karrah, Veena, Lin, maybe Genasia. Daric. He might have been locked up, but if I could get him out, he was my number one. The Riker to my Picard. Yet, I felt like another one was needed. Someone smart with a mind for potions. Someone trained, sort of, by another great potions maker. Trained by Abe, who would have been a no-brainer as an ally if he weren't dead.

"There's someone else we need," I turned to Rollan, about to make his day while giving us a great asset. "How would you like to take a little trip to Reta?"

"Q?" Rollan's eyes lit with excitement with my promise already coming to fruition.

"Yup, Q."

"Who is this Q?" Eisele asked, curious at the excitement his name conjured.

I smiled at Eisele, knowing how much she'd like him. How much he'd like her. "Eisele, Q is a genius, who happens to have access to Abban. Well, Abban's mind anyway."

Her interest was piqued.

FORTY-FIVE

A PLAGUE ON DREAMS

THE PROBLEM with wanting to recruit Q presented itself shortly after the idea formed. We couldn't exactly portal there without alerting others a portal had been opened. Since we weren't scheduled back for some time yet, and we'd already pretended to portal there, we couldn't risk it.

Neither did we have the means to contact him to let him know we needed him. The D.C. only made calls from Reta. We really needed him.

Eisele had excused herself to tend to her animals, offering to stable our horses as well, while Rollan and I debated the best way to get Q there inconspicuously.

"If only there was a way to get this damn thing to work," I tossed the Q's communicator onto Eisele's empty chair in frustration. Q's natural take to potions magic irritated me even more. My magic refused to present itself no matter how hard I tried, and he mastered potions from the get go. Then again, Q seemed to be a natural at everything.

"What is that?" Eisele returned just in time to see the device fly into the seat. She picked it up, turning it over and over in her fingers.

"Q made it. It's a cell phone, a device used to talk to people that aren't with you. They're pretty much a necessity on Reta. Anyways, Q worked some miracle on this one and another one he has. They're connected, so we can stay in touch. Problem is it's a one way thing. I can get calls, but can't make them."

"Now we are at an impasse on acquiring Q to our cause," Rollan added with a pout.

"Interesting, indeed," our hostess assessed. "How about I give it an overhaul, see what I can add to it?" I had no problem with it, and told her so. If anyone could get it working, I'd be grateful. Though, I didn't hold out much hope. "Also, I may be able to help get him here secretly, if that's what you are wanting to do."

"How?" I was curious how she thought she could.

"I happen to be a master alchemist. One of the potions I've created makes untraceable portals. How else do you think I get my supplies?"

"But you said the tracker was fake."

"It is, but portals are tracked as you know. I could not get around to get what I needed if I used them. So I developed something more discreet. I can portal anywhere I like, and do."

"Other worlds?" I motioned to a plant she had hanging near the entryway, what appeared to be a large, pink opalescent paddle succulent with dripping string of pearls succulents hanging below. It made me think of jellyfish. I'd never seen a plant like it before, and I was pretty sure I'd seen everything in Drem's lair.

She followed my gaze, then turned back with a chuckle on her lips. "You are clever. No wonder Drem despises you. Yes, I go to other realms. I would go mad with boredom if I did not. You see, I had the option of having supplies brought to me. I declined, to avoid cabin fever. Then I came up with my portals."

Her revelation sounded too goo to be true, but amazing. "If you really can, we can travel to the portal site in the morning."

"Did I fail to mention, I can portal anywhere from right here? I am sure I said something to that matter. You just need to know exactly where you want it to open."

I wondered why she stayed in her self imposed exile. She had no one checking on her, a tracker that didn't track, and the ability to go anywhere at a moments notice. If I were in her shoes, the world would be my oyster. All the worlds would be. I wouldn't sit on my laurels in the middle of nowhere, no matter how beautiful the scenery. I'd see everything I ever wanted and then some.

A life like that sounded like a pretty good alternative to what I'd face if I couldn't stop Drem. I wondered how hard it would be to get her to supply me with some if that happened.

"It's settled then. We get Q in the morning, then we get to work."

"We should call it a night, then," Rollan advised. "Despite not needing to travel more, I am sure our day will be busy." We left Eisele to her own preparations for the morning and returned outside to set up our tents. Eisele's cabin was so small, we didn't want to take up what little precious space she had between all her flora and belongings, even though we'd much rather have a roof over our heads.

I tried my best to assist Rollan in setting up. Because of my avoidance of camping in my past, I had no clue what to do or how to do it. Leaving Rollan with the lion's share of the work made me feel bad. He insisted he didn't mind, it was part of his job. I felt differently. I was just happy I'd be able to make it up to him for the lies earlier and connect him with Q in the morning.

A sense of satisfaction fell over me while I watched Rollan erect our tents. Things finally felt like they were falling into place. The shaky ground beneath me had finally calmed enough for me to make real progress. I thought a lot about how much Eisele was going to help us, thankful that she turned out willing to help us. That she wasn't like her brother.

Their relation still had me in shaken disbelief. They were so different in personality that if they weren't so similar looking I'd swear they weren't really related. Despite her younger appearance, Eisele actually was the older sibling, but only by a few minutes. They were twins. Yet, she had all the power between them. Not to mention real imagination when it came to potions.

Her untraceable portal had already given me ideas for immediate use. Namely, getting Daric back; as well as nabbing ourselves a few allies. I needed Q to make more devices for that though. If I thought making multiple trips into the villa would be safe, I'd have asked to go get Daric first. Immediately.

I stayed lost in thought, planning out who we'd recruit once we were ready to, until Rollan finished with the tents. We made short work of getting our things ready for the night after that.

WITH EISELE on our side and a plan to get Q, I should have had a peaceful night. The foundation for the fight against Drem had been lain after all. Instead, I tossed and turned through nightmare plagued sleep. Dreams worse than the ones that haunted me for so many years, likely brought on by the whole Drem situation and my irrational anxiety about camping.

The dream started out at Eisele's. She and I sat in her sitting room with Rollan and Q. Sunlight glittered through the windows, bringing with it warmth and hope. We chatted happily over tea, her birds sang and wind chimes tinkled in the background. The next minute, the warmth in the room got sucked away, and a shroud of darkness descended on the cabin. The sudden stormy weather set my teeth on edge. Gray clouds hid the sun. Lightning flashed dangerously close, its crack married to the thunder rumbling in the sky. The clouds began to seep in through the cracks of the cabin. They snaked closer and closer until they descended on out small group. The dark tentacles of atmosphere wrapped around my companions hungrily. They all screamed and writhed in pain until the clouds enveloped them completely.

Untouched by the malicious clouds, I jumped to my feet, ready to save them. I plowed through the clouds to get to my friends, but they weren't there. They'd been swallowed whole by whatever unseen thing lived in them.

The clouds began to dissipate once their prey vanished, seeping back through cracks and crevices to the outside. Even though I knew it would be useless, I attempted to give chase. I needed my friends back. I wouldn't let them be taken so easily. As I opened the door to follow, the ground opened up in a massive sink hole that swallowed everything within thirty feet of Eisele's cabin. Everything she held dear gone in moments. I tumbled with the falling ground, the great gaping hole gobbling me with the ground and plants. I fell for what seemed a lifetime before it spat me out in the middle of Neala's garden.

I stood, realizing I wore the charcoal dress I'd worn to that last dinner with Daric and my mother, only it no longer had the sea green sash I'd altered it with. The sash had been replaced by fraying ropes blotted with black ink.

The garden sparkled with tiny floating lights, just like the ones from my memory under the flowering tree. They danced to the airy music around the flower beds and over the statue that sat in the middle. Unlike my memory, the lights felt off. They weren't natural. Beautiful, yes, but unsettling. Whenever they neared me, I shied away from their unnaturalness. Something told me if they touched me, it would not be pleasant.

Mingling amongst the strange, eerie beauty were dozens of people, all dressed in finery befitting a royal party. I pushed my way through the swaying crowd, searching for anyone I recognized. As the bodies thinned, I could make out some familiar faces at the back of the garden. Everyone was there; Daric, Rollan, Eisele, Veena, Lin, and even Q and his parents. They flanked the sides of a bride and groom.

My stomach fell instantly because I knew who that bride and groom were. Drem and Neala. To make matters worse, my friends, my allies, all stood by watching the wedding with empty, adoring eyes. My mother wore the same dress and accessories from the dinner as well, paired with a long veil of lace finer than spider silk. On closer inspection the veil wasn't what it seemed. It connected to strings that led to Drem. He was the puppet master of the night.

I began to backpedal from the sight, the worst thing imaginable. Drem had gotten to them all. They were all under his influence, and I was alone.

I stumbled through the wedding guests, their faces began to blur into greasy smudges. As I went, their hands grabbed at me. They tried to prevent me from leaving. Every hand that landed on me left hideous bruises, no matter how briefly or light the touch.

I almost made it to the garden entrance when arms wrapped around me and held me against my will. As whoever held me began dragging me back to the wedding. I flailed against my captor with all my might. I caught a brief glimpse of them over my shoulder, horrified and heartbroken and the discovery. Daric.

The dream ended.

When I woke from that dream, I felt a sword hanging over my head. The loneliness from it lingered heavily on my soul. It was my worst fear, being alone and abandoned by the ones I loved. In my dream, Drem had figured out how to make that happen. I wouldn't put it past him to try in real life. It would be the only way I'd ever stop fighting him. The only way he'd ever truly win.

FORTY-SIX

RECRUITING Q

My nightmare clung to me, leaving me unfocused and anxious. Rattled to say the least. I dragged ass getting up and ready, even with the promise of seeing Q soon. There was so much to catch him up on. Knowing I'd have to rehash the past week with him to do that, swirled my emotions. The two were not a good combination.

Eisele and Rollan were a flurry of activity, more than making up for my lack of motivation. My guard, and friend, broke down the tents to not damage the grass surrounding Eisele's home. Eisele, already looking picture perfect, bustled about the garden gathering ingredients both for breakfast and for her invisible portal potion. I watched her from a distance, trying to decipher what she harvested as she went. Trying to logically guess which ingredient would be used for what. I wanted to know how to create this portal for myself, even if I completely sucked at potions and magic.

"For a Princess with gumption, you do not seem very motivated this morning," Eisele commented without pulling her attention from her task. "Interested in what I am doing, but not enough to come closer." Her hands plunged back down toward the dirt and came up with some leafy greens. Breakfast, for sure. In all my studying I never saw any potion with greens as an ingredient. I could still be wrong. This was Eisele, after all. She claimed her potions were secret to her. Unique. There could be anything in it, she seemed the think out of the box type.

Feeling called out, I hauled myself up and trudged over to the garden. Immediately the older woman shoved her hand basket into my hands, "Be useful, girl, and ask your questions. How can you expect to learn anything if you do not speak up?"

I cracked a half smile, her teaching style already proved different, and much better, than her brother's. He was entirely in control and didn't like questions at all. "Would you be willing to help me with something else while we're getting our heads together?"

"You mean help you with your defunct magic?"

I was taken aback by her astute observation yet again. She had the knack for seeing more than she was told, even though she wasn't psychic. "Uh, yeah. How did you know that?"

She rolled her large blue eyes, sending a shudder down my spine. God, she looked nearly identical to Drem sometimes. "I was not born yesterday. Trauma, plus early portal travel, compounded by years of being away from Vale. Naturally your magic would be in a shambolic state. Did my brother not tell you this or offer any sort of crash course in magic?"

It was my turn to roll my eyes. "Really? Drem offer me real help? His theory was firmly on the *I had to remember everything on my own* side. No help unless it came from him in potion form. That went over real well." My empty stomach curdled at the memory of the garbage smelling potion he forced me to drink.

"How counter-productive," she grimaced as she put another handful of herbs into the basket. "Well, I have all I need now. Shall we?" she motioned to the cabin. She didn't have to ask me twice. We wiped the dirt from our hands and went inside to wash up.

Eisele, being nearly as bossy and secretive as her brother, ordered Rollan to prepare breakfast while she put together the potion. She wouldn't let me watch her do that, keeping her unique magic to herself. No matter how much I wanted to observe and learn, I didn't blame her. She did, however, promise to help me with my own magic. When we got back.

Rollan tried his best in her kitchen. Following the simple veggie quiche recipe Eisele left for him, which did not include the greens she pulled from the garden, he managed to make something edible-ish. It wasn't pretty, and came out rather lumpy with a few egg shells in it, but it tasted all right. He did good considering he probably never cooked before in his life.

I offered to help early on, but he sent me away. A wise decision considering all my cooking ventures were near nuclear disasters. Much worse than his attempt at breakfast for sure. My cooking skills lacked the talent to satisfy my love of food. Seriously, I'd been known to burn water. I'd starve if left to my own devices.

After our breakfast, we gathered in the sitting area again, "Elle," she easily adapted to using the name I asked her to, dropping all formality. A fact that made me like her more. "You will be in charge of our portal to Reta. I will control our return. When taking the potion, visualize where exactly you want it to open to. You must be very focused, or you could go wherever your mind wanders." She handed me the vial of fresh potion, still warm from being made. It wasn't all that different in appearance to Abe's silvery blue concoction that sent me to Vale. The only difference being her silvery-blue potion sparkled inside the thin glass tube it sat in, and it appeared thicker.

"Got it. Drink and focus." The instructions were easy enough.

Eisele nodded once, "Rollan and I will hold onto your hands as we pass through. This is the biggest difference between a regular portal and mine. It will only let through the one who drinks it, and those in contact with them. Whereas a regular one stays open long enough for several to go through unassisted. Understand?" she looked at the pair of us, and we nodded in response. "Good. Now, get on with it. I want to be home in time for tea."

Standing, Rollan gripped my right hand and Eisele my left wrist, leaving my hand free to drink the potion. I popped the tiny stopper, getting a whiff of gingerbread as I did. The potion tasted just like it smelled this time, but was unpleasantly thick. I didn't complain though. What was a few moments of unpleasantness when the steps you took led to accomplishing your goals?

No portal opened. Instead, my skin began tingling moments before we were suddenly whisked away from Eisele's cabin and found ourselves stumbling in the middle of the Queen family's guest room. Rollan landed too close to the bed and ended up falling backwards onto it. His hands flailed wildly as he went, knocking over a lamp in the process. It reminded me of teleporting in a science fiction show, only less gracefully.

"Whoops," I grimaced. "Not where I meant to land."

"You let yourself be distracted?" Eisele accused, throwing her hands in the air.

"Only a little bit. We're still in the right place, just not at the front door." When I thought of Q's home, my mind wandered to staying in their guest room with Daric. It had been the first night we spent together without worry of getting into trouble. Nothing had happened, other than some great kissing, still it made an impression. I couldn't help it, or the warmth that spread across my cheeks at the memory.

The door burst open with a high pitched screeching cry. Janice armed with a pink flower fly swatter jumped into the room, with Q on her heels. Her screech morphed into fits of laughter when she recognized me, "Oh, it's you!" she giggled in relief.

Q skipped around his mother, who turned and went back to whatever she'd been doing before we crashed in. She wasn't worried about my sudden presence anymore, not caring I'd popped out of nowhere with two strangers. Q swooped me into his arms, "Damn girl, you could've warned us you were coming. Scared the living shit out of Ma."

"I can't, remember. Your device is a little faulty."

"Oh yeah, I guess you're forgiven then," his gaze fell on Rollan.

"And you brought me a gift!" he exclaimed as a flirty look took over his face. He swooped his silvery gray and hot pink hair from his eyes, "Hey, Rollan," he ticked his head up and offered a devilish smirk. The guard, blushing furiously, managed a little hello in return

"This is your genius?" Eisele eyeballed Q in his black sweat pants, baby pink muscle shirt, and matching nails.

"Who's this?" Q eyeballed her in return, looking both impressed and appalled. Eisele had dressed smartly in her dark harem pants and beaded tunic, a look Q approved of apparently. His hesitation, I assumed, came from her similarity to her brother.

"I am Eisele, and I will be the judge of your genius. Elle believes you vital to our mission, so we are here."

"She is Lord Drem's sister, former adviser of Vale, and one of us," Rollan filled in the blanks of Eisele's identity. "You look good, Q." The men both blushed at each other, Eisele mocked the display; her eyes rolling.

"So where's Officer Man Candy?" he asked after Daric, using his favorite nickname for my hunky boyfriend. "He's usually glued to your side." His question brought tears to my eyes, "Is everything okay?"

"Daric's been arrested," I choked back a sob.

"What!" I gave Q a quick, annotated version of recent events, ending with our coming to him for help. He didn't even wait a beat after I finished to respond. "I'm in. You guys hang tight. I'm going to fill Ma in and pack up. Want me to bring Abe's stuff too?"

Bringing up Abe made me think we were still missing something in our team. The four of us could probably handle Drem on our own, especially with Eisele. Her magic and intuition were so strong. Stronger than I'd seen in anyone so far. That wouldn't be enough, though. We didn't have any clue what was happening in the villa, or the village outside of it. We needed eyes and ears in both.

"Definitely, and some of those old phones you keep lying around. I think we're going to need them if we can work out the bugs with mine." At the last minute, I added, "Grab your camp stuff too."

"I thought you said this Q person knows Abban?" Eisele asked once Q left.

"He did. Abe is, was Abban." I gave her an annotated version of how Q had been trained in potion making by Abban's ghost, leading him to be able to go to Vale and see me.

"That man, he was a genius. An innovator of magic, like me. Too bad he is gone. He would have been a wonderful ally to have." There was a note of grief in her voice as she reminisced on Abe. Either she admired him a great deal, or she loved him deeply. Perhaps both. She wouldn't offer any more information when I prodded her though. Eisele was right, he would have been the best ally to have at the moment.

"At least we have Q," I reassured her. "He has Abban's notebooks he kept in his hideout at the institute. They haven't led Q astray yet, as far as I know."

"I hope he is as good as you think, that is all I am saying," she eyeballed me. I chilled under the glare. No matter how nice she was, her resemblance to Drem made me uneasy from time to time. With time, I imagined, that would change.

Q returned a few minutes later, toting the box of books and powders Abe left to him, and a fully supplied camping backpack. Unlike me, Q loved camping. As far as I could tell, he always had his gear ready to go.

FORTY-SEVEN

A CASE OF MAGIC BLOCK

"TRY HARDER." Eisele commanded harshly, thwacking her palm with a switch she'd plucked from her tree. I flinched every time the twig snapped against her palm. At least she didn't turn it on me. The way she moved and spoke were nearly frightening. If I didn't know she stood on our side, I would've been.

"I'm trying! What does it look like I'm doing?" we'd been at it for hours. She had me trying to conjure the firefly lights since that was the only magic I could remember doing before. According to her, the spell could be done by novices within an hour of practice. I'd yet to produce a tiny flicker. My frustration grew with every critical prod from my teacher.

I threw myself down on the lawn in protesting mental exhaustion. The wind tousled the tree top, the rustling seemed to taunt me. "I'm never going to be able to do this. Maybe Drem stole my magic," I scoffed in jest, not really meaning it but using it as an excuse for my failure.

Eisele let out a pregnant breath, "Well..."

"You don't think?" the idea was horrifying and plausible as far as I knew. I still didn't know fully what happened to me the night I was abducted.

She settled next to me, running her long fingers through the grass and producing tiny butterflies as she did. Show off. Her skill with magic was alchemy, but she also had some nature conjuring ability. She was rare. "No, Drem could not have taken your powers. They were not fully developed. He despised children, said their powers were useless until they came of age."

"Are they?"

"Sometimes," she wryly chuckled. "There are some that are formidable even in youth."

"Like you?"

"Yes. Like me. Like Abban. Like your friend Q would have been if his magic were not so diluted through generations. What he can do is impressive for one from Reta."

"Please don't tell him that. I don't think his head needs to get any bigger right now." I gazed across the open land that surrounded Eisele's home to watch Q and Rollan spar at the water's edge. Q's ego had definitely gotten a boost being near the cute guard, all the attention and compliments of flirting always had that affect on him.

"Anyway, on the lines of Drem taking powers. I think there is a chance your powers could have been blocked, and need to be unblocked slowly. If I am right, your powers have grown as they would have normally. With them being blocked, that is years of bottled up magic dying to come out. If it all came out at once, it could be bad." She paused, looking up into the tree as if what she wanted to say were up there. "Do you... can you think of anything that happened the night of your abduction that might have been done to block your powers?"

I didn't remember much from that night yet. Mainly the events leading up to being shoved through a portal to Reta. Everything else I knew came second hand. Closing my eyes, I let my thoughts wander to that afternoon under the blooming tree with Daric, and what he told me happened. Rather than immediately sharing his words with Eisele, I tried to visualize them.

I blank the landscape of my mind lightened and glazed over. As the glaze cleared, revealing a clear image of a young Daric's laughing green eyes, I felt that long gone familiar pull of hallucination. Instinctually, I shied away and Daric began to evaporate. I steeled myself with a deep breath through my nose and slowly released it through my mouth, and fought the revulsion trying to take over.

Slowly he reappeared in absolute clarity, down to the freckles playing across his cheeks and nose. I felt the tingle of a first kiss lingering on my lips, the flush of my cheeks. My fingers laced into his, familiar yet new and unmarred from years of toiling work. Excitement built into a torrent of butterflies as we both leaned in for another.

A hand grasped my shoulder and yanked me backwards. My field of vision shifted from the eager, smiling face of my friend to a flustered, sad eyed Abe. His mouth contorted in wordless shouts, making me realize the memory had no sound. I didn't fully remember yet. Daric's retelling still drove it.

In moments, Abe dragged me to my feet and out of the domed tree. My feet stumbled along the dirt path as be pulled me. My steps faltered, often, making me fall only to be pulled back up. Blood trickled from the subsequent scrapes. Finally at the villa wall Abe stopped, but didn't relinquish his hold on me. If he had, I would have ran right to my parents.

Using all of my child-sized strength, I flailed against his grip. I sensed his actions were about more than catching me kissing Daric. The need to flee paused briefly when Abe turned his face to me. Pain etched itself deep in every pore of his skin and tears were streaming down his cheeks. Again, his mouth moved wordlessly, too fast for me to even attempt to read his lips. He reached into his sweater pocket and pulled out a vial of clear liquid.

My sympathy only lasted a moment longer, before instinct set in. I knew the only clear potion was a sleeping potion. He intended to knock me out. He drew me in closer, trapping my arms with one of his so I couldn't fight. It wasn't long before I felt the potion running onto my face. Immediately I knew something else had been added to it. It smelled wrong. Felt wrong. My body grew tired and heavy, just like the potion design intended. But, everything felt tingly and cold. That wasn't right.

My vision went blank. I opened my eyes, back in Eisele's little world. "Abe altered the sleeping potion. It made me cold and tingle all over." I shuddered on the warm grass, feeling the effects of the potion lingering over me.

Eisele's hand rubbed my back, drawing my focus to her. Her eyes startled me. Seeing sympathy and caring in those familiar eyes somehow changed her. Made her separate from Drem. "I am sorry, truly. Abban did block your magic, using a potion I created and had notes on. Notes I was forced to leave behind."

"So, I'm screwed," I fell back into the grass with a huff. Just like that, I became useless in the fight against Drem. I'd have to rely on everyone else to do all the work. Be the damsel in distress. The idea festered in my bones.

I stared beyond the leaves, turning them into unfocused blobs of color. Why was it my luck to have all these obstacles in my way? Obstacles that were not of my own creation kept coming at me, keeping me from being whole. I felt destined to always be incomplete.

Eisele's face interrupted the sea of leaves and sky above me, ego filtering into her face. "I would not say that. It is my potion after all. Of course I know how to remove the effects."

I bolted upright, "Really? Let's do it!"

"It takes time. Like I said, getting your magic back all at once would be detrimental. Even if I reverse it today, it could be days or weeks before you see the first sign of it. Understand?"

I nodded eagerly. My magic coming back meant everything. I didn't like it would take a while, but better slow than not at all. The sooner we got to it, the sooner the magic would trickle in. "Let's get to it then."

"I have to make the potion. This one takes some time to become potent after making. Patience." She was talking to the wrong girl if she wanted patience. Seeing how I had no other choice, I'd have to deal.

Eisele promised she'd be ready to help me over the latest magical hurdle in the morning. No surprise there. Every thing she did required the most precise preparations, with every caution taken. I didn't blame her for her anal retentive attention to detail when it came to magic. Not after what happened with King Tor. I'd have been the same way. Those kinds of errors were bitches on the conscience.

I left her to do what she needed without interruption and watched Q and Rollan spar for a little bit before they ended their session. They invited me to go for a swim with them as they cooled down from the workout. I declined and walked along the water until they were finished.

While I walked, I allowed myself to fantasize about what my life would have been like if none of this ever happened. I'd have both parents, magic at my bidding, and every reason to be happy. I'd never have been pushed from home to home, or been an outcast. There wouldn't be this ball of anxiety taking up residence in the center of my being, worrying constantly about saving my mother.

Laughter and splashing drew my attention to Q and Rollan. Suddenly, I realized what I'd be missing if my life had been what I fantasized as perfect. I wouldn't have Q, and there was no guarantee I'd have Daric either. Who knows what would have become of them if I weren't in their lives. They'd have been fine, surely, but I couldn't help but think they'd feel less than complete. Like I did.

My friends didn't swim for long. The moment Q came out of the water I snatched his hand and led him to his tent. We needed to get working on another important aspect of my plan.

"Okay girl, what's the rush?" he asked digging through his bag and coming out with a towel. He draped it over his pink and gray hair as he sat on the sleeping bag, not caring if he got it wet.

"You know the extra phones I asked you to bring?"

"Yeah."

"We're going to need more D.C.s for our spies." He raised a perfectly formed eyebrow with a devious grin. " I want to go to the villa and enlist a few people to keep tabs on things for us," I blurted in my excitement. "Oh and get Daric."

"Obviously. You need your man," he tossed the damp towel at me. "One problemo, they don't work from here."

"Eisele says she can get them to."

"She's scary."

"She also says you have a lot of natural magical talent considering."

"I do like her, though." Flattery got one far with Q. I couldn't help but laugh at his ego, as usual. "I'm guessing you have a time frame in mind?"

"As soon as possible. The longer Neala is with Drem the worse she gets."

We got to work right away with Q doing the heavy lifting and me helping the best I could. Mostly I handed him things he needed. Since he'd brought his supply of powders from Abe, we didn't need to bother Eisele for any of her supplies. We'd only need to pull her from making the block reversal to configure the communicators to fully function in both worlds.

Time flew by as we worked. Before we knew it, night fell. We were far from being finished, and Eisele was still working on her own project. Rollan brought us packets from the provisions Veena packed for us, sparing us from his horrible cooking. He stayed and kept us company for a little while before going to his own tent to sleep. Of all of us, he was the only one keeping a regular schedule, thanks to his years as a guard. He liked the rigidity of that life. The dependability.

It wasn't long, though, before my eyes were too heavy to keep open. I fell asleep curled up on Q's sleeping bag while he worked diligently into the night. When he had a project, he became singularly minded until it was done.

FORTY-EIGHT

JUST CALL ME SECRET SQUIRREL

THE ONE DOWNSIDE to any plan; there had to be a sacrifice. Even if that sacrifice wasn't death, it could be painful. Unfortunately, Q bore the brunt of that. In order to return to the villa without raising suspicions, Rollan would have to return to his normal duties once we arrived. There was no way around it. That way there would be no consequences for Rollan, when Daric and I disappeared back to Eisele's. Once I freed Daric and used the portal, Drem would know something brewed against him. Hopefully he wouldn't figure out what that was.

Needless to say my flamboyant friend felt a little pouty the morning we set to leave back to the villa. Not even assuring him Rollan would be left with one of the communicators cheered him up much.

"Sorry Q, if there was any way to do this without losing Rollan we'd do it. Last thing we need is for Rollan to become a target. He'll be much more useful to us out of lock up, taking the lead for the team in the villa."

"I get it, but I'm not gonna put on a pretty smile just yet."

"On a brighter side, you get to play with Eisele all day. I know you're dying to dig into magic."

"She also needs a few lessons with the communicators. She did a wonder getting them to work, but she's clueless in using them."

"That's why she needs you here. Why I need you here," I jabbed my finger into his shoulder, "and not distracting Rollan." Q's eyes had drifted from me, over my shoulder. I knew what distracted him. A quick peek back confirmed it. Rollan worked hard breaking down his gear for the return trip. I looked back to Q, "Hopefully, everyone will be back together soon."

Q gave in reluctantly, knowing Rollan and I needed to get going. The ride back to the villa took most of the day. Plus we needed to stop and open a portal to match our cover story. I went to check my bag, packed with Rollan's tent and extra supplies, and Zenobi's saddle bag. Eisele provided me with a few small vials of her special portal potion for my return. I'd nestled them into the saddle bag, wrapped protectively in a swath of rabbit skin. Those vials were the only important things I'd packed for the return. Everything else, just for show. Even Rollan didn't fully pack his things up. Daric would need things after his escape. Although, Rollan's clothes would be a bit small for him, they would have to do.

The vials sat secure just where they should in their soft shroud. Satisfied with their safety, I felt ready to get this leg of the mission over with. My only wish; that Eisele's reversal of the block on my magic had already worked. I wanted little more than to be able to feel magic coursing through me, to make my own potions, and discover what else I could do. Impatience waiting for it to happen put an added edge on my nerves over what I was about to do.

THE SPARKLING GLASS roof of the records office winking in the sun was the first part of the villa I spotted from a distance, followed shortly by the warm tiled roofs and swaying tree tops in the gardens. My heart sang at seeing glimpses of home, caused by the warm fluttering of the few happy moments I'd had there. The song felt laced with grief, though, knowing home wasn't what it should be. What it could've been if Carradoc hadn't died. Hadn't been murdered. The only thing that lay behind those walls I had any right to be happy about came in the form of Daric; in the idea of rescuing him.

It would be hours before I'd be able to do that though. So much more had to be done first, including a brief check in with Neala. More importantly, getting my spies in the loop. Their importance in keeping me informed about life in the villa, about Neala, meant some sort of peace of mind for me. We couldn't let Neala succumb much further into the brainwashing. I feared she'd be irretrievable if she did.

We paused our horses at the cresting of a hill just outside the tree line of the woods. Peeking over the rooftops flew the flags of Vale, waving us in home. It took a moment and a second glance to notice something off about them. The Vale flag flew in all its green and gold glory. The royal flag, the one that displayed the crest of my family in the center of the field of green, was gone. In its place flew a green flag striped through with aubergine and trimmed in black.

"Well, shit," I looked to Rollan, exasperated and crest fallen. "I hope we aren't too late."

"Me too," his eyes took on a stony quality and his face looked grim. We both knew the flag change meant nothing good. Definitely that Drem's claws had sunk even deeper into my mother. Into Vale.

Zenobi nickered uneasily as I prompted her to get moving once more. It seemed even she sensed something amiss at home. I felt bad she had to stay behind when Daric and I left. "Promise you'll take good care of Zenobi for Daric?"

"Of course. If I can I will find a way to get her to you at Eisele's."

At first I liked the idea, but realized it would be pointless. She'd end up left behind again when we came back for Drem. Riding in wouldn't be an option. Alarms would be raised the moment we were spotted. We were going to have to portal in. "No, no need, I think we'll be using portals get back again. Element of surprise and all."

He nodded once in response, saying nothing the rest of the ride to the villa. We both stewed in apprehension as we watched the walls grow taller the closer we got. When we entered the gates, the high, smooth, white walls of the courtyard felt like they were swallowing us alive. The air felt entirely different, negatively charged and eerily heavy. The guards we passed barely acknowledged our presence. Their sharp eyes dulled under their helmets with brewing frustrations. Their minds obviously lay somewhere other than their jobs.

We rode up to the stables, dismounting and beginning to remove our bags. The stable hands rushed to greet us as we did. As I turned to hand Zenobi off, I was taken aback to see Karrah reaching for the reins. She dressed in the sturdy brown jumper and boots of a stable worker, her rich auburn hair fell in waves over her shoulders. I'd never seen her with her hair down, let alone out of uniform.

"Karrah, why are you in the stables?" I handed off Zenobi curiously.

Her dark eyes flashed angrily as she rolled them and grumbled, "Women are no longer allowed to be guards."

"What!" Rollan and I exchanged glances. This was a change we hadn't seen coming. Drem's aspiration before we left had just been to have my mother all to himself, nothing more. This though, this removal of women from powerful positions, reeked of something else. A power move. Whatever his venomous lips were pouring into Neala's ears, convinced her to do it.

"Who became Captain?"

"No one. We have no captain," she seethed through gritted teeth. "Queen Neala put Lord Drem in charge of managing the guards, until a Captain emerges from the current guards. In other words, no one is capable or worthy of the title in her eyes. Daric was next in line after Seylah, but you know. I have a hard time believing what he's accused of doing."

My eyes shot to the grassy ground, fighting against the tears coming. "Drem's a liar. Daric is innocent," I said more to myself than in response to Karrah. My mind forwarded itself to what I planned on doing later that night. What if the guard on duty doesn't let me in to visit, if he answers to Drem? My eyes snapped up to meet Karrah's, "Are the men falling in line? Being loyal and obedient to Drem's orders?"

If Karrah's eyes rolled any harder they would've ended up in her stomach. The guards weren't in Drem's pocket yet. "Why would they? We are, I mean they are, loyal only to the Queen, you, and themselves. Everyone is baffled by Queen Neala these days. Ever since King Carradoc died she is less herself with each passing day. Once a champion for us all, now feels female guards set a bad example for her impressionable, grieving, recovering daughter. She has lost her mind."

My insides swirled with lava. Not because Karrah believed my mother's words. I'd only confided what I knew to a handful of people. I raged internally because Drem's influence over her began to leak into Vale itself. Others were seeing it, and not knowing its true source, thought Queen Neala had lost her mind in grief. That she was crazy.

That implication burned more than anything else. Years of being accused of the same made it a highly sensitive subject. One I didn't want anyone else to be wrongly accused of. "It's not Neala, Karrah. Drem's brainwashed her. I have a plan to get things back to normal." Rollan cleared his throat behind me, a reminder of his help so far. "We have a plan," I corrected as I pulled a D.C. from the saddle bag and handed it to her. She rolled the device around in her hand, studying it.

"Your communicator?"

"No, your communicator. If you want to help us by keeping tabs on my mother and Drem for me," I stated hopefully. "It wouldn't just be you, so don't feel pressured."

"You mean to leave again?"

"Yeah, I'm just here for a few hours." I left my answer at that.

There wasn't any reason to give her more information than that. She'd know the reason later. It'd be the talk of the villa.

"I will prepare a horse for you, and keep you informed about Queen Neala's condition."

"Thanks, it means a lot. But no horse. I won't need one. Don't ask," I replied. Karrah stared at me like I'd lost it for a minute, then shrugged it off. I liked that about Karrah, she didn't press too hard; she trusted completely unless her gut told her otherwise. That quality held a majority of the reason I chose her as a contact.

"Hey, I need to run. A lot to do in a little time. Rollan will catch you up on how to use the communicator, okay?" I didn't give either the time to respond, or myself the time to feel guilty about just dropping all this on them. My time ran in short supply, and I still needed to get Veena on board.

VEENA WAITED at my door for me. As usual, when dealing with me anyway, she had a tray of food and tea. Her dark hair looked hastily thrown into a messy bun and hid beneath an aubergine kerchief. Yet another rapid change implemented in the short time I was away. She smiled in greeting, shifting the tray from both hands to one and holding out the now free one like she waited for something.

"Hand it over," she demanded.

"No hi or hello? How was your camping trip?"

"No, Elle. I am not about to sit here and exchange pleasantries when you sorely need rest and recharging. Just give me the communicator, so you can do that."

Sometimes I forgot Veena's abilities stretched beyond knowing when someone wanted food and what they wanted. She was one of the rare psychics of Vale that did not have a limit to one specific area. She didn't advertise that, though. If the wrong person knew, it wouldn't be good for her. She only let those she trusted know about it. I played coy about her demand, giving her a sliver of plausible deniability. I'd never stop trying to protect my friends in the smallest of ways, where I could. "What are you talking about?"

"Stop trying to protect me." I caved and handed her a D.C. from my bag, leaving me with one I meant to give Lin. "See, not so hard. Now, take this tray and get some rest. You will need it for tonight."

"I need to return something to Lin, though. So I'll just head off to the archives." If I'd calculated the days right, he'd be there until late in the night. He needed to be brought up to speed about the whole shebang. I especially wanted to hear his opinion on the functionality of the map I'd used to find Eisele.

"He has not been in archives all week. He has other pressing things on his mind. You can go to him at the library in the village later," she forcibly handed the tray to me and walked away. After a few steps she turned back, "Do not call for anything. I will not answer, for your own good."

Amused by her bold candor, I shook my head with a silent laugh as I entered my room. I placed the tray on the sideboard table by the door and grabbed a bunch of blackberries from it. The dark sweetness burst across my tongue. I could have eaten a mountain of them.

Hours remained before I'd be able to venture to the jail, under the guise of sneaking gin to visit Daric. All the time I thought I didn't have suddenly lay before me. I thought I'd spend more time with Veena and then head off to the archives to see Lin. Since neither of those things were happening, there was nothing to do but wait.

The long day on horseback began to feel like a heavy coat. Dirt and sweat coated my skin. My brain felt foggy and my eyes wanted to close. Veena was right. I needed rest before trying to rescue Daric from his wrongful imprisonment. First, though, I needed to clean myself up. Otherwise, I'd have a hell of a time relaxing.

I showered, spending more time than I usually would have under the hot water. It felt wonderful after weeks of cold baths in the lake beside Eisele's home. Afterward, I put on an over-sized tee that hung off one shoulder and was long enough to pass as a dress. Finding it stashed in the back of my wardrobe made me happy I'd kept some clothes from Reta. I still felt much more comfortable in them.

Before crawling into my large, downy bed, I nibbled on some more fruit and a buttery scone from the tray of food Veena left. A full stomach would make it easier to rest. I knew I needed every little bit of help I could get to sleep. My mind tended to wander, and over think on the easiest of days.

To my surprise, sleep came quickly for once.

FORTY-NINE

THE PRINCESS DOES THE RESCUING

As Karrah suggested, the guards in the jail gave me no problems when I arrived asking to see Daric. One even voiced their surprise over how long it took me to defy my mother's orders. It was strange not seeing and females amongst their ranks. Women had once equaled the men in numbers in the guard, often holding higher positions than their male counterparts. Neala felt the steady female head to be ideal for the line of work. I hated Drem's changes deeper with every reminder of them. After we stopped Drem, though, everything would go back to normal. As long as everything went as planned.

Despite the loose permission, I tread lightly once inside the jail. Who knew what other changed had been made on the inside. My footsteps echoed quietly off the dark stone walls that were a vast contrast to the light coloring of the rest of the villa.

A large open area awaited at the bottom the stairs leading down into the jail. Three cells, separated by floor to ceiling, stone barrier walls sat in a row, taking up a portion of the space. The first two cells were empty, except for the standard small cot and open toilet in each. A large figure sat nestled in a corner of the third. Daric. He had his back up against the barrier wall, long legs out before him with one knee crooked upwards, and one toned forearm hanging through the bars next to him. He still wore the shirt and pants from the night of his arrest, though they were filthy and torn in places. His sandy brown hair hung in greasy strands over the side of his low hanging head.

Despite his posture, he didn't give off an air of defeat. The tense muscles in his arm and shoulders screamed his determined strength. He hadn't given up.

Quietly, quickly, I padded up to the cell he sat in. There wasn't any reason for me to be nervous, or to sneak about. The guards weren't going to snitch. I waited until I knew Neala would be sleeping, which meant Drem likely would be too. That or he'd be in his lair cooking up whatever evil he needed to have some powers. My caution purely stemmed from me; and from the crime I was about to commit.

Dropping to my knees, I ran my hand over his exposed arm and wove my fingers with his, "Daric."

His head swiveled at my touch, bringing his mossy eyes to mine. Mist formed in the corners, framing the pain and surprise swirling in them. "Elle?" a tinge of disbelief hung in the question. "You are back?" he pulled my hand further through the bars, bringing it up to his face and nuzzling my palm with light kisses. His growing beard tickled against my skin. My heart caught and soft chills raced through my body. After weeks of worry, I relished the feeling .

"Just long enough to get you out." I tugged his hand upwards, guiding him to his feet. I knew we needed to hurry, just in case.

"How do you plan to do that?" his eyes studied me, landing on the bag hanging across my chest. "Only you would be able to talk a key from the guards."

"Funny. No. We're going to portal," I couldn't help but do a little shuffle. With Daric being a portal sensitive I was excited to introduce him to Eisele's portaling capabilities. To see what he thought of it.

"Elle, that is not possible. Portal magic, magic in general is blocked in here." I knew that already, knew that he'd bring it up. It didn't matter. Not with Eisele's potion. I checked with her before leaving that it would. Since it her portals were untraceable, they weren't bound by magic blocking.

"Trust me. I know what I'm doing Daric." I dug into the messenger bag and pulled out one of the portal vials. "Hold on to my hand tight, and don't touch the bars. We don't want to take them with us. I don't think Lin would appreciate them crashing into the library."

"Lin?" he raised his scarred brow at me.

"I need to return the map to him, and ask him a favor. Then we can go back to Eisele's."

"So you will not need the map to return?"

"We'll portal back." He moved to say something else in response, but I cut him off, "I know portals can't be opened in the village, blah blah blah. Trust me. Now, hang on." Keeping my eyes locked on his, I popped open the vial and swallowed down the contents while thinking specifically about the library in the village. The thick ginger-bread flavored liquid coated my throat on the way down. The moment I swallowed the tingling sensation crept over my scalp and down to my toes before whisking us away from the jail.

This time, I wasn't distracted. We appeared in front of the library in the village just as planned. Daric's eyes stared widely and his jaw hung slack. I'd never seen him so shocked before. "What was that?" he asked, slowly slipping his hand from mine."

"Untraceable portal. Eisele's secret formula. I knew you'd get a kick out of it, that's why I didn't spoil it." I turned my attention to the library. A dull light shone behind the main window. I wondered what had Lin in the library so late rather than in his home above it. At least I wouldn't be waking him.

We padded up the few steps to the library door, knocking gently on the butter yellow door. Seconds later Lin's tired face appeared in the cracked opening. Relief swept through his features upon recognizing us. "Princess, Daric, what brings you to my door so late?"

"Returning the map," I patted the messenger bag I carried.

He opened the door wider, waving us in, "Come in, quickly." His paranoid behavior worried me. Immediately, I noticed the library felt out of sorts. A quick glance would show nothing out of place. The shelves sat as orderly as ever, filled to the gills with gleaming leather tomes and the occasional potted plant. Little tables scattered between shelves let off a freshly polished citrus scent.

Only two things seemed out of place. A small fire danced in the fireplace at the front of the room. Nights had warmed some in the last few weeks, negating the need for extra warmth. Remnants of paper curled in the low flames. He was burning things, but why? Also, there was a small, disorganized pile of luggage huddled beneath one of the tables as if they were hastily shoved there.

Upon second glance, Lin himself looked frazzled. His usually smooth black hair didn't lay flat and his stormy eyes were ringed with tired worry. "Everything okay?" I motioned to the pile of bags under the table.

He ran his fingers through his hair, looking back to the mess I indicated. When he turned back the weariness in his face appeared ten-fold. His mouth stammered wordlessly as his eyes shifted from me to Daric repeatedly. Whatever went on in his head had him more than paranoid.

"Lin, you can tell me," I prodded. His eyes shifted one more time to Daric, revealing why he felt so uncertain. Daric was known as a well trusted guard. That reputation lingered despite his incarceration. "You can trust Daric, after all we're here clandestinely returning a map after I broke him out of jail. We aren't gonna rat you out for anything."

"Our solemn word," Daric added in attempt to assuage Lin's fear.

Lin's head bobbed in rapid relief. "Moirann," he called out with a hint of calm. His lips sealed in a thin line and his eyebrows raised nervously while he waited. A minute later a young woman stepped out from behind one of the shelves towards the back of the room; her belly swelled with child. As she stepped out of the shadows, I could see her golden eyes were filled with the same stress in Lin's.

Moirann stopped before us, placing a delicate hand on the top of her belly and weaving the fingers on her other hand into Lin's. Her long golden waves bounced over her shoulders as she settled. She reminded me of Janice Queen on many levels, from her petite frame and delicate features, to the warmth she emanated despite her nervousness.

"This is my wife, Moirann," Lin introduced her. "Moirann, this is the Princess, Elle, and Daric. They are safe, we can trust them implicitly."

"Safe?" Daric questioned.

"Yes. Safe. I do not know who to trust from the royal villa anymore. But knowing your opinions on Drem mark you as ones to trust in my book. We are preparing to leave this realm. Perhaps travel to Reta, I just need to find a reason for a portal to be approved before it is too late."

My mind backpedaled into confusion, "Wait. What do you mean too late?" Something else obviously happened while I had been away. My stomach began to churn knowing that it was bad enough to send Lin running.

"I think we need to talk," Lin gestured to one of the tables without their bags underneath. We moved our gathering there. The men pulled chairs out for Moirann and myself, and we all settled in for what I could tell would be a serious discussion.

As I sat I pulled the map from my bag and slid it across the table to Lin, before I forgot to return it. "I suppose it's pointless to return this, with archives being closed. Still, I don't need it anymore. Besides, it's useless."

"You did not find her then?"

"Oh no, I did. The map just doesn't really work the way you said." Lin looked confused by my revelation, I explained how Eisele wasn't being tracked. That she went into isolation of her own accord and Neala helped her stay that way with a fake banishment.

"Wow, that is not what I expected to hear," Lin ran his hand over his weary face. "Very interesting." He stared at the map in his hand for a long moment. Suddenly, he got up and hurried to the fireplace and threw the map inside. "Since it is useless, no reason to keep it," he commented as he sat. I didn't fully buy his reason for burning the map. There had to be another reason. I wasn't about to pry though. "Did you learn anything useful?"

"Eisele is a good fountain of knowledge on Drem. She's his sister." That news bomb set off a series of gasps from my company. Each person at the table looked at me like I'd suddenly betrayed them. "Don't worry. She's almost nothing like him. She's helping me. Us.

Anyway, what's happening that has you spooked, Lin?" I changed the subject, not entirely ready to dive deeper into what I'd been up to. That would take all night, which was time we didn't have if Daric and I were to get back to Eisele's before dawn.

I could see the wheels processing in Lin's head as he formulated his words. "Well, to put in simply, I am hearing whispers of some changes coming to Vale. I want to protect Moirann from them."

"What kind of changes?"

"More oppression of women. I am sure you know about females being kicked off the guard. Now, or so I've heard rumored, Neala is preparing and order to bind the magic of all women."

"Not my mother..."

"I know. Drem is behind it."

"Did you hear a reason why?"

"You. Your lack of powers. Wanting to help you feel less apart from the rest of Vale."

Suddenly it became crystal clear what Drem intended. Not only did he seek to isolate me from any sort of support, but he sought to make me hated by the whole damn land. To make me the reason freedoms were taken away. Such a malicious move just to keep his claws in my mother. I was the threat he needed to eliminate in order to really have Neala for himself. "Mother fucker."

"So you see my urgent need to get Moirann out of Vale. She is a natural healer, her magic is too vital to take away. Many depend on it."

"Not to mention we do not know the harmful effects it will have on our child," Moirann added, her lilting voice trembled with fear.

Lin's plan threw a possible wrench in my growing spy network. I felt it necessary to have someone in the village keeping track of how Drem's actions affected it. Especially if the rumor Lin heard came to fruition. I'd need someone fighting for me amongst the disgruntled people of Vale.

I hoped I could talk him into staying and being that person, and I had a good idea on how to do that. "I'm gonna level with you, Lin. I didn't just come to return the map. I need your help, and I think we can help you too."

"I am listening."

"Daric and I can take Moirann with us back to Eisele's. It's not another realm, but it's safe from Drem. Plus our method of travel is untraceable. No one will be alerted to a portal opening, so no investigation will be made. In return, I hope you'll consider staying in the village and keep an eye on things for us. Report back any big events so we can prepare accordingly. Run interference for my good name if it comes to it."

I pulled the last communicator out of my bag and handed it off to Lin. "You'll have this the whole time, and can contact Moirann whenever you want. Hopefully, it won't even be that long."

"We will do everything in our power to make sure your wife stays safe," Daric added. "Please, put your faith in us. In Elle. She puts everything into keeping her word and getting results. I know with your aid, we will take Drem down and save Vale from becoming an oppressed land," he reached for my hand and gave it a squeeze. His vote of confidence, though biased, made me feel better about asking.

Lin stared at the device in his hand, his eyes distant with thought and misting over. What we asked of him included a lot of risk. A lot of uncertainty. If I were in his shoes I'd hesitate too.

After a few minutes of deliberation, Lin placed the device onto the table and turned to Moirann. "I think you should go with them, my love. You will be safe there, and comfortable. Surrounded by friends I trust rather than being in a strange place we know little to nothing about."

Moirann's head nodded in contradiction to the swelling tears in her eyes. "Will you be safe, though?" the question fought past the emotion caught in her throat.

"Of course," he leaned in, planting a sweet kiss on her forehead.

"We'll check in often, Moirann."

"First sign of trouble, we will bring Lin to us," Daric added.

Moirann sniffled and ran a hand over the top of her belly, "Okay. To keep her safe is what matters most."

Once Lin agreed to help us, to send Moirann back with us, we wasted no time gathering up her bags and portaling out of there. We couldn't spend much longer in the village without rousing suspicions from the merchants that would be up shortly to begin their days. Plus we needed sleep.

FIFTY

FIREFLIES

A COOL NIGHT breeze accompanied the swath of bright galaxies in the sky when we landed just beyond the large oak outside Eisele's place. Lights still burned inside the home, Eisele was still awake. Knowing what little I did about her, she had to be burning the midnight oil fretting over her brother. She carried a lot of guilt over her actions in the past.

The moment we arrived she came bustling out the front door, her black nightgown flowing behind her like the petals of a parrot tulip and her hair hidden beneath a matching scarf. She looked as glamorous in her night time get-up as any quintessential Old Hollywood actress.

As we approached her, the minimal light from the windows illuminated her just enough for my companions to get a decent look at Eisele. Moirann gasped in surprise, and Daric tensed as they caught their first glimpse of the master alchemist; sister of the man we all despised. I didn't expect their reaction to her to be any different, even though I'd already told them who she was. Hearing something didn't always prepare one for actually seeing it first hand.

"It is about time," she huffed, "though you are a person heavy, two persons heavy." Her eyes lingered on Moirann and her round belly. With a heavy sigh she ushered us into the house, "I cannot in good conscience allow a pregnant woman to sleep on the ground in a tent. These old bones will make do suffering on the window seat." She wrapped her arm around Moirann, mothering her. It wasn't the reaction I expected from the older woman. I thought for sure her cantankerous streak would rear up and she'd make a big fuss about having too many people in her home. Instead, she went right into caretaker mode with a hint of her usual grumpy self.

"How did you know we arrived?" I commented on her instant appearance on our arrival.

"A little motion activated spell I cooked up while you were gone. Your initial arrival surprised me, and I do not like surprises. No more surprise guests for me." She began ushering Moirann into her home, "Come on then."

When I tried to follow, a jerk on my arm stopped me from taking more than a step. My eyes followed back, down my arm to mine and Daric's linked hands, then up to his face. The past few weeks were etched in deep, exhausted lines around his mossy eyes; which still gleamed despite how tired he was. "I will leave you ladies to settling Moirann in. I need to get that jail off me," he motioned to his self with his free hand.

"Of course. All I can offer you is the lake. Eisele may be helping us, but she's really picky about her personal space. Moirann is lucky she's pregnant, otherwise she'd be out here with us. There's soap in my tent, and Rollan left you some clean clothes, though they might be a little snug."

"No worries, I would rather bathe in glacial waters and wear too small clothes than remain as I am."

"I'll leave you to it then," I smiled and closed the distance between us, giving him a quick kiss before heading into the house.

I found Moirann in the sitting room, next to the long-tailed doves. Her golden eyes were wide with wonder while she drank in the opulent plants taking up every spare inch. She looked small against the flora surrounding her. Almost pixie like, and reminding me even m ore of Janice. Perhaps they were distantly related.

Eisele hovered nearby, pouring steaming, lavender tea into cups from a shiny, silver teapot. She turned a large blue eye on me as I entered. Without a word she began pouring another cup. My cue to have a seat as well, and that she wasn't done with me. I settled onto the window seat, fidgeting as I waited for the inevitable ass chewing she was about to lay down for bringing yet another person into her sanctuary. I wondered if she regretted agreeing to helping us.

She sat next to me when she finished. Still, she said nothing. Eisele sipped her relaxing tea, looking over the brim of her cup at me with an intimidating spark in her eyes. The inaction unnerved me until I couldn't take the silent torture anymore.

"Well?"

"Well, what, Princess?" she batted her eyes, though they were heavy with knowledge of her actions. She knew what I implied and intended to make me squirm. "Did you want something else with your tea?"

"You're being nice."

"Can I not be nice to my tired guests?"

"No. I mean, yes," I added hastily after falling into her verbal trap. "You know what I mean. I know you didn't expect me to bring Moirann back, and I didn't think you'd be so cool about another person invading your sanctuary," I breathed the words out quickly, slurring them together near unintelligibly.

"Oh, that. Yes. I would normally be upset over it. While you were away I came to realize I just needed to let go and go with the flow." I glared at her warily, knowing she held back. After a minute she gave in to my silent pressure, "Fine, I am bothered, but am not fighting it anymore. The sooner we get you where you need to be, the sooner I get my home back. Just, no more unauthorized new comers."

"I think you secretly like having all this company," Moirann quipped quietly from behind her own cup. Her assessment surprised me, but with a moment of thought I didn't think she was wrong.

There had to be some part of her that relished in having people around after so many years of solitude. She had to be lonely, any normal person would have been. The smirk hiding behind Eisele's cup all but confirmed the pregnant woman's theory.

"Well, she called you out," I prodded at Eisele. I couldn't help it. For once, I had a small upper hand in our new friendship. If you could call it that. I couldn't help feeling she merely tolerated me so she could correct the mistakes of her past.

She squinted daggers at me in return, I couldn't tell whether or not there was any heart in them. "I am too old and too tired for this. We will talk tomorrow before working on your magic." She stood and ushered me from my seat and towards the door. "Come on, Moirann. Let me show you to your room," I heard her say as I left.

As I exited her cabin, I couldn't say I felt disappointed about being thrown out. I had someone waiting for me that I couldn't wait to spend some time with.

The faint glow coming from my tent quickened my pace. By the time my hand reached for the opening, my insides vibrated with excitement. We'd only been apart a short time, but it felt like forever.

I ducked into the tent, seeing Daric hanging his wet clothes from a hook on the far side of the tent. He'd taken the time to wash his jail soiled clothes during his bath in the cold lake. At least he'd have them in the morning, and didn't have to stay in Rollan's too small clothes for long. His wet hair dripped down his bare back. My eyes hungrily followed the lines of his glistening muscles. My heart wrenched at what I saw. His torso was mottled with the shadows of bruises. Dropping my bag, I stepped up and gently touched one. The muscles in his back rippled tensely as he turned to me. I couldn't imagine the guards roughed him up like that.

"What happened? Did they?"

"No, this was all me. I happened. My comrades would never hurt me, even under the strictest orders. The first few days, I railed against the cell that held me; tried tearing it apart. When that failed, I fruitlessly tried to portal even though I knew it impossible. Both efforts left me battered."

"I'm sorry," I hung my head down, my forehead resting on his chest. He smelled clean, cold, and masculine. In the short time we were apart, I'd missed his scent. The warmth he brought to my coldness. He was the sun, and I was the moon.

"Do not blame yourself for my pain, Or for my imprisonment. You are amazing. Look at all you have done in these weeks," he whispered before bringing his lips down to mine in a gentle, knee melting kiss. My insides quivered with the heat spreading through them.

His kisses moved along my jaw, down my throat, and along my collar bone to my bare shoulder. My eyes closed, savoring the ecstatic feeling coursing through me. Every atom of my being felt electrified, magnetized towards Daric and not able to be close enough. The buzzing feeling grew with every flutter of his lips against my skin until I felt like a sun going supernova.

My lead lolled exposing my neck, relishing in the attention and inviting more of it. I opened my eyes, for a brief moment before closing them in ecstasy again. A flicker of movement and light appeared in that small window of time. It took a moment for my hormone addled brain that the light hadn't been the soft glow of the lamp. In surprise, my eyes snapped back open and I became briefly immune to Daric's insistent kisses. Surrounding us, were dozens of tiny floating white and yellow lights. My fireflies. They flickered in and out of existence, timed to the exquisite chills raking my body with every kiss against my skin. They were the embodiment of my happiness.

"Daric," I breathed out his name. Not understanding I tried to get his attention, that my whisper of his name wasn't an expression of pleasure, his grip around my waist tightened and the kisses continued with fervent intensity. His desire grew, heightened by our brief separation. My eyes fluttered against just giving in to his persistence, forgetting about the lights. "Daric, stop!" I insisted when he didn't.

His eyes came back to mine, confused and concerned, "What is it?"

"Look around." His gaze drifted upwards at my command. The lights reflected in his eyes, making the green sparkle like polished gems. Wonder and pride intermingled in his features while he watched them dance about the tent. When he looked back at me, his smile was nothing short of dazzling. "Your lights, see you are amazing. When did your magic come back?"

"It hasn't. Not fully. Eisele gave me a potion to counter the block we discovered on it. This is the first time I've done anything magical at all. I didn't even realize I was doing it. I think you brought them out." Warmth spread through me, sharing this moment with Daric. This display of magic became all that more special because of it.

In a way, it was fitting too. The last time I used magic, I'd been with him in our hideout. We'd shared our first kiss among my fireflies. Sweet and innocent. That my magic came back during a kiss seemed serendipitous. Fated. They brought a specialness to the night that only ignited our passion further.

Waiting until my life had settled became a distant thought. There would be no regrets. We tangled into each other's arms, where we stayed until morning.

FIFTY-ONE

BRILLIANT, IF I SAY SO MYSELF

Laughter filtered through the tent canvas with the bright light of late morning. I didn't have to look to know Daric had already risen. Initially, I'd woken when he did, at the first rays of light. He, like Rollan had long formed service habits that kept them running like clockwork. The hour proved too early for me, so I snuggled deeper under the blanket we'd shared and went back to sleep.

The sound of his laugh warmed my soul and steeled my resolve. With him beside me, I had no doubt I'd get stronger faster. Especially after last night. He'd brought out the first traces of my magic, a discovery that led to a little magic of our own making. I tingled at the memory.

Rolling out of the blankets, I reached for my discarded tee-dress and quickly pulled it on. I didn't care what it looked like. I felt renewed and more ready then ever to dive into training. A quick rummage through a bag produced a loose pair of cotton pants with wide legs that I threw on before heading out of the tent.

"She did!" Q exclaimed, bringing a hand to his mouth. Daric said nothing in return, just nodded his head.

"She did, what?" I interrupted crossing my arms over my chest, feeling like I caught them in the middle of a recounting of mine and Daric's night.

"Daric was just saying you did some magic last night. That's bad-ass, Elle."

My defenses dropped, guiltily. I should've known better. Daric wasn't the kiss and tell type, let alone the type to brag about his conquests. My arms dropped to my sides again, "Yeah. I did. It was pretty... magical."

"A pleasantly surprising ending to a long day," Daric added with a shy smirk and wink. He took my hand in his and pressed his lips to it.

Q, never one to miss an innuendo, or a wink, gave a beaming nod. "It's really good news, Elle. I can't tell you how happy I am for you. Finally getting a little magic." His double meaning wasn't lost on me.

"What is good news?" we turned to see Eisele and Moirann approaching our little circle. Eisele carried a pitcher of clear pink juice and a small tray of cups. Over her arm, she draped a blanket of quilted stars. Moirann, a step behind her, carried a basket overflowing with muffins, cured sausages, and berries. My stomach rumbled at the sight of the picnic brunch offerings.

"I produced my fireflies last night." Eisele seemed unimpressed by my revelation, she merely made a humming noise in response as she passed us and continued on to the large tree nearby. The three of us exchanged questioning glances before turning to follow them.

Under the tree, Q and Daric took the pitcher and tray from Eisele; I helped her spread the blanket out. I figured she brought it out mainly for Moirann as we hadn't bothered with one before. It wasn't much of a cushion from the hard ground, but it was something at least.

Q took the basket from Moirann and helped her settle on the ground before settling next to her himself. I wondered if he saw what I did in her. His mother. The feeling she gave off was uncannily like Janice. She was breezy and effervescent, though quieter than Mrs. Queen.

I took a seat next to Eisele, hoping to entice her into saying more about what I did last night. "What do you think?" I asked, reaching for a still warm muffin. I broke it open and nibbled at it, pleased to find the flavor sweet and fruity. "About my magic?"

She rolled her head dramatically to face me, her large eyes bored, "You want me to hold your hand and praise a little display of magic?"

"Rude much," I scoffed. "No. It's just great, though. I can really start training and have a chance at beating Drem now."

"No, sweetheart. You cannot expect to match Drem's stolen powers having just gotten yours back. To beat him with magic, you would take years to get there. What we need is a plan to neutralize him."

"But you agreed to train and help me. Help us beat him."

"I did. I never said you could do it alone. Or with magic. I said magic would be helpful. Not the answer."

Her response deflated me. Left me without any means of having a real hand in saving Neala. I'd have to rely on others to do the heavy lifting when push came to shove. It made me feel helpless. A thing to be pitied. Those feelings transported me right back to where I was before all of this. Looked at like a delicate thing that needed to be saved from herself. I hated that.

I picked at my muffin as I drew my attention to the leaves above to fight against the tears threatening to spill. The wind danced through the boughs, loosing a few leaves that floated away with it. In that moment I envied those leaves. I wanted to float away too. But, I wouldn't. Couldn't. Not now that I had a life worth fighting for waiting on the other side of what we were doing.

What if that other side never manifested? If we failed...The errant thought churned like a typhoon inside me.

"Isn't that right, Elle?"

"Huh?" the utterance of my name pulled me from my darkening thoughts. The group stared at me, waiting for an answer I didn't know the answer for. I swallowed down the embarrassment and the remnants of the nausea swelling in my stomach, "I'm sorry I spaced."

"I told Eisele what Lin had said he heard. The plan to block the powers of all the women in Vale."

"Yeah, that's what he was saying," I agreed, still half distracted by the errant thought of defeat.

"Rubbish," Eisele dismissed the rumor. "My brother wouldn't do that. Not when he relies on others to supply his magic. Fewer people with it would mean less for him, or his trick being discovered because he'd be taking more from those who still had it."

"Sorry," Moirann piped up, "but did you just say his magic is not his own? How is that even possible?"

"His ring, an old one with a purple stone," Eisele said off-handed. I knew the ring she spoke of, remembered seeing it on his bony fingers. He fidgeted with it often, especially when he was challenged by someone else. When he felt powerless.

"How do you know?"

"I am afraid that is my fault too," she admitted heavily. "I gave it to him years ago, when we were young. I felt bad he had no magic, so I made a ring that would hold a little of my own. Every day I put a little magic in. It was not enough to keep him from being ostracized by our peers though.

During my tenure as royal adviser, he figured a way to recharge the ring without my help. He spelled it to act as a siphon, taking in small amounts of magic from his surroundings. From the people around him. I did not think he would abuse it, so I let him keep it. I am sorry I ever made it. My good intentions have hurt Vale more than not."

I wanted to be mad at Eisele. Everything I've gone through could've been avoided if she hadn't made the ring in the first place. I would never have been kidnapped, my father would be alive. Neala would be herself. Yet, anger didn't come. She meant no harm when she made it. She was trying to help her brother.

"So we just have take out the ring," Q mused between big bites of muffin.

"Easier said than done, dude. Can't get close enough to the jerk to take it, and he never takes it off. I don't think." I didn't want to think about any situation where he'd take the ring off. Or think about him at all anymore. Unfortunately, he was a permanent feature for the time being.

"What if we don't need to get close to the ring at all to disable it?" Q chewed his lip as he spoke. For as long as I'd known him, that meant he was on to something brilliant.

"What do you mean?" Eisele leaned toward Q, taking obvious interest in what he said.

"Is there a way to perhaps shield everyone's magic so that it can't be siphoned?" his idea seemed to spring board off the false rumor of powers being taken away from all the women in Vale.

Eisele pondered Q's question, looking up to the sky. Her head tilted to and fro, as if she were weighing options; playing out scenarios and potions in her brilliant mind. "It is possible, a mass scale enchantment potion delivered all at once. It would be tricky, though. There would be inevitable misses. Maybe a series of applications, to make sure everyone is affected. The question would be how to deliver it."

"What about Elle? She can conjure her fireflies, send them through the village and villa," Daric suggested. "They could carry it." I appreciated his suggestion, it made me feel less useless.

"Too conspicuous. It would not be natural for a swarm of lights to course through a place more than once. A fog would be better." Eisele dashed the idea with her pragmatic answer. Unless I could conjure the fog too.

A picture of me standing in the middle of the villa came to mind, fog pouring from my hands and enveloping everything. Creating shielded magic Drem wouldn't be able to drain. "Can you teach me to conjure it?"

"No."

My fantasy dissolved with her one word answer, "Are you even capable of saying yes?"

"Let me finish. You are a moon child, born under a frost moon, the full moon that comes with the first frost of the year. Yes, your magic is conjuring, but limited to light. Your fireflies, as you call them, is one way to conjure light. When you are more in touch with magic, then you can control your lights to obey you. So, no, I cannot teach you to conjure fog when it is not in range of your specialty." She turned her attention to Daric and Q, "Is she always this foolhardy?"

"Dives in head first and wants to do everything herself, you mean?" Q laughed. "Yeah." Daric nodded in agreement. They weren't wrong. Not completely anyway. I didn't want to have to do everything on my own. I was just used to it. Used to everyone else failing me.

Eisele turned her sleepy eyes on me, "You need to work on that. Learn to rely on others that are willing to help. You are not alone in this fight you know."

It was the nicest thing she'd said to me since my arrival. "I know. I'm trying. Old habits and all."

Like a general, the older alchemist took charge of the planning. Q, along with herself, would create a series of fog producing potions. Each one would be imbued with a shielding agent that would bind a person's powers to them, protecting them from being siphoned away if they were in proximity to the ring. Once it was ready, we'd portal to the edges of the villa and surrounding village, unleashing the fog on them, two nights in a row. The third night, the whole village and villa would both be shielded and Drem's ring would eventually run out of power. When that happened, it would be time to strike.

We'd take the fight to Drem. He would never expect me to do that, or to disable his magic. We would have the upper hand.

FIFTY-TWO

IT HAD TO GET WORSE

I wanted to sulk. Wallow in my uselessness. Instead, I spent the next week working with, well everyone, on coercing my magic to grow. Q would ease me into my day of training. Together we poured over Abe's old notes and attempted to make simple potions. After lunch, Eisele would work me through rigorous magical exercises. With her help, I'd gotten as far as being able to conjure the lights at will, as well as a singular orb by accident. Moirann, had me meditating, and reflecting on my magic. She insisted the calm hour of reflection would be just as beneficial to strengthening my magic as Eisele's drills.

In the evenings, Daric would train me in combative techniques. He knew there was a chance I'd need more than magic in my arsenal when I came up against Drem. He worked me into a dripping, sweaty mess with sparring practice and taking runs along the river. Each session ended in a cold swim. He also had his own means of helping entice out my magic, once the day had ended.

Everyone insisted I made great progress for the short amount of time I'd had magic back. Impatient me, thought otherwise. I wanted to do more, push myself to my limits every day. I would've too if everyone had let me. My mother and home were on the line, and I didn't want to be the one standing on the sidelines. I needed to do my part. So, I worked as hard as I could, as long as they, and my body allowed.

I came to one conclusion. Magic was exhausting.

I did little other than eat, train, and sleep. Boy, did I eat. If Veena thought I was annoying with my constant need to feed before, she'd probably have killed me if she were in charge of meals while I trained with Eisele. There were days where I wished she were there to annoy with constant requests. While the food had been good, it was the same simple fare day in and out.

"When are you going on another supply run? You have to be needing one with all of us here, taking up all your stuff," I pestered Eisele while she prepared tea. As if to prove my point, her spoon scraped the bottom of the tea canister.

"My garden and livestock are keeping up just fine, despite your best efforts to eat me out of house and home."

"Why don't you let someone else cook tonight? Take a break? No one would mind if you had to get away. Don't you want some quiet?"

"The only one annoying me right now, is you, Princess," she added water to the kettle and set it on her little stove to heat up. "Who do you recommend cook? The very pregnant lady? One of the men? You?"

I couldn't cook for crap, and Moirann didn't need to be on her feet for so long. Q, while having great taste in food, didn't cook either. His parents spoiled him that way. Daric could cook, but it was all survival skill stuff and not anything that'd taste like anything but the color brown with seasonings.

A chime from the D.C. in my pocket interrupted me begging Eisele to cook something new. I pulled it out and saw the light flashing green. Veena.

I flipped the device open, and brought it to my ear. Maybe she'd talk some sense into my host, "Thank God. Can you explain to people the importance of a varied diet, Veena?" The line remained silent, crackling a few times in the void of sound. "Hello, Veena?" I questioned after a minute of continued silence. Still there was no answer. Assuming she'd just mastered her first butt dial, I prepared to hang up, until a faint sobbing froze me in my tracks. My palms instantly slicked with nervous sweat and my heart began to race."Veena, is everything okay?"

"Hello, Elloe," Drem's molasses voice echoed on the other end of the line. My breath stopped at the sound of his arrogance. "I am afraid your little spy has been indisposed. All of your little spies," he chuckled darkly. Hoarfrost settled over my skin and seeped its way deeper in, freezing me to the core.

"Drem," I seethed into the device. Eisele's eyes widened before setting to steel. She placed a hand on my shoulder and mouthed she'd get the others before leaving in a hurry. "What do you want?"

"Your mother wants you home, and frankly is a little hurt you came back and left again before seeing her. Makes me wonder what you are up to."

"That's none of your business."

"I do not that think that is the case. I think it is my business. Maybe with a little persuasion your friends will enlighten me."

"Friends?" Who else did he have if not just Veena? I wasn't worried he'd find our plans. We hadn't divulged them to any of our allies back in Vale. I did worry, however, he'd find out where I was. Who I was with. I could only image how he'd react and what he'd do if he did.

Still, that worry was minuscule. Eisele still had more power than he did, no matter how much he took from others. What I worried most about was what he'd do to my friends to get that information.

"Yes, friends. Veena, of course. That know-it-all librarian. Those guards so close to your Daric, who I assume is with you. A feat that has me baffled, so congratulations there. And that insufferable, young, new maid that idolizes you so."

I understood who most were right off the bat, he had Lin, Veena, Rollan, and Karrah. All of the people that had communicators. The new maid took another minute to figure out. Genasia. What didn't make sense was why Drem had her. She wasn't on the team, and I barely even talked to her. Barely knew her. Still, I didn't like that he had her. It told me anyone that showed loyalty to me would be targeted.

"If you hurt them..." my words failed at the sight of Daric and the others rushing into the small kitchen. Every face painted with worry and interest. I switched the communicator to speaker mode, so they could hear what was happening for themselves, and motioned for them all to be silent. Drem couldn't know he had a larger audience.

Drem clicked his tongue and drew in a slow breath, "It is a little late for empty threats, Princess. But you would be proud of your rag-tag team. Tongues of steel, even on that naive little maid. Loyal to a fault, each one."

"You asshole," I bit back.

"There is no need for such language, Princess. I am a flexible man, willing to come to accords. Come back and give up on this inane crusade against me. Let me have my happiness, and there will be no need for me to continue to coerce information from your friends. It is all I want. My chance at happiness. You understand that, do you not?"

Sadly, I did understand. My strongest memories still resided in my life before this. I was an outcast, with no home or family. "I do. I understand being the outcast. The freak. Being lonely. There used to be nothing I wanted more than my share of the happiness everyone else had." I looked at my gathered friends, some new and some old. There wasn't anything I wouldn't do for them. "But, never in my wildest dreams would I ever consider doing what you're doing to obtain it. A false happiness is all you have, all you will ever have. I will not stop trying to save my mother from the prison you've trapped her mind in. And I will not let you hurt my friends."

With that I smashed my finger on the end button. I had no interest in anything else he had to say. It was only after the fact that, after staring at the shocked faces of those around me, it registered what I'd done; moved up the time line for our plans considerably in order to save our friends from Drem's wrath before saving Neala.

The severity of my lack of power hit me like a ton of bricks, "Well, shit. What did I just do?" the tea kettle whistled angrily, as though it felt my frustrations too.

"Started a fight that you are glaringly not ready for," of course Eisele would state the obvious like that. She removed the kettle from the stove, "Guess I need to make you something to help your magic out, you are going to need it."

"No. I don't want to use other people's magic. I don't want to be anything like Drem." The idea of borrowing magic unsettled me. Could I say I was any better than him if I did that?

"Not a siphon, or an object imbued with someone else's magic. An object enchanted to enhance your own magic. What is already in you, waiting to come out."

That sounded doable. "Let's get to it then. Daric and Q, start a plan on getting our allies freed. Eisele and I have a lot of work to do."

"What about me?" Moirann chimed. "I want to come and help too."

"Sorry, Moirann. We can't risk it. Lin wouldn't want you or the baby in any danger. Besides, we might need your skills as a healer, waiting here for our people."

We all had our jobs to do. In 24 hours we'd start our plan with the first wave of fog. In 72 hours the shielding would be fully in place. Then it was go time.

Eisele immediately wanted to work on boosting my magic. For the first time since I met her, she invited me to venture further into her home. She took me to her apothecary. The space was small, barely big enough for a table, and bursting with even more plant life. The rest of her home made up for that lack of space, as she used it to grow and store the rest of her ingredients. Despite the size, it was more impressive than Drem's lair.

She worked like Abe, a flurry of activity flitting between plants both in and out of the apothecary to gather fresh ingredients. "Don't you keep already prepared ingredients?" I wondered, thinking it'd save her a lot of time and energy to do so.

"Fresh gets the best results, always. It may take more time, but worth in the end it is worth it."

I leaned across the table, resting my chin in one hand and drumming the other's fingers on the hard surface, while I waited for her to finish. Soon, the table was covered with various plants. She pulled two pestles from under the table and began putting blooms, roots, and leaves in them. Once one was filled, she pushed it across to me, "Grind those up, would you?" It was more of an order than a question.

The air filled with the smell of the combined ingredients as we both worked our mortars over them, pulverizing them. I pushed my bowl back to Eisele and she mixed the ingredients into her own bowl. "I'm going to need that necklace of yours," she ordered, motioning to the stone hanging around my neck.

"The spell won't hurt it, will it?" I caressed the necklace. It was more than precious to me. If this plan of ours went sideways, it would be all I had of my parents.

"Not at all. The spell will even fade away once your magic is fully restored down the line." Wordlessly, I took the stone off, sliding it to her. "No, not me. You. You need to put it into the potion." I pulled it back to me, holding it against my chest while I waited for her to say when.

She transferred the ingredients into a jar of moon water, mumbling a spell to finish off the potion. She was mesmerizing to watch. Her focus on her work had no match in intensity. Her love for what she does showed plainly on her face, making her radiant. As the potion completed, the murky, meshed colors of the ingredients transformed into a translucent gray liquid with no smell.

"Put it in now, Elle." The concoction bubbled when the stone and chain hit the surface, once again transforming in color. The clear gray slowly became opaque purple. "There. We let that sit in there for a day, at least. It would be better if it could steep for longer, but we do not have the time. You need to practice at least once with it before we finish unleashing the fog."

She was right, of course. I needed all the practice I could get in the small amount of time we had left. If only there were a way to slow down our time line, but there wasn't. Lin, Karrah, Veena, Genasia, and Rollan had to be rescued as soon as possible. There was no way I'd let Drem hold onto them for too long. If I could have, I'd have taken a portal then and there to get them.

FIFTY-THREE

THE BAD GUY IS ALWAYS PREPARED

"That is the stupidest plan!" I didn't like what Daric proposed one bit. He wanted to get re-captured. It was completely out of the question.

"Elle, honey, it is the best option to get to our friends. I am more than certain Drem will lock me up with the others. I will wait an hour or so before I can portal everyone out. Then, I shall return and protect Neala." He took my hands in his, holding them in assurance of his plan.

Untraceable portals were the best option. I knew that. Still, I didn't like him putting himself in danger. "What if he doesn't? What if Drem locks him up somewhere else?" I put the question to Q. "Tell him it could happen, Q."

"Elle, dude, it's not a bad plan. If he takes enough vials he can portal himself out, then ask one of his old guard buddies where the others are and get them. Just make sure he has enough to get them out individually if needed. He also has the most combat skill if it comes to that, which it won't."

"I do not want to involve my old comrades if I do not have to. I know it is a play you have used as well. So you cannot be against it."

He had me there. The fewer that knew what was going on, the better. "I still don't like it," I pouted.

"Do you think I like you insist on taking on Drem yourself? Especially given he has years of experience on you?"

I felt called out. "I won't be a lone though. Eisele will be nearby. Just in case." I'd already made an agreement with the woman that, if it came to it, she would be the one to kill Drem. I really didn't want it to come to that, even though it's what he deserved.

"You won't have back-up," I added. Q chose to stay behind with Moirann, to help with possible injuries. Unlike me, he knew his limitations and talents. Besides, he felt his part done, having gone with Eisele the past two nights into Vale to release the fog potion. That night, it'd be me, Daric, and Eisele releasing the fog and hunkering down until the time came. Or so I'd thought. Daric wanted to head in before we released the fog." I can't let you do this."

"Then who will, Elle? You? You can not do it all yourself. I am doing this with or without your approval." He pulled me into his chest, planting a kiss on top of my head.

"Fine," I groaned in protest against him. "But when this is all over, no more danger."

"Look who's talking," Q jabbed, to which I shot him a glare. Most of the danger in my past was hardly my fault. Things I'd been thrown into. Circumstantial. I didn't argue though. He'd witnessed me "poking the bear" as it were, numerous times. I couldn't help it. Sometimes I had to mess with people, or snark people into oblivion.

Whether or not I accepted his plan, Daric had to leave for things to begin rolling. Soon. Too soon. The unease in my stomach told me that if things didn't go as planned, this could be the last time I would see him. The last time I'd look into his shimmering green eyes. I tiptoed up and landed a light kiss on his full lips. He wrapped me tighter in his arms in return.

"Everything will be all right, love. I promise."

Daric's promise felt hollow. We had no idea what would happen once everything fell in motion. We could only hope. Still I gave a slight nod. He'd delay leaving until he knew I felt comfortable with it. As comfortable as possible. "You need to go get ready."

With another kiss, he slipped away to prepare. A thousand what-ifs swam through my head the moment the security of his body next to mine disappeared. There were so many variables we had no control of.

"Hey, it'll be all right," Q sided up to me, wrapping a lanky arm about my shoulders.

"As long as the guards are still on Daric's side," I worried.

"Of course they are, Eisele explained Drem can't influence anyone other than your mom. He wouldn't risk his hold on her slipping."

"You're right," meekly, I agreed. Worrying wasn't going to do me any favors. I just needed to trust Eisele's expertise on her brother, and Daric's capabilities. Besides, I needed to get ready for my own part in this too.

THE EARLY EVENING night sang on the outskirts of the forest outside the village. The bushes we hunkered in offered enough cover to prevent being seen, yet enough line of sight we could keep an eye on the comings and goings of the village. From what we would tell, nothing had changed that indicated anyone knew they'd been tampered with.

We'd left Eisele's picturesque home an hour after Daric, ample time for him to get himself captured and get his bearings for his specific part of the plan. My mind kept wandering to him, wondering if he was okay. I wouldn't stop worrying until I got confirmation he'd returned to base with our friends. Until then, the communicator in my pocket felt like a stone weighing me down in an ocean of uncertainty.

When the sun began its descent into the horizon, the evening bells chimed proclaiming the day was done. Merchants and vendors would begin to pack their wares and close their stores. People would bustle between their own homes. Little did they know they'd all become just a little safer as they ate their dinners and laughed with their loved ones before the night was out. That when the morning broke ,their Queen would be free from a cage they didn't know held her.

The bells stopped tolling, it was time.

We stepped out of the bushes, donning our long cloaks; me in Daric's storm colored guard's cloak and Eisele in one the color of a black amethyst. With our hoods drawn we made our way into the village and to the fountain in the center.

As the center of the village emptied, Eisele removed the stopper on the vial and poured the odorless contents into the still water. In seconds a thin fog seeped up, wrapping its ghostly fingers up and around the center statue. Soon it spread, enveloping the whole village in a light cloud of magic. The fog wasn't so dense that we couldn't easily see, like the famous fogs of London or San Francisco. What Eisele created was lighter, barely visible so not to arouse suspicions.

The fog became the children to our piper, following us as we marched toward the villa. When we reached the boundary wall, we stopped; the fog continued on to weave its final layer of shield around those inside.

The D.C. in my pocket buzzed, causing me to jump. I scuttled to the wall, pressing myself up against it, and answered the call in a hushed voice.

"They are here," here being Eisele's cottage by the waterfall. Daric sounded winded on the other end of the line.

"How are they? How are you?"

"They are okay, mostly shook up. Karrah is a little bruised ego wise, Lin and Veena are a little scraped and bruised, but no worse for wear."

"What about Genasia?"

"The young maid? She is hanging in there, really rough shape mentally." I hated hearing that. I don't know how she got wrapped up in all this. She wasn't as strong as the others, or as experienced. She didn't deserve whatever was done to her for information she didn't have.

"Are you okay?"

"I am fine, my comrades are still on our side. There was nothing to worry about."

I breathed a sigh of relief. Both my friends and my boyfriend were safe. All that was left to do was save my mom. "I'll have Eisele call when it's time for you to come for Neala. I love you."

"I love you," he parroted before hanging up.

Talking to Daric, knowing he and the others were safe, boosted my confidence. Not worrying about them allowed me to focus. I didn't need the distraction going up against Drem. Hopefully his stolen magic would be low or out entirely by the time we came face to face.

Handing the communicator to Eisele, I took a moment to gather my thoughts and center myself. I thought about the best place to go looking for Drem and Neala.

The sun was nearly set. One thing I knew about Neala, she loved spending twilight in her garden. She went every day to watch the golden light fade away into purples and grays, counting stars as they appeared. She also loved sharing that time. That's where I decided to look first.

I hoped her habits hadn't changed since my leaving.

As we wound our way through the villa, I couldn't help but realize how surreal this all had to be for Eisele. Self-exiled, she never expected to step foot there again. Then again she never expected an up-start princess to show up at her doorstep and tell her that her brother was a murderer. In that moment I felt more thankful than ever she wasn't like him.

Strangely, we didn't encounter anyone while making our way to Neala's garden. It was like a ghost town. The lack of bustling people set me ill at ease. Something wasn't right.

It didn't take long to get to the garden. A sinking anticipation settled the moment we crossed into the verdant area. Soon, I'd know if my hunch was right or not. My feet, as if on autopilot, traversed the trails leading up to the statue where she liked to sit. Just before the bend in the path, I spotted them. Neala and Drem sat side by side looking off into the distant sky. Neither spotted me.

I stopped Eisele next to me there, and whispered, "Call Daric. Tell him she's at the monument in her garden. I'm going in, getting him away from her so he can portal her out. Once she's out, be ready to help me."

"I anticipate it." It hurt a little she didn't have faith in me to do it on my own, but I understood. My magic was new-ish, and I hadn't mastered it yet. Even with the enchantment on my necklace to enhance my power, I still lacked compared to Drem. In the short time I'd trained with it, I only managed to control the lights twice. At this point I was banking on fight or flight kicking my magic into gear.

I watched long enough for her pull the communicator out then headed around the bend. One step beyond it, I felt a sudden rush of cold air. Lit rune symbols hung in the air and lay in a pattern along the ground, seemingly in a circle. I turned about, barely able to see Eisele where she stood. She saw what happened, and worry etched her features.

"What's this?"

"A barrier," a voice that chilled me added behind me. "No one in, no one out. Best of all, magic is nulled in here. Well, except mine."

Shit.

Panic filled me. Somehow he'd known we were coming and set a trap. Did we have a traitor in our ranks, in our group of allies? "What about Daric?" I mouthed to Eisele, to which she only shrugged. She didn't know if her portal could work against the runes.

FIFTY-FOUR

FOR ONE NIGHT ONLY, ELLE VS. DREM

"How DID YOU KNOW?" I spun on my hell to face Drem.

He smirked, " I set up a little surveillance of my own across the villa after finding out about your little friends spying on me and *my* Neala." My eyes darted over his shoulder to her. She sat, still gazing up towards the sky, completely unaware of what was happening. Or maybe she did know, but was too far gone to care anymore.

I wanted to cry. Run to her and shake her to her senses. Make her see what Drem was up to. I almost did, until Daric flickered into existence next to her. No cold wind appeared with him, nor did the runes light up. The barrier hadn't sensed him pop in.

He held a finger to his lips and whispered something to Neala. She nodded and slipped her hand into his. Moments later they were gone. Relieved the untraceable portal out-smarted the rune barrier, I gloated, "She's not yours, not anymore."

"She will always be mine!," he spat back, spittle spraying over his lips.

"Oh, yeah? Then where is she?" I laughed.

Drem spun around to find her gone. His robe flew behind him as he ran to the bench where Neala had sat moments ago. When he turned back to me, his face was like a beet, "How did.. Where is she?" he demanded, stomping his feet like a toddler while he came back at me. He was positively frantic.

"Daric used a portal to take her away, untraceable. Something I picked up from a new friend," I smirked, enjoying winning that small battle against him immensely.

"You like it, brother?" Eisele's voice sounded from right behind me.

"Eisele, sister," he drawled maliciously. "I am hurt you stand against me."

"I would have done it sooner, if I had realized what a monster you were sooner," she spat back.

"A monster you aided," he hit her low with that remark. He knew it would flood her with guilt.

"Unknowingly. Unwillingly," she sniffled in an uncharacteristic show of emotion. Her brothers actions obviously weighed more heavily on her than she let on. This had to be hard on her. Her brother, whom she tried to protect from ridicule, whom she tried helping, turned her love and help into something vile. Rather than being grateful and a better person for the kindness given him, he became selfish. A man that thought he deserved what he wanted no matter the cost. "I never should have helped you gain magic."

"But you did. That makes what happens next entirely on you, sister dear," his scowl spread into a malevolent smirk, his extreme blue eyes darkening with intent. His arm shot out and he grabbed onto my cloak, flinging me sideways into a patch of ferns speckled with tiny, white night blooming jasmine more than six feet away. There must have been something other than his own strength behind the move because he couldn't do that on his own.

He came at me again. Desperately, I tried to produce an orb to blind him, slow him down, but it proved useless. I tried again and again as he drew closer, panic thrumming in my ears. "Why won't you work?" I growled to myself in frustration right before remembering what Drem said. Only "his" magic worked inside this barrier he'd made. Assuming most of the magic he'd stored in his ring came from my mother, I was screwed.

Neala, like me, had conjuring magic. Only hers wasn't limited. The crown of the queen expanded her magic to be full spectrum conjuring and alchemist. My best shot at coming out of the fight would be making him use up every last drop and tire him out. The barrier would fail then, giving me my only shot at beating him. If I lasted that long.

Barely managing to roll from his grasp, I scrambled out of the flowers, bits of leaf and petal sticking to me. Daric's long cloak tangled around my feet with every step. With one hand I loosened the clasp and let it fall away. I didn't need it slowing me down.

A blast of air behind me threw me forward. My body collided with the stone bench, knocking the wind out of me. I slid off, the rough imperfections of the stone scraping my arms as I fell to the grass beneath it. Forcing myself up, my side burned with pain. There was no time to assess or recover, though, I had to keep going.

I glanced over my shoulder as I stumbled into the statue. Hurdling at me was a small fireball, which I narrowly ducked by diving to the left, landing on my back. The fireball left its mark on the statue, right where my head used to be. I heaved my body over, ignoring the new scrapes and pains, and army crawled under the thatch of hydrangea nearby.

Drem grabbed onto my ankle before I could fully disappear beneath the branches. He pulled be back, with conjured strength. The safety I sought in the bush became weaponized against me. The branches caught on my clothes and tore at my skin as my body dragged under them. Once again Drem hurled me across the sealed of section of my mothers garden. I collided with the barrier and crumpled at Eisele's feet. The barrier flickered on contact.

"Get up," Eisele hissed at me. "The barrier is weakening. His supply is beginning to wane."

"Easier said than done," I huffed back, staggering to my feet.

Drem was already advancing at me again. The pain searing my

muscles felt like nothing I'd ever experienced before. I didn't know how much longer I could go on like this. If I only had anything to defend myself with.

I slunk along the edge of the barrier into the plant beds and worked my way along it, all the time keeping my eyes on Drem. The gleeful malice on his face filled my veins with crackling frost. I felt as though his next attack would make me shatter.

He began lifting stones from the garden, using magic to hurl them at me. Most narrowly missed hitting me without me having to dodge them. Whether or not he intentionally missed to taunt me, I don't know. The few that hit me were small and did little to slow me down. It seemed he picked smaller ones to not exert his magic, which I knew he must have felt slipping.

All the while, I tested my lights in hoped the barrier had weakened enough to allow me some sort of defense. After what felt like ages, I managed an orb hardly big or bright enough to see. But not enough to hide it from Drem.

He bellowed in frustration, willing the stone bench to rise into the air. He meant to launch it at me. Panic swelled like a balloon in my chest. If that hit me, it'd be over for me. He'd have that victory, even though I felt certain Eisele would have no trouble finishing him off soon after.

I couldn't let him have it, couldn't let him rip me away from Neala. It would crush her. Desperately, I called for my lights again. This time, a large orb, brighter than the sun, flared before me. While I shielded my eyes from the blinding light, another bellow cut through the air. A crash followed shortly after.

When the light faded I saw the bench, or what was left of it, shattered at the foot of the statue. The statue itself was missing chunks from where the bench collided with it, and teetered unstably.

Drem was no where to be seen. Franticly, I searched for signs of where he hid, waiting to ambush me. I thought I caught a glimpse of his robes peeking fro the other side of the statue just as fireballs began to rain form the sky. Uncontrolled and random, he wasn't directing them anywhere in particular. Just hoping they'd hit their mark.

Fires bloomed in my mother's beloved garden every place they landed. His firestorm would kill me, if I couldn't stop him. After studying the falling flames, I did notice one pattern. None landed near the statue, confirming that was where he hid.

My life on the line, I formulated an insane plan. If it failed, it was over. I had to take him out in a big way if I wanted to live. I hoped it didn't do more than maim him, I made a promise that I didn't want to break. I didn't want to be a killer.

I turned to Eiesele and mouthed, "I'm sorry," just in case. Her face fell, understanding this was a last resort. She nodded once, absolving me of my promise.

Stepping away from the barrier wall, I bounced on my feet; hyping myself up. Two deep breaths and I was off, sprinting as fast and quietly as I could at the crumbling statue. On approach, I squinted my eyes closed and leapt, flinging my whole body at it. The monolith swayed on impact, finally giving in and collapsing.

The cacophony that flowed to my ears as I fell with it was nothing short of horrifying. My screams blended with Drem's and the sound of stone crumbling against the ground. I felt my body tumble from the cold stone onto the crisp grass. My whole body ached, and the pain radiating from my right hand made me think I'd broken it.

Opening my eyes, I flopped onto my back. The air, thick with dust, was free of fireballs, though the scent of ash and smoke hung heavy; along with a faint whiff of copper. Using my left hand, I swiped at my nose. Red stained my knuckles. I never wanted to do anything like that again.

I sat up, carefully, my bones protesting the short journey that left me winded. My neck creaked as I turned to survey the damage. My heart broke at what I saw.

Eisele knelt at the toppled statue, her dark head hanging low. Grief draped over her shoulders. An arm lay visible coming from beneath the rubble. Between two pieces of broken statue, a sliver of

Drem's face peek out; blood running in a rivulet over his opened, life-less blue eye.

Cradling my injured hand, and ignoring the pain raking my body, I scooted to her. The reality of what I'd done began to settle in as I approached her. Instead of feeling relieved at being free from him, guilt for killing Drem sat in my stomach like a stone. It was Amanda's accident all over again. The more I thought on it, the more nauseated I became. In the short few minutes it took to slowly drag myself to Eisele, I broke down into uncontrollable sobs.

I took her hand in my good one, "I'm so... I can't... there wasn't... I didn't...," words failed me. There wasn't anything I could say that would fix this. She looked up at me, her cunning eyes wet with coming tears and her face contorted. I was ready for her to ream me.

Instead, her arms flung around me; my forming bruises wincing at the added weight, "I am so sorry you had to do this, dear girl. I did not want the weight of killing a man on you. You do not deserve it." Her graciousness moved me, bringing an impossible amount of tears. I didn't know it was possible to cry that much.

We sat huddled together, crying and supporting one another for what felt like an eternity. When they hadn't heard from us, Daric, Rollan, and Karrah came to the villa looking for us. They found us still huddled together, grieving over the battle just fought.

FIFTY-FIVE

WITH ALL SAID AND DONE

A few weeks after defeating Drem, his death still haunted me. A wild conflict still raged in my heart between relief and guilt. I was happy his influence over my mother was gone, that he wouldn't be able to hurt anyone anymore. Yet, knowing my intentional actions killed a man, no matter how evil he was, left a dark spot in my soul.

I couldn't help the feelings, the memories of being treated like a dangerous crazy person returning. The accusations Amanda, Dr. Preble, and his brute squad threw at me felt justified in some little corner of my mind.

The thoughts were nonsense. I knew they were. Time would tell if they'd let up, if I'd stop giving them any credit. Part of me knew I would. I had to heal from this, just like I began healing from all the other traumas in my life.

That battle took backseat to Neala. For a few days after the battle, we feared the state Drem put her in had become permanent. She'd spend hours dazing into space, hardly acknowledging anyone, and barely ate. She became easily agitated when we wouldn't let her see Drem, so we decided to wait until her faculties were her own before telling her Drem had died. We worried she'd hurt herself if she found out.

Eisele agreed to move into the villa, to help her recover. I believed it was her similarities to Drem that made Neala accept her help. The day she began helping was the day we started to see improvement in my mother. She explained to us it would take time, be a slow full recovery. Just like my magic, which grew incrementally every day.

It was slow going and frustrating, until finally, she began to show signs of her old self. That meant the time had come to tell her the truth about Drem. All of it. Even if she didn't want to hear it.

I rapped softly on my mother's bedroom door. I wasn't looking forward to this. Worries of how she'd react plagued my mind. I feared she'd go off, or spiral back into the near catatonic state. I feared what the truth would do to me, too. The biggest fear: what if she hated me for it, rejected me for being a killer?

"Come in," Neala's voice filtered through the heavy wooden door. Nervously, I turned the handle and stepped inside.

Laughter greeted me as soon as I entered. We followed the musical sound, eventually finding my mother and Eisele seated on her bed, laughing like old friends with hands clasped together. It was the most relaxed, the happiest, I'd ever seen the solitary alchemist.

They turned to us as we approached, my mother flinging her arms wide beckoning me in for a hug. She glowed warm and bright, her smile reaching her eyes for the first time in ages. She was my mother.

Neala's demeanor wasn't the only noticeable change. Her room once again reflected her light and loving personality. All the belongings Drem had removed sat proudly back where they belonged. Most notably, things that had belonged to my father. Small touches of Carradoc.

"Mom!," I cantered to her at her wordless invitation, throwing my arms around her. Her warmth radiated from her. Every inch of me tingled happily, breathed a sigh of relief. I felt immensely better, like her being herself again, healed me just a little too.

"Oh, my dear girl. I have missed you so."

"I'm sorry I haven't been here much," I apologized for my absence she probably wasn't entirely aware of.

"I know you needed to grieve your father in your own way. It really is unfair his illness took him from you just as you found us." Her words were proof Eisele was right. She believed my absence came from Carradoc's death, like she had no memory of the time since he died.

She released our hug and turned to Eisele, "Have you met my amazing daughter yet, Eisele?" once again she demonstrated the effects of Drem's brainwashing.

"I have, she is an incredible girl."

"Incredible?" I asked. I still had my suspicions that she didn't like me much, even after that night we comforted each other.

"She is indeed," Neala agreed. "I am absolutely delighted you decided to come back to us. I just wish your brother were here to enjoy your return. It is not like him to disappear like this. Drem is usually so reliable."

I bit my lip, nervously, "That's why I'm here, actually. I need to talk to you about him. I know why he isn't here," tears welled across my lashes. We were about to find out how she really felt about Drem. About to learn if she'd still accept me after she learned the truth.

Seeing my distress, she guided me to sit between her and Eisele, "What is it, my dear Elloe? What has you so distressed?"

There was no putting it off anymore, "Drem is dead." The image of his death flashed in my mind, causing me to dip my head in shame.

"Oh, that is terrible," he hand fluttered to her chest in disbelief. "Dear, I had no idea he meant that much to you. I assumed you did not care for him after all that fuss you made about him helping you." She didn't faint, or burst into an emotional wreck. The pressure on my shoulders eased a tiny bit.

"I didn't. I hated him, Mom. Hated him more than anyone I've ever known. He was awful."

"Then why are you so upset, sweetheart?"

"I didn't know how you'd react to his death. I was worried you'd hate me when I told you."

Concern knitted her perfect eyebrows together, "Why would you think I could ever hate you?"

"Because, I," emotion choked me, and I needed to pause for breath." I killed him."

Neala leaned back, shock mixing with the worry etched in her features. Her reaction skewered me, and my tears finally fell hard and fast. "Why would you say such a thing?"

Unable to speak myself, Eisele jumped in and began recounting the whole story to my mother, starting with King Tor's untimely death. She explained Drem's obsession with her led him to murder not only once, but twice.

Through tears and sobs, I filled in my parts. The night of my kidnapping and the realization Drem had killed my father too. She listened, rapt and dismayed, when we told her of Drem's brainwashing. How he stole powers from the kingdom at large. Daric's arrest and my leaving, the truth about where I'd been. The changes he'd begun to make to ensure no one would take her from him.

Finally we told her about the night we stopped him, "I didn't want to kill him, Mom. I just wanted you back. I wanted him to stop hurting you and pay for what he'd done to our family." I dropped my gaze to my hands in my lap, which fiddled together nervously. When I looked up again, her tears matched mine.

"Is this all true?"

I nodded, "Yeah. Others can confirm if you need it. Lin, from archives, Daric, some of the guards, and even Q. They all helped us along the way. Helped us get you back." My mother broke her eye contact, looking to the ceiling then to her own lap. I saw her emotions warring with each other. Saw the wheels in her head processing what we'd told her. She stayed silent, head bowed. I felt sure we'd lost her.

"I know it is a lot to take in, my Queen," Eisele prompted when Neala stayed silent. "I assure you no one involved has or would lie about this. Please, do not punish your daughter for doing what was right."

Neala's head snapped up, "Punish her? No. Never. From what you say, she saved me. Avenged my father and my husband. Yes, this will take time for me to understand. To wrap my head around. Believe me when I say, I cannot be anything but grateful to her. To you all."

DESPITE SAYING she needed time to work through everything that had happened while she was under Drem's spell, my mother insisted we celebrate immediately. That night she ordered an impromptu banquet in my honor, as well as honoring everyone that was involved in saving her; including Genasia, even though her part was only circumstantial.

The dining hall went through a speedy redecoration. The heavy decorations that hung while Drem sat by Neala's side were discarded, making way for lighter fare. Gone were the dark banners and flowers, which were replaced with bunches of white and blue hydrangea intermixed with sunny lilies. The high back chairs were left bare, and the windows covered in sheer drapes. It was bright, peaceful, and perfect.

The banquet didn't boast multitudes of guests. Only those of us being honored joined my mother for the sumptuous meal It was her way of thanking everyone. By the time I arrived, most everyone had seated. Q and I were late. We had to make a run to Reta so he could dress properly, and extend Neala's invitation to his parents to join us. I took the opportunity to get myself a light dress that even surprised myself; a white chiffon, spaghetti strap number with barely visible gray and blue flower print. White had long been a color I avoided wearing due to my general paleness. After everything, learning who I really was, I decided it was time to embrace the pale.

Mr. and Mrs. Queen were delighted to receive Queen Neala's

invitation, and marveled over their quick portal trip to the villa. Janice especially. Her gasps of joy were audible as she floated into the dining hall, her monarch wing print summer dress trailing behind her like her own wings. Her flight path honed directly on Moirann, who broke her shyness instantly under the enigmatic Mrs. Queen's friendly advance.

Mr. Queen, wearing a smart seersucker suit, ever the opposite of his daring wife, took up an empty seat across from her. He beamed adoringly at the budding friendship before him. Q of course made a beeline for his crush, Rollan, who looked just as dashing in his dress uniform as Q did in his black, slim fit pants with matching button down shirt and tie. They greeted each other with a chaste kiss. Perhaps they'd become more than crushes.

As soon as I took my own seat next to both Neala and Daric, the meal commenced. Veena, who sat opposite me in a soft pink dress, couldn't help herself in ensuring every dish brought in met her standards. She wasn't used to relinquishing control of her kitchen, though the menu indicated she'd not done so entirely. Every dish, from the seafood pasta in white sauce to the delicate custard orbs filled with warm caramel, screamed her name.

At the end of the meal, as we all enjoyed sipping on dark flower brew, my mother stood and began to give her thanks. "I want to thank all of you gathered here for your aid and loyalty. Without it, I fear Vale might have become a very different place.

And to my Elloe, my incredible daughter. If it was not for you, there might not have ever been justice for my father and yours. I love you, sweetheart."

"I love you too, Mom."

"This dinner tonight," she continued, " is not just about thanking you all. I have an important order of business to address. Due to recent events, I find myself without an adviser. I would like to ask, in front of all of you as witnesses, for Eisele to consider ending her exile permanently and returning to her old post. It would mean the world to me."

The entire table turned their eyes to Eisele, who wore a look of happy shock. She placed one hand on her perfectly in place pin curls and the other played with the dark lace ascot tucked into her prim white blouse. "I accept, gladly, on one condition."

"Anything," Neala gazed at her old friend adoringly.

"I must have an apprentice. I know, the last one did not turn out so well," she chuckled, the rest of us joining her, "but I firmly believe in having one to balance and check me."

"Done. I shall put the word out that my new adviser seeks one."

"No need. I have one in mind already, if they are willing to accept." Eisele pointed her gaze directly on Q. "Quentin, you have shown as much natural ability in alchemy as the best trained of us. You would make worthy apprentice, one I know I and the crown can trust."

My smile broadened. Her pick in apprentice was more than fitting. Q would make a perfect apprentice, and, selfishly, I would love to have my best friend with me. Q, if at all possible, looked even more excited by the prospect than I felt.

"Hell yeah," he crowed. "As long as I can jump between here and Reta as needed. I gotta stay close with the fam too. I mean, if it's okay with Ma and Dad?"

"Of course it is!" Janice exclaimed immediately. "Plus I'll get to come visit too, learn to expand on my aura reading." It was the answer I expected from her. Janice Queen was going to be here more often than Reta, and would fit right in.

"It is settled then," my mother announced, "Eisele will immediately resume her duties as adviser, with Q as her part time apprentice." The table cheered, congratulating the pair. I, for one, was really excited about these new changes.

AFTER DINNER, I floated on a blissful cloud. For the first time ever, I knew true happiness and peace were possible. I still had a long way to go, to recover fully. If that was even possible. But, I definitely came a long way from the insecure girl I'd been before.

Daric and I walked lazily, hand in hand along the path to our hideout. Millions of stars twinkled in the inky purple sky, and my lights danced and zoomed along the path around us. Conjuring the firefly-like magic came as easy as breathing now. More often than not, they'd appear without me thinking about them, especially when I felt happy.

At that moment, I felt beyond happy. My mother was safe and healthy. I had a home. Q was coming to Vale to work with Eisele. Nobody rejected me for looking strange or being weird. I was in control of my own life. On top of it all, I had Daric.

It had to be fate so long ago that landed me in The Kendrick Institute. If that hadn't happened, I'd probably still be miserable and lonely in a world I now knew I didn't belong in. I never would have met Abe, learned magic existed, found my family, my home, or someone I loved more than I could express.

We paused outside our blooming tree, Daric sweeping me into his warm embrace. "I told you we'd win," he smiled that crooked grin I loved so much, his eyes twinkling like they had stars in them too. He leaned in, enveloping my lips with his own.

"I don't think tonight could be any more perfect," I sighed, leaning my head on his chest after our lips parted.

With a gentle hand, he raised my face up once more, "I think it can." His green eyes sparked hungrily just before his lips took mine again. This time, the kiss was urgent. Demanding. I melted into him, allowing his strong arms to lift me against his body. My legs wrapped around his waist, needing to close any space between us.

Daric swept open the white flowered curtain and carried me inside.

ACKNOWLEDGMENTS

I want to thank my family, all of you, the born into, extended, and found, for your continued and enthusiastic support. Without you, I would fall boneless to the ground and be a slithering mess.

To my husband, how you tolerate me constantly being buried in books and writing taking up my hyper-focused attention, I don't know. I love you, even on Tuesdays and bank holidays.

Thanks to Emily and Bug for letting me pick your brains, with some fava beans and chianti.

Thanks to all the critters in my life, so I am covered in fur and scales and protruding hairs making, me an animalistic set of armor to blend into nature with. The camouflage is appreciated.

And to my readers, I love you. Thank you for loving the worlds I create, and your blind acceptance that I'm just not normal.

ABOUT THE AUTHOR

Dawn J. Braithwaite is an emerging author from the glorious Pacific Northwest, relishing in the rain and weirdness found there in abundance. A mild mannered geek with a dark sense of humor, Dawn thrives on nerd and pop culture, and the written word. She lives with her three children, husband, and small menagerie of furry and scaled animals. For years she dreamt of sharing the worlds in her mind, saying, "I am too small to contain the worlds within me".

Like the Moon is Dawn's second book.

Of Secrets and Crowns

9 789898 626 1225